SUSA

HIDDEN WORTHINESS
The Pagano Brothers II

THE FREAK CIRCLE PRESS

ALSO BY SUSAN FANETTI

The Pagano Brothers:
Simple Faith, Book 1

The Pagano Family:
Footsteps, Book 1
Touch, Book 2
Rooted, Book 3
Deep, Book 4
Prayer, Book 5
Miracle, Book 6
The Pagano Family: The Complete Series

Sawtooth Mountains Stories:
Somewhere
Someday

The Northwomen Sagas:
God's Eye
Heart's Ease
Soul's Fire
Father's Sun

Historical Standalone:
Nothing on Earth & Nothing in Heaven

As S.E. Fanetti:
Aurora Terminus

The Brazen Bulls MC:
Crash, Book 1
Twist, Book 2
Slam, Book 3
Blaze, Book 4
Honor, Book 5
Fight, Book 6
Stand, Book 7
Light, Book 7.5

4

You are worthy.

And it is very much lamented ...
That you have no such mirrors as will turn
Your hidden worthiness into your eye,
That you might see your shadow.

~ William Shakespeare, *Julius Caesar*
Act I, Scene 2, lines 55-58

~ 1 ~

Donnie Goretti pulled his Porsche Cayman onto the Pagano Brothers Shipping lot and parked in his usual place. The mid-week summer evening had aged into night, and the lot was nearly empty. But not as empty as it should have been. As he cut the engine, Chubs Falcone, one of their associates, ran up and opened his door, pulling it wide. The fish-tinged aroma of Quiet Cove Harbor hovered low on the muggy air.

"Boss."

"Chubs." Donnie stood and watched as the kid closed the door with a careful, solid *thunk*. "Where?"

Chubs swallowed and gestured toward the harbor side of the lot and building. "Along the side. Under the don's windows."

With a nod, Donnie headed in that direction, letting the associate trot to keep up. Before they crossed the lot, a bright flash of headlights and the distinctive roar of a muscle car announced Angie Corti's arrival. Donnie stopped and waited. Chubs ran over to the parked Hellcat and opened Angie's door, too.

Angie had clearly been home for the night; he got out of the car in jeans and a t-shirt. Under normal circumstances, the top echelons of the Pagano Brothers, chief officers and capos, always worked in suits. But this was not a normal circumstance. Donnie was still in his suit only because he'd been at Dominic's for dinner when Chubs had called.

He said something to Chubs and then slapped the kid on the side of the head, hard enough to make him stumble sidelong and barely catch himself before he landed on his ample ass. Donnie didn't need to be in earshot to know what had provoked the strike — Angie was head of security and enforcement; Chubs should have called him first. Instead, he'd jumped over Angie and called Donnie directly. No mere associate should have presumed to make a direct connection with the underboss of the Pagano Brothers, much less leave the underboss to share the information downstream. He shouldn't have even had Donnie's number.

Had he called with anything less important than the information he'd had, Donnie would have hung up on him. But he'd had something extremely important to say.

With long strides, Angie met Donnie in the middle of the parking lot, leaving Chubs to trot to catch up again.

"Boss," Angie said with a nod. "You seen it yet?"

Donnie shook his head. "Just got here. Let's go."

Angie snatched the Maglite from Chubs. They walked side by each to the harbor side of the Pagano Brothers Shipping building, leaving Chubs to pant behind them.

This side of the building had something of a view—the moored ships, the harbor waters, the Atlantic Ocean beyond. There were floor-to-ceiling windows along the front third of the building, where the executive offices were located, making use of the light and the view, but they were made of bulletproof glass. The Pagano Brothers were more than a shipping company, and its officers needed security more than they needed a walk along the harbor.

There was no true access point to this side of the building. No path, no doors, no patios off the offices. Only a stretch of grassy berm. Normally, no one trod on this grass but the landscapers.

Tonight, Donnie, Angie, and Chubs walked along the top of the berm. Angie, always the watchdog, pushed out ahead, and Donnie let him do it, but there was no need. The violence had already been done here, and, for this night, in this place, the danger was over.

As they came up on the windows to the don's office, Angie stopped short. "Motherfuckers," he breathed. "Fuck, boss, that's Bobbo."

Donnie stepped around Angie. Lying on the berm were three bodies, carefully arranged in a row, head to foot, face down. The nearest body was unusually wide, straining the seams of its inexpensive suit. Like Angie, Donnie could tell at once that it was Bobbo Mondadori, and not only because of the rotund shape. It was the bright, striped socks inside the unremarkable leather loafers. Even in the oddly tinting glare of the flashlight, those socks stood out.

Bobbo was an OG enforcer who'd been made way back in the Ben Pagano era. He wasn't smart enough to rise above the rank of soldier, but he was loyal as fuck, tough as old leather, and hard as steel. A truly old-school Mafioso. Donnie and Angie had both learned the ropes at his wide side.

Donnie stared at what was left of Bobbo Mondadori, who had been their oldest, longest-serving man. His eyes fixed on those ridiculous socks, and a cascade of memories rushed over his mind—all the times he'd leaned over his considerable girth to yank up a pant leg and show off a new pair of absurdly bright and patterned socks. All the ribbing he'd taken with a grin and a fat finger.

"What—fuck!" Angie snarled, and Donnie's attention focused back on the present. Angie had shifted the beam of the flashlight so that it illuminated Bobbo's full body.

He'd been shot in the back of the head, of course. But arrayed across his back were five pieces of his body — eyes, ears, and tongue — laid out so they made a grotesquerie of a face.

"*Minchia!*"

Donnie snatched the light from Angie's hand and pointed it farther up the berm. Two more bodies, face down, their same parts making horrid masks on their backs.

Using his phone, Donnie took a photo of the row of bodies, and another of Bobbo alone. "Who? Chubs, talk."

The associate scrambled closer. "I came for my shift. I was … I was —" He cut off, and Angie wheeled on him, grabbing his shirt in an angry fist.

"You were late, you piece of shit. You were *late!*"

Donnie turned and studied the scared kid. Late was bad, it was unacceptable, but being on time would have put four bodies here, most likely — four bodies at the beginning of a security shift, left for hours to be found in broad daylight. Whoever had done this had known just when to strike.

Whoever — right. He knew. There had been rumblings lately about the return of the Bondaruk bratva to the States. The bodies arranged so artfully were obviously meant as the announcement of their return. And their declaration of war.

11

"I was late, yeah. I'm sorry! When I got here, I couldn't find nobody. The cars were—but they—I looked around and found—I'm sorry!"

Angie slapped him again, and the kid's knees buckled.

"Who?" Donnie asked again.

Angie answered. "It was Bobbo and Mike on first, then Lenny was on with Chubs." He pointed along the berm. "That's Lenny, then Mike. Fuck."

There were three Mikes in the Pagano Brothers, and two of them were enforcers, but Donnie recognized the body as Mike Caputo—a compactly built gym rat. Who'd gotten married three weeks ago.

Donnie crouched beside Bobbo's body. "They were dead when they cut them," he mused, staring again at Bobbo's eyes, ears, tongue. *See no evil, hear no evil, speak no evil.* "Almost no blood, even from the tongue."

He took out a neatly folded handkerchief and opened it over the dead back. Then he picked up each piece—the fleshy ears, the eyes still dangling their stems, the tongue, so much longer than people imagined—and set each one on the crisp white linen. Then he folded it carefully around the pieces and held the bundle up. When Angie took it, Chubs folded over and puked onto the grass.

"I am gonna turn your face inside out if you don't find your balls, kid," Angie snarled. He tossed his keys, and they landed behind Chubs' feet. "My trunk. There's a black case. Bring it."

As Chubs grabbed the keys and ran back to the lot, Angie went to the next body—Lenny's. He set the bundle gently on the grass and took out his own handkerchief.

Giving Bobbo's body all the respect it was due, Donnie turned the heavy head so it lay on one earless side. He looked into empty sockets. Little blood there, and no more than a trickle of blood from the corner of his mouth.

They weren't tortured. They were killed and desecrated, then left in a line exactly even with the span of the don's office windows. Not a quest for information. Simply a message: *We are here, and you are vulnerable.*

God, Sherrie—Bobbo's wife. Their kids were grown and strewn all over the country. She was alone here.

No, she wasn't.

The wobbling rumble of Chubs running back with the black case seemed to shake the ground. Donnie looked to Angie in the dark. "You got this? I gotta get to Nick."

"Yeah, 'course. Call in help or keep it quiet?"

"If you can handle this on your own, keep it quiet. Nick'll want to see the bodies, but he should decide how the men are told."

"I'll put them on ice across the harbor and wait for the call."

Chubs came up with the box, and Angie took it. A smallish art supply case, with trays separated into

13

compartments. Donnie had seen him use this box and others like it to hold similar items when those items were meant for messages from the Paganos. Tonight, they would hold Paganos themselves.

"You will hold your tongue, Chubs," Donnie said, standing up. "You spread this news before the don has it, and I won't kill you before I take it out of your mouth. *Capisci*?

Bathed now in sweat, and panting from his run, Chubs nodded. "Yeah, boss. My mouth is shut."

Leaving Angie and Chubs, with a last look at their fallen soldiers, Donnie walked down the berm to the parking lot.

~oOo~

The wide blue door swung open, and a pretty little imp grinned up. "Hi, Uncle Donnie!" The big, soft body of a Golden Retriever pushed past her hip and onto the porch, tail wagging.

Well practiced in compartmentalizing his emotions and his activities, Donnie grinned back at Nick's youngest daughter, Carina. "Hi, sweet girl! What are you doin' up on a school night? And hey there, Snuggles." He ruffled the dog's ears as they stepped into the foyer.

Carina rolled her eyes, and Donnie saw the teenager the little girl had become only weeks before. "It's summer for another week, duh."

"Cara, watch your tone." Nick came into the foyer. He had a kitchen towel over his shoulder, and his hands were lightly dusted with flour. "Hi, Donnie."

"Nick. Sorry to intrude on your night."

Nick knew to expect him, but he kept his business and his family as separate as humanly possible. He hated to do any business at all in his home, but tonight there was no other choice. Bev, his wife, was out of town with their two oldest girls, a week touring colleges. It was too late for their housekeeper, so Nick was alone with their two youngest, Carina, just thirteen, and Ren, who would be twelve in a matter of days. Both were unruly ruffians and couldn't be trusted on their own.

So Nick had left Donnie to handle the scene tonight, and called him here to report and discuss.

"No intrusion. You can join us."

"You have good timing, Uncle—we're making pizzas! Come on, you can grate cheese."

As Carina and the dog headed to the kitchen, Carina moving her hips like she'd just discovered she had them, Nick's expression darkened. "Tell me."

Donnie knew to be short and sweet now; they'd talk in more depth when the kids were in their beds for the night. "Bobbo, Lenny, and Mike Caputo." He tapped his ears, eyes, and the tip of his tongue. "Message."

Nick's eyes were fiercely green and seemed to get brighter with anger. Now they were beams of laser heat. "Bobbo. Fuck."

"Yeah." To lose three men was a bad blow, but to lose a beloved old warhorse like Bobbo was a grief.

"Angie's on it?"

"Yeah. He's keeping it quiet. They'll be ready for you to see in the morning."

Nick looked down at his floury hands. "We'll talk. For now, family." His expression eased, and he was again a relaxed father making a late dinner with his children.

Donnie followed suit, and smiled as he nodded at his friend's hands. "Pizza? You?"

"Carina. She gave me the job of rolling out the dough."

~oOo~

Of Nick's four children, Carina had the biggest personality. Elisa, the eldest, was serious and quiet. Lia, next in line, was dramatic — one might say melodramatic — and creative. Ren, the youngest and their only son, was more or less a typical pre-teen boy, a little sullen and antisocial, more interested in games and comics than anything else, but he was barely more than a year younger than Carina and easily drawn into her schemes.

Carina—oh, Donnie loved this girl. He loved all Nick and Bev's kids, but Carina was something else. She could be an absolute pain in the ass and was even sometimes a little mean—or, really, just thoughtless, not malicious—but he loved the way she took the whole world on as a challenge to be conquered. If she wanted it, she went for it, and it didn't occur to her that she couldn't—or shouldn't. To Carina Pagano, the word 'no' was a dare.

Donnie hadn't been anything like her as a kid—he'd been more like Ren—and he'd been witness to Nick and Bev's struggles to keep her safe and corralled, so he didn't think he'd want to parent her, but damn, he loved to stand on her sidelines. She was going to be something else when she grew up.

Donnie had a child of his own, a son. Thomas was grown now, twenty-three years old, and Donnie had supported him well throughout his childhood, but they hadn't had a relationship since he was in diapers.

He'd never been married to Thomas's mother, or even especially committed. The pregnancy had been an accident, and neither of them really wanted to make a family together, though they'd tried for a while. She'd hated the Pagano Brothers, and she'd made visitation difficult from the moment they'd split up.

17

He could have threatened her, forced her, but it sat wrong on his conscience to threaten the mother of his child. At the time, when he was new to the organization and dealing with a lot of hard consequences for his decision to join, he halfway agreed that his kid was better off without him.

He hadn't seen his son since the first time Thomas had seen Donnie's newly scarred face. He'd been three years old then. He'd screamed hysterically and hadn't stopped until his mother scooped him up and hurried him from the room.

One of the worst days of his life—right up there with the day his head had been forced down onto a hot commercial grill until most of his skin and tissue had been burned off.

Donnie had stopped fighting Thomas's mom for access to his son on that day, and Lissie had moved out of New England not long after. He had no idea what Thomas had been like as a kid.

Nick's kids were the closest thing he'd ever get to kids of his own, and he loved them all as if they were his own. But Carina, she was something special. That girl would light the world all the way up.

Or burn it all the way down, depending on her mood at the time.

He stood at the kitchen island and grated mozzarella cheese while his don made crusts and Carina prepared the meat and ordered them around. Snuggles snuffled around the kitchen floor, sucking up bits of cheese that escaped from the pile Donnie grated. Ren sat on the sofa in the hearth room, playing on his phone, laughing when somebody made a crack or the dog did something dumb. In the heart of this warm family scene, Donnie could almost forget that this was a night of death and bad trouble. Except for the slight shadow between Nick's brows and the hot gleam in his eyes.

A Pagano man had to carry his life in a little black case, with compartments for anger and grief, for violence and war, and for love and warmth and family, keeping it separate, keeping it whole.

~oOo~

Nick studied the photos Donnie had taken and handed the phone back. "Not see no evil, hear no evil. Blind, deaf, and dumb. That's what it means."

Donnie felt like a fool not to have seen that. "Of course. I'm sorry."

The don waved off his apology and crossed to the French doors that looked out from his home office onto his expansive back yard. The pool was lit for the night, and blue light wavered across the glass.

Donnie sat where he was and sipped his scotch. "It's Bondaruk. Gotta be."

"Yes. We knew Yuri would send another son and rebuild. These past eleven months haven't made him calmer or smarter." He turned from the view and sat in a nearby armchair. "I won't go to war with this vermin, Donnie. *L'aquila non fa guerra ai ranocchi*. We'll deal with this quietly and thoroughly."

"Agreed. But he'll send another son. He's still got eight left. Should we find a way to end them at the source?"

"The source is in Ukraine. Not even I have that kind of pull."

"*La famiglia italiana* might."

Nick laughed darkly and finished his scotch. "This is not the time for spending favors in Italy—or here at home. No, we can handle this ourselves, and we will. We'll end the son here now, and if and when he sends another son, we'll end that one, too. He'll either learn, or he'll mourn."

At the word, Nick stopped and sighed quietly. "I'll go to Sherrie in the morning and—what's Mike's new wife's name?"

Donnie had to reach for it himself. "Katie, I think. Yeah, Katie."

"I'll see her, too. Get me her number and address."

Donnie forwarded the info from his contacts to Nick's phone. "Done."

"All right. Don't stray tonight, Don. Who's on you?"

"Nobody. I was at Dominic's when I got the call, and I sent Jake on with Sonia." The memory pushed a sour chuckle to his lips. He'd just broken up with her, not thirty seconds before he'd gotten Chubs' call. Usually, when he ended things, he took some time to smooth things over, but tonight, he'd bundled an angry, weepy woman into Jake's SUV.

He never understood why women cried when he ended things with them. Though sometimes they said the words, they didn't love him. He knew that for an absolute fact. And he didn't love them. He made sure of that. He was not lovable, so he would never love.

Nick never missed anything, but he let the chuckle slide with nothing more than a keen look and a pause to let Donnie explain if he wished. He didn't wish.

"You can't be alone. Call Jake back, and make sure the capos aren't running loose tonight. Get eyes on Dumas, too. We heard anything from West Virginia?"

Trey Pagano, Nick's cousin, and the only other Pagano in the organization, was in West Virginia with his wife, on a belated honeymoon. Lara Pagano was Nick's cryptologist and thus an extremely high value target. The Bondaruks had already hurt her more than once.

21

They had guards with the couple, keeping watch from a safe distance. They called in at the end of each day with a clear check when all was well. "Angie didn't say. He would've if the call had been missed. But I'll check in with him anyway."

"Put somebody on Carlo, too. They have the baby this week." Trey and Lara's four-month-old son, Frank. Carlo was Trey's father, and Nick's cousin. It wouldn't be beneath the Bondaruks to go for an infant, if they were aware he existed. They didn't keep to the same code that held families sacrosanct.

Donnie nodded. Though it was unlikely the Ukrainians would make another move tonight, it would be stupid not to guard against it.

He would be up through the night, but it wouldn't be the first time. He knew Nick would be as well. He was calm, because he was always calm. But Donnie knew him better than almost anyone except his wife, and he saw the rage that flamed under the surface.

"I won't play with this vermin, Donnie. I will send Yuri Bondaruk's sons back in boxes, one by one, on a fucking assembly line."

~ 2 ~

The tinny music coming from the school's sad little sound system wound to its end, and Ari and Julian froze in position. The applause started slowly, from the teachers first, and then the children. Julian drew Ari up, and they stood. Julian bowed, and Ari swanned into her curtsey, as if she were on stage at the Met and not standing on the scratched floor of a multipurpose room at Lincoln Elementary School in Washington Park.

School wasn't in session yet, but the district ran grant-funded summer programs. Apparently, the grant didn't cover air conditioning, and this room was hot and stuffy. A couple of lazy fans on poles rattled back and forth in the corners.

"Thank you very much!" one of the teachers cheered as she stepped in front of Ari and Julian. "That was really beautiful!"

They bowed again and moved off to the side, where two plastic folding chairs awaited. Julian picked them both up and brought them in so they'd sit facing their audience.

"Children, now Ms. Luciano and Mr. Trewson will answer your questions. Who would like to ask the first one?"

A host of hands shot up, and Ari smiled. She liked these outreach programs, where dancers went to schools to showcase their craft to children who might follow in their footsteps, vastly more than what she faced in a few days: the premiere gala for the company's fall season. Hobnobbing with Providence's snooty elite over middle-shelf champagne, being eyed up and down like a racehorse, was not her idea of a good time. If she was going to wear tight clothing and uncomfortable shoes, she'd rather be dancing while she did it.

This gala was the first time she'd be in the position of prize racehorse. Devonny Allera, the company's prima ballerina, had torn her Achilles tendon, possibly ending her career and certainly sidelining it for the season, and Ari had been tapped to take her place as the lead of the fall season's premiere ballet. She actually hated the story of *The Phantom of the Opera*—Erik was a creepy stalker and not romantic at all—but it was a crowd pleaser, and who was she to sneer at anything about her chance in the spotlight?

The spotlight on the stage. Out in the world, she didn't like to be noticed. A leotard and tutu were her armor. Without it, she wanted simply to fade away.

The gala was a masked ball, and Ari was glad. She would dress as her character, Christine, and she could be the belle of the ball in armor.

A boy asked the first question, and directed it to Julian. "Do you get teased for being a ballerina?"

Hardly the first time such a question had been asked. Sometimes a kid — usually a teenager — asked it like a joke, and laughed with his buddies as he did it. But just as often it was asked as this boy — probably eight or nine years old — had: shyly, turning red as boys around him laughed. He was interested. And embarrassed. But he'd asked anyway.

Julian smiled and honed his focus on the brave boy. "Well, we don't call boy dancers ballerinas. We're ballerinos, or danseurs. Or just dancers. But yes, I got teased a lot when I was a kid. More than teased — really bullied. But I loved to dance from before I ever went to school, and I tried to ignore all the jerks and do what I loved. And now, I spend every day with some of most beautiful, elegant women in the world, and I'm stronger than any of those stupid boys who bullied me" — he flexed his arms, showing his impressive biceps, and Ari noticed that his focus had shifted to the laughers — "I can lift a woman with one hand, so gracefully you'd think she was

25

made of feathers, lift her over my head, and carry her across a stage on the palm of my hand. None of the men those stupid boys became is half my strength, and none of them is doing what they love now. But I am. When people tease you, it's because they're scared, or they're jealous. They're trying to bring you down because they know they're not as good as you are."

The boy who asked the question smiled with secret happiness. The boys who'd laughed at him sat quietly, and for a few seconds, Julian's strong wisdom overtook the room. Then the teacher in charge cleared her throat. Julian had basically called out several children in the room for bullying, called them jerks, and stupid, and weak, and jealous. Ari was curious how the teacher would handle it.

She didn't. "Yes, thank you, Mr. Trewson. Who would like to ask the next question?" Hands went up again, and she selected a little girl with long, wild black hair, dressed all in pink. A glittery image of ballet slippers adorned her t-shirt.

"When did you start dancing?" she asked in a soft voice, her eyes downcast. She hadn't indicated whom she meant the question for, but Ari exchanged a glance with Julian and took it herself.

"I'm like Mr. Trewson, in that I've been dancing since before I could stand. But I've been in real ballet classes since I was three. You don't have to start as early as that to have a career when you're grown, but if you haven't started yet, you should soon. And there's never any time you're too old to start if you just love to dance and learn. I teach a class with seniors—grandmas and grandpas—who are just learning." She leaned in and stretched out one leg, going into full point, affecting a balletic pose while seated on a cheap folding chair. "I like your shirt. How old are you, sweetie?"

"Eight," the little girl in pink answered.

"Do you take classes?"

"I took one, but my mom said it was too expensive. It was fun. Miss Paz said I was good. I watch a lot of videos online."

Ari knew Gloria Paz; she'd retired from the Rhode Island Ballet a year or two after Ari had joined. If Gloria had, in fact, told this girl she was good, then she was good. She made a mental note to leave brochures with the teacher for the company's community classes. There were low-cost and free opportunities for students that showed talent and fire.

"It can be expensive, your mom's right. But there are ways to help with that, too. We'll leave some information with your teacher, and maybe you can show your mom, okay?"

Smiling brightly, the little girl sat back down.

"Is it hard?" was the next question, and Julian and Ari fell into a rhythm of answering the questions that always got asked.

~oOo~

Ari hated to eat right before a fitting, but she'd taken a pain pill last night after a grueling day of dress rehearsal, and she'd nearly overslept their first school visit. Julian had finally dragged her from her bed with just enough time to shower, dress, and grab her gear, so she'd skipped breakfast. She couldn't skip lunch as well.

All her life, meals had been highly organized and scheduled activities. There were times of the year she could be a bit more flexible, and she didn't deny herself every gustatory joy, but her body was her work, and food was fuel. She spent hours of her days at peak physical effort, so she didn't fuck around with how she ate. Protein. Vitamins. Fiber. Calcium.

Julian ate well, too, for the same reasons, but he had more room for flexibility. He needed bulk on his frame. Also, he'd had his final fitting last night. Ari couldn't help but glare at the pumpernickel roll slathered in butter as he took a bite.

She sighed at her grilled salmon salad. Salmon was one of her favorite meals, actually, but right now, with her stomach lamenting its missed breakfast and her best friend nomming on a yummy roll, fish and lettuce didn't really appeal. Knowing what she'd face at the fitting tonight, these few calories hardly seemed worth it.

Baxter would be there this afternoon. Their director and choreographer was a supercharged control freak who had to have everything exactly to his microscopically detailed specifications. He'd even dictated her costume for the gala, and he made a nuisance of himself at every fitting.

He was angry at her, had been angry at her throughout rehearsals, yelling and demanding, threatening to replace her with each tiny misstep or question. Somehow, he blamed her for Devonny's trouble, as if she'd done something to his muse to bring on the injury.

She stared at her salad again, thinking of all the cruel bullshit that would spew from Baxter's mouth if she had even the teensiest food belly—and she would. When you ran at less than ten-percent body fat, and wore skin-tight clothing, a little bit of food in the belly showed.

"You have to eat, Ari," Julian said, and stuffed the last of his roll into his mouth.

"I know. I'm just psyching myself up for Baxter." It wasn't just children who were bullies.

"Baxter thinks he's a tortured genius and can do what he likes." Julian picked up her fork and speared a piece of salmon. He held it up, and Ari took the bite. "But remember, he's nothing more than the director of the

Rhode Island Ballet. He's never stepped foot on a stage in New York, and you have."

Her brief sojourn in the *corps de ballet* of the American Ballet Theatre. "Yeah, and I failed."

And Baxter had come from a leading ballet company in Europe. The fact that he'd never been in a New York ballet company was about geography, not talent, so Julian's attempt at making her feel better was pretty pathetic. But it worked, because he'd tried.

"You didn't fail. You're a soloist here, doing what you love."

Her friend's eternally upbeat outlook on life. He could find the bright side of a black hole. It didn't matter that his argument was circular and nonsensical. He'd simply shone light until the world looked brighter.

He offered her another bite of her salad, and she took it. "Fine. Baxter is a jerk because he's a failure, but I'm a huge success in the exact same place."

His wide grin showed all his beautiful white teeth. "Precisely!"

~oOo~

"Can we *please* do something about these? How many times do I have to ask?" Baxter grabbed Ari's breasts

30

with all the sensitivity of a man complaining about the quality of the produce. "She looks like a bloody tavern wench."

She was hardly buxom; she barely filled out an A cup. But Baxter complained about the slightest hint of tit in the line of a costume. In his mind, the most beautiful female body was starving to death.

Bastien stepped in, pushing Baxter aside without seeming to have done so. "This is the Hannibal costume, Bax. It should be alluring."

"Alluring, not tawdry. Take it in, tape her down, do *something*." He let her go with a little shove and twirled away in disgust.

The bodice was already so tight it threatened to constrain her breath and movement.

"If I can't breathe, I can't dance," Ari said. She spoke quietly, half hoping her mild protest would be missed, but he heard her and turned back.

Pointing his finger, he drove it into her stomach. "Maybe you should think of that before you shovel slop into your mouth like a pig." His weaponized digit came up and poked her in the nose. "Besides, you should get all the air you need and then some through this thing."

Ari knew she was a pretty woman. She had seen thousands of photos of herself, and she knew it. She had a beautiful body, strong and sleek. Long dancer's legs and arms, slim hips and waist. Her breasts were perfectly average in the dance world and sufficiently perky for the real word. She had a graceful neck many of her colleagues coveted. Long, thick hair, dark with lots of natural highlights. Big blue-grey eyes. A nicely shaped face, almost oval.

She knew she was pretty. The factual evidence was everywhere. But when she looked in the mirror, all she ever saw was her nose.

It wasn't a sideshow exhibit. It wasn't oddly shaped or weirdly placed. It was just a nose. She could look at any one of the many photos—professional and otherwise, retouched and natural—that showed her face and see that it was just a nose.

But it was a bit too much for her face. Just a bit bigger than was proportional. It had been even bigger, relatively speaking, when she was little; she'd grown mostly into it during her teens.

From the first time a schoolmate had run up to her on the playground and yelled HONK HONK! in her face, she'd been self-conscious. In high school, as she was becoming good enough to plan for a career in ballet, she'd begged her father to let her get a nose job. Just a little narrowing, maybe some shortening. A nip and a tuck. Nothing more.

Her father had refused, insisting that she was beautiful just as God had made her, and that he absolutely would not allow her to be cut on solely to conform to somebody else's arbitrary standard of beauty.

So she'd learned to contour.

As an adult on her own, she'd planned to have surgery as soon as she could afford it, and when she'd been brought on at the ABT as an apprentice, she'd been sure it was just a matter of time before she'd be beautiful. But apprentice dancers made very little money. They didn't make much more in the corps. She'd lost her place in the company without rising higher than that.

Here she was, in Providence, a soloist in an inconsequential company, sharing an apartment with her best friend because neither of them could afford to live alone in anything like a decent neighborhood.

She was thirty-one years old, probably at the peak of her anemic career, and she was still wearing the nose God gave her.

And still self-conscious about it, still seeing nothing else about her face. Baxter knew it, he'd seen the sheen of her insecurity the second he'd noticed her at all, and he went right for it whenever he felt she needed to be put in place.

He also knew that it worked. It hurt too much for her to do anything but drop her eyes meekly.

"If you can't dance, there are a half a dozen girls in this room who could take your place right now. Is that what you want, Ari?"

Half a dozen girls watching this scene, thanking their lucky stars they weren't in her place exactly right now. At least half of them would console her later, if she wanted it. The other half would climb over her bloody, moaning body for a chance at the lead.

"No." She hated how powerless she sounded. How powerless she was.

"I didn't think so." He turned to the costume designer. "Tape her down, or whatever you have to do. I want a clean line."

When Baxter's snit had carried him far enough off, Bastien leaned conspiratorially close. "Don't you worry, kitten. You are beautiful, and I'll make sure you can breathe."

~oOo~

Julian spread a towel over his lap and held out his hands. Ari lifted her feet from the soaking tub and gave them to him, stretching out on the futon as he wrapped her feet in the towel and massaged as he dried them. She crossed her arms over her eyes and gave over to the sore calm.

Today had been an easy day, just a few brief performances of the Raoul and Christine *pas de deux* for kids in summer programs and residents of an assisted living center, but Ari couldn't remember a day in her life when her feet didn't hurt in some way. In fact, she was afraid to contemplate the prospect — if her feet were ever pain-free, it would only be because she'd stopped dancing.

"You need to toughen up, Ari. If you let him get too deep in your head, he'll break your confidence, and then it'll be New York all over again."

"New York wasn't a break in my confidence. It was a reality check. I wasn't good enough for New York."

"You were good enough to make the *corps*. That's more than I ever achieved, and I graduated from fucking Julliard."

His thumb pressed more firmly into her arch, and she flinched. With a little hiss of apology, he backed off.

"I wasn't good enough to stay, though."

"You could have been. You let the pressure get to you."

He was rubbing too hard again. Ari sat up and covered her hands with his. "I don't want to talk about New York. And anyway, this is different. Baxter is a jerk, and I hate the things he says, but he doesn't intimidate me. He's not Balanchine or Wheeldon or anybody of note. He's just a bully, and like you said, bullies try to knock you down because they feel so small. He's not in my head, Jule. I promise."

She meant the promise sincerely — to her friend and to herself. A few nights from now, she would dance her first starring role. Almost thirty years since she'd first stood at a barre, she was finally starring in a ballet. It didn't matter where the stage was. She was dancing, and she was starring. She had what she wanted. Baxter Berrault would not ruin it for her. No one would ruin it for her. No one was in her head but Christine Daaé, the target of the Phantom's obsession.

She took her feet off Julian's lap and stood up. "Your turn. I'll heat up some more water."

~ 3 ~

As don, Nick Pagano was an amalgam — or maybe the word 'chimera' was better. Like that mythical beast, he was made of distinct parts into a powerful whole. Just as the Mafia itself was both whole and separate.

In the common consciousness, the Mafia in its entirety was New York and New Jersey — *The Godfather* and *The Sopranos* — and, in fact, those cultural touchstones marked important changes in the American organizations and in their reputations. When *omertà* broke in the Eighties, taking down key players from dons to capos, John Gotti most famous among them, that crisis had caused a quake in all of *La Cosa Nostra* that changed the business materially. Not only had the Families been broken, but that break left a chasm into which swarmed other organizations — Russians, Ukrainians, Albanians, Colombians, Salvadorans, Dominicans, and more, in a seemingly endless rush. They all had their own ways, their own cultures, and they changed everything.

When Gotti went inside, it was said, when the code of silence was broken, the old ways died. The new ways of the Mafia that rose up again had an entirely different attitude.

In the public eye, that shift looked like the great Don Vito Corleone giving way to classless thug Tony Soprano.

The New England Council of Five Families was not part of New York or New Jersey. They were barely affiliated with each other, beyond the strong but mainly metaphorical connection that was *La Costra Nostra*. Their businesses were, as a rule, entirely separate. They were friendly neighbors, but not associates.

New England had not been caught up in the federal snare of the 1980s. They had observed their neighbors' trouble and had taken good counsel from it, and they had survived. *Omertà* held. And yet, as the cultural image of the Mafia changed overall, many of the trappings of that change made it to New England. Three-piece suits and silk ties gave way to track suits and gold chains. And even among the dons who kept the old ways in dress, most had allowed the new ways of business into their work.

Not Nick. Nick was a traditionalist. In the Pagano Brothers, a made man wore a suit and comported himself like a professional businessman. Period. From soldiers up the chain, Paganos dressed for success. He didn't care about associates, those dwellers on the bottom rung who might or might not have what it took to make their bones. Their more casual dress was a sign to everyone that they were not yet worthy of his notice.

He was traditional, too, in his steadfast adherence to the old codes. Not only the code of silence, but of conduct. Families were sacrosanct, even the families of his enemies. So were innocent bystanders. If there was a foreseeable chance for 'collateral damage' in a strategy, he wanted a better plan.

Like his uncle before him, he understood that the best cover for his organization was the public itself—and that they provided that cover not because they feared him but because they respected him. They even admired him. He gave with both hands in his community. His wife was a beloved leader of community fundraising. When someone in Quiet Cove had a problem, they knew they could go to the don or his wife and get help.

Everyone in New England was perfectly aware that Nick Pagano could erase them from existence with one nod of his head. But few outside their world saw him as a threat or the Pagano Brothers as a stain on their community. They knew what he did to make his money. They also knew that he respected them and protected them. He made their community better.

That was a lesson he'd learned at the side of Beniamino Pagano, and he never wavered from that old-world understanding.

But he was a modern man, too. He keenly understood the ways of this world and didn't pretend that his business existed anywhere else. Under his leadership, the Pagano Brothers had developed a surveillance and intelligence division that was practically military-grade. Their financial people worked sophisticated digital programs that buried the organization's assets, and their deeds, under miles of complicated code. A growing percentage of their income came from enterprises which required no handoffs or pickup, no physical exchange of goods at all. It all happened online, all over the world, in parts of the internet deep below the place where Nonnie saw pictures of the grandkids.

So yes, Nick was a chimera, made up of old ways and new. He understood tradition and progress equally well. He was both honorable and ruthless. He was not averse to change.

But no one in a track suit crossed the threshold into his office.

Angie locked Nick's office door and came to the desk, standing before the leather chair that was a mate to Donnie's own. He unbuttoned the coat to his custom suit and sat down.

"Tell me," Nick said as soon as Angie was seated.

More than a day had passed since Bobbo, Lenny, and Mike had been killed. Nick had spent most of the day before with grieving wives. Donnie had spread the word through the organization and worked with the capos to beef up their defenses. Angie had been managing the intel.

Angie leaned forward as he answered. "There's no Bondaruk son stateside yet, as far as we can see. We got movement in Jersey again, but there's no material business happening. Just setup. Everything we see says there's an advance team but nothing else."

"Their advance team hit us?" Donnie tried to make sense of that. Normally, an advance team kept their heads down. You didn't want to make your presence known until you had strong ground to stand on. A year ago, the Paganos had disemboweled the last Bondaruk crew on American soil, killing Yuri's two oldest sons and his favorite nephew. He would have expected their second attempt to be more careful than their first.

Nick sat back in his chair and stared at a point over his desk. Donnie and Angie waited to hear what he'd say.

"How many?" he finally asked, turning his attention back to Angie.

"We've marked four. They're in different motel rooms in and around Asbury. The watch shop is pretty quiet. One guy went in yesterday and came back out in about twenty minutes."

The Bondaruks used a watch and clock repair shop as their front, with their headquarters in the back. After the crew had been wiped out last year, the shop had gone on working legit, by all signs, and Nick had let it stand. They'd kept an eye on it since.

"They're acting like an advance crew, staying lo-pro," Donnie mused aloud. "Then why the fuck did they make that big piece of performance art with Bobbo and the others?"

"Bondaruk wanted me to know. He's telling me he's undeterred. He means to come for me, but it doesn't change his plans. He's telling me what we did last year had no impact on him."

It was obvious bluster—Bondaruk had been out of the American game for a year because of what the Paganos had done in their own retaliation. But the message wasn't about the business. Yuri's message was that his sons were replaceable.

Angie's face twisted with disgust. "We got four men in sight and nobody else moving. Four is the full team. You say the word, and all four of those roaches will be in our roach motel in two hours, ready for you."

Nick's bloody brutality when he sought revenge was the stuff of legend. But now, he shook his head. "No. Keep an eye on them, but nothing more.."

"Don?" Shock sharpened Angie's voice, but Donnie thought he understood.

"You want to wait."

Nick smiled. Little more than a twitch at the corner of his mouth, the expression had no humor, but a bitter kind of resolve. "I do. I told you the other night, Donnie. The Bondaruks are vermin. I won't play their game. They think they declared war, but this is nothing but a slap fight. When we strike back, that won't be war, either. It will be extermination."

"Nick, they killed Bobbo," Angie said. "They desecrated his body. We're just gonna brush that off as a slap?"

The only men in the Pagano Brothers who could argue with Nick were sitting in this room with him. And probably the only men who were brave enough to do it.

The don sat forward, setting his elbows on his desk. "Bobbo was made before I was. I loved that old man. He was past seventy and still doing anything asked of him, still keeping watch and breaking balls. Losing Bobbo is not a slap. What they did to him, and the others, is not a slap. But I will not weaken what they died for by slogging through the sewer with men so far beneath me. We will not trade blows. We will not strike until I am holding a Bondaruk son's eyes and ears and tongue in my hand. And then I burn down everything Bondaruk.

"You want to take them down in Ukraine?" Angie asked. Donnie was surprised himself. The other night, Nick had suggested that he wouldn't strike Bondaruk at home, that he didn't want to call in the favors he'd need. But what he'd just said seemed to indicate a willingness to go that far after all.

The Pagano Brothers had never made an international move against another organization. It would take monumental effort and planning—and alliances Donnie wasn't sure they had.

"I want decisive action, and I will wait to strike until I have what I want," Nick answered, leaving the core question unanswered. "For now, leave the vermin to rebuild their little nest, and when a son steps into it, then we'll make a move."

~oOo~

That evening, Donnie stood on his deck with a glass of Macallan and watched the ocean. His house perched on a rise near the southern reach of Quiet Cove, on the corner of a tiny inlet. From here, he had a view of the vast Atlantic, past tall grasses and a rocky beach, and of the cozy solitude of the inlet. If he walked to the side of his deck, he could look up at the houses on and around Greenback Hill, the lights in their many windows making them glow like golden castles. He knew which of those houses was Nick's, and knew his friend was home with his family, setting aside his business concerns to be the husband and father they loved.

Here down below, Donnie was alone.

He rubbed at his ruined cheek. Even twenty years after he was burned, the grafted skin still hurt, but by now the sensation had become normal. It wasn't pain, exactly, because that side of his face, all the way to the mass that had once been his right ear, was almost wholly numb. The numbness itself was a kind of ache. And the stretch. The scars and grafts were more fragile than normal skin — pulled more tightly, dried out more quickly, broke more easily. No number of years seemed sufficient to make that discomfort and inconvenience something he could disregard. It was normal, but he still felt it. Maybe because truly normal skin, and his past self, adjoined it. A constant comparison between what had once been and what would ever be.

On that day twenty years ago, however, Donnie had experienced pain beyond expression, beyond comprehension, and every pain since, even the agony of endless surgeries and procedures, of debridements and grafts and rejections and more debridements and grafts, had paled in comparison to that night. He remembered every millisecond of the horror — his head held down, the grill heated up beneath him, growing warm, then hot, then hotter, until his skin sizzled and burned and melted away. He remembered the pain, like ravenous fangs clawing through his sanity. He remembered the smell of meat and hair. He remembered the sound of his screams, and of Bev's. Nick's wife had been there, forced to watch his torment before she endured her own.

Twenty years ago, he'd been a newly made Pagano man, still young and stupid, still learning the ropes, still scared most of the time. Twenty-six years old, disowned by his family, trying to be a weekend father to a preschool son, trying to figure out what kind of man he would be. He'd looked to Nick as a mentor, but barely made his notice. Until that day.

On that day, when Donnie had failed to protect Nick's woman but had given up half his face in the attempt, Nick had seen Donnie completely. He hadn't pulled him up from the ranks with undue quickness, but from that day, Donnie had known the boss, and then the don, was keeping an eye on him. When he was strong enough again to work, it was Nick's attention, and not the goggling stares of the rest of the world, that gave him the strength to forge his life as he wanted.

Women couldn't look at him long enough to love him. His own son saw him as a monster. As a soldier, he'd endured years of being called 'The Face.' But he'd had Nick, and Bev, and their family had become his family. Their children saw only their Uncle Donnie. He had put all his energy, all his will, into the Pagano Brothers. He had become a man to be respected, or feared, not for his looks but for his deeds. And he had risen to become Nick's right hand.

Now, no one called him 'Face' where he could hear it. Now, when he walked into a room, men dropped their heads not because they couldn't bear to look on him but because they didn't feel worthy to meet his eyes. He was a wealthy man who wielded great power. He had friendship and family. He had the physical pleasure of a woman whenever he wanted, with *comares* like Sonia — steady companions who enjoyed his company, and his wealth, enough to overcome their disgust with his appearance — or with girls like the one he'd called for tonight.

In truth, all those women were the same. Some took payment in cash, and others in gifts, but Donnie had no delusions that any woman was with him, for a night or for a year, because they wanted to be with him.

The doorbell rang, and Donnie finished his scotch and went in through the wide French doors. He set his glass beside the bottle and headed to the front. Mrs. Alfonsi, his housekeeper, worked only through dinner, so he was alone to answer his own door. There was a guard — in fact, tonight it was Chubs — on the house, but he knew to keep a distance.

The woman on his porch was just as he'd requested: small and flat-chested, her hips slim and her legs long. She was blonde, and she wore skyscraper red heels with a microscopic white dress that clung to every nonexistent curve. She tried not to react to his face—he paid extra for that, and no doubt she knew exactly who he was, so she'd been ready—but he saw her brown eyes trace the lines of his scars, and saw the tension in her face as she resisted a reaction.

Quickly, she focused on his eyes, and she smiled. "Hi, baby. You called for me?" she said, in a voice too high-pitched for those words to sound sultry.

He stepped back and let her in. She took in the sight of his house, what she could see from the foyer, and seemed impressed. When he reached for her bag, she turned slightly away.

"It's one thousand, up front."

Donnie took the prepared fold of bills from his pocket and handed it to her. She flipped quickly through the fold before she tucked it into her bag, and then she handed the bag to him.

As he set it on the table near the door, he asked, "Would you like a drink?"

"Sure. Gin?"

With a sweep of his arm, he indicated the direction of the kitchen.

He poured her a glass of gin but didn't bother to pour another scotch for himself. Taking note of that, the girl—he never bothered with their names; they were fake anyway—set her glass down after a single sip and reached out as if she intended to cup his face. He grabbed her wrist before she could, and spun her around on her red heels so she faced the island.

He didn't kiss women, and he damn sure didn't let them touch his face. He wouldn't allow a woman like this to touch him at all.

"Oh, okay. Rough is okay, too. Just don't hit my face, and don't leave marks."

Donnie opened his trousers. With one hand, he drew the condom from his pocket, while the other hand yanked her dress up to her hips. She wasn't wearing underwear.

Pushing her down onto the granite with a hand between her shoulder blades, he kicked her foot so she spread her legs. Then he wrapped himself up and shoved himself in.

At first she grunted and muttered "Shit," and he liked that. That was real. But then she caught up with herself and started in on the hooker prattle. "Oh yeah, baby, oh God, it's good."

Without losing the beat of his driving hips, Donnie leaned over her. "Shut the fuck up," he growled at her ear. She shut the fuck up.

With his eyes closed, he fucked the whore he'd paid for and imagined himself the way he might have been, with a woman he might have had. This was the only time he ever allowed himself the fantasy. Before that night at Sassy Sal's diner, he'd been too young and stupid to want love. Since that night, he'd been too damaged to have it—or to ever believe the words when they were said. So he never allowed himself to imagine what it might have been like to be loved, except like this, with a nameless, faceless, meaningless woman.

He held her down, kept her quiet, closed his eyes, and fucked the fantasy in his head.

After he finished, he told the hooker to finish her drink and get out.

~oOo~

"Good morning, Mrs. Alfonsi." Donnie came up from his cellar gym and into a kitchen bright with morning sun and redolent of bacon and bread. His housekeeper treated him more like a son than an employer, and she insisted he start each day with a real breakfast.

"Good morning, Mr. Donnie. I have a bacon and cheese omelet and fresh biscuits for you. Would you like juice, too?"

"Just coffee this morning. And it smells delicious as always." Before he sat at the table, he opened the doors and let the sounds of the morning ocean in. Labor Day was coming up, and there was always a rush of bustle at the beach and boardwalk right before, a last hurrah before the summer was over, but this early, there were only a few surfers and dogwalkers out, and the sounds were natural and soothing.

He sat at the table, where the morning paper was ready for him — and something else, too. He picked up the engraved invitation he'd thrown out the day before. His motherly housekeeper was meddling.

"I told you I changed my mind."

Mrs. Alfonsi brought his coffee and breakfast over. Steam rose from the plate and the cup, and Donnie's stomach rumbled enthusiastically. "But it's such a shame. You love the ballet so much."

He did love the ballet, and opera, and classical music in general. He was a top-tier member of the donors' councils of both the Rhode Island Ballet and the Rhode Island Philharmonic. "And I have my usual box for opening night. This isn't the ballet, it's a party, and I don't go to parties."

"You made plans for this one. It's special."

Special because tonight's party was a masked ball, and he'd had a wild, weak moment when he'd thought he could make use of that. Cover his face and pretend to be normal. Make that fantasy real for an evening. The idea had held him long enough that he'd actually commissioned a custom mask, one that covered three-quarters of his face and concealed the place where his right ear should have been. Hell, he'd even bought a costume cape and told himself it was a great idea to go as the Phantom to the Rhode Island Ballet's gala for their *The Phantom of the Opera* ballet.

He figured he was having some kind of a midlife crisis, because no other explanation made sense. Donnie Goretti, the underboss of the Pagano Brothers, had actually been considering cosplaying the Phantom of the Opera. All so he could party with the pretty people, people who meant nothing to him. The frivolous nerd he'd been as a teenager, with a room papered in *Star Wars* posters and a comic book collection that had filled dozens of long boxes, had creaked briefly back to life and made him forget his truth.

He'd remembered himself just in time and tossed the invitation. The ridiculous mask and cape were in boxes at the back of his closet.

And wasn't it just a little bit on the nose for the disfigured man to use a masquerade gala for *The Phantom of the Opera* to mingle amongst the beautiful people? So on the nose as to be pathetic?

Yes. Yes, it really was.

"Mrs. Alfonsi, don't meddle. My omelet is getting cold, and I'm sure you have work to do." He handed her the invitation. "You can start by putting that in the trash where it belongs."

She took it and stood beside him, her lips pursed tightly, as if holding back a torrent of argument. Donnie ignored her and dug into his breakfast.

As she walked away, she said, "You should allow yourself some joy, Mr. Donnie. You deserve it. You are *worth* it."

Those last words stopped Donnie in mid-chew, and he looked over, but she'd already busied herself with cleaning up, and she didn't look back.

By the time he finished his breakfast, she'd moved on to another room, another chore. Donnie picked up his dishes and took them to the sink.

The invitation was propped up on the counter, leaning against the utensil crock. A chocolate chip cookie sat before it, resting on a folded paper towel. Like bait on a trap.

Donnie couldn't help but chuckle. He took the cookie and headed up to prepare for his day.

~ 4 ~

"So. Many. Phantoms." Julian turned from the door with a wry grin. "It's like a convention."

Ari nudged him, and he made room for her to peer around the jamb and over the railing to the entering guests below. The gala was a masquerade ball to celebrate the premiere of the season and the debut presentation of *The Phantom of the Opera*, but the invitations had not specified that guests should arrive in costume as characters from that ballet. They could have worn any costume they wished. And a fair number had done so. Still, there must have been dozens of Eriks, in white masks and black capes, among the male guests below, and nearly as many Christines, most of them in either the negligée or the wedding gown. She didn't see a single Raoul.

Ari rolled her eyes. First, it was a bit pedestrian to dress as the characters of the ballet, wasn't it? She, Julian, and Sergei were all themselves in costume as Christine, Raoul, and Erik, but that was different — they would actually play those characters, and in fact would descend the stairs tonight in character. Second, all those women in filmy dressing gowns or flouncing wedding dresses had really missed a bet. There was an actual masquerade ball in the story. Ari was wearing an evening-gown version of that costume herself, and it was the obviously best choice for tonight. But she only spied a handful of sparkling violet and pink confections in the elegant throng below. Third, though *The Phantom of the Opera* had been a novel, about a dozen movies, more than one Broadway musical, an actual opera, and a ballet, virtually every guest below had chosen their expensive-but-commercially-made costume from the 2004 movie. Which was, like, one of the objectively worst versions.

And finally, she would never understand why people loved this story so much. It wasn't romantic. Was it tragic? Sure, okay—for *Christine*, it was tragic. For Raoul, too. But Erik? Fuck him. He stalks Christine. Kidnaps her—repeatedly. Terrorizes her—constantly. Manipulates and gaslights her. Threatens the people she loves. Yeah, he has a sad history, but boo fucking hoo. Experiencing abuse is no excuse for being abusive.

All those women below wearing the *wedding gown costume*? What the hell? Did they not get that Erik forces Christine into that dress and tries to force her to marry him by threatening to kill the man she truly loves? Ari could not comprehend why women swooned over these 'dark,' 'dangerous' men who were just entitled psycho assholes.

If she were really Christine, she'd have set fire to the bastard herself.

Ari smiled privately. She did not have a romantic personality. She was not a magical thinker. It was probably her chief failing as a dancer—indeed, it had been called out as such by a few teachers and choreographers. Most classical ballets told classically romantic, classically tragic stories. Most of the girls she danced with swooned over Erik and every other dark hero and sad heroine just like the women in the audience. Dancers like that saw the ballet as the literal embodiment of such deep, painful emotion. Their body expressed their soul, and transcended the physicality of movement.

When Ari danced, her body was her soul. She felt every atom of her own physical being keenly and completely, and she felt fully present and powerful in it. Not transcendence. Immanence. She was a physically masterful dancer and experienced true joy on the stage, but she didn't 'leave her body,' the way many of the girls she knew said they did. She was a competent actor and could pretend to be Christine, or Juliet, or Giselle, but she could not become them.

She was always Arianna, dancing.

That was why she was in Providence and not New York.

But she was dancing.

"Here comes Bax."

At Julian's observation, Ari peered along the second-floor mezzanine and saw their director strolling toward them. He wore no costume, just his usual classic tuxedo with a white silk scarf. He stopped just at the top of the grand staircase, and the string quartet below gave over unassuming background music for fanfare. She felt Sergei come up behind them and peer over her head.

When Baxter had the attention of the guests below, he smiled warmly, a beneficent god granting favors. "Welcome, *Mesdames et Messieurs*, to the Fall Gala of the Rhode Island Ballet. Tonight we celebrate our fall season, and our debut presentation of *Le Fantôme de l'Opéra*, with a masquerade. As ever, we are most grateful for your patronage and your enthusiasm, and we are delighted to share this night with you." He extended his arms in regal invitation.

"And that's our cue," Sergei muttered.

Smiling, Julian shifted his posture and held out his hand, becoming Raoul. "My darling?"

Ari took his hand, and they strolled out in a classical walk along the mezzanine toward the staircase. The guests below applauded when they reached the top. As they descended, their eyes on each other, Julian stopped at the midpoint and did a simple lift. In the way they'd decided, she went into *pas de chat* position, and he tripped lightly down the next three steps as he turned. Polite applause brightened with delight, and Ari smiled up at Julian as he set her down. They descended the rest of the steps normally. The music became Christine and Raoul's, and in the small arc of space left by the guests at the foot of the staircase, he lifted her again, a straight lift, above his head. Ari arced over him, her arms swanning back. Julian turned her, and she came down winding sensually around him until her feet touched the floor again. She wore dress pumps, and Julian wore dress shoes as well, so none of it was as beautiful as it would be on the stage, but their moment of make-believe lovemaking had captivated their audience nonetheless.

The music changed again, became more forceful, and they lost their audience's attention to Sergei, descending the staircase as Erik. Sergei played the role with more menace than pathos, a decision Baxter endorsed and Ari appreciated. In their performance, he was the villain, not the victim.

As Raoul, Julian tucked Ari protectively under his arm, and they melted into the costumed crowd.

Now that was how to make an entrance.

~oOo~

Drowning in a sea of white gowns and black capes, her ears going numb from the constant barrage of the same meaningless drivel spewed by a multitude of mouths, Ari had had her fill of the gala by the end of the first hour. The mask over her eyes was hot, her feet hurt in a purely mundane uncomfortable-shoe way, and she'd had just about enough champagne that she was having trouble remembering to be charming and mind her manners.

This was the beginning of her first moment in the spotlight. Everyone wanted to talk to her, to touch her, to say they had met her. They all wanted to show their knowledge of the ballet as well. The talk among Providence's cultured set was that Devonny Allera was most likely finished, and Arianna Luciano was poised to take her place permanently. These patrons of the arts all wanted to be able to say they'd supported her from the beginning. Truly, she was glad of them and their support.

But the only spotlight Ari had ever wanted was the one that would shine down on her on the stage.

Julian loved any spotlight he could get. He was charming and handsome and adored the swooning attentions of shy teen girls and blue-haired widows alike, so he moved through the crowd like Jesus through the Red Sea. Or was that Moses? She'd never paid that much attention at Mass. Anyway, Julian was in his element and soaking up every batted eyelash and overheated giggle. Sergei, too. He stayed in character all night, hamming it up as the Phantom, putting all the Bob's Costume Shop wannabes to shame.

Using a need for the ladies' room to effect her escape, she loitered there as long as she could, until it was getting a little weird to be standing in the corner like an overdressed washroom attendant.

Back out amongst the fabulous people, she went to the bar for a fresh glass of champagne. Rehearsals tomorrow weren't until the evening. She could get drunk tonight, and as long as she remembered to drink water and take vitamins before bed, she'd be fine by then. If she didn't remember, Julian would. He always took care of her.

Servers were carrying trays of champagne around the party, so the bar itself was nearly abandoned, except for the service staff. But there was one Phantom at the end of the bar, leaning there like he'd decided to try and grow roots.

Ari spared him a glance, then turned her attention to the array of glasses the bartender was filling with bubbly, never lifting the bottle, but never losing a drop of liquid, either. When she could take a glass, she did so, and turned to face the beautiful battlefield before her. As the star of the show, probably she should be out there, charming all the deep pockets.

Sighing, she put the glass to her lips again. One more glass for fortitude.

"You're Arianna Luciano." The lonely Phantom at the end of the bar had spoken.

Ari put her charming smile on her face and in her voice. "How can you be certain?" She tapped the glittering silver mask over her eyes.

His own mask was fairly remarkable, now that she was looking straight at him. Not a 2004-movie-whose-dumb-idea-had-Gerard-Butler-been version, but one like she'd never seen before. It was both obviously a Phantom mask and obviously unique. Professional quality, the finish done so that it seemed to be made of actual porcelain. It tied in back with silk, rather than an elastic band. And it was much bigger than most of the masks. It covered everything but his left cheek and the left side of his nose. On the right side, it even had an ear.

The shape of its face was simple, no more than a rise at the brow, a slope of nose, a curve at the cheek, a sweep of lips. No expression at all, neither victim nor villain. Nor lover. Just nothing. It was the best Phantom mask she'd ever seen.

The mask was this man's only costume. In every other way, he was dressed for a night at the theater—a well-cut tuxedo, a fashionable black tie, leather shoes polished to a sheen.

"You've made an impression tonight," he said.

So had he, suddenly.

"I hope that's a compliment."

"It is. I've watched you for a while. You're the best dancer in the company, I think."

Ari thought so, too. But she was more athlete than artist, so the opinion wasn't universally accepted. Baxter certainly didn't share it. "Thank you. You're a regular attendee, then?"

"Season-ticket holder, yes. For about ten years or so." He moved closer, bringing a glass of whiskey or something like it with him, and nodded at her surprisingly empty glass. "May I buy you another?"

The booze was free here, of course. And she really should be out in the party being fabulous, not tucked back in this corner alone with a masked man who said he'd been 'watching' her.

She looked out at the bright, swirling party. All that mingling. All those people, remarking on her arms and legs and neck.

Back here, they weren't actually alone. The bartender was right there. Servers came back and went forth regularly. And of course this man had been watching her. She was a performer. People watched her all the time. That was the job.

She smiled and picked up another glass of champagne, lifting it up as if in thanks before she took a sip. "Thank you."

"It was nothing." The half of his mouth she could see twisted up wryly.

From the tiny bit of information available to her, she thought he was handsome. He had a very nice jaw, at least, and his mouth had a very nice shape. He wore a bit of beard, fashionably short and neatly groomed. The grey that glittered through it, and the noticeable grey of his short, otherwise-dark hair, suggested that he was past forty. He was on the tall side of average, with good shoulders over a trim build. His tux was custom and fit him perfectly. That mask had set him back several hundred dollars at least, and that tux was at least a few thousand. So he was rich, too. No surprise, here in the land of the oldest money.

The eyes behind the mask were jewel-rich blue. He wore a bit of makeup to add shadows under the mask, but that blue was so vivid that Ari could see one eye didn't open as well as the other. His baritone voice had a strange, muffled cast as well. Maybe the mask constricted the movements of his face.

"You're staring," he said, and white teeth flashed in a brief smile.

"Sorry. I'm admiring your mask. Custom made, right?"

"Yes."

"Well, it's a work of art."

"I'll pass along your compliment to the artist."

They stood awkwardly together, their small talk dried up, and then he said, "I thought your performance as the Stepmother in *Cinderella* this spring was really impressive."

She'd loved dancing that part. It wasn't the lead, but the Stepmother didn't have to be beautiful, and the solo was choreographed to show her as rough and harsh, so Ari was able to ham it up and really put her body into it.

That was an actually decent compliment—not necessarily substantive, but it was about her art rather than her body, and that alone made it a real step up from the flutterings of the guests in the ballroom beyond. Pleasure warmed Ari's cheeks, and she smiled. "Thank you."

With a nod, he handed her another glass, and ordered a new drink for himself with a wave.

"You know my name. What's yours?"

"Erik."

Catching the eyeroll before it happened, just in case it was his actual name, she asked, "Is that coincidence or subterfuge?"

Another droll smirk. "Masquerade."

Now, she rolled her eyes. "That's hardly fair, since you know my name."

"But you're a public person. I'm not. And this is a masquerade. So tonight, I'm Erik."

"Then should I be Christine?"

"Is that who you want to be?"

He'd come even closer, so close she had to look up to meet his eyes, so close she could smell his cologne—expensive, subtly applied. The scent of it mingled with the champagne and effervesced her senses.

"I prefer to be myself."

"I can understand why." His hand came up to her face, and his thumb brushed over her cheek, along the edge of her mask. "You're very beautiful and very talented, Miss Luciano."

Was he going to kiss her? The room was beginning to swish around on a sea of champagne, and she thought she'd let him. Why not? He was nice, and respectful. Seemed even to have a sense of humor. He knew the ballet. The evidence suggested he was handsome and rich. Checking off all the boxes, and some bonus boxes, too. Also? Champagne. So why not? What harm would a kiss do?

She raised her hand, meaning to mirror his touch of her cheek, intending it as an invitation.

He stepped back, so quickly Ari felt the rush of air fill in the spot where he'd been. For a moment, they only stared at each other.

"Darling?" Julian's voice broke her bubbly confusion. He took her hand. "I've been looking everywhere. Baxter wants us to get people dancing." He sharpened up into Raoul's regal posture. "Come waltz with me, my love. Excuse us, sir."

As Julian drew her toward the ballroom, Ari looked over her shoulder, but all she saw was a beautifully crafted and perfectly expressionless mask.

"I didn't know Baxter wanted us to dance again," she said, woozily, as Julian spun her onto the dance floor and led her into a waltz. "I've been enjoying the free champagne."

"Bax doesn't care if we dance. He's schmoozing. This is me rescuing you, you beautiful fool."

"Rescuing? I was fine."

"Do you know who you were talking to?"

She grinned. "Erik, obviously."

"Ha. Ha. Ha. That's Donnie Fucking Goretti. You of all people should know that."

The name rang a bell, but that bell jangled in a bubbly sea. "Donnie who?"

"The Pagano guy? Right hand of the don, or whatever they call it?"

Now she got it—and also that weird 'you of all people' crack. Her Uncle Mel, back on Long Island, was a shylock for one of the New York Families. Julian thought that meant she was In with the Mob.

Donnie Goretti was the underboss of the Pagano Brothers.

"That's Donnie Goretti?"

"Yes, dummy. You were over there flirting with a killer. So I rescued you."

"How do you know it's him?"

"Some of the guests were talking about him. He's a regular, I guess, and a big donor, so they all know him. They were saying how funny it was that he'd come to the masquerade. Because, you know, his face."

His nickname was The Face. When newspeople talked or wrote about him, that was always how they referred to him: *Donnie 'The Face' Goretti*. Because he'd been horribly scarred in some kind of accident.

And he'd come to the gala tonight masquerading as the Phantom.

People were gossiping, saying that was funny? She thought of the beautiful mask that hid so much of his face, and thought it wasn't funny at all.

She looked back toward the bar, but he was gone.

~oOo~

Left to right: Nick Pagano, his wife, Beverly, Donnie Goretti, and an unnamed woman leave a performance of "La Traviata."

Donnie "The Face" Goretti (left), and two unnamed men entering the Biltmore Hotel last Friday, around 10 p.m. Tyrone Bederman's body was found the next morning, when housekeeping entered his room. Bederman was under federal indictment. No cause of death has been released.

FREE TO GO: Donnie "The Face" Goretti leaving the federal courthouse this afternoon after all charges against him were dropped.

Opinion: Donnie "The Face" Goretti: Saint or Sinner?

ORG CHART FOR THE NEW ENGLAND FIVE FAMILIES: THE PAGANO BROTHERS, RHODE ISLAND

The roof was repaired after the school received a donation from Donnie Goretti, of Quiet Cove.

Ari clicked through the images and read their captions. When one caught her interest, she read the post it was attached to. It was dumb—she'd probably never see the guy again, and she didn't want to, anyway—but she was curious. What had he been hiding?

She'd been wrong—most of the news *didn't* identify him with his nickname, but it made an impression when they did. But most of the stories that called him 'The Face' were focused on his criminal activities, and there were surprisingly few legitimate news stories about him as a mobster.

Most of the stories that called Donnie Goretti out as a criminal came from shady sites and blogs run by crime-obsessed nobodies. For a mobster, Goretti kept a surprisingly low profile. Uncle Mel would say he was 'old school.' As an influential citizen of Rhode Island, however, Goretti made the news fairly often—donating sizeable amounts to charities and non-profits, patronizing the arts, enjoying the best the city of Providence had to offer.

In any photo he knew was coming, he showed only the left side of his face. It was the shots taken without his knowledge that showed what he'd hidden beneath that beautiful mask. He'd been burned. The whole right side of his face, hairline to jawline and back to his ear, or the place where his ear should have been, was a mottled, melted scar. Shiny and smooth in some places, rough and raised in others — a combination of skin grafts and burn scars, she assumed. His nose, his mouth, and his eye were all partly melted.

The scars were horrible, but not horrifying.

He wore a short beard. Ari found that fascinating. It was stubble, not a full growth, but still, she would have expected a man who could grow hair on only half his face not to grow hair on his face at all. Instead, he seemed to have decided that he would look the way he wanted to look, wherever he could look that way.

Where he could be, he was very good looking.

Whatever had happened to him to leave such ravaging scars behind must have been painful beyond imagining. Ari looked and looked for a story about a fire or something like that, but she found nothing. There was a story about a nightclub bombing in Providence twenty years ago, in which Nick Pagano had featured prominently, and for a second she thought she'd found the answer. But Goretti wasn't mentioned in that story or any of the follow-ups she found.

After an hour online in the dark of her bedroom, Ari knew what Donnie Goretti looked like. She also knew he lived in Quiet Cove, was forty-six years old, and had never been married. He was on the board and/or the top donors' circle of every major arts foundation in Rhode Island and high on the donor lists of several charity organizations as well. He'd been indicted for murder, but the charges hadn't stuck. But of course he'd killed that man. He was a mobster. A Mafioso. At the top of the 'org chart.' Don Pagano's close right hand.

A philanthropist Mafioso who enjoyed the ballet. She found that absolutely fascinating.

Out of nothing more than curiosity, she decided she'd ask in the office where his seats were. They kept track of their most prominent donors, sent gifts to their seats. She could probably finagle that information if Bernard was in the office. He liked her.

Once the house lights were down, she wouldn't be able to see the audience, and while she was dancing, she wouldn't care. But she wanted to know where Donnie Goretti sat.

No reason. Just curious.

~ 5 ~

Nick's grandfather, Gavino Pagano, had started Pagano Brothers Shipping as a one-man, one-truck delivery operation and slowly built it up to a modestly successful shipping company. In Gavino's day, the enterprise had been nothing more than that—strictly aboveboard. After he dropped dead in his own warehouse, the two oldest of his three sons, Beniamino and Lorenzo, took over the company. And they saw an opportunity to make the Pagano name hold sway.

With Ben as don and Lorrie his right hand, the Pagano Brothers organization began there, while the family still mourned the death of the father. During the following decades, from their base in a tiny town in a tiny state, Ben and Lorrie built up their power until they controlled or influenced most of Rhode Island's government and business and had weight throughout New England. They did it in the old way, preferring to make friends rather than threats.

When Nick ascended to the head of the family, he followed in Ben and Lorrie's footsteps, keeping to the old ways even as he brought the organization into a new era. He made no effort to adjust their identity, honoring his father and uncle by insisting that the Family continue to be known as the Pagano Brothers. And he increased his power even more. Under his leadership, the Pagano Brothers now led the New England Council of Families. Nobody did anything significant in New England without Nick's knowledge and input. Not even the other dons.

Donnie had joined the organization while Ben was don. He'd been young, barely a teenager, when he'd started working for the Paganos—running messages for Freddie Fingers, the bookie operating out of the shoe repair shop at the end of his street, for ten bucks a run. Once he was eighteen, he got his own sheet, and a reputation as an earner. He was good with numbers, and working the gamblers have him plenty of opportunity to play with the numbers and shape the odds in the Paganos' favor. He also got a reputation as a hardass. It had been, and still was, his own little secret that he'd been so uncompromising and willing to do violence not because he was naturally brutal but because he was terrified of letting his bosses down. Deep inside, back in those days, he'd still been the shy geek who'd done his first errand for Freddie because he was afraid to say no.

When Carmine 'The Knife' Coltello, the capo back then for the shylocks, heard of his head for numbers, he'd pulled Donnie over and given him a territory of his own. Donnie had been twenty-three years old. The youngest shylock in the organization. Ever. That was still true. As a shylock, he'd maintained his reputation as a hardass earner for the same reason: fear of failure. He earned his bones, and was made.

His blood family had disowned him on that day, but Ben had stepped in and taken him under his arm. From that day, Donnie had loved Ben like a father. He'd worshipped Nick like an older brother, but, much like an older brother, Nick had hardly noticed him until three years later, after Pagano enemies blew up Nick's car outside Neon, a Providence nightclub. Donnie hadn't been anywhere near Providence that night, but after the explosion, they'd beefed up security, putting double teams on all the major players in the organization and their families, and on Beverly Maddox, a woman Nick had picked up in the nightclub and had planned to bring home for a one-night stand. She'd been hurt in the explosion, and press coverage had linked her to Nick, so she got bodyguards, too. There hadn't been enough security men to cover so much, so they'd brought soldiers in from around the organization. Donnie had been called in to cover her.

It was while he was guarding Bev, who by then was far more than a one-night stand to Nick, that Donnie had been burned. And Bev had been badly hurt as well.

It was the greatest failure of his life.

Nick should have killed him for what he'd failed to protect his woman from. Instead, Nick had been grateful for his sacrifice, as had Bev. They'd brought him into their private circle. They became his closest friends. Eventually, while Donnie was still in his thirties, Nick made him underboss and gave him the keys to the office adjoining his own.

Pagano Brothers Shipping was the front for their underground business, but it was, in fact, a legitimate business, contributing substantially to their assets. All of the officers and most of the soldiers worked straight jobs in PBS. Donnie was Chief Financial Officer. When Nick had been underboss, he'd been in charge of operations, but Donnie's talent for numbers made CFO a better fit for him. Angie was COO. For the most part, all three men ran both sides of the business together, so the titles were paperwork more than anything else. But not always.

On a day like today, Donnie had been trapped at his desk, buried behind virtual stacks of coded spreadsheets, analyzing reports from all corners of the Pagano Brothers empire, dark and light. The similarities between the shipping company and their underworld concerns had always struck Donnie as amusing. The great majority of so-called 'mob' work looked a lot like regular work: people to collect from, people to pay, products to deliver, relationships to foster, relationships to sever. It was all work, all done for the same reasons as everyone else's work: paycheck, advancement, acquisition.

And everybody was working the system as hard as they could.

His phone chimed, and his assistant's voice came into the room. "Mr. Goretti? Miss Evans is calling. Would you like me to put her through?"

Sonia Evans—the woman he'd broken up with last week, on the night the Bondaruks had killed Bobbo and the others. Getting that call in the middle of their ending had made the ending fairly abrupt. She'd been crying when he'd handed her off to his guard to get her home.

Fuck, he hated those tears. She didn't love him; she couldn't love him. But she liked the life he offered, the fancy dinners and expensive box seats, the glittering gifts. They were all the same, the women who'd spend time with him—willing to bear looking at him, fucking him, for the payout.

Sometimes a woman almost seemed not to care what he looked like, or to get used to it quickly. Those women, he kept around for a while—a few months, occasionally longer. But sometimes, they would want to settle into the lifestyle, and they'd try to pretend they loved him. He was willing to tolerate their pretense of affection — and even to enjoy it himself — until they tried to make him believe they could love him. That was a lie too far. When he ended things, often they cried. And fuck, he hated those fake tears.

Fake. Endlessly artificial. Like Arianna Luciano's sparkling smile and flirtatious banter. He'd regretted his weakness in attending the gala from the moment she'd turned away. So stupid, so pathetic. Now the image of her in that starry gown and glittering mask had fixed itself to his mind's eye. He'd been so taken in, he'd gotten so close to her, there'd been a moment when he'd thought he might kiss her, and he hadn't kissed a woman in twenty years.

She was obviously with the dancer who'd whisked her away. Their chemistry of their coupleness had blazed out around them. And yet she'd flirted with him. As fake as all the others. Of course, it was a masquerade, and he'd been pretending, too. To be normal. To be desirable. She hadn't owed him honesty, or attention. She'd simply been charming, when it was her job to be so.

He really wished he hadn't gone to the gala. He really wanted to stop thinking of her. That long, sleek neck, the way the tendons showed at the base. Her pert mouth, her pointed chin. A subtle hint of cleavage rising up from her gown. Ballerinas were the most beautiful women in the world; he'd thought so since he'd first seen one, in a middle-school field trip to see a dress rehearsal for *The Nutcracker*. He'd seen Arianna Luciano's head shot in multiple ballet programs and knew very well what she looked like without a mask. She was beautiful in a different way. She looked like someone he could know.

Irritated at his inability to quit picking at the itch she'd made in him, Donnie was not in the mood for Sonia or any woman. "No," he answered his assistant. "Tell her I don't have time."

"Right. Sorry for the interruption. Do you need anything?"

"I'm fine, Tara. Thanks."

Just as the line closed, there was a knock on his door, and it swung open. Angie leaned in. "Hey, boss. Got a minute?"

"Yeah. What's up?"

Angie came in and sat before Donnie's desk, stretching out his legs and settling in. "I had Marty in this morning. He's got a problem."

Marty Bianchi was the capo in charge of the runners, the men who ran errands or deliveries between the men on the streets and their clients, and up to PBS. Other Families had runners in each division, but the Pagano Brothers had always kept the runners separate, assigned to the bookies or the shylocks or whoever needed them by a capo in charge of them all. Marty's team was the lowest-ranking men, many of them unmade and not even soldiers yet. Where Pagano men got their start.

Since his men were not made and had not yet taken their vow, they were also the greatest source of potential trouble. Marty was an OG Pagano, a crusty old grandfather type who led with a guiding hand and a closed fist. He kept keen eyes on his men, and he dealt with trouble as it came. If he'd come to Angie with a problem, then it was one that would be solved with blood.

Donnie sighed. Bobbo's visitation was tonight, his vigil and funeral tomorrow. He really did not want to get his hands bloody in between. "What?"

"He's got a runner swinging out."

Skimming was virtually impossible in their organization—there was so much sophisticated oversight that a capo would have to be involved, and capos were men whose loyalty had been tested and proven. But occasionally, a runner would get it in his head that he could pick up some side jobs on his runs, do some extra business with or for Pagano clients. Off the books. They called this 'swinging out,' and it was a good way to get, at the least, jumped out of the organization. Depending on how far out a runner swung, it could mean the painful end of his life.

It didn't happen often. Once every couple years, maybe. Marty handled it himself unless the betrayal was significant enough to earn death. Angie was sitting here, so the betrayal was significant. Donnie sighed again. "Who and how?"

"It's Alex Di Pietro, and it's bigger than the swing."

The name was only faintly familiar. "Which one is Alex?"

"He runs for Al on the south coast."

Donnie's old route. Al Rizzo was the bookie who'd taken over after Freddie Fingers died. "Right. What's he doing?"

"One of Marty's eyes saw him at a meet in Charlestown. Plates on the sedan he met up with were Jersey." Angie pulled his phone, swiped around on it, and held it out to Donnie.

As he expected, there was a photo on the screen. "Fuck." One of their runners had met up with two of the men they'd ID'd as the Bondaruk advance team. "Fuck. Where is he now?"

"He's loose and stupid. Marty let him run until we made a call. He's got eyes on him round the clock."

"Good thinking." Donnie handed the phone back, and Angie put it in his pocket. "What about Al?"

"Al brought it to Marty. He's clear." Angie slammed his fist on the leather arm of the chair. "These Ukie shits are camped in Jersey. Why the fuck are they pissing in our yard? They gotta cross through New York to get to us."

"I guess back in the old country, they bought into the hype. Everybody knows the New York and Jersey Families. A hundred bucks says they thought New York was too big to fuck with and New England was bent over and waiting."

Angie laughed. "*Stronzi.*"

Donnie didn't laugh. "We have to take this shit with the runner to Nick. He and Bev are with Sherrie at the funeral home, but I don't think it can wait."

"You need me with you?"

"You got something else to do?"

"I thought I'd head south myself and nose around. We don't know what this *figlio di puttana* is giving them. I'd like to know that when I put my hand in his guts."

It was good to go into an interrogation with as much information as possible. "Yeah, go. Just don't miss the visitation." Their third funeral in as many days.

"I won't. I'll be there."

~oOo~

Since he meant to go back to the office and finish his paperwork before the visitation, Donnie left his Porsche in the PBS lot and rode to the funeral home with Dre, his bodyguard.

For a long time, he'd resisted having a full-time guard. He lived alone and could handle himself. When he went out with a woman, or some situation in which he'd be in a crowd, he'd call for a guard, but he preferred being left alone. Nick had put his foot down a few years earlier, when the Council had been working on pushing out a New York gang trying to get an in along the New England coast. An SUV full of bangers had driven by and sprayed his house and car with bullets. Donnie had jumped to the front of his car — a Corvette at that time — and been spared. He'd caught some shrapnel and nothing else, and the Paganos had crushed the shit out of the gang days later. But on the day of the drive-by, Nick stopped humoring Donnie's willfulness regarding security.

Dre parked the SUV in the funeral home lot. He came around, doing his usual check, and opened Donnie's door. Donnie went into the building knowing that Dre would hook up with Ray, Nick's guard, and keep watch at the exits.

He followed the sedate signs — black velvet with plain white plastic letters — to the room Bobbo was laid out in. The afternoon was for family only: Sherrie, their three kids, the grandkids — and Nick and Bev.

Like everywhere else in the building, the room was so quiet it seemed to be packed in cotton. Bobbo's wife and daughters sat with Bev on a silk sofa along a wall. The grandkids played quietly, also along the side of the room. No one seemed to want to fill the space in the middle, aligned with the casket at the far end.

The casket was a large, pearl grey model, and a narrow, dark purple satin cloth lay over it, a trio of white crosses embroidered into the pointed end. Brilliant floral arrangements filled the nook the casket was centered in and spilled out along the sides. The lid was closed—his face had been too abused for an open viewing; besides the dismemberment, the bullet had exploded through his forehead.

A placard propped on a brass easel beside the casket showed an enlarged photo of Bobbo smiling at the center of a professional family portrait—his wife, two daughters, a son, two sons-in-law, a daughter-in-law, four grandsons and two granddaughters. And the incredibly annoying and equally ugly little miniature mutt he'd loved like a fourth child, perched in his hand. The words beneath that photo read *ROBERT ANTONY MONDADORI Now In The Loving Arms of Our Lord.*

Bobbo. Fuck. The old bastard had lived through almost all the wars. Old as he was, he'd deserved to go out in his bed, asleep beside his stalwart wife, not executed while he was stuffed into a suit, working a security detail. But Bobbo hadn't wanted that. Nick had offered him retirement once, and the tough old warhorse had burst into tears. He'd wanted to work, and he was good at it.

A stir in the back corner of the room, where Bobbo's grandkids were playing, caught Donnie's attention. Knowing what he'd see when he looked, he turned to the right. The kids had seen him, his face, and they were all focused on him now. Three were staring. One of the smaller ones was yanking on the arm of her brother, or he might have been a cousin, trying to ask a question. Kids of that age often came right up to him and asked what was wrong with his face. And he always gave them a kid-friendly answer. That innocent curiosity was so much better than furtive stares.

The toddler began to wail.

That was the worst. There was no length of time that could pass and inure Donnie to the sight and sound of a child crying in fear when they saw him and thought him a monster. He'd learned long ago not to bother trying to ease their fear; it only made it worse when the monster tried to talk to them.

Nick broke away from Bobbo's son and came over. Before he'd left the office, Donnie had called to tell him he was coming, and give him the broad strokes as to why, so Nick came straight for him and indicated that they should leave the room. Relieved, Donnie followed him out.

They went across the hall, into an empty visitation room, and Nick closed the door.

"Tell me."

Shaking off the scene in the other room, Donnie told him, filling in all the details he had and offering some commentary as well. Nick listened as he always did, his focus complete and his posture still. "He's still on the street, and Marty and Al are acting like everything's good.

Angie went down there to get his own look. He'll be back in a couple hours."

Now that the report was finished, Nick reacted. "Fuck this scum. Let us bury our dead, goddammit!" After that growled curse, he was calm again.

"Do you want to act now?"

He didn't hesitate. "No. The plan is good. They want us to react. They're ready for it. No. We don't play their game. They play ours. So we wait. But this Alex—"

"If we keep him on the streets, we can feed him some poison and let him take it to the Ukies."

"It's a good idea, Donnie. Yeah. But we are on him like glue, every second. I don't want that little weasel taking a shit that I don't get a report on its color and smell."

"Understood."

"Who brought him in?"

"Al did. He was a neighborhood kid, hanging around the repair shop, just like me. He's been running about four years."

"How old?" Nick was better than Donnie about keeping the names and details of his employees straight, but Alex Di Pietro was a bottom-rung guy, and it was hard to keep those details right to hand.

"Nineteen."

"Fuck."

"Yeah."

By the time this was over, Alex Di Pietro would be dead; there was no other result to a betrayal like this. Nick hadn't bloodied his own hands for several years, but Donnie knew he wouldn't assign this kill. Alex wasn't made, wasn't truly one of their own, and he'd betrayed the Family, but he was still a damn teenager. Nick wouldn't put his death on anyone but himself.

With a deep breath, Nick regained his center. "You're going into Providence tomorrow night, right?"

It was the premiere performance of *The Phantom of the Opera*, and Donnie kept season tickets for a full box on premiere nights. Six seats. Often, Nick and Bev accompanied him, and he brought a date, and occasionally, they filled out the other two seats with business associates, or Donnie invited Trey and his wife, Lara. At Christmas, he worked it out with the theatre so he could squeeze in a seventh seat and invite Nick's whole family, in what had become a traditional outing to see *The Nutcracker*.

But tomorrow was Bobbo's funeral, and the wake after, which would go on into the night. Besides, he was alone, and not in the mood to sit alone in a theater box. "No, not with Bobbo's funeral tomorrow. I'll let the box sit empty."

"No, go. I want you to touch McCauley, but I don't want to make a thing of it. He'll be there, right?"

Parker McCauley was the mayor of Providence. "He usually is. What do you want?"

"I want to know if he's seeing Ukrainian movement in the city and what it is."

"Okay, I'll go."

~oOo~

Tonight's visitation was open to the public, and the funeral home that night was packed. Friends and family, the people who knew and loved Bobbo and his family, came and stayed. Quiet Cove citizens and Paganos business associates, the people who knew Nick and wanted to be sure to pay their respects to the don as well as to the deceased, moved through more fluidly.

Standing some distance from her husband's closed casket, near enough to be convenient for the vague condolences of people she didn't know, but not so near that a crowd amassed at the bier, Sherrie stood and shook hands, accepted hugs. She smiled softly and was unfailingly gracious, but she was obviously exhausted. She was younger than Bobbo, about Nick's age, Donnie guessed, but since her man's death, she'd been aging right before their eyes.

She needed some coffee or something to get through the rest of this evening. Donnie looked around for a grunt to send on the errand, but the room was too crowded, so he made his way to the door himself. As he entered the hallway, he came face to face with Sonia Evans.

A defensive reflex threw his hands up to grab her arms. "What are you doing here?"

She shrugged him off. "I'm not here for you, Donnie. I'm here to pay my respects. I called to let you know I'd be here, but you wouldn't take my call."

Sonia was an attorney; Donnie had met her when one of the PBS attorneys had brought her in for advice on a legitimate business idea they'd considered. She specialized in international business law. She was tall and beautiful and smart—and among the toughest of the women he'd dated long-term, one of the few he didn't intimidate in some way. He'd really enjoyed her company. But she'd tried to convince him she'd fallen in love, that she wanted things he knew damn well she didn't want, and she'd ruined what had been a good thing.

None of that was relevant now. Tonight wasn't about them, and she had no reason to be here. She didn't even live in the Cove. "You didn't know Bobbo."

"Sure I did. We were together almost a year, Don. I met him several times. I had a couple nice talks with him. He was a good guy."

"Fine." He stepped out of her way. "Pay your respects and go."

Her brown eyes narrowed. "You are a sad man, Donnie Goretti."

He had his hands around her arms again, and before he knew what he was doing or why, he was dragging her to and through the nearest closed door, into an empty visitation room. She stiffened but didn't fight him. Sonia was not one to make a scene.

As soon as he stopped, though, she shoved him away. "What the hell, Donnie?"

"Watch how you talk to me." The words came off his tongue with serrated edges.

The anger she heard made hers flare. "I didn't mean it as an insult. I meant that you're sad, and it makes me sad."

"Fuck off, Sonia. I don't need your pity, and I don't want to hear any more of your bullshit."

"Donnie. It's not bullshit. Or pity. You've got more than enough pity for yourself. All I wanted was to be able to kiss you. We were together ten months, and you never kissed me once. I just wanted to be closer to you. I was falling in love, and I was doing it alone, because you're so fucking scared."

He laughed at her sanctimonious, wrongheaded judgment. He wasn't scared. Over twenty years, he'd built himself into a man who could win with the hand he'd been dealt. His scars had never held him back. Every day, he moved through a world that looked on him with horror, but he'd become a man people either feared or respected too much to show their revulsion. Yes, they called him 'The Face' behind his back, but they knew better than to show him anything but respect. More than respect— obeisance. They were afraid of him, not the other way around.

The people he trusted, those he knew truly cared for him, to those few, he was only Donnie, as he'd ever been. He understood how rare those people were, and how valuable.

Romantic love and sexual attraction were something else entirely, though, and he understood his limits there. The only thing about him women could be attracted to was his wealth. He knew better than to trust any word they said otherwise.

"I'm not scared. I'm a realist."

"No. You're a pessimist. You hate yourself so much that you can't believe anyone would love you, and you won't even open yourself to the possibility. You think every act of desire for you is a fiction. That's fear—and it's sad as hell."

The anger was so strong, the urge to do violence so acute, that his hand became a fist and began to rise. Sonia noticed it with a glance, then met his eyes again. "You won't hit me. That's not who you are."

She was right. He never did violence with hot blood. He had control over himself, in every way. "Things with us were good, but you fucked it up. You don't love me. You don't want this mouth on you. You couldn't."

"Things *weren't* good with us. I was hurt and frustrated trying to love you and not feeling anything like it back. There's a massive steel cage around your heart. You think I'm so shallow your scars are all I see of you. You're the shallow one, Donnie. Your scars are all *you* see. But your face isn't the ugly part of you. It's your fear that's really ugly."

His control was slipping; he hadn't been this angry at a woman since Lissie took his son from him. No woman had ever said such things to him before. "You need to get away from me. Pay your respects to Bobbo's wife and get the fuck out."

For a few seconds, she simply looked at him, calmly, her eyes locked with his. Then she nodded. "You're going to die alone, Donnie. Because you hate yourself so much you won't let yourself feel love."

She walked away, leaving him alone in the dim, silent room.

Donnie stood where he was with his fists clenched.

~ 6 ~

There was no serious rehearsal on premiere day. Dancers warmed up, they worked through any choreography that had been particularly difficult to master, but otherwise, they saved their energy for the performance and took to their own premiere-day rituals. Ari, Julian, and Sergei had met up first thing that morning for a last run through the final act, which was particularly intense in both emotion and movement. After that, Sergei went off to the PT room for a massage, and Julian left the theatre altogether. It made him nervous to 'lurk' around — his word — waiting. He thought the energy of the building was too 'noisy' — also his word.

Ari knew what he meant. The anticipation in every room was nearly audible — and she loved it. It matched the same buzz she felt inside, the one that made her heart pound. She stored all that energy up like a battery and brought it onto the stage with her.

That was true when she danced in the corps or had only a solo. Today, when she'd dance the starring role, the same energy felt a bit more brittle, a bit too loud, and she almost wished she was hanging with Julian at the movies for the afternoon.

But she had her premiere-day rituals, and she was too superstitious to set them aside. So, after a lunch of a single grilled chicken breast and a bottle of Pellegrino—she needed the protein but needed not to feel full—she sat on the floor in the far corner of the main rehearsal room, her legs spread wide and covered with her favorite pair of black-and-white-striped legwarmers. While corps dancers worked on their own around her, she broke in her performance pointe shoes.

A ballerina's pointe shoes were nearly as important as the feet she put them on, but they didn't last long. Each dancer in the company had her own favorite brand, and each shoe was custom-fitted for her. Ari liked Freed shoes. Her foot was a bit wide across the ball, and the Freed's shape fit her right and gave her pointe a nice, smooth line. The shoe room upstairs kept dozens of each girl's shoes in stock all the time, and dyed them to match costumes when that was necessary.

The *eight* costumes she'd wear for *Phantom* didn't require dyed shoes, and Ari would have time for only two dressing-room costume changes—at the intermissions. All the others would occur just off stage, a quick addition or subtraction to what she had on. So, barring catastrophe, she'd wear one pair of shoes all night, and that pair would be demolished by the time she took her bow.

Like most of the girls, Ari went through about ninety pairs a year. At nearly a hundred dollars a pair, the annual cost was significant, but the company paid for them. New shoes came out of the box rigidly shaped, so hard you could knock them on the floor and get a hollow sound. Because they lasted so briefly they were essentially disposable, a dancer could not break her shoes in with wearing. They had to be nearly destroyed out of the box and rebuilt for the fit the dancer liked.

All dancers had their own tools and methods. Ari used a small hammer, its ball wrapped with gauze. First, she ripped the lining out and bent the shoe in half, back and forth, until the satin softened. Then she took her hammer and smashed the toe box. When she had the box right, she painted its inside with floor wax to firm it up again. While the wax dried, she darned the platform of the toe for extra durability, sewed a small strip of elastic to the inside of the heel, and then sewed the ribbons to the shoe in the exact place she wanted them. She used dental floss as thread. Real thread broke, and a broken ribbon was a disaster. Dental floss held.

Inside her shoes, before she put on her costume tights, Ari would prepare her feet: bandages around her pinky toes, tape binding her second and third toes together, gauze around all five. Kinesio tape across the backs of her heels and around her arches. Even with so much preparation and protection, Ari's feet were like every other dancer's: veiny, full of corns, calluses, and blisters, and freakishly muscular. Both big toenails were thick and yellowed from falling off and growing back in so often. There was a whole lot of work, a whole lot of strength, a whole lot of pain, and a whole lot of ugly packed into those dainty little satin slippers.

She did all this for all her pointe shoes, practice and performance alike, but on premiere day, she sat in this spot, in these legwarmers, the other dancers all around her, all engaged in their own preparations, and let the bustle around her create a cushioning quiet in her mind, where all her focus could go to an imaging of the ballet. There was nowhere else she would be, nowhere else she could be.

Never moving from her spot, never stirring at all, Ari danced in her head and prepared four pairs of new shoes. She hoped she'd wear only one pair all night, but she was ready if a problem arose.

When she was finished, and looked around, hours had passed. She had just enough time for a glass of water and a protein bar before she went to put on her makeup get into her first costume. The one Baxter thought she looked fat in. He'd finally thrown up his hands in defeated disgust and given up trying to get the costume, and Ari, to conform to his expectations.

His constant belittling had begun to worm itself into her head, but today, infused with the energy of the art, Baxter could get fucked. The costumes were beautiful, and she was beautiful in them. Her makeup would be beautiful, camouflaging her flaws and accenting her best features. Tonight was her night, and no one would poison her confidence. She was good. She was ready.

She was Arianna, dancing.

~oOo~

The Hannibal costume was the first, and the easiest to dance in—a fitted bodice, striped in jewel tones and seemingly strapless, and strips of the same colored ribbons for the skirt. Ari's hardly noteworthy cleavage was still apparent, but she stayed in the bodice and could breathe. Her hair was mostly loose, only the front part pinned back in a firm coil of braid. She didn't like to dance with her hair down, but it was right for the costume.

The next costume would change out the ribbon skirt for a dark, ombre-dyed, princess-length tutu. And then a filmy cover of a dressing gown over that. That dressing gown was the most complicated costume, long

95

sleeves always felt like they were in the way, but the steps of that scene were fairly simple. A full change at the first intermission, with a strapless-illusion leotard, three different tutus, and a small velvet shrug, would accommodate the next three costumes. In the final act, the Don Juan dress would become the wedding gown.

It was all very complicated and took almost as much rehearsal as the dancing, but Ari could hardly wait.

She stood now in the wings, just at the edge of the curtain, and watched the audience roll in. Behind her, a soft chime sounded, and one of the office staff announced over the PA, "Fifteen minutes to curtain. All Act One dancers should prepare to head to the stage."

Already where she belonged, and alone there, Ari scanned the house. This was part of her performance ritual as well. There were a few different types of people who came to the ballet, and for the most part they clustered together in different places of the theatre. First, there were the season-ticket holders, a few subgroups of those. Season tickets were sold first, and the best seats of each section were reserved for people who laid down anywhere from several hundred dollars for a single season ticket in the rafters to many thousands for a private box. In this theatre, the premium seats were either the boxes or straight up the center.

In the most of the boxes were the people everybody recognized: the dignitaries of Providence. Politicians, cultural figures, high-powered businesspeople, what passed for celebrity in their town. They dressed formally, in tuxedos and gowns, and sometimes used opera glasses. In the main sections, the people in seats near the stage were also dressed up, but more 'cocktail' level than 'meet the Queen' — lovely dresses, expensive suits. As the seats stretched farther from the stage, the dress became generally more casual, and the farther out to the sides, the people were less likely to be devotees of the art.

Not to say that all the box-holders loved the ballet. Some had tickets because it was expected of people in their elevated circumstances. Those boxes were status symbols. Sometimes, the glow of a phone screen emanated from high on the side of the theatre as some bored CEO played on his phone during a performance.

She'd asked Bernard about Mr. Donato Goretti, dangerous Mafioso and benefactor of the arts, and knew he had one of the private boxes, and which one, and that his tickets to that box were for opening night. Acting on instinct and not allowing herself to think too much about it, she'd asked Bernard to include a note from her with the gift from the company that would be waiting for him.

She'd spent more than an hour figuring out what to write, and ended up with, *If you're free, will you have a drink with me tonight? If so, meet me under the big tit in the main hall.* Seventy minutes to come up with two sentences. The 'big tit' was what they all called the obnoxiously enormous crystal chandelier that greeted everyone who came through the front doors of the theatre. Ten feet across and six feet deep, an inverted dome made of strands of crystals, with an ornate round medallion in the center. A big tit.

Seventy minutes for those two sentences. At first, she'd tried to be classier about the way she described it, but that took too many words and was awkward as hell, and anyway, *everybody* called it the big tit. Also, casual and coarse was probably not such a bad idea, since she wasn't entirely sure why she wanted to see him. She just wanted to. He'd not left her head much since the night of the gala. She wanted to see him as himself.

Also, he had a private box, six seats, which very strongly suggested that he would be with a date, and probably a small group, so she'd been audacious to ask him for a drink in that way.

Oh well. He could simply ignore the note. No harm done.

"Five minutes to curtain. Dancers, please come to the stage."

It looked like her invitation, written on one of her favorite lavender—scent and color—notecards, would go unread. Donnie Goretti's private box was empty.

Strong arms came around her waist, and she turned and smiled up at Julian.

"*Merde,* darling," he murmured and kissed her cheek.

She wrapped her arms around his neck and returned the ballet world's traditional wish for good luck. "*Merde.*"

~oOo~

At the end of the first intermission, dressed in her Rooftop costume, Ari stood in her usual place and watched the crowd return to their seats. The box she was most interested in was empty. During the first act, she'd been too busy, and the stage lights had been too bright, for her to be aware of an audience at all, much less a particular seat in a particular box. But she had no reason to believe it had been anything but empty the whole time. Donnie Goretti had decided to skip the ballet tonight. Oh well.

Hearing Julian and Sergei talking behind her, Ari took one more look around the house — all those people here to see her do the thing she was best at, the one thing she was truly good at — and turned around.

A flash of movement caught her eye, and she looked back. Donnie Goretti had come into his box. The movement had been the door opening. He closed it now and stood for a moment looking over the house.

He was alone.

While it possibly made her note less awkward, seeing him standing alone in that box was almost as sad as learning why he'd worn such an elaborate mask to the gala.

He saw her. Freezing in the act of taking his seat, he stared down at her, and then stood straight again. For a moment, they stayed just like that, a *tableau vivant*. Then Ari smiled and curtsied. He smiled back and gave her a courtly nod.

A ruffle of applause in the house surprised her, drawing her attention. Without realizing she'd done so, she'd walked closer, onto the stage, beyond the shield of the curtain.

"What are you doing?!" Julian hooked his arm around her waist and walked her backstage.

"Sorry, I wasn't paying attention." She glanced over her shoulder. Donnie was sitting now, no longer smiling, but he was still staring.

"Get your head back in the dance, darling. It's time to make love for the masses." Their most complicated *pas de deux*, when Raoul and Christine declare their love for each other, opened the second act.

"I'm good. I'm in it. Just had a moment, that's all."

~oOo~

When the final curtain came down and the house lights went up, Julian grabbed Ari and spun around with her.

"You were splendid! Oh, so beautiful! I'm in awe of you!"

Ari laughed and hugged him. "You didn't suck, either." The crowd's cheering was like a wave lifting her high off the stage. She hadn't missed a single step. The best performance of her life, probably ever, had just happened.

"Me? I was a Frankenstein lurching around the stage compared to you!" He set her down and did a few *soubresauts* of pure joy. Sergei came up with a grin.

"You were wonderful, Ari. But ..." he gestured toward the curtain. It was time to take their bows.

Ari took the hands of her leading men, and they walked to the curtain together as it rose again. The crowd's cheering redoubled, and Ari heard calls of *Brava! Brava!* meant for her.

As Julian stepped downstage for his solo bow, a stagehand ran in from the side with a bouquet of white roses, and the crowd got even louder. Julian took the flowers and dropped to one knee, offering them to her as if in supplication. Ari curtsied and took the offering, then came downstage and gave the audience a full curtsey, folding to the floor and rising up again.

Brava! Brava! Bellisima! her audience cried. A Niagara of emotion thundered through her blood. She had been her best at the thing she was best at, and all these people had seen it. It had really happened. Even Baxter Berrault was grinning and clapping at the side of the stage.

When she stepped up and Sergei, playing the Phantom himself, came down, the crowd went even wilder. Ari didn't mind. Julian and Sergei had both been perfect as well. They three had been absolutely in sync from the first step to the last. She had actually become Christine, felt that elusive transcendence, without losing her sense of immanence. She'd even been in love with Raoul for a little while, and felt a little afraid of and sorry for Erik.

As the stars stepped aside and made their bows with the corps, Ari looked up to Donnie Goretti's box, but it was empty.

~oOo~

Backstage, Baxter came up to her, still smiling. He spread his arms—he wanted a hug. Ari was too high on her accolades to care that he'd done nothing but berate her for weeks. She let him swallow her up, crushing her flowers against her chest.

"You did okay, kid," he said at her ear. "Not too shabby."

From Baxter, that was as good as a *Brava!* and she hugged him a bit harder with the one arm she had around him. "Thank you!"

As he let her go, his hand took full position of one of her rear cheeks and squeezed.

She jumped back with a little squeak and looked around, but no one was paying them any mind.

Baxter was still smiling the same proud-papa smile. Had it maybe been unintentional? Baxter wasn't into her — he thought she was fat and ugly, an opinion he made known at every chance. Besides which, he was with Devonny. They were a Thing and had been for as long as Ari had been with the company.

As she chased her confusing thoughts through the chill fog of revulsion his fingers at the cleft between her cheeks had brought on, he stepped closer and leaned down to her ear. "Let me take you to dinner tonight."

Normally, she went out with the other dancers for a drink and then home to soak her feet, but tonight she'd made an exception for the possibility of a date with a mobster. She didn't know if that was a go or not, but it didn't matter. She was glad to be able to tell Baxter with the emphasis of honesty, "No, sorry, I have plans."

A sneering frown passed over his face like the shadow of a fast-moving cloud. When it was gone, the smile didn't come back. "Rehearsal tomorrow, ten a.m. Don't you dare be hung over when you get there." He stalked away.

"What'd you say to Bax?" Sergei asked, coming up beside her.

"Nothing. I don't know." She shook off the whole weird scene and smiled up at him. "Whatever. He's Bax. I'm going to get changed!" She had a date to at least loiter under a big crystal boob for a while.

It took her five more minutes to get to her dressing room, wending through the backstage crowd, accepting hugs of congratulations from the other dancers and the crew, and those friends and family of the company who had easy backstage access.

As one of the stars of this ballet, she had her own dressing room, such as it was. The Rhode Island Ballet was a small regional company with resources commensurate to their reputation. Though the historic old building they called home was beautiful and the public areas were grand and stately, the parts the public couldn't see were … less so. The ancient pipes leaked, so the ceilings leaked even on the lowest floors. The linoleum was cracked and pitted. The private dressing rooms—there were three—were eight-by-eight boxes that barely fit the one person assigned to each with their gear and costumes.

Also, they smelled like maple syrup, strangely, which probably meant mold lurking somewhere.

Still, it was her first time with a private dressing room, and it could have had a dirt floor and its own resident rat — they had rats, too, in the subbasement — and she still would have loved it.

When she opened the door, there were two vased floral arrangements taking up the whole of her dressing table, and a long white box resting across the arms of her chair.

See? The room was beautiful. She skipped in and set her stage flowers aside to read the cards.

The first vased arrangement, a typical commercial assortment of colorful flowers, were from the Mayor McCauley — he'd been in the audience, and he usually came backstage after, but she hadn't seen him. He made it a tradition to send flowers to the star ballerina of a performance he attended. The card had been printed off at the florist. Probably an online order. *Best wishes, Mayor McCauley and the City of Providence*, it read.

The second, larger arrangement, of purple calla lilies in a wide, simple, clear glass vase, was from her father. *Merde, cara mia! Love you, Daddy*, the card, also printed, read. Ari laughed — three different languages in six words.

The box — obviously one that long-stemmed roses came in — offered no outward clue as to their sender. She lifted the lid and folded back the emerald green tissue.

At least two dozen long-stemmed roses, in identical bloom, each one the same vivid shade of orange, rested neatly in the box. A small ivory envelope lay across the stems. She picked it up and pulled a small ivory card from it.

Handwritten. Bold strokes of black ink: *Only if you are truly free. 'Erik.'*

'Erik.' In quotation marks. Ari smiled. Donnie Goretti had gotten her note, and didn't seem horrified by her audacity. But how had he accomplished this? He was at the theatre. He was responding to her note, obviously. So how had he managed to get two dozen perfectly matched *orange* roses to her dressing room with a handwritten note?

Orange roses. One of her ballet instructors when she was a girl had insisted that dancers needed to be more than simply graceful and good on their feet. They needed to 'live the dance' — in her exaggerated, indeterminately European accent the words 'live' and 'dance' had been stuffed with miles-long vowel sounds — which meant they needed to know a whole bunch of Victorian nonsense. Including the meanings of flowers.

She couldn't brew a pot of tea from loose leaves, and she couldn't use a fountain pen without making an unholy mess of herself, but she remembered the meanings of the flowers.

Orange roses meant desire.

Did he know that? Probably not. But any florist most certainly would.

A shiver bounced through her at the sudden image of Donnie Goretti reading her note, making a call during the first intermission and ordering two dozen roses that meant 'desire,' then arranging to write and include a personal note before they were delivered by the final curtain.

Oh, this guy was interesting. Oh yes, he was.

~ 7 ~

Donnie stood in the main hall of the theatre, where the masquerade gala had been held, and waited. As the crowd thinned and then trickled until only a handful of guests lingered with him, he felt more and more ridiculous.

She'd known who he was, he told himself. She must have done some research. She knew what he looked like. Even if she hadn't looked up photos when she'd learned his name, she'd seen him tonight, looked straight at him, and smiled. He'd felt a softly magnetic thrum between them, for just a moment. She knew what she was getting into.

But what if the distance between his box and the stage was too great for her to see clearly? What if she hadn't seen photos?

Normally, his first meeting with a woman, and her reaction to him, was the test by which he knew whether to express—or to feel—any interest in her. Women who showed curiosity or surprise but didn't let his scars distract them, he considered. Women who gawked or stuttered, he did not. Nor did he consider women who avoided looking entirely, or who suppressed any reaction at all. That was the most false reaction of them all.

He didn't meet women for drinks unless they'd seen him and he knew they could hold a real conversation with him without obsessing about his face or obviously working not to. He didn't expect love, but he did expect companionship.

The urge to leave, to call Dre and have him bring the car around, pulled Donnie a few steps in that direction, but he locked his knees and stopped. She'd asked him. She'd gone to the trouble of finding his seat and leaving a note. She had to know what she was getting into, right?

He looked up at the sparkling crystal monstrosity over his head. *Meet me under the big tit*, she'd written and made him laugh. He'd never heard that before, but he'd known at once what she meant.

He'd been thinking about her since the gala. Tonight, watching her dance so beautifully, with so much grace and emotion, he could hardly help but imagine her body in his hands. That was dangerous business. All his sexual life, from practically his first wet dream, he'd been attracted to dancers, their grace and strength, their sleek, small bodies, their fluid limbs.

Arianna Luciano was already sunk deeper into his head than most of his *comares*, the women he kept exclusive with for months at a time.

He'd assumed that she was in a relationship with her partner, Julian Trewson, and tonight's performance hadn't convinced him he was wrong. The chemistry between them lit up the stage. Still stinging from Sonia's rebuke last night, Donnie had felt a strong throb of jealousy, for the emotion even more than the woman. To have a woman look at him like that—but it was impossible. He didn't consider love, didn't dwell in fantasies, because no woman ever would, ever could look at him that way and mean it.

If Arianna was not with Trewson, then she was an excellent actor, and that was dangerous business, too.

"Mr. Gor—Donnie?"

He turned at her voice, swinging to the left, and faced her directly. Every atom of his attention narrowed to her reaction. In that glimmer of a moment, he saw nothing at all of her but her face.

Her eyes met his, then shifted away, taking in his scars. When she met his gaze again, she smiled. "Thank you for being here."

It was a near-perfect reaction, according to his mental scorecard. Acknowledgement without fascination. Still not sure what to think, but ready to consider the possibility that she might truly want to share a drink with him, he opened his focus and saw the rest of her.

Her dark hair was down and loose, flowing over her shoulders and down her back. She'd removed her stage makeup and showed a fresh-faced, natural beauty. She had the kind of face Donnie thought of as 'Italian' — strong-featured, almost regal. Large, light eyes, possibly grey, under dark, arched brows. A pointed chin, a shapely mouth made for smiling. A strong, aquiline nose.

Her slight frame was dressed casually, in a flowing flowered skirt that nearly reached the floor, and a pale pink t-shirt, a bit loose, with a neckline that scooped and showed most of her perfect collarbones and the fair skin of her chest. On her feet, just peeking out beneath her skirt, was a pair of white sneakers.

And she carried the roses he'd sent, cradling the open box in her arms.

She glanced down at her own attire. "I'm sorry about my outfit. I didn't think to bring anything better to wear." She laughed, a soft, nervous titter. "Honestly, I wasn't sure you'd be waiting." Her arms tightened around the box of roses. "Thank you so much for these. They're spectacular."

"You're welcome. You know who I am? Really know?"

"I do, yes. As much as I can know from what other people say."

He liked that answer. "And you're free?"

"I am."

"What about Trewson?"

Now she laughed. "Julian? No. We're best friends, but that's it."

"You danced tonight like lovers."

"That's the ballet, and we're both good. But we're just friends. Julian's into big girls."

"Please?"

"You know — big girls. Curvy. Zaftig. Plus-size. Fat. Pick your adjective, he likes big girls. He says he fondles skinny girls for his job, so fucking them on his off hours is too much like work." She blushed hard then, maybe because of her coarse language, but Donnie liked that. It spoke to a level of ease.

He didn't like the idea of Trewson fondling Arianna, but it was certainly an apt verb for their performance tonight. "And you?"

Her grin was sly and enchanting. "I'm not into big girls, no."

She'd made him laugh again. "Are you into anyone?"

"Well, it's a bit too early in the date to know for sure."

None of his alerts had yet gone off. As she'd been in those few brief minutes at the gala, Arianna was spirited and friendly, with a fizziness to her humor he found charming — and unusual.

He took a step closer; there was little more than another step between them. "Have you asked me on a date, Arianna?"

Her eyes traveled the full terrain of his face and returned to his gaze. He saw no revulsion there. "I guess that depends on you. Are *you* free?"

"I am."

Her smile opened wide. "Then I could eat. But I need a minute to find someone to help me get my beautiful roses in water."

"Bring them along. We'll find you a vase." Donnie held out his hand, and Arianna, this delightful little ballerina, set an elegant, long-fingered hand in his.

~oOo~

There was still a kiss of the day's summery warmth in the cool night air, and Donnie had Dre drive them to a hotel on the river, one of the better hotels in the city, with a little Italian café that had elegant seating on a convertible deck. Donnie was known to the staff here, and he and Arianna were led at once to one of the best tables, a cozy booth right on the edge of the deck. The lighting was low enough that he didn't notice any of the other diners react to his face as they followed the host to their table. Good. He could forget and be himself, maybe.

Arianna sighed happily and turned to the view. The river glittered with light cast by the buildings on its banks.

"Thank you," he said to the server as they were seated. Donnie took the seat that put his left side to the rest of the restaurant.

"Of course, Mr. Goretti. May I bring you cocktails to begin your evening?"

Donnie turned to Arianna. "If I order a bottle of wine, will you drink it with me?"

She smiled. "I thought you were a whiskey man."

"Scotch. But I like a lot of things. Will you? And do you have a preference?"

"I will, and no. I trust you."

And he trusted the chef here. "Ask Daniel to send out his best recommendation for a night after the ballet." He nodded at the box resting on the back of the booth, near Arianna's head. "And we'd like a vase for these, please."

The server bobbed his head. "Of course, Mr. Goretti. Right away, sir."

Arianna watched him go and turned back to Donnie. "You can just ask for a vase? How do you know they have one?"

"It's a hotel. They'll have a vase. And if they don't, they'll find one."

"People just do whatever you want them to?"

He shrugged. "Usually."

She laughed and opened her menu. "That must be cool. I spend my days getting ordered around." They perused their menus for a moment, and then she cleared her throat. "Um, this is embarrassing, but there aren't any prices here. I don't think I can afford this place."

Donnie peered over his menu at her. "You thought you were paying?"

"Well, yeah. I asked you out, remember?"

She had; he remembered. A first in his experience. "I do remember. But you're not paying, Arianna." He had no doubt that this restaurant was too expensive for her credit card to bear, but he wouldn't have tolerated her paying in any case.

Her big eyes narrowed, and Donnie expected her to make a totally ineffective protest. Instead, her expression opened again, and she said, "Thank you. My friends call me Ari."

"Is that what you want me to call you?"

Before she could answer, the server was back with a bottle of red and two glasses. Another server came around, cradling a large crystal vase half-filled with water in one arm and carrying folding service table in the other. She set up the table, put the vase on it, and held her hands out. Arianna handed her the box, and she began arranging the roses.

"I'm not sure how I'll get those home now," Arianna muttered, watching.

"We'll work it out. Don't worry."

Their server presented the bottle of wine to Donnie, laying it over his arm. "The chef sends out this Montepulciano. Bold and fruit-forward, an excellent complement to a late, light meal on a fresh summer night. If you'd like a heavier meal, he has another recommendation."

Donnie considered the label. At Nick's side, and Bev's, he'd learned more than how to earn and how to run the Pagano Brothers. He'd also learned how to enjoy the fruits of his labors. Ballet and opera, the symphony — that had all come naturally to him, long before he understood they were the pastimes of the rich and powerful. He'd grown up listening to and watching performances with his grandfather. But wine and food, cars and clothes, the way to comport himself like a powerful man and not some dumb dago who'd struck it big in the Powerball, that he'd learned from Nick — and from Bev.

He wasn't a connoisseur, or even an enthusiast; he didn't follow which years were good years, and he didn't have all the lingo down. Most of the enthusiast stuff was silly. But he knew how to taste a wine and what to look for, and he knew many of the key vineyards and their labels—and he trusted Daniel. This was a good wine. Assuming that Arianna wouldn't eat a heavy meal, he nodded, and their server opened the bottle.

Arianna watched as he performed the tasting ritual. Donnie felt self-conscious about the way his mouth worked, but he buried that and went on with the task. When he nodded again, accepting the wine, their server poured their glasses and set the bottle on the table. "We have two specials tonight, if you're interested—a fish course and a risotto."

"What's the fish?" Arianna asked.

The waiter described the specials, and they each ordered one—the swordfish for Arianna and the tomato-basil risotto for Donnie, who'd spent the afternoon grazing the casseroles and finger foods at Bobbo's wake. He wasn't at all hungry, but he didn't want to sit and watch Arianna eat. He wanted her to be comfortable.

When the server left and they were finally alone again, she sipped her wine. "Oh, it's good."

Donnie took a sip as well, carefully. He sometimes had difficulty drinking from certain glasses, when the size and shape of the mouth of the glass didn't work well with the way his own mouth opened. His burns had gone down to the bone, and he didn't have the muscle composition on the right side of his face to make his mouth work as it should. Several muscle grafts had failed. So he was simply careful.

He smiled across the table at her. The orange roses now overwhelmed the side of the table. The blooms and their sweet scent dangled between them, making a slight screen between Arianna and the scarred side of Donnie's face.

"You never answered my question. Would you like me to call you Ari?"

She returned his smile with one much prettier. "Actually, I like the way my full name sounds when you say it. I feel like that wine."

"Please?"

"Sweet and … elegant, I guess." One graceful shoulder lifted. "Chosen." She blushed and dropped her eyes. "Not that you're choosing me. I just like how it sounds."

Donnie never asked women how they felt about the way he looked; there was no answer they could give that he'd trust. But he was sorely tempted to ask Arianna now. She honestly seemed unaffected by his scars—not blind to them, just not bothered. Maybe even more than that. If he could trust his perception, she seemed *attracted* to him. Not attracted to him despite his scars, or because of them, like a weird fetish. But simply attracted to him, who was scarred. His instincts screamed that it was impossible, but his senses promised that it was true. If only he could just ask her, and believe.

"Arianna," he said, wanting her eyes on him again.

She looked up. Her embarrassment over what she'd said deepened the tint of her cheeks to a rosy glow.

"Do you want to be chosen?"

"I don't know what that means."

"It can mean different things. It could mean we have our dinner and go into the hotel, and I book us a room for the night. I take you home in the morning, or earlier if you want, and we leave it at that. Or it could mean we spend more time together than that, that we date for a while."

Her collarbones lifted as she took in a deep breath. "You move fast. Our salad hasn't even come yet."

He smiled. "Yes. I'm decisive. But I'm not the one who brought it up."

"Can I have dinner to think about it?"

Before he answered, he studied her, looking for signs that she needed time to psych herself up to fuck him. All he saw was a young woman who seemed a little overwhelmed by the turn of events.

His instincts screamed, and his senses made promises. So he said, "Of course," and resolved to pay close attention during dinner to any clues she offered.

~oOo~

While they waited for their salad, and then ate it, they chatted lightly about the ballet. When Arianna understood that his knowledge of her profession was deep enough that he could follow most of her technical talk, she let herself go, and told lively stories about a near-disaster backstage with one of her costumes, and a tardy dancer in the corps during the second act. With only subtle prompting, she lost herself in an analysis of her performance and regaled him with descriptions of her preparations. Her voice was rich with passion and enthusiasm, and Donnie was charmed yet again.

She'd been brilliant tonight, her dancing so evocative that the whole house had barely breathed. In her breathless recounting, he saw her see herself—she knew how good she'd been, and she embraced it. No unwarranted self-doubt, no artificial self-deprecation. It spoke of a strong will and a clear awareness of herself.

He refilled their glasses, killing the bottle, and she stopped her bubbly stream of talk and had a sip. Then she laughed. "I'm sorry. I'm the worst—blah blah blah all about myself all night."

"Don't be sorry. I was just thinking how refreshing it is to hear someone talk about their accomplishments with real pride."

She shrugged. "I know what I'm good at. I also know what I suck at."

"Such as?"

"Usually, I'm not so good at conveying emotion. I'm a strong dancer, and I can make my body do anything I want it to, but the critique I get most often is that my dancing is cold. All body and no heart. I think that's too harsh, but it's not really wrong. I do struggle to get into my character. Usually when I'm dancing, I feel my body so keenly I it's hard to be anybody but myself. Tonight, I don't know ... I felt different. I really felt like Christine for a while there. Which is kind of funny, because I hate *The Phantom*. The story, anyway."

"You do? Why?"

Their entrées came, and conversation stopped as their dishes were laid out and Donnie ordered another bottle of the Montepulciano. When they were alone again, he repeated, "Why do you hate *The Phantom*?"

She had a bite of swordfish, and Donnie grinned as her eyes fluttered closed. "Oh God, this is so good!" She had another bite before she answered him. "It's more the way people think about it that I hate. Everybody loves the Phantom, because boohoo, he's had a terrible life and never known love, he's scarred and hideous and ashamed, and whatever. But he terrorizes Christine. He threatens to kill Raoul to force her to marry him. He kidnaps her. He's a monster."

Donnie had gone still around the word 'boohoo.' His fork hovered over his risotto, and his senses were honed to a pinpoint on Arianna. Her snide words felt a bit too carelessly close to dark things inside him—and outside him as well.

It wasn't until Arianna stopped, and he didn't fill in the space in their conversation, that it dawned on her what her words had touched. She gasped and set her fork down.

Donnie felt what had to this point been an unexpectedly delightful evening crumble.

"Donnie, I'm sorry. I didn't think."

On another night, with another woman, he might well have called a halt right here. But he wasn't ready to give up tonight. He set his fork on his dish. There was possibly something encouraging in her utter lack of awareness. She hadn't thought. His scars had not been foremost in her mind. She didn't see a comparison between him and the Phantom of the Opera. At least not until she'd seen him see it.

So he asked her the question he never asked a woman. "Do my scars bother you?"

She didn't answer right away. First, she looked at him, tipped her head to see around the spray of roses, and studied the right side of his face, a map of skin grafts and burn scars. No eyebrow, no eyelashes. Only the slightest hint of a nostril. An eye that opened ineffectively, pinched on one side like a teardrop, but could not make tears. Almost plasticine smoothness where his lips should be.

The small lumpen mound that was what remained of his ear.

"Only because it must have been incredibly painful, whatever happened to hurt you like that."

"I don't want pity. Don't feel sorry for me."

"*Of course* I'm sorry for you. I'm a human being, and I'm sorry when others feel pain. But it's not pity. It's compassion. I don't want to know the person who wouldn't feel sorry for your pain." She reached across the table and hooked her fingers over his hand. He'd been so wrapped up in his own feelings of this moment that he hadn't seen her move, and he jumped at her touch. "You want to know if I find you less attractive because of your scars, right?"

He didn't answer.

She went on as if he had. "No, I don't. I'd seen photos before I left you that note. I knew what you looked like then. Your scars didn't change my interest, and tonight has only made me like you more."

Donnie didn't believe her; he couldn't. But his reaction was different. Usually, he felt anger spike up from his gut when a woman lied to him, especially about what she saw of him. Now, he wanted her words to be true.

"Why?" The word sounded weak, but it was the only one in his head. Sonia's harsh judgment must have gotten in there somehow and taken root.

"You're fascinating, Mr. Goretti. You're charming and considerate, and you look at me like you really see me. And I like looking at you. Seeing you." She took her hand back and looked at her plate. "Well, we got through the salad course. After I finish this amazing entrée, I think I'd like to be chosen, at least for tonight. If you'd choose me."

For this night, he wouldn't ask more questions, demand more answers. For this night, he would enjoy the company of this lovely young woman who was a much better actor than she believed. He would let her lie, and for this night, he'd give himself the fantasy of belief.

"I choose you."

~ 8 ~

Ari was both surprised and impressed when Donnie paid for their dinner with an American Express Centurion card. Surprised because she hadn't expected a Mafioso to use plastic—her Uncle Mel did everything in cash—and impressed for the obvious reason. Though she lived her life in the world of high culture and danced for the wealthy every night, she herself, and all her friends, barely made ends meet. Only those at the pinnacle of their profession, the principal dancers in the most esteemed companies, made real money. She'd never seen a black Amex before.

After he signed for the bill, he stood and held out his hand. Ari took it and rose from her chair. His hands were good—not coarse, but strong, and nicely shaped—and when he closed his fingers around hers, she felt protected. With just that scant touch.

When he drew her from the table, she pulled back. "Wait—my flowers."

"Not to worry." With a tug, he pulled her forward, and she let him lead her through the restaurant.

He stopped at the maître d' stand and said, "We're going to take a room tonight. I'd like the roses at our table brought up."

"Of course, Mr. Goretti," the maître d' replied.

As they crossed the lobby, Ari laughed, and he smiled back at her. "What?"

"People really do whatever you want."

Still smiling, he gave her the answer he'd given before. "Usually."

At the front desk, he set his Amex down again and asked for a room for the night. The desk attendant's eyes widened just the slightest bit, almost unnoticeably, but Ari was fascinated by the power of that insignificant black rectangle, so she'd caught it. The attendant's demeanor shifted gears at once, but smoothly, from blithely professional to enthusiastically solicitous.

Donnie behaved like a man who expected nothing less than this level of devoted service. Ari, standing beside this powerful man, her hand in his, felt like a little girl he'd swept up from the gutter. Next to his bespoke tuxedo and Italian leather shoes, her thrift-shop boho skirt and top and forty-dollar Keds were little better than rags. She loved this outfit, she loved her style, but *damn*, she wished she'd remembered to bring her cute little black dress and vintage Chanel flats to the theatre. Tonight was an Audrey

Hepburn night if ever there was one, and she was standing here looking like Eliza Doolittle.

Key card in hand, Donnie led her to the elevators. There were seven sets of brushed steel doors — three elevators on each side, facing each other, and another perpendicular to those, in the wall between them. Donnie went to that one and waved his key card over a sensor above the call buttons. The door opened as soon as he pressed the 'up' button, and he led her inside. He waved his card over another sensor and pressed the button marked 'P.'

She'd felt so self-conscious at the desk that she hadn't paid attention to the room assignment. He'd taken a penthouse suite. For a one-night stand with a girl he'd just met.

Was it a one-night stand? It had to be, right? A little masked banter at a party and then a nice dinner a week later was hardly enough to base anything more than a brief fling on, right? Especially considering that he wasn't a regular guy. He didn't come home from a hard day at the office and complain about Bill down in Accounting. When he had a hard day at work, he probably washed somebody's blood off his hands. Or maybe that was a good day for him; she didn't know. Maybe he was a mobster because he enjoyed violence.

Ari was a bit more mob-tolerant than the average girl, but Donnie was a bit more mobster than the average mobster. The second-in-command of the Pagano Brothers was like mobster concentrate. Sharing a sexy night with him after sharing a nice meal was one thing, but she had to take a breath and really think before anything more than that happened.

If he even wanted anything more himself. Wasn't she getting just a bit ahead of herself here? She could have severed her own tongue for that stupid line about how she'd felt 'chosen' — what even did that mean? It made her sound sappy and besotted, like a teenager with a crush on her teacher. But she sort of felt that way. Everything about the night had her bewitched, from that moment during intermission, when his gaze had drawn her onto the stage, to finding the beautiful roses in her dressing room, and the handwritten note with them, to seeing him standing under the big tit, in his perfectly tailored tux. He'd taken her hand and led her into a fairy world of privilege and light, and yes, she was dazzled.

She barely thought about his scars. As the night had progressed, they'd factored less and less, and all she'd seen was a man who was interested in her, who listened when she spoke, even when she yammered on too long, who smiled at her with real enjoyment and maybe affection, who treated her with respect and consideration.

Besides, he was good looking. Really handsome. Not his scarred side, no. It wasn't pretty, what had happened to him, and when she imagined what kind of accident he must have had, she hurt for him. But his scars didn't lessen her attraction. They just were.

He didn't seem to believe that, but she really wanted him to.

While her brain had been spinning, the elevator had been rising, and Donnie had stepped behind her. His hands cupped her shoulders and slid slowly down her arms; at her wrists, his fingers retraced the path. Gooseflesh stippled her arms, and she sighed.

At her shoulders again, his fingers eased forward around her neck, enclosing her throat gently, and then dipped down, over her collarbones, her chest, into her t-shirt. She wasn't wearing a bra. He paused just inside her shirt, like a silent question. Asking permission. Wanting her consent.

Well, she wasn't heading up to the penthouse with him for a quick game of parcheesi. She tipped her head back and arched her back, offering her chest for his exploration.

He took the offer at once. His fingers swept around the curve of her breasts and then found her nipples. He plucked them, and when she moaned in response to that bright snap of pleasure, he grunted softly and plucked a bit harder. Flames of desire lapped through her blood, and she felt her underwear go damp. She put her hands over his and pressed her ass backward, finding the hard ridge she'd hoped to find.

The elevator doors opened. She'd sort of forgotten they were in one. Had all that happened in only a few seconds?

Donnie took her hand. "Come on."

The penthouse floor had significantly fewer rooms, each with a sleek double door. He found theirs quickly, as if he knew the layout already, and opened the door.

The room was dark, only the soft light of two sconces over a console table near the door. She set her little purse on the table. The first thing she really noticed, because it dominated the room, was the view—a full wall of glass, showing what seemed like the entire state of Rhode Island, twinkling beneath them, far and wide. Captivated, Ari walked through the room—a sitting room with furnishings she noted as elegantly modern without really seeing them—and went to the windows.

She even thought she could see the ocean, but that had to have been an illusion. The Atlantic was more than thirty miles off.

Lights came on behind her, and a glowing sketch of the room was superimposed on her view beyond. She saw Donnie, a shimmering shadow, come up behind her, undoing his tie as he walked. He'd shed his jacket already.

"You like the view?" he asked, standing behind her. His hands came to her hips and clutched, gently but firmly.

"I do. I've lived in Providence for a pretty long time, but I don't think I've ever seen it like this."

"How long have you been here?" One hand left her hip, and his fingers slid through her hair.

She sighed at the pleasure and closed her eyes, thinking back to that scary time, losing her position in the *corps de ballet* at the ABT, losing herself in the failure, curled in her childhood bedroom with the curtains drawn until her father had grabbed her by the shoulders and pulled her to her feet. They'd sat together for most of a day, plotting out her 'next chapter,' in his words. She'd found her place here at the Rhode Island Ballet as part of that plot.

"Seven years. Almost eight."

A knock at the door drew their attention, and Donnie went to answer it. Ari turned and watched a hotel staffer come in with her orange roses. At Donnie's direction, he set them on the desk near the window, and Donnie handed him a tip. He followed the staffer to the door and put the 'Privacy, Please' notice on the knob. Then he locked the door completely.

When he turned, he stood at the end of the little hall that served as an entrance to this suite, and, facing her, he unbuttoned his shirt. Behind Ari was a wall of pristinely clear glass, and the entire city beyond it, but dancers lived their lives displaying their bodies, so she wasn't shy about showing hers, whether in a flesh-toned leotard or simply her flesh. She grasped the hem of her top and lifted.

"No." Donnie said. "I want to do it. Turn around."

"What?" A faint tremor of fear goosed her knees. His tone had been sharp, almost adversarial, and a voice that had been AWOL to this point, gamboling around in four full glasses of expensive wine, piped up now and asked if it had been smart to come up to a Mafioso's hotel room on the first date.

His shirt was unbuttoned fully, and he'd pulled it free of his trousers. He wore no undershirt. His black tie was loose, hanging over his neck and down along the open sides of the fitted white shirt.

Oh, just that glimpse of his chest was nice. He was fit and firm but not overdeveloped. In that inch or two of gap, she saw a lean torso, a sweep of definition at the pecs, and a moderate covering of dark hair. Maybe a little sharpness at the inguinal crease. Oh, yeah.

He stood, relaxed and commanding, his body positioned so the light highlighted his left and shadowed his right, as if he'd arranged himself like that intentionally, and Ari saw a handsome, powerful, confident man.

That was the man she'd seen all night, in fact. But now he seemed unburdened.

"Turn around," he said again, in that same tone that brooked no argument.

Still feeling that wary zing, but too turned on to heed it—and maybe too drunk, though she felt only tipsy—Ari obeyed him. That was what it felt like: she obeyed.

When she did, and faced the window wall again, Donnie came to her. She watched him in the glass, coming toward her like a shimmering ghost. He picked up the hem of her top and lifted. Her eyes open and watching, Ari raised her arms high, and he took her top up and over her head.

"No one can see us up here," he murmured as he tossed her top away.

"I don't care if they do."

At that, his eyes met hers in reflection, and the moment paused.

Without breaking their spectral gaze, his fingers went to the waistband of her skirt. He found the tie inside the front as if he'd known it would be there, and pulled it loose. Easing his fingers along her hips, he caught the sides of her underwear, too, and pushed everything down until it was loose enough to fall the rest of the way. Ari toed her sneakers off as she stepped out of the pool of fabric, and kicked the mess away.

Now she was standing before a wall of glass in a well-lit room, before a man nearly fully dressed. That tremor in her joints wasn't fear anymore. Maybe it should have been. Maybe she was doing tonight the stupidest thing she'd ever done in her life. But it didn't feel that way. She didn't think he'd hurt her. Nothing about her interaction with Donnie Goretti had been threatening, not even his firmness now. He'd treated her kindly, and gently. Honorably. Like she was precious. Like she was chosen.

She wasn't afraid of him. Quite the opposite — she'd never wanted anyone this much in her life. This was, like, fantasy material here — an elegant suite, a beautiful view, a handsome man in a tuxedo, a little exhibitionism — and here she was, living it.

Donnie swept her hair over one shoulder and leaned down to the one he'd bared. Ari thought he'd kiss her, but instead, he brushed his left cheek over her, lightly grazing her skin with the stubble of his beard. At the same time, his hands smoothed down her arms to her fingers, slid inward, over her hips, her belly, up, sweeping around her breasts, up over her shoulders, around her throat, down her back, over her ass, and back up her arms. He touched her nearly everywhere, his strokes slow and focused, like he was trying to memorize her, but he didn't touch the parts that ached most for him.

Her legs began to tremble all over. She stepped her foot out a bit, opening herself in invitation, and arched her back, presenting the nipples he'd briefly teased in the elevator. She saw him smile in the glass, and felt his breath at her ear. Again, she expected to feel his mouth on her, but it was nothing but his breath.

With a whimper of burgeoning frustration, wanting more, more of his touch, more of him in any way, she tried to turn. She wanted to feel that chest, explore it, wrap her arms and legs around him, find his mouth and taste it.

His hands became steel grips and held her in place. "No." His mouth was so close, the words were hot breeze on her neck.

"I want to touch you."

"No. I touch you." He made the words true as he said them, taking her breasts in his hands, brushing her nipples with his thumbs until she shuddered and moaned and forgot that she wanted anything else but what he was doing.

He plucked at her nipples, again and again, softly, so softly, like he was trying to shape foam into peaks. Every kiss of his fingertips was charged with fire, making her swell and throb inside and out. She arched back more strongly, raised her arms, reached back for his head, but he stopped his feathery torment and caught her wrists. "No." He pulled her arms forward and set her hands on the glass. Now she leaned in a little, and when his fingers returned to tease her nipples, his pressure was firmer, almost a pinch now, and she cried out at the blast of hot need. He held on and pulled, and Ari made a sound more keen than moan. Dear God, her pussy ached. Her wet trickled down her inner thigh. She *hurt*, she needed so hard.

"Please, please, please," she heard herself beg, panting.

He stopped and let go. "You don't like it?" His tone suggested that he knew very well how much she liked it. He was teasing her.

"Please don't stop. Please."

"You want more?" He plucked again—harder, and added a twist.

Ari reared back, slamming into his chest. The rich cotton of his shirt was soft on her shoulder blades, and she felt the firm, hot chest beneath it. "Please. Yes, please."

One arm scooped around her waist, and he tucked his left cheek against her head. "What do you want, Arianna?"

"Make me come, make me come. Please make me come."

His other hand slid between her legs, through her folds, and the pleasure of that touch rolled her eyes up and stopped her breath.

"Ah, *stella mia*, you're dripping wet. That's what I like. You're silk in my hand."

He found her clit. At the same time, the hand holding her against him slid upward and claimed a breast. He pinched her nipple and flicked his finger over her clit, and Ari's head and body filled with throbbing, noisy pleasure. She couldn't think or talk or do anything but feel. She could scarcely breathe.

He brought her to orgasm just like that, relentless and perfect, and when she gulped in a shrieking breath and crashed over the crest of it, he stepped closer to the glass, pinning her between it and him, containing her flailing, spasming body. Before she could catch her breath, while her body still twitched, and flares of bright light danced before her eyes, he took her other breast, caught hold of its nipple, and the fingers of his hand between her legs pushed deep into her. He leaned over her, pushing her to the glass again, and delved deep, finding the intense, painful pleasure of her g-spot and slamming against it, hard, so hard, but not too hard, except she hadn't come all the way down from the first climax and already the next one was on her. She screamed this time, she felt it claw out of her throat, and she soaked his hand, and he kept going, pulling at her nipple, pounding his fingers inside her, keeping her coming and coming in waves, until all that was left of her was quivering, insensible ecstasy.

He let her go, let her rest her forehead on the glass, and she tried to pull her senses back from the wild reaches they'd scattered to. The lights of the world below shifted and spun. She heard his zipper, heard the soft crinkle of a condom packet, and barely understood what the sounds meant.

"Can you take more?" He asked when his hands came back to her, one resting now on a hip, the other rubbing gently over her back. "Do you want me?"

She didn't know the answer to the first question, but she knew how to answer the second. She had no idea what she was asking for, had barely seen any of his body at all, but she knew she wanted what he'd give her. "Yes. Oh yes."

With a foot still wearing an expensive leather shoe, he nudged the inside of her bare foot, and she her spread her stance.

Watching in the glass, her vision still hazy from back-to-back, mind-shattering orgasms, she saw the diffuse, transparent figure of Donnie Goretti, crime family underboss, tip his head back as he fed himself into her.

The lube of the condom was a shock of cool against her throbbing, swollen flesh. At the first press of his cock into her, she knew he was bigger, or at least thicker, than average. He filled her, demanded her body open more to take him, but she was soft and loose and soaking wet, and she took him in one sleek slide, until her ass and thighs firmly pressed to the summer-weight wool of his trousers. He was deep, filling her up. At first, he didn't move. Her pussy pulsed around his hot invasion, and she felt his body heaving with harsh breath, but he didn't move.

She found his eyes in the glass. While their mirror images locked gazes, he flexed his hips back and drove them forward, a sharp, determined drive until he could go no deeper.

"Oh fuck!" she gasped as he backed up. Before he could thrust again, she arched up like a cat, fearing that heavy slam of sensation as much as she needed it. It was like his fingers again — too much, too deep, too hard, but as soon as he backed off, she wanted it again. Now she really was a little afraid, she was tired and sore, but she didn't want it to stop. That was what scared her — her own reaction.

She'd never had sex like this. From behind, of course. Standing up, yes. But this feeling, this intensity, this fear and need, pain and pleasure, all eddying together into something she couldn't resist, with a man she hardly knew — that scared her.

When she flinched, he stopped. Their eyes were still locked in the shifting reflection before them.

"Arianna?"

She loved the way he said her name. It wasn't the sound so much as the feeling in it. He said her name like he could taste it.

"Do you want to stop?"

With that question, he quelled any doubt that she had about him. She still feared the sensation, but she still needed it, too. And now she felt sure she could trust him.

139

He would stop if she needed him to. She could trust him. He would take care.

"No. I want you. Fuck me, Donnie."

Her utterance of his name pulled a harsh, earthy growl from him, and he rammed forward, his fingers digging into her hips, binding her, controlling her. She cried out as he struck deep again, too deep and just right. He pulled sharply back and did it again, a fierce surge forward. Another, and another, and on and on, each one coming faster, fiercer. Ari could only find breath in her shrill gasps. She scrabbled her hands at the window as if she could get purchase there, and she tried to focus on their reflection, his body in hers, his eyes on hers, but it was nothing but shuddering light and shadows.

The climax storming toward her was enormous. She could feel it swallowing her sense already. "Oh God, oh God!"

"Don't come," he grunted.

"What?!"

"Wait. I'm close." His words came like drum beats, keeping tempo with the strike of his cock inside her. "Wait, and come with me."

She'd never stopped an orgasm before. Usually, she did everything she could to help the guy get her there. She chased them, embraced them. She'd been derailed, of course, by bumbling guys or external interruptions, but she'd never tried to hold one off on purpose, and she didn't have the brain power right now to figure out how.

This one was too big to learn on, anyway. It clouded her mind and tore open her body. She needed it. "Can't—wait—need—"

He changed his rhythm, doubled his pace, grabbed her hair in one hand, and slammed his other hand on the glass beside hers. "Then come! Come now!" he groaned.

And she did. Whether her body was following his command, or the feral sound of the words was the stimulus that pushed her over, or it was just time, she came right then, came until her throat ached, until her muscles were steel bands, until tears streamed down her cheeks.

With a long, deep, desperate groan, Donnie thrust a final time and froze there, his body rigid. His hand in her hair pulled and pulled until his release let him go and he relaxed, drooping onto her back, laying his bearded cheek on her shoulder. His body was humid with effort, his shirt noticeably damp. His belly was a bellows against her lower back, swelling and receding as he fought for breath.

Stunned, Ari sagged against the window and tried to reclaim herself.

"You're crying," he said quietly.

She was, and she couldn't stop. "I'm okay."

"I hurt you."

"No." Yes, he had, but she would let him do it again. No—she'd *want* him to do it again. She'd carry the tenderness of that pleasure with her well into tomorrow. "That's not why I'm crying. I'm okay."

He didn't ask her why she was, and she couldn't have told him if he had. She had no clue. He'd done something, found something, shown her something of herself she'd never known before. But she didn't know what it was or what it meant.

She didn't know what any of this meant. In some ways, this had been the most intense, intimate sex of her life, and in others, it had been the most disconnected.

Except for one brief clasp of his hand at dinner, when he'd nearly jumped from his skin, she'd never touched him. Every contact between them had been his hands on her, his body on her, his body inside her—even through all this wild, sweaty, screamy sex. She'd hardly even seen him—just that glowing shimmer of a reflection. It was like she'd been fucked to hysterics by a ghost.

"I'll take you home now, if you want," he murmured.

That was their agreement in the restaurant, not so directly stated, but clear nonetheless—he'd take her upstairs, they'd fuck, and then they'd decide what was next. Now, while she was splayed naked and pressed against this penthouse glass, his cock still inside her, his clothed body curled over her, he wanted to decide what was next. That felt detached, too.

Finally finding the end of her tears, she swallowed and searched for a clear thought. "Do you want me to go?"

The seconds before he answered hung like weights and slowed the clock. "No."

"I want to stay."

~ 9 ~

Donnie sat on a white leather sofa and watched the sky brighten and diminish the earthbound lights below. The windows of this hotel room faced east, and the sky was clear, so he saw a ruddy gold sunrise climb up from the horizon. He watched as the world beyond the window brightened enough to obscure the smeary print of Arianna's body on the glass. Beside the abstract impression of her body in wild movement was the clear realism of his handprint.

After a grueling performance on the stage and their enthusiastic romp against the window, Arianna had collapsed almost at once when he'd taken her to bed. She'd let him carry her in his arms and tuck her in. He'd lain with her until he was sure she was deeply asleep, and then he'd come out to sit and think, and occasionally drop into a light doze.

Sitting here at the side of the sofa, now that morning light flooded the room, he could see her, the fluffy cloud of white comforter that was her sleeping body, the ribbon of her dark hair on the pillows. She hadn't moved all night, except when he'd slipped her from his arms.

He hadn't slept; he rarely slept away from his own bed, and never on the first night with a new woman. For the past twenty years, sleep had been an inconstant and troublesome companion, especially away from the place he'd arranged just right to settle into it. With half a nose, his breathing was more easily compromised than normal, and in the dry air of a hotel, that could become a problem. Of course he could breathe through his mouth, but he snored when he did. Impressively. One of his *comares* had recorded him one night and played the recording at him the next morning. He'd dumped her on the spot, but he'd never forgotten the sound.

Though he'd never admit it aloud, he was simply too self-conscious to sleep with new company, so he never bothered to try.

There was a lot he was self-conscious about. People thought he had overcome his scars, that he lived as he wanted and didn't let his disfigurement figure in his life or personality, and it was true, or as true as he could force it to be, as true as he could claim it to be. Those few people who would speak of his scars to him had all, in some way, noted how impressed they were that he was who he was

145

despite what had happened to him, how he hadn't let misfortune and pain make him bitter or weak.

But it wasn't about living the life he wanted. It was about wanting the life he lived.

He hadn't overcome anything. He was bitter. He'd simply learned to keep his dark feelings buried deep, where they could torment him only during long night hours alone. He'd learned to accept the life that was left to him.

The night just past was one when the dark feelings had climbed up from his mind's catacombs and howled.

Allowing himself the fantasy of a night with Arianna Luciano had been a mistake. He liked her, more already than he should. She was sweet, and direct. A captivating balance of self-assured and self-aware that he admired. She ... effervesced.

God, the way she felt in his hands, the sinewy writhe of her fantastic body, the powerful, sleek muscles of her thighs, her ass. Her beautiful small tits, the dark, diamond-sharp points of her nipples, tightened with need. The husky sensuality of her sex sounds.

Could he make her his *comare*? What would she think of the offer? What would she think of his rules? Could he be with this woman and not want to love her?

Why was he asking himself so many stupid questions? Who cared what she thought of the offer? She would accept, or she would refuse. And he wouldn't love her, because it wouldn't be returned. He hadn't opened his heart in nearly twenty years. No reason to think the lock would suddenly fail now.

But should he make the offer at all? Why not take her home and forget her? One night. One fantasy. *Finito.*

Donnie raked his left hand through his hair and cocked his head back and forth, easing out the kinks of a night spent sitting up. The right side of his face pulled painfully, and he put his hand to that cheek. Though he had very little sensation on that side of his head, he could feel its inflexibility, like a sharp pull, that became painful the more inflexible it became. The grafts and scars were far more fragile than regular skin—stiff and, without sweat glands or sufficient pores, prone to dryness and damage. The hotel air that dried out his sinuses did the same to his face, and he hadn't planned to be away from home. He got up and went to the small powder room off the sitting room, in search of hotel lotion. It wasn't his prescription ointment, of course, but any oasis in a desert.

In the bathroom, at the mirror, he noticed the front of his trousers, marked with the remnants of their sex, where her wet, frantic body had slammed against his. He closed his eyes and felt her again, fresh memories rising up and taking shape and tone.

No. He couldn't jump down that chute. The time for fantasy was over. Rubbing ginger-scented lotion over his damaged face, he put his mind to plans for the day.

Call Nick and tell him he'd be in late—he could do that now; Nick was a habitually early riser. Get Arianna breakfast, and get her home. Get back to Quiet Cove and the life he lived.

After going to his jacket for his phone, Donnie took up his place on the sofa again. The lump of comforter that was Arianna still hadn't moved. He dialed Nick's number.

The don answered on the first ring. "Donnie. Good morning. What's going on?"

"Good morning. All is well. I'm still in Providence, though, and unless you need me, I'm going to take the morning off."

"Did you talk with McCauley?"

"I did, last night. As far as he knows, there's no new movement of concern in the city, but he'll talk to Gwynn about it and let us know." Ned Gwynn was the Providence police chief.

"Good. And you're okay?"

"Yeah. I just stayed over in the city, and I've got some personal things to attend to this morning."

Nick's tone took on a sheen of amusement. "Ah, I see. Then take your time. We're quiet here. I hope you're enjoying yourself."

Donnie laughed, and the night's dark creatures crawled back into their holes. "I am. I'll see you later."

When that call was finished, he went to the desk for the room phone. Standing beside a riot of orange roses shining in the new sunlight, their blooms a bit bigger and looser than the night before, he called for room service, ordering most of their breakfast menu, a pot of coffee, and a selection of juices and teas, and scheduling it for thirty minutes out, when it might be on the early edge of reasonable to wake her.

When he turned around, though, he saw it wasn't a worry. She stood at the bedroom doorway, wearing a black hotel robe that swamped her body. Her hair was a long, wild tangle, swept over her head to cascade over one shoulder.

"Good morning." He went back to the sofa and stood before it, facing her. "I just ordered breakfast. It'll be here in about half an hour. Do you want to shower?"

She stood where she was, squinting at him sleepily. "Did you sleep?"

"Some. I don't sleep well in hotels."

"You didn't stay in the bed with me, did you?"

"For a little while, I did."

"Then why did you want me to stay the night?"

He could make the offer. Either she would accept his terms, or she wouldn't. Either way, the questions would be answered, and he could put a wall around what this was or was not between them. "Because I didn't want you to go." Donnie sat where he'd been earlier. "Arianna, come talk me."

She came to him, gliding gracefully down the short set of stairs from the bedroom. He'd expected her to sit beside him on the sofa, but instead she went to her knees before him, set her hands on his legs and pushed herself between them.

He was still dressed as he'd been last night—his shirt open, his socks on, his trousers closed again, his belt fastened. Even his tie was still draped over his neck, under the collar of his shirt.

"This isn't talking," he said, but didn't stop her when she opened his belt.

"You didn't let me touch you all night." She pushed open his shirt, exposing his torso. Scratching lightly through the hair, making swirling patterns that left hot sparks of pleasure on his skin, her hands slid tantalizingly up his belly, his chest, over his shoulders, blazing trails everywhere she could reach. Donnie's muscles coiled tensely, into wary need. She found the scars on his right shoulder, where the edge of the grill had caught him, and he let her explore those ridges of hard skin. Her touch flowed through him and made him hunger. But when her hands moved in, headed for his neck, he grabbed her wrists.

"Not my face. Never touch my face."

He saw protest and curiosity, a million questions clamoring at once in her eyes, but with a faint nod she conceded, and he let go. She brought her hands down and opened his trousers, accepting the touch he'd allow her to have.

His cock had gone hard when she'd still been standing in the doorway. When her graceful, soft hand circled it and pulled it free, Donnie groaned and slouched down, giving her more access. She explored him fully with her fingers, every ridge and vein, the full length and circumference, from root to tip. Then, circling both hands around him, she took him into her mouth. Her tongue pressed into the hole at his tip, and he grunted and grabbed her head in both hands, twisted his fingers into her tangled mane, and rocked his hips up, deeper into her mouth.

She backed off at once, fighting against his grip on her head until she could look up at him again. "No. Don't fuck my mouth. Let me do it."

He didn't give women control. The reason he could handle having women in his life at all was his perfect control of their place in it. He drew the boundaries. He managed the risk. He said when and what and how much. Only him. When they tried to wrest control from him, tried to make him do what they wanted, tried to manipulate him with fairy tales, he sent them away.

But Arianna's beautiful hands were wrapped around him. She knelt at his feet and looked up at him with wide grey eyes, and he couldn't draw the boundary.

He dropped his hands, and she bent down and took him into her mouth again.

It took forever, because he couldn't relax. Her hot lips and tongue, her strong fingers, all felt amazing, breathtaking, and he climbed up to the top at once, but he couldn't let himself go over. She sucked and licked and pumped, every stroke, every touch an agony of need, and all he wanted was to fucking *come*, but he couldn't let go. He hovered at the peak until every muscle in his core ached, but he held on.

He didn't give up control. Not with women he'd dated for months. He couldn't give it up to a girl he'd had a single night with. Not even if he wanted to.

But then she changed it up. She took her mouth off him and brought her hands up to the top. Squeezing his cock to the point of pain, she slid her top hand up and down, just over the ridge of his glans, short, hard, fast strokes just there, while her grip forced all the blood to his tip.

"Jesus," he gritted over his choked breath. "Jesus!" His need finally broke its bonds and overran control. The orgasm slammed through him, as much pent-up pain as released pleasure, and he came like a geyser, straight up. It landed with force on his belly.

Still holding his cock in a slightly eased grip, she leaned in and licked up what he'd spent. .

Donnie grabbed every feeling he had and got them all in a chokehold, because the whole spectrum of emotions was loose inside him and digging into dark earth. What they could unbury would tear him apart.

When he had control, he put his hands around her head and made her look him in the eyes. "Sit down. Now."

She frowned. "Did I do something wrong?"

Yes. No. Both. He had no fucking idea. He grabbed her arms instead and stood with her, forcing her around to sit on the sofa. Then he went to the bar and snatched a towel off the rod by the sink. He wet it and wiped himself off. When he was cleaned and his trousers were closed again, he returned to the sitting area, but he chose a chair instead.

"Donnie, I—"

He cut her off. "Do you know what a *comare* is?"

"I do. I've seen *The Sopranos*—also, my uncle is connected. Fuck, Donnie. Are you married?"

He ignored her question for the more important thing she'd said. "Connected how? To who? Who's your uncle?"

"Carmelo Luciano. He's a shylock with the Romanos in New York. Are you married?"

Again, much more interested in this new development, Donnie didn't answer. If she had connected family, then she understood his life in a way few other women could. "Are you close to your uncle? Is he made?"

She shrugged. "He's made. He's my father's only sibling. They married sisters. My mom died when I was a kid, and my aunt did the mom stuff after that. So yeah, we're close. I only see them once or twice a year now, though. I'm not answering another question until you answer mine. Are you *married*?"

"No. Never."

"Then why are you talking about *comares*?"

"It doesn't just mean a woman on the side. It means a woman a man like me has an arrangement with."

"What kind of arrangement?"

"A woman I want to spend time with, who understands what that means."

"Isn't that just a relationship?"

"No. I don't have relationships. I have arrangements."

While she stared at him, eyes and mouth wide open, the room phone rang. Donnie got up and answered it. "Yeah."

"I'm sorry to bother you, Mr. Goretti, but we've got a room service order here, and the privacy tag is on your door. Would you like to reschedule breakfast?"

"Right. No, I'll let you in."

A minute later, two servers pushed two large room service carts in, laden with food. They began to set the table, but Donnie signed the receipt, wrote in a big tip, and got them gone.

154

Arianna was still staring silently when they were alone again.

He indicated the carts with a wave. "I didn't know what you ate for breakfast, so I got it all. Come, we'll talk while we eat."

Watching him like he'd sprouted fangs, she rose and followed him to the carts, keeping a noticeable distance. He helped himself to pancakes and sausage, a couple eggs over easy, and a cup of black coffee. Arianna chose fruit and yogurt, a few strips of bacon, and coffee with cream.

She sat across from him. Donnie noticed a twinge flicker over her face as her ass hit the seat. He'd been a little rough last night, but she'd wanted it. She'd liked it. Of that, he was certain.

She mixed blueberries and raspberries into Greek yogurt and had a spoonful. "You're asking me to be your *comare*?"

"I am, yes." He started with his eggs, adding salt and pepper and a dash of Tabasco.

"I'm afraid to ask, but what's the difference between a relationship and an arrangement? For you, I mean."

"I have rules. They're not negotiable. Break one, and we're done."

"Such as?"

"You never touch my head. Nothing above the shoulders, ever. And I won't ever put my mouth on you, anywhere. What you did for me just now, I won't reciprocate, and I won't kiss you. On the mouth or anywhere else."

"But—"

"I said it's not negotiable. I'll take care of you, make sure you're satisfied. Several times a night, if you want it. And I don't expect you to give me head unless you want to."

"The oral sex isn't as important as kissing. You won't kiss me? At all?"

"No."

"A kiss is the seed of a romance."

"This wouldn't be a romance. That's another rule. I will treat you well. For as long as we're together, I'll take care of you. I'll keep you safe and comfortable. I'll take you to the finest restaurants and events. I'll buy you nice things. We'll travel, first class. Sometimes we'll stay in. I'll enjoy your company and be good company. I'll support you in what you do. But I will not love you, and I won't tolerate lies about your feelings for me. Don't ever use that word."

Dropping her spoon in her barely touched yogurt, she pushed the bowl aside. "Not that it's feeling all that likely right now, but what if I were to fall in love with you?"

They always asked that question. Was he supposed to believe that they actually thought they might someday? He gave the same answer he always gave, but this time the stakes felt higher. Her shock at his rules, her obvious offense, felt different. Less calm. More real. More pained. A hot flare of shame had kindled in his gut.

He ignored it and kept to what he knew. The truth. "I won't believe you, because it will be a lie."

Her confusion and resistance became anger. She leaned back in the chair and crossed her arms over her chest. "This whole *Pretty Woman* thing you're doing here is impressive and all, but I'm not a whore."

That was where the offense always originated: image. Women didn't like things spelled out so starkly. They liked the manipulation, the pretense, the lies. They wanted him to pretend with them that they'd be with him for any other reason than the life he offered. Donnie saw things far too clearly to pretend.

When he laid out his terms, they often thought he was implying they were whores. But a contract with a whore was a simple thing: payment for services rendered. Now, he was merely setting his boundaries. Not a contract. Not a service. An arrangement.

"Of course you're not. We would be having a different conversation if you were."

An ugly cackle erupted from her pretty mouth. "Seriously, have you seen that movie? Because you're channeling Richard Gere really hard right now. Are you just taking me on a tour of all the toxic romantic clichés about damaged men? First the monster in a mask, now the ice-cold executive who makes contracts instead of love. What's next? I guess it'll have to be the stone-cold killer with the secret heart of gold. Or maybe not. Apparently you don't have a heart at all."

Donnie shouldered aside his keen disappointment in her reaction. The odds hadn't been on his side, anyway. He kept his voice calm and reasonable. "I'm being straight with you. I like you. I enjoyed last night very much. I'd like to see you again. But only if we have an arrangement."

"We don't."

Abruptly, she stood up. Donnie stood, too. For a moment, they stared at each other. Donnie could see that she wanted to say something, but nothing came. Finally, she stormed around the table and crossed the wide room to the window, where her clothes were in the same pile she'd shed them into. She grabbed them in a bundle and hurried to the small bathroom where he'd put lotion on his scars not long ago.

The door slammed. The lock turned.

Fuck.

It was hardly the first time a woman had been offended by the terms of his offer—not this outraged, but pissed enough. Donnie usually took it in stride. A woman who couldn't handle his boundaries was a woman who couldn't handle him. But he felt a powerful urge to *convince* Arianna, to explain, to make her see, to make her say yes.

Hearing strange sounds from the bathroom, Donnie went to the door. Before he got there, he understood what he was hearing: retching. She was throwing up.

That flare of shame shot up higher.

The toilet flushed. The tap ran. A few seconds later, she came out, dressed, and looking pale and sad. She seemed diminished somehow. Dimmer. Donnie clamped his jaw down on the apology in his mouth.

She went back to the window and picked up her little sneakers.

"Give me a minute to get my clothes back together and call my driver, and I'll take you home."

Facing the window, right in front of the smear her body had made, she said, "No. I'll call a cab."

The defeated tone in her voice was tinder for his shame. He was burning from the inside out, but he kept his voice calm. "That's silly. Just wait a sec."

"Fuck you, Donnie." She spun around. Tears flowed down her cheeks. "Fuck you. You just made me feel small and … and dirty. You took last night and twisted it until all the good bled out. I really liked you, but you're so broken you can't feel it. You're pathetic."

Fury quashed the shame and impelled him forward. He grabbed her arms and snatched her close. "Watch how you talk to me."

He'd scared her, he could see the fear, but she sneered defiance at him. "Why? Because you'll hurt me? You already did."

When she squirmed hard in his grasp, he let her go. Rooted in place, he watched her run to the door on her graceful legs, even now floating like the ballerina she was, and escape him. She hadn't bothered to put her sneakers on.

The crystal vase of orange roses mocked him from the desk. He recalled the night before, just hours ago. Finding her note. Seeing her on the stage, sharing a connection in a look. Calling the florist and explaining what he wanted to say, doing everything he had to do to get the order delivered with his own note before the final curtain. Seeing her come for him, gliding to him, dressed like a waif in a flowing, flowery skirt. Their delightful dinner. Their intense sex. Her trusting sleep.

She'd left here in tears. Running from him. Fleeing. And now all his dark feelings were loose in the light.

Fuck, how had it all gone so wrong?

Sonia's voice rose up in his mind, speaking the words she'd said at the funeral home. Less than forty-eight hours earlier. *Your scars are all you see. But your face isn't the ugly part of you. It's your fear that's really ugly.*

That was bullshit. He could look in any goddamn mirror, any reflective surface, and see what was ugly about him. He'd lived the last twenty years seeing what was ugly about him in the obvious shock and horror of the people who had the misfortune of looking his way. In the fucking *screams of children*. Of *his own child*. It wasn't his fear that told him no one would love him. The world told him that every single day.

He wasn't fucking afraid of any goddamn thing. His fear had been burned off him on a motherfucking commercial grill, while Nick Pagano's woman, his friend Bev, screamed on the floor at his feet.

Those vibrant roses mocked him. Orange for desire. How stupid he'd been.

He grabbed the vase in both hands and hurled it. It flung water and long-stemmed blooms like blood spray before it crashed on the wall and shattered.

~ 10 ~

It was still early, so early it had taken the doorman a few minutes to track down a cab for her, so early the city streets were quiet. When Ari went into her apartment, it had the quiet, cavernous gloom Julian preferred when he slept, with all their dark drapes pulled shut.

She hung her purse on one of the hooks on the wall by the door and dropped her keys on the bar-height counter that separated their tiny kitchen from their slightly less tiny living room.

There was a handbag on the papasan chair that wasn't hers. Julian had company. Of course he did; the dancers had gone out as usual to celebrate the premiere performance of the ballet, and he always liked to hunt down a pretty to bring home.

She went back to the door and took her purse down from the hook. She wasn't going to leave it around for a stranger to paw through. That had happened once and only once.

Then she ran out of drive. Shock and fury had gotten her this far in something that looked like calm. Out of that suite, to the elevator, through the hotel, to the cab, into the apartment, all in a thoughtless, hazy daze, but calmly. Intentionally. Now, closed up in her home, she could go no farther. She stood there in the narrow little hallway, her purse dangling from the strap in her hand, and couldn't move. She felt sick and weak and hurt. She felt battered. Violated.

Her body ached, but it wasn't that. What he'd done last night, she'd wanted it. She'd *loved* it. He'd treated her like a princess. He'd swept her off her feet. Everything inside her had spun and sparkled, and it hadn't been the wine. She'd been bewitched.

And then this morning a cold-blooded monster had been wearing his clothes.

He hadn't forced himself on her, but she felt violated nonetheless. He'd taken that beautiful encounter, and the newborn feelings fluttering through her, and clawed it all to shreds. He'd sat there, expressionless and calm, cold, and told her he wanted to make her his whore.

He'd made her feel stupid and small. Everything that had happened last night was now trashy and dangerous, and she should have known better. It was like he'd raped her heart.

Shit, she was going to be sick again.

Bolting for the bathroom, she didn't bother to try to be quiet. She slammed the door and landed on her knees, gasping at the hot strike of pain between her legs. Trashy and dangerous. Not just rough—cruel. He'd been cruel and harsh, and her stupid brain had told itself a fairy tale about a sad man in pain. Told her that her fear was really desire.

After she puked whatever was left in her stomach, she needed to wash. She needed to scrub every trace of that bastard from her body and her head. She stripped out of her clothes and stuffed everything into the trash, filling up the little plastic wastebasket. In water at the hottest temperature she could possibly stand, she scrubbed herself with a loofah everywhere he'd touched her, everywhere she could reach, except between her legs, which was too sore to scrub.

God, she'd had him in her mouth! She'd *licked up* his semen like a fucking dog! The thought made her retch again, violently this time, desperately, and she didn't have time to get out of the shower. She dropped to her hands and knees and puked at the drain. There was nothing left but acid, and it swirled down with the water.

Ari was on her hands and knees in her shower, her hair hanging around her face, her body aching in its deepest core, her stomach and chest throbbing. She watched her vomit swirl down the drain, and it was all just too, too, too much. The sobs she'd been battling all morning finally won the war, and she let herself fall over. Curling up on the shower floor, the scalding spray beating down on her like needles, she gave up and bawled.

"Ari? Jesus! What happened! Jesus!" The shower door slammed open and Julian was there, in the shower, turning it off, grabbing her up.

Ari sat up and fought the tears back again. She fought Julian off, too, getting to her feet on her own. She took the towel from his hands and wrapped it around her chest. "I'm okay."

"Bullshit! I haven't seen you like this since—oh fuck, Ari. Oh, love. That son of a bitch." He grabbed her arms and studied them, then took her chin in his hand and studied her face.

He didn't know whom she'd been with, only that she'd had a date. He'd already held forth on the dangers of Donnie Goretti, and she hadn't wanted a lecture from him last night, while she was buzzing from the high of those orange roses.

"No, Jule. No. Stop." She knocked his fussing hands away. "Stop. It's not—he didn't—" Donnie hadn't raped her. She'd wanted everything they'd done last night, even when she was afraid of it, even when it had hurt. She'd *begged* him for it. And he'd decided she made a good whore.

Her stomach rolled, and she dived to her knees and dry heaved at the toilet.

Julian hovered over her, holding her hair.

A knock on the door, and a strange female voice. "Julian? Is everything okay?"

"Fuck," he muttered. "I've got a guest. Let me get rid of her, and then I'm all yours, love. I'm so sorry." He kissed Ari's head and got up.

Ari stayed where she was. Short of ever laying eyes on Donato Goretti again, the last thing she wanted to do was come face to face with Julian's random fuck.

Hoping she finally had control over her stomach and her emotions, she flushed and stood. At the sink, ignoring her reflection, she brushed her teeth. Her robe hung on the back of the door. A black silk kimono. Nothing at all like the hotel robe besides the color. And yet when she put it on, the fresh memory of the morning bloomed fully. Waking naked in that bed, rested and content, hearing Donnie on the phone, ordering their breakfast. Getting up, smiling at the hot ache between her legs, putting the sumptuous hotel robe on, and wandering out to see him standing there, dressed exactly as she'd last seen him. The first inkling of trouble had been then — when she'd understood that he'd left her alone in the bed most of the night, though she'd fallen asleep with her head on his chest. His beautiful chest. His strong arm around her shoulders.

He'd fucking *carried* her into that bed. When she'd been too spent and stunned to move, he'd swept her into his arms like Richard fucking Gere and carried her to bed.

What had happened while she'd slept to turn the prince into the beast?

Nothing, of course. He was who he was. She'd simply been exactly the kind of woman she hated and fallen for all the clichés. She'd thought he was sad. She'd thought she was special. She'd thought he was broken and she could fix him. She'd thought she understood him.

Wrong. On every count. She was just stupid, stupid, stupid.

A knock on the door, and Julian peeked in, stretching his hand into the room. "Coast clear. Come talk to me."

Shaking off the echo of those same words in Donnie's voice, Ari closed her kimono, finger-combed her wet hair, and took her best friend's hand.

He ensconced her on the futon, tucking her in under an afghan, and sat beside her. The smell of fresh coffee floated over from the kitchen; he must have started a pot before he'd come back to the bathroom.

"I'm sorry you sent your girl away."

He waved that off with a flourish. "I got her number, and I think I got bonus points for taking care of my friend in need. Though I might have lost a couple because my friend in need is a beautiful ballerina."

"Sorry. Sounds like you like her."

"I do, maybe. We had a good time." He shook his head briskly. "But who the fuck cares? What happened, Ari? Who was it, and what did he do? Should we call the cops? I know last time—"

Among her growing list of things she absolutely did not want to do this morning was talk about 'last time,' five years ago, when she'd actually been raped, by a dancer in a visiting company, and going to the cops had been nothing but a new set of horrors and shames to contend with, until Baxter and the director of the other company had both leaned on her hard enough that she dropped the charges.

"No. It's not that. I wasn't raped. I thought I had a good night. I thought it was good. It was just … he was different this morning." *No he wasn't. He was the same. Last night, telling you what to do, not letting you touch him, not letting you look at him, doing what he wanted. It was all the same.* She shuddered and put her face in her hands, pressing her fingertips into her eyelids as if she might push the thoughts out of her head.

"Different how?"

She shook her head.

His hands closed gently around her forearms. "You're scaring me, love. Please talk to me."

She looked up, into Julian's worried eyes. "Last night, I thought he was kind. This morning, he was just …

168

cold. And I'm humiliated. That's all it is." She felt like an idiot for letting it happen, and a fool for being so upset about it now.

"That's not nothing. Fuck anybody who makes you feel like this. Is there any reason you ever have to see him again?"

He was a season-ticket holder, but she'd never noticed him before. "No."

"Is there any point in my asking his name?"

"No. It doesn't matter. I just want to pretend it never happened."

"Okay, then, we will. Let's do this: We don't have to be at the theatre for hours yet. Let's open this bad boy" — he slapped his hands on the futon pad — "and bring in all our pillows and blankets. We'll cuddle up and watch crappy TV until we have to go. Sound good?"

She was going to cry again, but now because she loved this man, who was truly kind, and truly cared for her. "Sounds perfect."

~oOo~

"Goddamn it!" Baxter roared and threw his water bottle. "What the fuck is wrong with you? Did you get hit on the head last night?"

"Chill out, Bax," Julian snapped back. He pulled Ari, who'd just nearly broken his nose flubbing—no, *destroying*—the entrance to a one-armed seat press, over to the barre.

The entire cast of the second act was in the rehearsal room, witness to the most embarrassing rehearsal of her career. They were about to be witness to the most embarrassing breakdown of her career as well. She clutched her arms around her middle, trying to hold herself together.

"You're in your head, Ari," Julian muttered. "Hey, hey." He grabbed her chin and tipped her head up. "Just look at me. We've done this hundreds of times. Just be with me. Like we were last night. You and me and nothing else."

Except she wasn't in her head. She was in her body, and her body was sore. A one-armed seat press was a complicated lift, and incredibly intimate in any case—the boy lifted the girl with one hand between her legs, high above his head. The entrance required perfect timing, and Ari had just kneed Julian in the nose—which was a ridiculously clumsy, amateurish result. Julian, ever the professional, hadn't dropped her like a hot rock.

And that was simply the latest and worst of five failed tries, each one more calamitous than the one before.

He was right: they'd done it hundreds of times, in rehearsals and performances alike. Last night, on stage, they'd executed the lift so flawlessly Ari felt like she'd soared, and the whole audience had reacted in gleeful awe.

The problem was his hand. He put his hand between her legs and lifted her, and it hurt. A lot. She felt all the ache of the night before, doubled. And then she *was* in her head, remembering how intense Donnie had been, how much she'd liked it. How he'd turned that all to shit this morning. Her humiliation exploded in a bright burst of pain, and then she was a total fucking mess.

Looking away from Julian, from Baxter, his contempt reflected in the mirror, Ari closed her eyes and pressed her fingers in. The night's performance was in two hours, and this rehearsal had been an absolute nightmare. Her confidence was shot. Everyone's confidence in her was shot.

"Maybe we should cut that lift tonight," Sergei suggested. He sat on a stack of mats in the corner.

"Absolutely not," Baxter snarled. Ari could sense him stalking toward her, but she still jumped when he grabbed her arm and wheeled her around. "You will not fuck up my ballet. I will cut your fat ass before I cut that lift."

"Jesus, Bax, come on," Julian muttered. The boys could get away with a lot more lip than the girls with Baxter Berrault.

Baxter ignored him and squeezed Ari's arm just a little bit harder. "If you can't do it, tell me now. Should I

171

call Jessi over? I'm sure she's ready to step into the role." He looked across the room. "Aren't you, Jessi?"

Ari didn't hear the answer, but she had no doubt it was in the affirmative. She straightened her back and took a deep breath. "I can do it."

"Good. Show me." He let her go and stalked away.

Julian cupped his hands around her face and smiled down at her. "I always got you, Ari. Fuck him, fuck that guy last night, fuck everybody everywhere but us. I got you."

The music started up again. Julian kissed the top of her head, and they walked back to the center of the room.

~oOo~

As she'd done hundreds of times before, she made the lift, in rehearsal and on the stage. She made all her steps, all her moves. The transcendence she'd felt the night before was gone, and once again, as usual, she was Arianna, dancing. On this night, however, she didn't feel even her usual sense of immanence, of deep presence in her own body, no sense of the art in her power. All the memories of last night were still alive in her mind and crashing into each other, keeping her too much in her head.

172

The recollection of a perfect performance. Of her excitement to have Donnie want to see her. Her enchantment with him at dinner. The intense, nervy desire she'd felt in his arms, with his hands all over her, controlling her, commanding her, overwhelming her. The next morning, with the sun shining harshly and throwing shadows over it all. His chilly, distant calm.

Distant. That was the thing—he'd been distant from the start. Detached. Even when their bodies were joined, he'd been nothing more than a shimmer on the glass. He'd given her nothing at all, and like a fool, she'd filled in all his gaps with wishes and fantasies.

She'd thought his reserve was caution. She'd thought he was self-conscious. She'd thought he'd been hurt so much, and felt empathy for his pain. So she'd offered him everything he'd take.

Naked against a window with a stranger, exposed to the whole city of Providence, and he hadn't even taken off his damn tie.

No wonder he wanted to make her his whore. She'd let him use her like one.

Her body danced, remembered its movements, but her mind could not let go of these truths. No transcendence. No immanence. She was only Arianna, dancing.

When Sergei carried her off the stage at the end of the second act, he set her down just in the wings with a huff.

"I'm sorry," she said at once, though neither of them had made a wrong move.

"We dance with a robot tonight."

"I know. I just can't get into it." The house lights were up, and the soft rumble of an audience freed to speak and move rolled into the wings. Ari turned from Sergei and went to the front. She looked out and saw the usual stream of people heading leisurely to the exits for their break.

The box she'd been so interested in last night now held three middle-aged couples. Of course he wouldn't be there. He didn't own that box. He had a premiere-night subscription. And why would she want to see him if he were there? Why was she even looking?

To know it and be warned. Just that.

She felt a hand on her hip and looked over her shoulder at Sergei.

He gave her a reassuring smile. "Come, Ari. Costume change."

A bad date. That was all it was—a bad date. Donnie Goretti was a jerk, but he certainly wasn't the only jerk she'd ever known. Or even the worst jerk. Just a jerk. It meant nothing. *He* meant nothing. And she was being even more stupid and weak than she'd been last night to let him ruin her art like this.

She took Sergei's hand and let him lead her away from the stage.

~oOo~

Ari sat at the mirror of her dressing table and smeared a third coating of Pond's over her face. Her wedding dress costume was off and ready to return to the costume department for cleaning and any repairs it might need. Wearing only her fluffy pink robe, open so she wouldn't get cold cream on it when she cleaned her neck, she wiped away the last of the stage makeup. The usual, musical chatter of dancers and staff in their post-performance bustle fill the hall beyond her closed door.

She'd wanted a star's private dressing room for as long as she could remember, from the days of tiny pink leotards and tutus and soft shoes. But now that she had it, she was a little lonely. The other dancers shared a room, boys and girls alike, and chatted and laughed and complained together while they prepared or unwound.

She was alone here, with nothing but her thoughts.

The third act had gone better than the first two. She'd gotten hold of the stupid, swoony chick who'd taken

175

over her brain, and she'd stuffed that flighty little twat in a trunk in the back. In the third act, which was mostly her and Sergei, Christine and Erik, the ingenue and the Phantom, she'd homed in on Sergei's portrayal of Erik as the villain of the piece, and she'd used her own emotions to fuel her Christine.

She wasn't perfect in the third act, but she was present. She'd done well enough for the audience, and her fellow dancers, to forgive her for the automaton she'd been for the first two-thirds of the night.

Donnie Goretti got exactly this: one day to fuck with her. Now, it was over, and she was over it.

When her face was clean, and she'd started pulling pins from her hair, the door behind her swung open, and Baxter stepped in. Ari dropped her hands and drew her robe closed over her chest.

He closed the door, came the tiny distance to her table, and leaned on it, facing her, his leg against hers. Ari held her robe close and looked up at him.

"Do you need something?"

His grin was slight, and probably meant to be friendly, but she saw predation. "I do. I need to understand you."

"I don't know what that means."

"It means in the past day, I've seen about six different Arianna Lucianos. I've seen a competent dancer. I've seen an abysmal failure. I've seen a clockwork doll.

176

I've seen an angry shrew. And I've seen a true star. Last night, you were sublime. Watching you dance, I was so hard for you I hurt."

She flinched at that, and his grin became openly feral. A snarl of bared teeth.

"Ah, you don't like that? That right there is your problem. You'll never be a star until you understand that. It's what the ballet *is*, darling. It's visceral. It's pure, untrammeled emotion. You should *want* me to be hard. You should want every cock in the house to be dripping with the need to fuck you. And every pussy, too."

"Stop, Bax. Please."

Ignoring her, instead he hooked his foot around her ankle and turned her toward him, forcing her legs to spread. Her robe fell open, and she knew he could see what he wanted to see.

The way Baxter treated her was nothing new, not for her, and not for most girls. And boys, too. Harsh teachers, abusive directors, predatory choreographers — the whole culture abounded with stories about them, so many that nearly every book or movie set in the world of ballet showcased just such a character. It was a profession in which people entered at a very young, tender, naïve age and were shaped to adulthood within it. It was a profession about the body, in which those young, tender, naïve children, all of them beautiful and graceful and scantily clad, were expected to accept the gaze and touch of nearly any person in a position of power over them, a profession in which they were called 'girls' and 'boys' throughout their dancing careers, no matter their age or experience.

It was a profession in which the people in power were used to being obeyed, to having dominion over young bodies, in which those people had also come up in the same way and now believed they'd earned the right to do the same to others.

From the time she was three years old, people had claimed possession of Ari's body, controlled it, demanded it do their bidding, berated her until she could make it obey. Shaped her body to their will with their hands and their voices.

She did not know how to have a will of her own in the face of her director's abuse. Not only did he hold her whole career in his hands, but she'd been trained for nearly thirty years to take what men like him gave. Men with power. Men who saw her as a thing to be shaped to their vision.

Men like Baxter Berrault.

And Donnie Goretti.

She wanted to be strong, to be her own person, to be Arianna, dancing. She'd told herself she was, that she was the dancer she wanted to be. But she was only wet clay, waiting for a man's hands to make her what they wanted.

In the past day, men had shaped away most of her sense of self. Maybe it hadn't ever been anything but a delusion anyway.

All she could do now was pull her robe closed and look away.

He leaned close and set his hand on her knee. "You only have this part because Devonny's injured. You're nothing more than her understudy. You'll never be anything more than an understudy, Ari, until you accept what dance really is. And you're running out of time. You only have a few years left on your toes, and then you'll be nothing at all." His hand began to inch up the inside of her thigh. "I can show you. I can make you *feel* it."

She put her hand down to block him. "Bax, please stop."

He set his hand on hers. "Do you understand that I can save your career? Or end it?"

Before she could understand if she had the strength to resist him, to put everything she'd worked for her entire life on the table in the balance against her sexual autonomy, Julian knocked briskly on the door and opened it.

"Hey, love. You about—oh. Bax." He stepped in and took in the scene. Ari caught his eyes in the mirror, and tried to send him an SOS. Baxter had removed his hand, but his posture was still intimately close. "Everything okay?"

179

"Sure," Baxter said, standing up. "Ari and I were chatting about tonight's performance. I'll see you both tomorrow. Don't stay out too late."

He walked out of the room like a man with no conscience.

Julian closed the door and locked it. He spun around. "Okay. You're in my dressing room with me for the rest of the run. You're not alone with him ever until he moves on from this sadistic twitch he's got for you. Once Dev's back, he'll behave himself."

Ari could only nod.

~ 11 ~

The timer on the treadmill flashed the end of his forty-five minutes, and the belt began to slow down. Not ready to stop, Donnie pressed the 'up' arrow and added another fifteen minutes.

He worked out at least five days a week, more than that if he could find the time. When he was young, he'd had the kind of physique and metabolism that was effortlessly fit—not obviously muscular inside his clothes, but lean and strong, and decently defined, no matter what he ate or whether he worked out. The long stretches of stillness after his injury had changed that, and he'd had to work more conscientiously since. After he passed forty, he'd had to work even harder to keep the same results.

Where he could, Donnie did what he could to be pleasing to the feminine eye. When he was a young man, a fresh Pagano soldier, he'd been pretty good looking. He'd been told often enough to see it himself. He'd gotten plenty of tail. But then he was scarred. After that, until he was made underboss, he'd dated only one woman, and she'd taught him well the lessons of the limits of his appeal.

That he'd been alone except for hired company from then until he stood at Nick's right hand had set the lesson in stone.

Power and money blurred women's vision. Since Nick had brought him up to underboss, he hadn't lacked for female company, but he understood quite well that when they looked at his face, they had to overcome it—he could see the struggle, even in the women he was with for some time. They built up a habit of looking at him in a certain way. So he kept his body fit. He wanted to give them somewhere to put their eyes that he'd see true attraction shining in them.

When he'd bought this house, one of the first things he did was build this gym in the cellar. He'd designed it to be a real gym for one person—a place where he could work out in private, and do anything and everything he wanted. A couple times a week, he lifted and did a little work with a heavy bag and a speed bag. At least three times a week—and every day if he could—he ran on the treadmill.

That was by far his favorite workout. In the rhythmic beat of his feet on the belt, the steady pace entirely in his control, the complete lack of unexpected stimuli, Donnie could free his brain to lift the heavy weight of hard thoughts. Whatever was pressing on his mind or heart, he could explore it and know it, master it and set it aside.

Usually, his heavy thoughts were about his work. He'd never had the taste for violence and blood that Angie had. He did what he had to do because it was his job, and because he would always do anything for Nick. He'd die for his don. He had certainly killed for him, and he would again. And again. He understood the need for the dark work, and he did it. But even against their bitterest enemies, when the taste of vengeance was pungent on his tongue, he got no enjoyment from the work. Satisfaction, perhaps, but not enjoyment. It always weighed heavy.

On the treadmill, he could lighten the load.

For the past few days, his heavy thoughts had been about himself, and they leaned on him harder than any death he'd caused. They weighed on him now. So he kept running. When the next fifteen minutes timed down, he added ten more. Then he really had to stop and get ready for work.

In all his years in the Pagano Brothers, in all his years as a man on this earth, never had a woman run from him before. Women had acted as if he'd hurt their feelings before—and he might truly have; not all of his breakups had been gentle. They'd been angry before. They'd stormed out. But Arianna had *fled*. She'd run barefoot out of the room, so desperate to get away from him she hadn't taken a moment to put on her shoes.

That weighed.

He liked her. Images of their night together flashed through his head, distracting him from his work. Her keen wit, her sunny smile, her directness, her openness. She was nothing like him at all. Bright and beautiful and graceful. Sweet and open. Her fantastic body had molded itself to his hands. Giving to him. He'd been so charmed he'd almost let his guards down. He *had* let his guards down for that night. Maybe because Sonia's parting words had cut him deeper than he'd realized, he'd let himself really feel Arianna. Let himself pretend.

Had he been too harsh the next morning? Or was she simply more fragile than he'd realized? He'd made the offer he always made, laid out the same rules. He'd *told* her he liked her. And yet, she'd run. Crying.

In any case, it was for the best, for both of them. If his offer hurt her so badly, then she wasn't as strong as he'd thought. And it would have been too risky to make her his *comare*—he'd given too much of himself up that night, had allowed himself too much.

Still, it weighed. He couldn't get his thoughts of her worked through and set aside. Those memories—of her smile, of her sinewy body arched in ecstasy, of her tears—flashed, vivid as when they'd been made.

He'd given too much of himself, let her in too deep. He wanted the chance to really be with her, the chance to feel more than attraction and companionship. That was the weight, the pressure, the thing that chafed and ached: with Arianna, he wanted to know what it would be like to feel her love.

And that was just fucking impossible.

He hit the kill switch and stopped running.

~oOo~

At his desk later that morning, Donnie struggled to keep his mind on the figures before him. Usually he was good at keeping the shifting codes of their off-the-books work straight, but today, it took a force of will, and he'd had to check his key a few times. He rarely needed a key once a code was in use. He made a point to memorize them before they went wide through the organization.

The knock at his door offered a welcome break. "Yeah, in!" he called.

Trey opened the door. "Hey, boss. Got a minute?"

"Yeah, sure. Have a seat." Donnie closed his tablet and laptop.

Trey was a young man, only twenty-seven years old, and he had not yet been made, but he held power in the Pagano Brothers that Donnie wasn't sure the kid realized. As the only other man in the organization with Pagano blood, Nick meant Trey to take his place on his retirement.

Donnie had suspected as much since Trey had joined the organization, though Nick had only recently told him, and still had not made his intention widely known. He'd also understood how cataclysmically dangerous that plan was. Trey was only half Italian. In the ways of *La Cosa Nostra*, ways established many generations ago in Sicily and held sacred throughout all Italian Families, only fully Italian men could lead.

Even to make Trey would cause a schism through the globe, and possibly an international civil war. When Nick said he didn't want to call in favors over the Bondaruks, Donnie knew he meant to save those favors for the day he made his young cousin, who called him Uncle, and thereby made clear whom he meant to take his place.

As second in command, Donnie had a right to think of himself as next in line to take the lead, and he would take it, if, God forbid, something should happen to Nick before Trey was ready, and if he didn't lose a challenge for the seat. But he had no strong ambition himself to be don. He was too suspicious and cynical to be a good leader. Nick often had to talk him back from the most pessimistic possible perspective on an issue. Angie was better at seeing things pragmatically, but he was also a hothead.

In the limited evidence thus far, Donnie saw that Trey would someday make a good don. He was levelheaded and loyal. He was smart. He had compassion, but he knew its limits. His stomach was strong, and his will stronger.

But he had a lot of growing yet to do. Nick had demoted him a few months back, after he'd choked badly in a firefight.

Still, when the time came, Donnie would stand with Nick and fight any fight to get Trey made. And if necessary, he'd fight to put him in Nick's place, too, when the time came.

He hoped he'd be dead before then, frankly. He didn't want to live past Nick's era. His whole life had been framed by his relationship to the don.

"What's up?" he asked now. "Day or night?" That was how he thought of their work—legitimate shipping business in the day, their other work in the night. Which was true more often than not. His characterization had caught on with the men over time.

"Both," Trey said as he sat.

"Did you talk to Marty first?" Marty Bianchi was the capo Trey now reported to, since Nick had decided he needed more experience at the bottom. Trey had taken that hard, as Nick had expected, but he'd complied and put his full effort in his new place — also as Nick had expected.

"I did. He sent me to you."

"Then let's start with that."

"I got a call from Shelly Irwin at Cove Realty. Someone put a contract in on the Cyclone space. He wants to know what to do."

Cyclone had been Quiet Cove's first real nightclub, but its tenure had been short-lived. The brothers who'd owned it had not gotten with the program in town, a program in which businesses paid the Pagano Brothers a monthly insurance premium, for which their businesses were protected and allowed to operate. When threats and minor-to-moderate consequences — including one of the brothers having half his leg shot off — had not brought them to heel, Nick had ordered the business destroyed.

What was left was a structurally intact shell and not much else. And the Swinton brothers were long gone and far away.

The shell had sat empty for months now.

Still, for night work, this was pretty light. "You got the specs?"

"Yeah. Shelly sent them over." Trey swiped the screen of his tablet a few times and handed it to Donnie.

He glanced through them, taking note of the offer price and the attached business proposal. In the Cove, a historic New England seaside town, new businesses had to be approved in deep detail by the town council. And the town council made no move without Nick Pagano's okay.

This was a proposal for another nightclub. The space was right for something like that, and the proposal seemed sound, but after Cyclone, Nick would be reluctant to go there again.

The offer was signed by someone named Billy Jones, whose limited liability company had a stupid fucking name.

"Who is NyteLyfe LLC? Billy Jones is not a name that narrows anything down."

"I did a quick search before I went to Marty. It's a new company—formed for this purchase, I think. Billy Jones is almost local. She's from Boston, but she summered here with her folks when she was a kid." Trey laughed. "She's twenty-eight, and her Instagram is full of surfing shots. I probably shared a wave with her at some point."

Donnie was still stuck on his assumption shifting to a different fact. "She?"

"Yeah. Wilhelmina Jones. Billy."

A twenty-eight-year-old woman wanting to run a nightclub seemed a stretch in several directions. "Where's she getting the money?"

"I'm still looking into that, but she's descended from old Boston money. Her grandfather owned a bunch of newspapers. He died last winter. It looks like her uncle got most of the inheritance, but my guess is however the rest of the spoils fell out, she got enough to put this offer in."

"I'm not impressed, but I'll take it to Nick. What's in the daylight?" In effect, Trey had the same job for the shipping company that he had for the Family. He was an account manager in the day and the night.

"Empire Toys. They want to start shipping to Europe, and they need to know Nick's mind on it. What kind of RFP should they put together?"

Companies that worked with Pagano Brothers Shipping gave Nick right of first refusal for their transportation needs. PBS did some international work, but only a few runs a year. Most of their traffic was continental. "That should go to Angie first. He's got his hands on the routes."

"Okay. It's the first time I've worked with something international. I wasn't sure whether to start with the money or the process."

"It's the same as anything else. Always start with process. We have to know what we're doing before we can know what it costs or what to charge."

"Right. Of course. Sorry."

Donnie waved off the apology and handed Trey's tablet back. "Send this proposal to me, and I'll talk to Nick. That it?"

"Yeah. Thanks, boss." Trey stood.

Before he turned, Donnie asked, "How's Lara? And that baby boy?"

Nick's chosen successor grinned. His face shone as bright as a lighthouse lamp. "They're fantastic. I think Frank grew in the few days we were away." Trey's eyes shifted to the window and took on a dreamy aspect. "All this is pretty cool. Being a dad, having a wife. I feel like I had no idea who I was until I had them."

Things Donnie couldn't have. When he was younger than Trey, his life had been doomed to solitude. He hadn't even gotten the chance to be a father to the son he had.

When he didn't respond, Trey blushed and refocused. "Sorry. That was … sorry. Anyway, they're great. Thanks for asking."

~oOo~

Nick leaned back in his chair, the reading glasses he hated perched on his nose, and studied the nightclub proposal. "What do we know about this girl?"

Donnie settled back in his usual chair before Nick's desk. "Not much yet. Trey did some preliminary research. She's twenty-eight, from Boston, from Mayflower money.

Her folks were summer people here. He thinks she inherited the funds to buy the nightclub."

"No loan, then?"

"First blush, it looks like no. She didn't list a lender on the proposal, and it's not a contingent offer."

"NyteLyfe. What a stupid fucking name."

Donnie chuckled. "My thoughts exactly. It's probably some kid slang thing"

Joining him in laughter, Nick lowered the tablet. "You, my friend, aren't old enough to be talking about 'kids' like an old fart. Elisa was an only child still in diapers when I was your age." Elisabetta was the oldest of Nick's four children, now a senior in high school applying to colleges.

He flipped through the proposal a few minutes longer, then sat forward and put the tablet aside. "I don't think we need a nightclub. We never needed one before. I don't want another outsider with big ideas stomping in our town and thinking she can change the way things work."

Donnie had expected just that response, but he wasn't sure he agreed. Nick had always been uncompromising in his principles and demanding in his practices, but he'd also always been flexible enough to recognize and exploit progress. As he aged, he was beginning to get a bit set in his ways, but he was still willing to listen to his trusted advisors. "I have some thoughts. If I may?"

Nick nodded and crossed his arms on his desk. "Tell me."

"You're right that we did fine without a nightclub before, but Cyclone was a hit while it was open, and now, people miss it. They got a taste for it."

"By people, you mean kids."

"Young people, yeah. Right now, that space is empty, and we're paying the town's upkeep on it. It's an empty socket, right off the boardwalk. That's money everybody's losing. If it's not this proposal, I think we should consider finding somebody else to buy it, with a proposal we like. We work somebody who stays in their lane. The Cove wins, we win."

Nick picked up his tablet again. "It's not a terrible proposal. The offer's in a negotiable range. It looks like she wants to do a Gatsby theme? Jazz and red velvet? How's that going to go over with the demographic?"

"I don't think the music will be jazz. I think it's more like the Baz Luhrmann version of Gatsby."

The don's expression was patient, waiting for an explanation. Though Nick and Bev went to all the high-ticket cultural events, he wasn't much of a moviegoer. He did, however, have a wife, three teenage daughters, and a screening room in his home.

"The Leo DiCaprio version."

"Ah. Right." Nick made a face, and Donnie chuckled.

"Anyway," Donnie continued, "I like her proposal, and the season just ended. She'd have the fall and winter to get up and running. That's plenty of time to get her on board with the way the Cove works." After all these years, he knew exactly how far to push an alternative view, so he stopped there and let his don think.

"Okay. Get Calvin to dig deep into this … Billy Jones. Billy?"

"Yeah. Wilhelmina, apparently."

"I want Calvin to dig deep. If she doesn't stink after what he turns over, we'll talk to her."

"Okay. I'll put him on it now."

Nick nodded. "What's the word on Di Pietro?"

The stupid runner who'd swung out on his own and made contact with the Bondaruks. "Nothing so far. We had Marty plant something, but it hasn't sprouted yet. We're on him like skin, but he hasn't met with them again. Maybe they tried to reel him in and he didn't bite."

"If that was the case, why didn't he tell his capo?"

Donnie suggested the most obvious answer, the one Nick himself knew just as well. "Fear. Even bringing it up turns suspicion his way, and he's a kid who doesn't know which way is up."

"If he's not moving, bring him in. Have Angie lean on him. If he's still standing after that, maybe he'll be okay."

Nick's phone rang before Donnie could respond. After a glance at the screen, he picked it up. "It's Beverly." He answered, and shifted smoothly from the don who'd just ordered one of his men to be tortured to the husband who adored his wife. "Hi, *bella*."

When Donnie gestured an offer to leave, Nick shook his head, so he sat where he was, turned his deaf ear to Nick, and tried not to listen to a husband's conversation with his wife.

It was something about one of the girls, something disappointing. Nick mostly listened, and sighed a lot.

Then Donnie heard his name and turned back to Nick. "Donnie and I are just wrapping something up. I can be home for lunch." He listened, and then looked at Donnie. "Beverly is inviting you to dinner tonight. Are you free?"

While Angie's evening had just been planned, Donnie's plans consisted of being home alone, with no company but his recently energized dark thoughts. Nick's family was the one home besides his own where he felt truly comfortable. "Sure, I can be free."

"He'll be there. And I'll see you in about an hour. We'll talk to her, and I'll talk to the school. *Ti amo, bella.*" He ended the call and became the don again. "I'll talk to

Angie about Di Pietro. You get with Calvin and have him work this nightclub proposal. I want to know who this Billy Jones is."

Father, husband, businessman, don. Nick Pagano was indeed a chimera.

~oOo~

After a typically delicious, typically chaotic dinner, while Nick helped Ren with his homework, Lia left for a friend's house, and Bev and Elisa cleaned up, Donnie went looking for Carina, who'd left the table in an angry huff.

She was outside, sitting at the far end of the pool, curled into a chair, looking over the back fence to the ocean beyond. Carina in stillness was a rare sight.

The night had a brisk chill of new autumn, and he zipped his black hoodie up all the way and slid his hands into its pockets as he walked along the side of the pool that had been closed for the season a week or so ago. When he pulled up a chair and sat beside her, he got no reaction, so he looked out at the ocean and stayed quiet with her.

Donnie hadn't been surprised to arrive at Nick and Bev's that evening and discover he'd been *conscripted* more than *invited* to dinner. It wasn't the first time he'd been brought in as a buffer in times of parent-child conflict.

Particularly where Carina was concerned. Sometimes, he could talk to her in a way her parents couldn't, because he wasn't an authority over her. He was just Uncle Donnie.

He thus also hadn't been surprised to learn that the 'she' Bev had called Nick about earlier was Carina, who was in trouble, again, at school.

From the time Carina was old enough to get around on her own little feet, she'd been stirring up trouble at every opportunity. The older she got, the more inventive she got. She'd been into so much mischief for so long, when her trouble had a root of good, it took the people around her some time to see it.

Also from the time she was toddling, she'd had a special affection for her Uncle Donnie.

Donnie couldn't really say why. Back then, he was still having surgeries fairly regularly—failing grafts replaced, new attempts to reconstruct his nose, poor healing repaired—and at times, he'd looked more monstrous than when his skull and teeth were exposed. But Carina had seen only Uncle Donnie, no matter how horrifying he'd looked. Sometimes her sisters would shrink back a little until they got used to his swollen, shredded face, but Carina never did. She'd climb right up on his lap and want to know what was going on on that side of his head.

There was virtually nothing she could do to lose his devotion. He loved all Nick's kids like he'd had a hand in making them, but Carina was his girl.

"I'm not stupid, Uncle Donnie," she finally said. "I know you're out here because I make Mamma cry and Papa mad, and they gave up and made you talk to me."

"Nobody made me, sweetheart. I'm just here if you want to talk."

She was quiet a few moments more, staring blades at the Atlantic. "It's not fair. If I'm suspended, I can't go on the New York trip. And I didn't do anything wrong this time. Even Papa says I was right!"

She'd beaten up a sixth-grade boy. That boy had been running around the cafeteria snapping girls' bra straps. He hadn't snapped Carina's, but she'd seen him coming, and she'd slammed a tray into his face and then proceeded to tear up her knuckles on that face. He was in the hospital tonight.

"Your papa didn't say you were right, exactly, though, did he?" What Nick had said was that the boy had been wrong, and that he deserved to pay for it, but Carina had to be aware of her power and take appropriate action. "Do you understand what he means?"

She nodded. "He didn't deserve me to hurt him so bad. But Noah does stuff like that all the time. Girls complain about him every day. He stands under the stairs and looks up our skirts, he snaps bras, he runs after us making kissing noises. It's gross. Father Brennan says to just ignore him."

"Maybe you should. If he's not touching, he's just being a pest. You need to remember who you are, Carina. You're older, and stronger, and you're a Pagano. You have a lot of power. When you're powerful, you have to be careful how you use it. Do you know what the saying means, 'don't punch down'?"

She rolled her eyes at him. "I'm not a little kid. I know what things mean. It means don't pick on somebody weaker. I don't do that. I didn't pick on Noah."

"You didn't?"

"I taught him a lesson. Like a Pagano. I can't forget who I am, ever. Everybody knows Papa. But Noah's not just a pest, Uncle, and I don't care that he's younger and smaller. Snapping bras is touching, and it's not okay. You don't know what it's like to be a girl. Did anybody ever grab your junk when you were in school?"

He laughed. "Only if I wanted her to."

He'd managed to draw a smile from her, but it didn't last. "Gross. But see? Girls don't do that to boys. But we're supposed to take it from boys like it's fun. It's not. It's embarrassing. Everybody laughs, and it feels bad. So I didn't punch down. Maybe I did too much, but I didn't do wrong, and it's not fair I can't go to New York."

Donnie had listened at dinner, while Nick and Bev had tried to talk to her. Carina's parents presented a united front, they worked out their disagreements in private, but their very different personalities were obvious nonetheless. Bev was a nurturer. She wanted to get deep into an issue and salve everyone's hurts. She wanted to help her daughter understand and navigate the world—but she was also a woman, and had wanted her to stick up for herself. Nick was a leader. A problem solver. He was a fiercely and openly loving father, but he was also the ruthless don of a powerful organization. He wanted to crucify the boy for coming anywhere near his daughter with ill intent, but he was also aware that every time one of his children drew attention, they drew it to him as well.

During the afternoon, after he'd spoken with Father Brennan at the school, Nick and Donnie had gone to the hospital to check on the boy. Nick had spoken with his parents there, and Donnie was sure that Noah Connelly would never touch a girl—or look at her, anywhere—without her consent again.

Carina was right—the boy was in the wrong. But she'd broken his nose, blacked his eyes and knocked two permanent teeth from his mouth, and left him with a concussion, and she'd done it with the entire middle school for an audience.

Frankly, one-hundred percent of the grownups in this house tonight were one-hundred percent in awe of this girl and what she'd done. But she was a Pagano, and the Paganos did not make ostentatious displays of their power. When Nick sought revenge—he called it rendering justice—he did it in the dark. Night, not day. Decisive, but not declaimed. A man who had to shout his power had none.

So Nick Pagano had sat privately with the school principal and brokered a solution for his daughter, one that showed the other students and parents that the Paganos didn't wield their power injudiciously. Carina was suspended for three days for fighting. And Noah was suspended for ten days for fighting and dishonorable conduct.

Then Don Pagano had gone to the hospital and made sure Noah's parents understood the danger should their son ever behave dishonorably again.

Eventually, Carina would be able to hear her parents on this matter. When the sting of the lost trip had faded. For now, Donnie said, "You can't act in rage, Carina. A hot head explodes. A cool head controls."

Again, she rolled her eyes at him. "I don't want to be don of Christ the King School, Uncle. I just wanted Noah to stop."

Donnie laughed and reached over to pull her into a hug. "Well, then, you accomplished your goal. And I think I'd better let your parents give the rest of the advice."

"Carina?" Bev called from the house. "Come on, honey. Homework."

Leaning on Donnie's shoulder, Carina sighed. "I'm suspended, and I can't go to New York this weekend, but I still have to do algebra. It's not fair." But she kissed him on his cheek—she and her mother were the only people who kissed him, or who were allowed to do so—and got up.

As she went in, Bev came out and took Carina's chair. "Did she talk to you at all?"

"She did. Nothing you don't know, though. I don't think I'm the right audience for this one. I don't get the female middle-school experience."

"She doesn't want to talk to me because she doesn't think I get her. I'm too nice, she says."

Donnie didn't know anyone as nice as Bev Pagano. She truly was a kind soul, all the way through. Gentle and sweet, open to everyone. The kind of woman people spoke of as a saint. The day to Nick's night.

Never had Donnie let anyone down the way he'd let her down. She'd been savaged because he'd failed to do his job and protect her. And yet, she loved him. She'd never blamed him for her attack. She'd blamed herself for his.

"Carina will be fine," he told her now. "She'll calm down once the trip is over and her friends stop talking about it."

"I know." Bev sighed. "She's so much like her father. So strong, but so uncompromising. It's hard to get her to see anything but what she thinks is right. And she's not wrong this time, so it's even harder. I'm glad she hurt that boy. She's right, it's not harmless. Boys like that are the ones that date rape girls later because they think they're entitled to sex. And you and Nick are both wrong that there was a better way. I understand why he let her be suspended, I understand what he's telling the other parents by allowing it, but Carina is right this time. That boy needed to be shamed, and she needed to shame him, where people saw. It's not fair that she's punished for doing what she needed to do, but Nick's position comes first. If that boy behaves, it won't be because he respects Carina or any woman. It will be because he fears her father." She sighed. "I wish my daughters didn't have to live in a world where every public space they walk through is a potential danger zone. They have to wonder if every man they meet might be a predator, or if every man who offers them friendship is really just waiting for something more. I hoped it would be better when they were becoming women, but it's not. We are under siege every day we live in this world."

Donnie stared at Bev's profile, all his dark thoughts bursting to life. Was this why Arianna had run from him? Had she seen him as a threat? Of course that was it—why else would she have run? But what had he done that was aggressive? Threatening? Predatory?

As underboss of the Pagano Brothers, he was a dangerous man, an apex predator. That was his role, and who he was. But he had no wish to hurt or frighten women. He wasn't Nick's right hand when he was with a woman. He was only Donnie. He needed control because there was so much danger for *him*.

All he'd done was tell her his rules. Women were sometimes offended by them, but none had ever been *threatened* or *hurt* by them. They existed to prevent hurt, not create it. Had Arianna seen them as a threat of some sort? How? Why?

And why did it matter? Why couldn't he let this go?

"Donnie?"

He blinked and climbed out of his head. "Sorry. Just thinking about your girls. They'll be fine, Bev. They're Paganos, and they're strong. Nobody will dare fuck with them."

She smiled and took his hand. "I love you, Donnie. But you really have no idea what it's like to be a woman in the world."

~ 12 ~

Ari walked along the line of girls at the barre, checking their form in *penché*. Though most instructors she'd had when she was learning had moved her body into position and expected her to hold where they'd placed her, she used a different approach, talking dancers through as they moved their own bodies.

After *The Phantom of the Opera* finished its run, the second and final ballet of the fall season was a showcase of up-and-coming dancers and choreographers in the area—mainly high school and college students. Ari had a few weeks off, with only regular classes scheduled as workouts. Dancers in the company earned their keep during their downtime in community outreach—school visits, guest instruction at affiliated studios, and in the dance programs at area colleges.

Today, she was giving instruction at a dance studio in the 'burbs, teaching a group of middle-school girls. This was a critical age, where an 'activity' became an ambition.

These girls had every advantage—the best studios, the best teachers, parents with the resources, both money and time, to ensure their daughters' best success. But here was the point where those resources could do only so much. Once these girls entered their teens, if they didn't have the talent and body and drive for ballet, none of which could be bought and paid for, they would never be ballerinas.

Pausing near the end of the barre, where one of the smaller girls struggled to find the highest point of her arc, Ari said, to the whole group, "I bet you've heard the thing that you should imagine there are strings running through your center, pulling you up to the ceiling, and through your arms and legs, pulling them in the way they should go." Though these preteen girls were already too well trained to break position to nod or speak, she could see in their faces, reflected in the mirror, that they were familiar with the instruction. Several made an effort to improve their *penché*, as if she'd given the instruction. "Return to first position, please, and turn to me."

The girls came off pointe, gracefully returned to first position, turned, and resumed first. They all stood in their practice leotards and filmy practice skirts like figurines waiting for their music box.

"I think of that instruction as 'the marionette.' Have you all seen a marionette show?" She mimed a marionette herself, and a few of the girls laughed softly. "It's a good idea, because if you can imagine yourself like that, everything loose and pliable, then you can strive for the fluid grace a dancer needs. It's like we don't need gravity, right?" To demonstrate, she ran into the middle of the room, and did a series of *grands fouettés* into *fouettés rond des jambs en tournantes*. Every eye was fixed on her, devouring her movements, coveting them.

She stopped and faced them again. When the girls applauded, she curtsied lightly. "But I always had trouble imagining somebody else was pulling my strings. I saw a few of you who maybe have the same trouble. So, if thinking of strings doesn't work, you can try what I do and see if that works better. I think of myself as trying to reach something I'm not supposed to reach. So I make myself as tall and long as I can. Instead of a string pulling on me, something outside myself, I'm inside myself, pushing every part of me to be go as high and far as it can."

She went *en pointe* and into *penché*, extending her leg to the ceiling, her arm to the wall. "No one is pulling me. No strings. Only me." Taking a turn around the studio, she performed a short series of *grands jetés* and returned to the center. "I don't defy gravity because I'm being pulled from the floor. I defy it because I can fly. Okay. Let's try again. To the barre. *En pointe.* And *penché.* Good!"

~oOo~

After class, most of the girls clustered around her like star-struck groupies. They wanted her autograph. They had a million questions each. Ari took as much time as she could, trying to answer all their questions, take their selfies, and sign their notebooks. She hadn't needed to star in a ballet to have the admiration of girls like this. As long as she'd been dancing professionally, girls in studios had wanted to be her.

When they asked questions about what dancing professionally was like, she tried to strike a balance between realism and fantasy. Girls like this already knew about the pain and hard work. There was more of that, and she was honest about it. She was honest about the competition and disappointments, too—they had some experience in those areas as well. But she skirted some of the seamy underside, not speaking directly about men like Baxter Berrault. Instead, she told them that their body was their own, and while their bodies would always feel the discomforts of hard work, they should never be made to feel uncomfortable in their own skin.

Lessons she tried to master herself, and she'd thought she'd done well at it. But in the past month, she'd been shaken.

The last performances of *Phantom* had gone well enough—nothing like the premiere, but more true to herself than the second performance. She'd shoved Donnie 'The Face' Goretti into her personal scrap heap of bad dates and dumb mistakes and stopped thinking about him. For the most part. And she'd successfully avoided being alone with Baxter, mainly because Julian, and Sergei, too, had made it their purpose in life to keep her company in the theatre. She'd given up her dressing room to squeeze in with Julian, and her partners had been her shadows for the rest of the week.

So no more horrible moves from Baxter, but he was vividly aware that she avoided being alone with him, he showed his displeasure just as vividly, and she knew she was going to pay. Tomorrow was the first winter season planning meeting, a mandatory, company-wide affair, and Ari fully expected to be humiliated in front of everyone. At a minimum, she expected him to announced auditions for the role of Clara.

Devonny, six years older than Ari, had never had to audition for the starring role of any ballet in all the time Ari had been in the company. But Devonny was not yet ready to dance again. Ari was inarguably the next-best dancer — arguably the best dancer — in the company. Baxter had given her the role of Christine — not necessarily with good grace, but without question. But he would make her audition now, she was sure. And depending on how angry he was at her rejection, he might well give the part to someone else. Jessi, most likely, whom he often held up as her chief competition.

Jessi wasn't close to the dancer Ari was, in art or craft, but she was emotionally and mentally pliable, and her body was less evidently muscular than Ari's. More Baxter's type. Baxter despised *The Nutcracker*, and hated that ticket-holders demanded the ballet every December. Ari absolutely believed that he'd sacrifice the quality of their 'kiddie show' on the altar of his unsatisfied penis.

For the past few weeks, she'd felt the constant weight of Baxter's angry, petulant, vindictive gaze. No matter where she was, how far from him she was, what she was doing, that feeling never left her. He had control of her career, and she had little else of value in her life.

Once all the girls had left the studio for the changing room, Ari sat on the floor. She removed her pointe shoes and slipped into a pair of split-sole shoes instead. She pulled legwarmers over her tights and wrapped a pashmina shawl around her shoulders. The girls' teacher, an elegant older woman named Marlene, who'd danced professionally in the Midwest, slid her arms into a well-worn cardigan.

Ari prepared to make small talk. She preferred to wait and change to her street clothes when the girls were gone and the studio was quiet, and she knew that the instructors liked their time with her as well. Most ballet instructors had been professional dancers of one sort or another, and they all liked to talk shop and relive a life when little girls and demanding mothers were not part of their daily grind.

"You know," Marlene said, watching Ari gather up her gear, "what you said about pushing your body rather than allowing it to be pulled, I'm not sure I agree. I think the grace comes in the way our bodies seem to be controlled by something greater than ourselves."

Ari smiled. "You mean God?"

"If you wish. But something more powerful than our petty human selves, certainly."

"I understand. But we work hard for our art. We hurt for it. We don't wake up one morning with the ability to do the things we can do. It takes years of real, painful effort."

"Of course, yes. Like all artists, we suffer."

"Then why give credit to something other than ourselves?"

"It's not credit, dear. It is still the dancer, herself, on the stage. But the art is in making hard work look effortless."

Marlene was right, obviously. Ari had been told often enough that her dancing was too 'strong' for true greatness that she understood: her strength was her weakness. But it chafed. It particularly chafed that this old dancer who'd never achieved enough success even to fail at the ABT thought she could offer unsolicited advice.

Since she wasn't a diva, though, she let it slide, and she put a point on the conversation. "You're right, I know. I didn't mean to confuse your students."

"You didn't. It's good to have different ways to think of things. Do you have time to share a cup of tea?" Marlene asked.

Though she was no longer in any mood to hang around in this studio, Ari smiled. "Of course. I'd love a cup of tea."

"I have shortbread cookies, too. Do you dare?"

"I think I can dare a cookie, yes. That sounds lovely." She followed the woman back to her office, which she knew would be a cramped, dreary, disheartening space.

And a look into her own future. Maybe her near future.

~oOo~

"If he does" — Julian met her at the back of his car and pushed the trunk lid open — "you should talk to a lawyer."

"I don't think it's a prosecutable offense to make me audition." Ari reached in for her dance bag, but he brushed her hand away and took them both.

"I'm not a lawyer, and neither are you, so we don't know. But everybody knows you're the best girl in the company. I think you're better than Dev, too. There's nobody even close, and everybody knows it." With both bags hooked over one shoulder, he offered his hand, and Ari took it.

"I love you, Jule. You've always got my back. But Bax has never liked my look, and I'm not perfect. I don't have the artistry that Dev does."

"Okay, yes, that's true. But still, there's nobody else close to you, technically or artistically. Jessi looks like she's run a marathon at the end of an act. Carijean makes the boy work way too hard in lifts. And they're the best girls after you and Dev. If Bax puts either one of them in the lead, that's nothing but an attack on you."

They'd reached the door, and Julian dropped her hand to open it. Ari felt an odd, paranoid tickle up the back of her neck, like she was being watched. It was strong enough to stop her in her tracks.

With the door open, Julian turned to see that she was a couple steps back. "What?"

Ari looked behind her; there was no one around. The afternoon was getting a bit old, and the shadows were long, but she could still see clearly down the sidewalk, to the parking lot. They were running almost late, and she recognized the cars of the rest of the company. A few others as well, but nothing that stood out. The typical bland sedans, a couple dark SUVs, Baxter's bright yellow Corvette.

"Ari?"

The feeling of being watched persisted, but she spun back to her friend and smiled. "Sorry. Goosed by a ghost, I guess."

Her own words kicked a memory into the open, from a few weeks back: when she'd had the thought that being with Donnie Goretti in that hotel room had been like being fucked by a ghost. She turned and looked back again, but still nothing.

"Ari, what?"

She was being ridiculous. And she was supposed to keep all thoughts about coldhearted Mafiosi stuffed in the back of her mental closet. "Sorry, sorry. Baxter's got me all kinds of paranoid, I guess."

"Well, come on. Let's work out, and then we'll see what he does in the meeting."

~oOo~

Between ballets, dancers worked out regularly but a bit more lightly. Rehearsal schedules were grueling, so in those few weeks that they weren't rehearsing or performing, dancers took it as easy as they could while staying sharp and in shape.

From choreography to rehearsals to costume design to set design, it took weeks to prepare a ballet. The Providence company put on seven ballets every year: two each in spring, summer, and fall, and an extended run of *The Nutcracker* in December. Each normal run lasted about a week; *The Nutcracker* ran two and a half weeks. Each non-holiday season's schedule included one classic, crowd-pleasing ballet, like *The Phantom*, and another production that was more obscure, or experimental, or a brand new piece by Baxter. In the fall, they did the regional showcase.

The Nutcracker was one of those ballets that was like a fast-food burger. Wherever you went in the US, if you ordered a Quarter Pounder at McDonald's, you knew exactly what it was going to taste like. If you were someone who went into a McDonald's and ordered a Quarter Pounder, you probably did so because you knew exactly what it would be. If somebody at the grill decided that brown mustard instead of yellow would really make that burger sing, or added a couple of jalapenos, the person who bit into that burger would likely be very unhappy.

People who went to *The Nutcracker* had similar expectations. For many families, the ballet was part of their Christmas traditions. They came every year. For matinees, children came dressed in character. They had every step memorized, and they were not happy when any step deviated from their expectations. They wanted the sets the same, the costumes, everything.

Ari thought every dancer in the company could probably dance *The Nutcracker* in a coma, even the parts they hadn't danced. They all knew every single step. This was why Baxter despised it. But it was their chief money-maker. Every single performance sold out within a week. Their press coverage doubled. Season-ticket sales spiked. Producing *The Nutcracker* every December kept the Rhode Island Ballet solvent and paid for Baxter's poorly attended experimental productions.

But he was always in a sour mood when it was time for *The Nutcracker*.

About twenty minutes before the meeting was scheduled, he came into the rehearsal studio, where the company had been gathered for about an hour, in their own tradition of working out together before the big season meeting. He sat on a chair in the corner, crossed his arms, and glowered.

Ari's neck prickled with that sense of being watched, and now she knew she wasn't being paranoid, but she tried to ignore him and do her thing. She and Julian were playing around with the parts of Clara and the Nutcracker Prince. She hadn't admitted it, and didn't want to really believe it herself, but she was kind of hoping it would serve as an audition.

She knew the part. She was the best choice to play Clara. She hadn't embarrassed herself as Christine—she'd gotten close once, maybe, but she'd recovered, and she'd been truly brilliant once.

The second the clock hit the meeting time, Baxter stood. He clapped loudly and called the company together. They all stopped their stretching and dancing and chatting and sat on the studio floor.

He started as usual, with a debrief of the season that had just ended. Reading from a paper, he gave ticket sales information, read excerpts from reviews—which all the dancers had already seen, of course; they all read their notices, and all told other dancers what a bad idea it was to read your own reviews—and other financial minutiae Ari didn't have much interest in. Then he gave out praise. The company called these his 'crumbs'—he didn't give spontaneous praise often, and this time in meetings was set aside as if it were something he'd been forced to do. He read his praise from a piece of paper as well. Sergei and Julian got a monotone sentence or two. Travis, who'd played The Persian, got a nod. A few girls from the corps, including Jessi.

Ari wasn't mentioned. She knew then that she'd have to audition for Clara.

So did everyone else. When he set aside his paper of crumbs and moved on to talk about the holiday season, Julian grabbed her hand. Other dancers looked her way.

217

Maybe they all did; she looked straight ahead, at Baxter Berrault, and tried not to see anyone outside that field of vision.

"Okay," Baxter said. "So, no great shock, but we'll be cracking nuts for Christmas. The holiday gala the Saturday after Thanksgiving. Premiere performance the first Friday of December. Set design is on the usual short schedule, just buff everything up. Costumes are designed; we just need measurements and fittings for the cast. Four-week rehearsal schedule, starting week after next. Julian, you're our Nutcracker Prince. Sergei, the Cavalier." He looked straight at Ari then. But she was prepared, so he didn't get the satisfaction of seeing hurt or shock or shame or anything else when he said, "Auditions for all other parts start Monday." The corners of his mouth sharpened into a nasty grin.

Ari only nodded, keeping her disappointment and anger pressed down deep inside her, but the rest of the company reacted. Gasps and murmurs and more looks.

Dissatisfied with her flat reaction, Baxter put away his sneering grin. "If you've got questions, find your own answers. If you don't know how things work around here by now, I don't know what to tell you." With that, he turned and left the studio.

Julian squeezed her hand. "I mean it, Ari. You should talk to a lawyer."

"He's being an asshole, but he hasn't done anything wrong. I don't have some sanctified right to the lead. If anybody does around here, it's Dev. If I don't get a named part, then maybe."

"I don't know why he's being so shitty to you. He's still with her, isn't he?"

Dancers gossiped like any group who spent hours in close proximity together, but Ari hadn't heard that their director and prima ballerina had broken up. It didn't matter, though.

"I don't know. Bax has always been shitty."

"Yeah, but you're getting a double dose lately."

Ari shrugged. Before she could decide if there were words to add to the gesture, Jessi came up to her, smiling sweetly.

"Hi, Ari. I just wanted to wish you good luck next week."

Frenemy bitch. Ari smiled back just as sweetly. "Thank you. You, too. *Merde*."

"*Merde*!"

How fitting that the ballet world's wish for luck was the French word for 'shit.'

~oOo~

Julian took her out to a tiny, dark cavern of a bar that night and got her very drunk. Legless. Snockered. Pissed. Ankled. Rubbered. Plastered. By the time she was back in his car, leaning on the window and watching the streetlights swirl and sparkle, she didn't give a flea's rashy butthole about Baxter Bonehead Berrault and his stupid cracked nuts.

When Julian opened her door, the seatbelt got stuck or something and wouldn't let her go. He leaned in and fixed it, then helped her to her feet. The sidewalk was squishy, and it was hard to walk, but Julian was there, his arm around her, making it easier.

"I love you, Jule. Julie. Julian. Julius Caesar."

He laughed. "Okay. I love you, too. But I think we're going to put tequila on time out for you for a while."

"It was good. You get a lime. And people cheer."

"They don't normally cheer, love. You were giving them a show."

"Oh. Was I good?"

"Brilliant as ever."

The skin on the back of her neck prickled, and Ari pushed Julian off. She almost fell off the sidewalk, but she caught herself and turned around. "BAXTER! FUCK YOU, YOU FUCKER! GO AWAY!"

"Ari! Ari, what? Calm down."

"He's here! Creepy fucking creeper. He's following me."

Julian hooked his arm around her shoulders and squinted out into parking lot and around the grounds of their apartment building. Ari squinted too, but things were all sparkly and hard to make out.

"I don't see anybody."

"He's out there. Creep. He makes my neck all prig-pric-puckery."

"Okay. Well, let's go in and lock up snug, okay?" He pulled her around. The ground heaved, and she almost fell, but Julian swept her into his arms.

She dropped a grateful head onto his shoulder. "I love you. You got my back."

"And you've got mine. Let's get you inside."

~ 13 ~

Donnie got back into the passenger seat of the SUV and pushed his hood off his head. "Okay, let's go."

"I don't like it when you go off on your own like that, boss. Not the way things are right now."

"It's not your place to have an opinion about what I do."

"It's my job to protect you, though."

Donnie turned and leveled a look at his bodyguard and driver. He let that look be his rejoinder.

With a terse nod, Dre went back to his driving. He eased the GMC out of the corner parking space and pulled to the exit. He left the lights off until he was back on the road. "Does she need a detail on her?"

With that image of her in Trewson's arms, the sound of her voice saying *I love you*, he was tempted to say no. Four times before today, he'd found himself driving alone to Providence, checking on her, each time thinking he'd go up to her, confront her, get her to listen.

If only so the last thing she'd done with him wasn't run away from him. Maybe then he could stop thinking about it. It burned, that she'd run from him.

But each time, the thought that he'd scare her, showing up out of the blue, had stopped him. He couldn't take it if she ran again.

Why it mattered — he wouldn't let himself think much about that.

He just wanted her to know he hadn't meant her harm.

It shouldn't matter, but it did. He should forget that night as he'd forgotten countless others, but he couldn't.

"Boss?"

He was tempted to say no. She'd lied to him. Julian Trewson was obviously more than a friend. She'd lied to him, and she'd run from him, and there was no reason at all he should feel the need to protect her.

But he thought of that thick envelope of photographs, left at the desk at PBS, so that Nick's poor assistant was the first to see them. Surveillance shots of Bev, and of their kids. Of Angie's sister and her kids. And of Arianna. Their one night turned into a weapon. Their dinner on the riverside had been surveilled.

Far worse than the surveillance shots were the doctored images that accompanied them. The heads of the women and girls, superimposed on violently defiled bodies. Not skilled photo manipulation. Barely better than taping one head over another. But the point was made.

Since the Bobbo and the others had been killed in August, officers and their families had been under constant guard, and the Paganos had been on high alert, paying close attention to New Jersey. The only move the Bondaruks had made since August was to try to flip one of their runners, but Alex had withstood their pressure, and Angie's. The kid hadn't swung out. He was solid, and he was therefore still breathing.

Clearly, the Ukrainians had grown frustrated at the lack of movement. They wanted a war.

Now Arianna had gotten caught up in it.

Nick thought the envelope was full of a lot of bluster and provocation. The images were vile, and the don had been enraged, but when it came time to decide how to respond, he was calm and thoughtful. He said if the Ukrainians could do what those photos threatened, they wouldn't have bothered with doctored photos.

Donnie agreed. But his chest had frozen solid at the sight of Bev's head on a naked, bloody, broken body. He'd seen her body bloody and broken before; he'd spent years reliving her screams in his dreams. They'd been muffled by the phantoms of his own maddening agony, but he remembered.

To see her like that again, even falsely? And the others, too, all of them innocent? Elisa. Lia. Carina.

Arianna. Photos of her at dinner with him. Entering and leaving the theatre. Her headshot from the Rhode Island Ballet's website. And her head, her hair in its ballerina bun, with a little cluster of dark flowers on one side, affixed on a naked body, bound from shoulders to ankles and whipped to bloody stripes.

Nick had doubled the details on the women and children. He'd seen the images of Arianna and him at dinner, and the fake images of her torture, and demanded Donnie explain who she was. After he had, Nick had left it up to him whether she needed protection.

"Yeah, we'll put a shadow team on her. Until they get here, park out front so I can see her windows." There was no good way for him to tell her of the possible danger, so it was best she didn't know she was being watched. He pulled his phone and dialed Angie.

~oOo~

Nick handed Donnie a manila folder. "Lara finished the new codes."

Donnie opened the folder and flipped through the few pages. Trey's wife was the Pagano Brothers' master cryptologist. She created codes to obscure their night work, and she broke the codes of their enemies. She herself was the key to their empire, though they kept that fact quiet and let her father appear to hold the position.

Every couple months, they changed codes throughout the organization. Shylocks, bookies, and bagmen had to keep up, learning whole new languages in a few hours. When the key to a new code was on paper, the organization was at its most vulnerable; anyone who got their hands on the paper could learn enough to bring Nick to his knees. So it wasn't on paper long, and everybody had to have it down.

Donnie, in charge of all the men who worked directly with money, tapped the sharpest minds for the work, from capos all the way down to the lowliest errand boy.

Lara provided decryption to Nick, and he shared it with Donnie and Angie. But that was even more precious, so only the officers had access to it. Everyone else had to memorize.

"I'll get this out to the capos this afternoon." Before he did, he'd get to know it himself. He wasn't anywhere close to Lara's freakishly genius level, but Donnie was pretty good with numbers and patterns. Despite his access to Lara's decryption program, he memorized all the codes he required his men to know. After years of working with Lara, he had a sense of the different arrays of patterns in her coding. She called it the 'grammar' of the code and said all coders had a grammar, because they only had one brain.

"Don," Angie said when Nick returned to his chair. "Can we talk about those pictures?" At least once a week, sometimes once or more a day when things were tense in the underworld, Angie and Donnie sat like this, before Nick's desk, and discussed any big organizational issues. When it was business as usual, the meetings were brief and pro forma—sharing new codes, updates about new business or changes to old business. When there was trouble, sometimes the meetings got tense. Angie and Donnie were the only people who could push Nick and expect to be heard.

Now, Nick nodded, but it was clear Angie had a short leash. "We can talk. But you better have a new angle. You know my feelings."

"I do. And you know you have my undying respect. I will follow your play. But are you sure it's the best thing to pass this by? The things in those pictures! If they act ..." He stopped and let them fill in the rest themselves.

Nick had decided not to respond at all to the envelope of incendiary photos. They were meant to enflame, and he had decided not to take the bait, except to increase the security coverage on families.

"Do you have new intel for me? Is there a Bondaruk son on the ground in the States? New Jersey or New York or New England?"

Angie shook his head. "No, not that we've seen. They got two advance teams now, laying pipe to get their business back up. But no Bondaruks yet."

"Cannon fodder. That's all they've put in play. You know how I felt seeing my wife and daughters in those filthy images. I know how you felt seeing Tina. I will not forget. Ever. But if we react to this, when there are no targets of value on the ground yet, we make ourselves look weak and foolish. I hope you agree that I am neither of those things."

"Of course not, don." Angie eased from his assertive lean forward. "I'm sorry if I offended."

"You didn't. I know what you're feeling. I feel it, too. When I get my hands on a Bondaruk, he will feel the full consequence of our outrage. Until then, we will show them that they are beneath our notice."

"There's a chance," Donnie put in, carefully, "they will amplify their messages until we can't ignore them. If they make a move on Bev, or Tina, or the girls …"

"Or your tiny dancer," Angie added. His mouth canted up in a muted impression of his usual teasing grin. "What's her name again?"

"Arianna. And she's not my anything. She was a one-night stand, and she's just caught up in this by bad timing. She's nothing to me. But she's innocent, and I don't want her hurt, either."

"Beverly was a one-night stand who got caught up in our business, too," Nick said.

Donnie wasn't sure what to say to that, but he'd watched in stunned disbelief last year as Nick had conspired like some old nonna to get Trey and Lara together, so he wondered if the legendarily ice-blooded don was trying to make a similar connection here. Apparently, as Nick aged, he was getting a soft spot for romance.

If he was, Donnie ignored the attempt. "My point is, Bev and Tina have already been hurt by our business. And the Bondaruks went for Lara *twice* last year and really hurt her. I think we make a mistake if we discount them."

"I agree," Angie said.

Nick leaned back and steepled his fingers before his face. "Do either of you have a suggestion for how to respond that doesn't make us look the fool?"

"At a minimum, don, they disrespected us. Even if they only meant it like a nasty middle finger, it was a threat to our loved ones." Angie felt strongly about this, clearly, because he was pushing dangerously hard.

"You're giving me more argument, Angelo. You made your case. If you want me to change my thinking, give me a suggestion I will consider."

Donnie had it, he thought. "We do it quiet. We take them down—one team, or the team leaders, or every one of them on the ground, we take them down. But we don't say a word. We make the ones who put that envelope together hurt, long and hard. Then we put them in the ocean and go on. No message. No claim. We just do it, and move on. Put Bondaruk back to square one."

Nick thought about that. At Donnie's side, Angie finally relaxed. He liked the idea.

"To be quiet, we'd have to take them all, in a single sweep. No witnesses." Nick asked Angie, "Can you do that? Two teams of how many?"

"Eight men in all. I need a couple days to put it together, but yeah, I can. They're not using the watch shop. They've got a new base in the back of a video store—one of those places that rents movies from the old country. After hours, it's just them. Might be some collateral loss of a couple hangarounds, but that's it."

"That's a lot of moving parts to get in sync." After another moment's thought, Nick stood, and Donnie and Angie stood with him. "You pushed for this, Angie. And you, too, Donnie. I'm going to let you run with it. If you get it done, I will gladly make these insects who threaten our women suffer. But if you fuck this up, and hang me out in the air, that's not a mistake you come back from. *Capite?*"

There was no backing down now. Donnie and Angie both nodded and answered, "*Capiamo.*"

~oOo~

What the fuck was he doing?

He could tell himself he was checking up on Arianna's guard detail, and that was exactly what he'd told himself when he'd left the house. But why had he taken his Porsche and left Round Ollie, his own detail while Dre had some time off, to chase after him?

Now he'd seen that Keith and Sandy were on her, staying back at a shadow distance, doing their job, so why was he still here? Why was he on the theatre parking lot, twice as close to her as her guards, sitting behind the wheel in a black hoodie like a goddamn stalker?

The hoodie was just what he'd been wearing when he'd left the house. The hood was up because—he didn't know why. He didn't know when he'd put it up. Probably some shame reflex because he was being a fucking idiot.

Six weeks since their single night together. He'd almost set it aside, stopped digging at the strange sore spot she'd left in his psyche, stopped wondering if he'd kicked away something good, something real, if he'd spent the past twenty years of his life kicking away the chance for something good and real.

No. He knew he had not. He had all the good and real he ever would, and all the proof he needed that that was true.

He'd almost mastered this unpleasant twitch in his head that wouldn't forget her, he'd almost reclaimed his equilibrium, and then that envelope had arrived. Seeing her threatened, those awful images of the threats envisioned, had awakened something inside him in a place deeper and darker and more desperate than he'd known before.

What the fuck was he doing? Making sure she was okay. Seeing her with his own eyes and knowing it was true.

She was in a relationship with Trewson; she had to be. She'd lied to him, the evidence of that had been obvious from before he'd spoken a word to her, but now he'd *heard* her tell Trewson she loved him, saw him carry her as he himself had that night, sweeping her off to bed.

It pissed him off, but it didn't matter. He needed her to be safe. She'd shared a late dinner with him, and now she was caught in the net of his night world.

The stage door opened, and Donnie's attention narrowed. A couple of dancers he vaguely recognized, women, came out. He knew Arianna's schedule; Calvin had hacked in or jacked in or whatever he did—he'd gotten access to the theatre's computers, so they could use her work information to build a plan to shadow her.

Arianna was signed up for an hour of private rehearsal time this evening and tomorrow afternoon, and she had an audition at one o'clock on Tuesday.

Her hour had ended twenty minutes ago.

He didn't need to be here. Keith and Sandy were here to watch over her.

But he couldn't leave until he saw her.

Another ten minutes passed. Where was she? Could somebody have gotten to her inside the theatre?

Once that thought struck home, he couldn't shake it. He had to know. So he got out of his car and headed toward the stage door. He didn't bother to be stealthy. He wasn't trying not to be seen. Now he just had to put his eyes on her, any way he could.

The door opened when he was about ten feet away. Arianna stepped out, with fucking Julian Trewson right on her heels, as ever.

She was finishing a sentence, looking back at her lover as she spoke. Donnie stopped where he was, and she nearly ran into him when she turned around. Reflex had his hands up and around her arms before she did.

In the space of a breath, her expression went from simple surprise at the near collision, to confusion, to shocked recognition, to an infuriating, gut-wrenching dread. The dread held. Her body went stiff.

"What? Why? What are you …?"

"We need to talk."

Behind her, Trewson was just catching up and sensing danger. To his credit, he didn't pussy out. He tried to yank her back. Donnie gripped more tightly at first, but when she winced, he let her go.

Trewson put Arianna behind him and stood to his full height—a couple inches shorter than Donnie—and puffed up, almost bumping chests with him. "Who are you and what do you want?"

Remembering that his hood was still up, Donnie pushed it back. The lights outside the theatre threw long shadows and cast an eerily gold tint over everything they illuminated, but Donnie saw the guy go pale with fearful recognition. Good. His fucked-up face was worth at least this: making assholes afraid.

At the same time, he heard the deeply familiar click of a nine-mil's slide being racked, and he spun and sidestepped, pulling his Beretta from his waistband and putting himself between Arianna and the bullet coming their way.

It was Round Ollie, who pointed his gun to the sky the instant he was aimed at Donnie. "What the fuck, boss?"

Donnie turned the muzzle of his gun toward the sky as well. "Stand down, Oll. I don't need you here."

"You sure?"

"Yes. Go back to your truck."

"It would be easier to do my job if you'd tell me what you're up to."

He hated having a round-the-clock guard on him and resented having to check in with underlings. If for no other reason than this weeks-long pain in his ass, he wanted Bondaruk blood. "Go back to your truck. I'll let you know when I'm ready to leave."

Round Ollie hesitated another few seconds, long enough for Donnie to consider aiming his gun again, and then backed — slowly — off.

Donnie turned to Arianna and her lover. Both were frozen in front of the door — no one else had come through it and into that scene, thankfully. Trewson had his arm around Arianna, holding her back from Donnie. Donnie wanted to cut that arm off and shove it up the bastard's ass.

To Arianna, as he put his gun back in his waistband, he said, "I'm sorry to come up on you like this, but I do need to talk to you."

"Why?" She gave Trewson a gentle push and extricated herself from his clutches.

"Wait, Ari — you *know* him?"

Arianna ignored him. "Why are you here? What could you possibly want?"

"I've been plain. I want to talk. It's important."

"So talk." Her tone dripped poison. "Or wait—if it's your oh-so-generous *offer* again, don't bother. My answer is the same. Find yourself a real whore."

"What the fuck is going on, Ari?"

Donnie noticed that Trewson's protective courage had cooled quite a bit since he'd understood whom he faced. Since then, he'd been little more than a baffled audience, throwing out questions neither Arianna nor Donnie heeded.

"It's not that. I'm not here to bother you or hurt you. But I do need to talk to you."

She crossed her arms in defiance. God, she was beautiful. Her hair was up in its perfect, sleek bun. She wore no makeup he could see, and had on a dusky jacket over dark sweats, legwarmers, and sneakers, but she was as elegant as if she were in costume as Giselle.

"So talk," she said again, in that decidedly bitter, inelegant tone.

"Ari, dammit!"

Donnie glared menace at Trewson. "Not here, and not with him around. In private."

Trewson laughed. "Forget about it. Ari, tell him to fuck off and let's go."

But she didn't tell him to fuck off. Instead she stared at him, her wide, lovely eyes narrowed in concentration. Her cheeks quivered lightly, as if powerful emotions were barely contained, barely concealed beneath

236

their surface. Donnie wanted to reach out and hold that face in his hand, to run his thumb over her trembling skin and soothe her.

"I don't want to hurt you, Arianna. I'm truly sorry that I did."

She blinked. "There's a diner down the street. Brightly lit. Lots of people. We can talk there."

"Ari, Jesus! Is this the guy who—? What the hell are you doing, love? This is not okay."

Donnie wanted to rip out the tongue that called her 'love.' Shit, he was jealous. Violently, dangerously jealous.

"It's okay, Jule. I'll be okay." She looked back at Donnie. "Right? I'll be okay?"

"You will. I promise. I need half an hour, and then I'll be gone." He hated brightly lit restaurants, so he wouldn't want to linger, anyway.

She turned to Trewson. "Julian, just go home. If you don't hear from me in thirty minutes, you can call for any help you want. But for now, just go home, and I'll see you later."

"This is so stupid, Ari. This is who had you crying for two days, isn't it? This is the dumbest thing you've ever done. He can do a lot of harm in thirty minutes. Jeremiah only needed five."

Arianna surprised them both by wheeling around and slamming her hands into Trewson's chest. "Fuck you for that. Go home."

Trewson glared for a second, then gave her an angry nod and stepped around her. He came up to Donnie, mastered his fear, and said, "I know who you are and what you can do to me, but if you hurt her again, I'll do what I can to hurt you before you send me to the fishes or whatever you people do."

"Go home," he replied.

Trewson looked back at Arianna, who tipped her head toward the parking lot.

"This is so fucking stupid, Ari." He walked away.

Donnie watched him go. When he was in the parking lot, far enough away that they had some semblance of privacy, he turned back to Arianna. "Who's Jeremiah?"

"None of your business. You want to talk, so let's go. I'm on a clock here."

Trouble in her past wasn't his chief concern, so he dropped the question and held out his hand. "Thank you."

"Please don't make me stupid again." She put her hand in his.

~ 14 ~

What the actual fuck was she doing?

As Donnie opened the passenger door of his Porsche and she slid in and settled on the leather seat, Ari tried to stir up the sense of doom the situation warranted. Summing up the past five minutes: Donnie Goretti had shown up right outside the stage door, out of nowhere, after more than a month. Within like a minute of that shocking development, a big guy had emerged from the night, pointing a *huge gun* right at her, and then Donnie had a gun, too.

He'd put himself in front of her. He'd heard the guy coming, or something, and he'd jumped in front of her.

The guy had turned out to be working for Donnie, but Ari didn't think he'd known it when he'd put himself between her and a gun.

Maybe that was why she was sitting here, in Donnie Goretti's fancy sportscar, now.

Julian was livid. If something happened to her, she'd never hear the end of it—not that his endless chorus of 'I told you so' would be her primary trouble. Even assuming she were alive to hear it.

That thought made little impact. She couldn't work up the worry the situation clearly required.

He got in behind the wheel. He reached to the passenger side, opened the glove box, and set his gun inside. She didn't know how she felt about a loaded gun resting so close to her, but she supposed if she needed it, she was closer to it than he was. Not that she knew how to shoot it.

"Thank you," he said again as he settled back behind the wheel.

Ari turned to him—and was struck dumb for just a second. From where she sat, as he faced front and started his car, she could see only the scarred side of his face. It occurred to her in a flash that she'd never seen him like this. In the time of their acquaintance, he'd always positioned himself so that she saw his left side—either only his left, or straight on. That might be because of his hearing, but she didn't think it was the only reason. He presented his best side every chance he could. He moved through the whole world always aware of the way he was seen.

Without realizing it, even when she'd been looking right at him, or imagining him since, she'd seen or thought

240

of only the left side of his face. It wasn't that she'd forgotten he was scarred. She could describe his scars as easily as she could the rest of him. But she didn't think of them. She thought of him as a handsome man, but this side of his face was devastating. God, what had happened to him?

The shock lasted only a second, but he seemed to sense it. His shoulders went stiff, and he put the car in gear—it was a manual transmission—and backed out of the space with more vigor than necessary.

"Turn left out of the lot, then right at the light," she said, raising her voice a bit to make sure he heard her. "The diner's three blocks down on the right. The Minuteman."

He nodded and followed her directions, but didn't speak.

When he'd taken her to dinner, they'd ridden in the back seat of a large SUV, and another man had driven. Donnie had sat on her right. To cover the tense silence, she asked, "That man with the gun isn't your driver?"

"Not tonight."

"So he follows you around? Is he following us?"

"Yes. He won't get in our way."

"I thought you just had a driver. You have a bodyguard."

He glanced at her, then back at the road.

Ari sat quietly and considered how dangerous Donnie's life must be. Uncle Mel was too low in his organization to warrant a guard, she supposed. Or maybe he had one and she just didn't know. It wasn't like she was a part of that world. She'd grown up thinking of what Uncle Mel did as a job, the same way she thought of her father's dental practice. Just the things grownups did. Not until she was grown had she really understood what Mel did. Even then, growing up where she did, in the Italian-American neighborhood that was the home ground of the Romano Family, she didn't think it unduly strange or have a lot of curiosity about the Romanos' inner workings.

She didn't have long to ponder on past or current events. Donnie passed the diner and turned the corner, finding a spot on the street about a block down. After he turned off the car, he reached over and collected his gun again. He meant to go into the diner armed.

"What's going on, Donnie?"

"Not in the car. We'll talk inside. Wait. I'll come around."

She waited, and he came around. Before he opened her door, he checked all around them. This was a level of caution and wariness he hadn't shown the last time they were together. Then, he'd been alert, but not on guard. Now, he was ready to take a bullet for her.

There was some kind of danger, and he'd just pulled her into it.

242

He opened the door and offered his hand. Ari sat where she was. The sense of doom the situation warranted had found her at last.

"What are you pulling me into?"

A slap of guilt went across his face, and he flinched — subtly, but unmistakably. "I'll explain inside, Arianna."

She'd deserve every verse of Julian's 'I told you so' chorus. She took Donnie's hand and let her lead her into the diner.

~oOo~

The Minuteman was just a diner, a seat-yourself, menus-on-the-table, pay-at-the-register diner — nothing like their evening as the most esteemed guests at a ritzy Italian restaurant. Since it was so close to the theatre, the dancers ate here fairly often. Tonight, Ari was the one the staff knew, and she offered a friendly nod to the servers they passed as Donnie led her to the back.

The place was as crowded as she expected on a Saturday evening, but not so packed there wasn't a place to sit. Donnie found a booth in the far corner and took that, directing Ari to take the seat that faced the wall. He took the seat that faced the restaurant, though it put his right side most on view. Now that she'd noticed his tendency to present his unscarred side, she couldn't help noticing when he didn't.

He was dressed much more casually than she'd seen him before. In the weeks since their date, she'd imagined him in the only way she'd known him: tuxedoed, in varying stages of put together. Tonight, he wore jeans and a black hoodie, with a plain white t-shirt under it. The hoodie wasn't a sweatshirt; instead, it was made of some soft, knitted material. Probably cashmere. He looked good. Maybe better than the tux, because it seemed more true.

She shook that romanticized bullshit right out of her head and reminded herself what a bastard he was.

"So talk," she said as he took the menus from their place between the napkin dispenser and the condiment caddy and handed her one. She set it aside; eating was not her purpose here.

"Wait," he said, and put the menus back.

A waitress Ari didn't know came over with two pots of coffee. "Regular or decaf?"

"Arianna?"

It was late for caffeine, but Donnie's little ambush had pretty much guaranteed a sleepless night, anyway. "Regular."

"And for me," Donnie said.

The waitress filled their cups. "You know what you want?" She looked down at the table when she spoke, not making eye contact with either of them.

"Coffee's enough for me," Ari answered first.

"Just coffee for now," Donnie added. "I'll let you know if that changes."

The waitress turned. She didn't look up until she was clear of the table. Weird.

Alone again, Donnie pushed the bowl of creamers her way. He remembered. "I need to tell you that I've put a guard detail on you. They're shadowing you now, so you won't see them unless there's trouble. It would be easier, and safer, if they could come closer. But I'll leave that up to you."

She froze with the little plastic cup of creamer hovering over her coffee. "A guard? Like that guy tonight?"

"Basically, yeah. It's two men, because you're not armed yourself. Like I said, you won't see them unless you need them, but you'll be safer knowing they're there."

"You've got two big guys with guns following me around, and that's supposed to make me feel *safe*?"

"Yes."

It didn't. "Why are they there? How long have they been there?" She thought of that maddening prickle on her neck. Several times in the past couple weeks, she'd been sure she was watched but had seen no one.

"Just since tonight."

Oh. Well, then maybe she *was* going crazy. Maybe it was just Baxter worming his big head into hers and making her generally paranoid. Wonderful. She went back to fixing her coffee and let herself figure out what questions she had next.

"Why? Who am I supposed to be safe from? And what difference is it to you if I'm safe? Since when do you care?"

"I care, Arianna."

"Right. Whatever."

He didn't like her response; a strong wave of anger flashed over his face. Just the left side. The right side didn't move nearly as much. There, it was only a faint crimping near his eye.

"When we went out to dinner, somebody saw you with me. They took photos of us at our table. They sent them to me and made threats. I know you don't want anything to do with me, but it's my responsibility to keep you safe now."

"So you're to the *The Bodyguard* chapter in your book of romantic hero clichés?"

"Please?"

Her hurt feelings were convoluting the issues here. He'd just told her some mobster had threatened her, and that was *way* more important than snarking about what a bastard he'd been six weeks ago. "They threatened me? Why?"

"They must have thought we were together. These men target loved ones. They must have thought you were that to me."

"But I'm not. You don't have loved ones. You only have *arrangements*." Welp. The hurt feelings would not be silenced.

He stared steadily across the table at her.

She'd just gotten him out of her head. Mostly. And here he was, being cold and detached, reminding her of the dazzling night they'd shared and the nasty mess he'd made of it the next morning. "I don't want to be part of this."

"I'm sorry."

"Are you giving me a choice in this?"

"No. If you don't want to see them, you won't. They'll stay back, out of your way. But they will be there. You don't have to see me again after this meeting, but my men will protect you until the danger is over."

She sipped her coffee and stared at the table, and she thought about what she felt. She wasn't scared. He'd told her there was a threat against her, somebody in his mobster world that wanted to hurt her to hurt him — because men sucked and always turned to women when they wanted to cause the most pain — but she wasn't scared, at least not primarily. Primarily, she was just hurt.

Old hurt and new. Heart and ego. She'd misread this guy *so badly*. That night, she'd been crushing on him so hard, skipping down the primrose path toward loving him, and then, in the harsh light of day, he'd simply said, *Yeah, I don't do love, but if you fuck me when I want, I'll buy you something nice for your trouble.*

So why did he care if she got hurt now? Was it some Mafioso honor thing?

Of course it was exactly that. The code. Their honor. Why they maintained they weren't criminals while they stood elbows-deep in crime and violence. They considered themselves honorable men. It had nothing to do with her at all.

"That night really meant nothing to you."

"That's not true. I told you then that I liked you, and I wanted to see you more."

"No. You wanted to fuck me more."

Again he stared silently at her, and again a riot of emotions flashed across his face in an instant.

"Arianna, look around this diner right now, and tell me what you see."

She looked, and saw exactly what she expected to see: a bunch of people eating hamburgers, chicken fingers, grinders, stuffed quahogs, drinking cabinets and soda— the usual. It was a diner. People were dressed casually, chatting casually. Some had children with them. Some were in larger groups, talking animatedly. Some were pairs, obviously on a date. Near the door was the big man who'd pulled a gun on her. Donnie's bodyguard.

That reminded her that Donnie had a gun stuffed in the waistband of his jeans.

She started to turn back and tell him he was the only thing of note in the place, when she caught something at a table near them. A group of four, three men and a woman. Young. Early twenties or so.

They were staring. One of the men pulled on his own right cheek, misshaping his face, and his friends laughed in that hunched, high-school way people laughed when they were being mean and didn't want to be caught. Laughing at Donnie.

Her lens refocused now, Ari looked around the diner again and noticed that a lot of people were looking at Donnie. Some of them with sympathy, many with shock, some with evident disgust. Most tried not to look but couldn't help themselves. The children stared most unabashedly, but their parents tried to make them stop. A few people, like the table near them, were casually cruel.

As she looked, she understood that just about every person in this place had taken their turn to stare at the man with the melted face.

When she turned back to Donnie, tears blurred her vision. With that cold, impassive expression, he watched her master them and said nothing until she had.

"You brought me to a restaurant where there's a fucking spotlight over my head, but I'm here, sitting here, explaining the trouble to you, because I do care. I do like you."

"I'm sorry." She couldn't think of anything else to say, could barely get those insignificant words out.

He waved her apology away, and tilted his head toward the rest of the restaurant. "For twenty years, this is the world I've lived in. I understand what people see, what they *feel*, when they look at me. I don't turn away from it. I don't hide. I live my life, and I don't pretend it's anything more or better than it is. I have arrangements because that's all I can expect."

Once again, he was sitting across from her, perfectly cool, upending everything she thought she knew about him. "But that's not true. Until you turned it all ugly in the morning, what I saw when I looked at you was a man I really liked." She tried to hold back the next words, but they pushed on anyway. "I even thought I could fall in love with you."

He left those words lingering in the air between them for an uncomfortably long time.

"Let's say I believe you. You say it now, while we sit here, and let's say I believe that you think you really like me. That the way I look doesn't matter, and you're honestly attracted to me. Not my power, not my money, *me*. Maybe you think you could feel more than that for me someday. Let's say that right now, we both believe that's true. But you don't know. If you were to spend some time with me in the world, when those stares that just made you cry are turned your way too, eventually it would be too much. You don't know, because you haven't lived in this world that I see every day. But I've been here for twenty years. I've been here with many women, and I know. Love doesn't grow in this world. So it's best not to pretend it can."

"But Donnie, how can you be happy if your heart is so closed off?"

"A closed heart is better than a broken one." He flinched, hard, as that sentence ended. He'd said much more with those few words than he'd wanted to. He'd said enough to make her heart ache. With a brisk shake of his head, he tried to take them back. "My happiness is not your concern."

"What if I want it to be?" She reached across the table and took his hand. The second time she'd touched him in this way. As the first time, he flinched, but let her hold on.

Julian would never understand, he'd never let it rest, but Ari felt herself slipping all the way back to her first feelings for this man. All the harsh things he'd said, they meant something different now. As he'd made her see the diner in a different way, he'd made her see him newly, too.

Finally, he spoke. "You're asking me to do something I don't do."

She responded by returning his silence.

"Are you with Trewson? Do not lie to me, Arianna."

"No. I've already answered that question. He's my best friend, and it's all he's ever been."

"You told him you love him."

"And I do. As I said, he's my best friend—wait." She took her hand back and thought for a moment, replaying her conversation with Julian as they left the theatre tonight, and came up empty. They'd been talking about the news that Devonny needed another surgery. "When did you hear me tell him I love him? Have you been following me? More than tonight?" Was it Donnie she'd been sensing at the back of her neck?

"Last night. After I got the photos, I came in to check on you. You were going into your apartment with him, and you told him you love him."

She didn't remember much of last night. Julian had gotten her drunk so she could forget that Baxter fucking Berrault was a fucking son of a bitch who persecuted her for no reason except she didn't want his dick.

"I don't remember. I was drunk. But he's just a friend. Who I love as a friend. Does it matter?"

"It does if you're willing to reconsider spending time with me."

She didn't like the way he said that — like he was offering her an arrangement again. "I don't do arrangements, Donnie. I do relationships. Two people with open, hopeful hearts."

When the silence stretched forward again, she added, "I spend my life being stared at, being judged for the way I look and what my body does. I know it's not the same at all, and I'm not suggesting it is, but I am good at filtering out whose gaze doesn't matter from whose does. The people in this restaurant don't matter. When I look at you, I see a man I want to be with."

Her phone rang right then, and she grabbed it to shut it off, but it was Julian — it had been thirty minutes since she'd sent him on his way. "It's Julian. I was supposed to call. If I don't take it, he'll send in the troops."

Donnie nodded, and Ari answered. "Hi, I'm fine."

"You didn't call. Where are you? You need to come home."

"I'm fine, Jule. It's good. I'm not in danger." Well, that wasn't true, but that was a much longer conversation not to have over the phone. "I'm not coming back yet, but everything's fine. I'll be back soon."

"Ari, please think about what you're doing. A guy pulled gun on us tonight!"

Looking straight at Donnie, she said, "I love you, Julian. I'm fine, and I'll be home soon."

"I love you, too, but you are being a fool. I'm calling every half hour until you are in this apartment."

"Fine. If it makes you feel better."

"It doesn't, but it's all I've got."

She ended the call and set her phone away.

Donnie stared at it, jealous contempt firing in his jewel-blue eyes. When he met her eyes again, he said, "Let's say I'm willing to try a relationship. I need rules."

"The no-touching, no-kissing thing? No."

"Then we're done. I need that."

"Why would you not want someone who cares about you to touch you? Why would you not want to kiss that someone?"

The waitress came back and refilled the coffees. Now Ari understood her unwillingness to make eye contact as something other than shyness, and she wanted to kick her in the face.

When she was gone, Donnie stared at his coffee. "Again, you ask me to do something I never do. I don't talk about this. Why do you expect me to?"

"Because I don't understand."

He exhaled frustration, but he answered. "As I said before, you can touch me, and kiss me, everywhere but my head. As for me kissing you, my mouth doesn't work right. I know you see that. I can't kiss you, and I can't do anything else with my mouth, because I don't have the motor control on half my face to do it right. It would feel wrong to you."

"How do you know how it would feel to me?"

"I've been told."

The insights were flying at her now, and she wanted to find the woman who'd fucked Donnie up so badly and kick her in the face, too. Repeatedly.

"That's why you don't want your face touched, too."

Another answer of silence.

"Okay, let's negotiate."

"I told you, my rules aren't negotiable."

She grinned. "You also told me you don't do relationships, so clearly everything is on the table now."

He laughed, and suddenly the atmosphere of their table changed completely, the sun breaking through storm clouds. "Make your offer."

"I'll table the question of kissing. I won't promise never to bring it up again, if things go well I'm sure I'll bring it up again, because I love kissing. But for now, it's tabled. In exchange, I get to touch your face at least once. We'll both be honest about how it makes us feel, and if it's awkward, we'll work through it. If you hate it, or I don't like it, I won't do it again. But I don't like being punished for something some other woman did to you."

"What makes you think it was only one woman?"

"Intuition. I think you put your hand on a hot stove and decided you'd never go near a stove again."

Again, he flinched hard at her words. She was like a human taser to this man. This time, though, he stunned her by laughing. His laughter held more surprise than humor, but it went on for a while, long enough that Ari felt herself smiling along, not quite understanding.

"It wasn't my hand on the hot stove, but I get your point."

"What?"

"That's what happened. I was held down on a commercial grill until my face cooked off."

Both her hands flew up and covered her mouth. The horror of that pain broke over her in a single, overwhelming burst. "Oh my God. Oh, Donnie."

His cold mask was back in place, and with it the dark clouds loomed overhead. "I don't want pity. I never want to see that look on your face again."

How could she not feel sorry for his pain? "It's not pity, Donnie. I told you before. It's empathy. It hurts that you were hurt."

He shook that off. "Call it what you want. What you feel for me, whatever it is, I don't want it to be about that. Don't be with me for that. Don't pretend you like me, or try to love me, for that."

"I won't. I wouldn't. You're more than your face, Donnie." He was, for example, the underboss of the

Pagano Brothers. How strange that a man so feared, so powerful, could be so raw and afraid.

"I *am* The Face, Arianna."

"Not to me."

He pulled his wallet out and put a twenty on the table. "We'll see. Come on, I'll take you home."

~oOo~

On the ride, Donnie was quiet, and Ari spent her time watching the side mirror, trying to decide which of the vehicles behind them was Donnie's guard, and hers. They were being followed by two different cars, right?

Though his guard had been in the diner with them, she hadn't seen him leave or get into a car or truck or anything. They were good, these Pagano Brothers men. Donnie had said she wouldn't see them unless she needed them, and even when she tried to see them, he was right.

"They're back there," he finally said. "If you agree, I'll have your detail move in. They can be right on you, if it makes you feel safer."

"Will I *be* safer?" She couldn't quite get her head around the idea that one of Donnie's enemies had threatened her. Why did they think she was important? Because they'd had one date?

"They can clear a space for you before you go in, make sure there's no trouble."

She didn't want to walk around like a movie star, surrounded by brawny men. "That's too close. That's in my way, and other people's, too."

"Then they'll just keep up with you. You'll know they're there, but nobody else will. They come in case of trouble, but they might not be able to prevent it starting."

"Do you think somebody will really try to hurt me?"

He pulled into the loading zone in front of her apartment building and cut the engine. Turning to her, he met her eyes. His expression had changed many times through this hour together. Now, he was the same man she'd had a lovely, romantic dinner with after the best performance of her life. "I hope not. But the threat is there. I'll do everything I can to keep you safe. You do your part, and be smart."

"Okay."

He smiled. "Okay. I'll walk you to your door."

"You don't want to come in?" Why was she asking that? She wasn't going to fuck him tonight. Possibly not for a while. First, she had to be sure he wasn't going to revert to that morning-after shithead again. But she wasn't ready to say good night, either.

"You live with Trewson, right?"

258

Oh, right. That was a definite complication — she had a big fight waiting for her inside. She laughed. "Yeah, I do. It'll probably be pretty chilly in there."

"Then I'll walk you to your door. But here." He took his phone out and handed it to her. "Call yourself."

She dialed her number, and her phone rang.

Donnie took his phone back, and she took hers from her bag and declined the call.

"This is my personal phone. If you need me, you call."

She nodded and stared at his number on the screen of her phone. Then Julian's face popped up, and her phone rang again. Another half hour had passed.

"Oh my God, I'm parked outside. I'll be in in a few minutes!" she said as soon as she answered.

"Five minutes, and I'm coming out."

"Fine, *Dad*." She ended the call. "He's being impatient. I should go in."

When Donnie got out, she waited for him to come around and help her out. She wasn't sure if it was an act of chivalry or caution, but she liked it. She liked when he took her hand and they walked to her building with their fingers woven together, too.

He walked her into the building and started to go up the stairs, but she pulled back. "That's my door just at the top of the stairs. You don't need to go all the way up."

"Is there a reason you don't want me to?"

She tugged his hand and walked him to the nook for the mailboxes. "We'll have more privacy here."

"I'm not going to kiss you good night, Arianna."

"I know." She put her arms up, meaning to wrap them around his neck for a hug, but he recoiled and caught her wrists, and she decided something. "I want my touch now."

"No. Why?"

"Because I can't think why I would wait." She let him hold her wrists, waiting for him to let go on his own.

Finally, he did.

He stood stiffly, watching her warily, like a trapped animal. Donato Goretti, underboss of the Pagano Family, feared by dangerous men, was afraid of her.

She put her hands on his chest, felt the rapid tempo of his heart. Moving slowly, keeping her eyes fixed on his, she eased up, to his shoulders, and in, to his neck, insinuating her fingers along the neck of his hoodie — yes, cashmere. When her fingertips touched his jaw — stubble on the left; tight, oddly hot skin on the right — he sucked in a sharp breath and pulled his head up, nearly out of her reach.

"Donnie."

The tension in his body was visible, it was *audible*, but he didn't pull further back. She moved her hands over his jaw, to his cheeks. He grunted, a sound of misery, but she didn't back off. She would have this touch. He owed it to her.

Both sides of his face felt as she expected them to. The left side was rough with his short beard, and his skin was warm and soft. The right side was waxy smooth in some places and uneven in others. Its temperature was different, warmer than the other side. That was the only thing she found surprising, and she wanted to ask why, but this wasn't the time.

Nothing about the right side of his face disgusted her. It wasn't aesthetically beautiful, but she didn't mind looking at it. It was Donnie's face, and she wanted to know it. What she felt most was sad. There'd been no accident—someone had done this to him on purpose. She ached for the pain he must have felt. And the pain he obviously still felt.

She touched his whole face, over the uneven skin at his ear, and around his head, until she could link her fingers on the back of his neck. "Thank you."

Donnie's eyes clamored in their sockets, and she didn't know what emotion rioted so intensely in them. Had she made him angry? Had she hurt him? Did her touch offend him?

"I liked that," she said, not knowing how to know his thoughts except to say her own. "I'd like to touch you more sometime, if you'd be okay with it."

He stared at her with those noisy eyes. "I … don't know."

That was more than she'd hoped for. Best of all, it was a real answer—warm and alive and vulnerable. "Okay. Will I see you again?"

"You want that?"

"Not an arrangement. A relationship. The start of one, anyway. Open hearts."

Before he answered, her apartment door creaked open. "Ari!"

"I'm down here. *God*, Jule!"

Donnie's expression became that of a man working very hard to be patient and running out of energy for the work. He cupped her face in his hands, and for the tiniest second, she thought he'd kiss her after all. His gesture was so kiss-ready. But he simply brushed his thumbs over her cheeks, said, "I'll call," and let her go.

He went to the door, and she went up the stairs. Julian stood on the landing, his arms crossed. But he hadn't come down to go toe to toe with the Mafioso.

A couple steps from the landing, she turned. Donnie was still at the door, waiting. Watching.

She blew him a kiss.

He left with a smile.

~ 15 ~

Donnie considered the map on the screen. "You put this together fast." Barely two days after Nick had given them leave to take down the advance teams, Angie had put together the intel and the resources for an attack that could take every Bondaruk-affiliated asshole in the States out.

"I want these motherfuckers, boss," Angie muttered. "They put my sister's head on a dismembered body. They don't get to walk around with that in their brains."

Donnie wanted them, too. Now that he'd wedged open the door of his feelings, Arianna was taking over his mind and heart both. Truthfully, she'd been annexing territory in there since the night of the gala.

Whether it was real intent or mere bluster, he wanted this threat against her gone. Immediately.

"Who are we calling in for this?"

"There's eight of them, plus maybe a couple grunts that hang around. Ten of us should make it quick. Three unmarked vans. Vio's offered those, so we can come in from the coast. I want guys that move fast. You, me, Jake, Tony, Dre. Paolo. I was thinkin' Alex Di Pietro—he's green, and he's not made, but I went hard on him, and he took it. He might do good with a chance for some payback on the guys that put him in my crosshairs."

"We can't have anybody who'll fold in heat. You think he's got it?"

"Like I said, he took what I laid on him, and I wasn't being nice."

Donnie chuckled. Poor Alex. "Okay. That's seven. Who else? What about Trey?"

Angie frowned. "I don't know. Like you said, we can't have anybody fold in this heat. He choked bad with the Bondaruks last year. Almost got himself and who knows who else killed."

"True, but ..." But Trey was Nick's chosen successor. It was far too early for that to be acknowledged as a truth, but Donnie and Angie knew it, and it was their job to make the kid ready. He absolutely had choked badly last year, but his own woman had been at risk then. It was worry for her, not fear for himself, that had jammed his circuits.

Angie glanced at Donnie's closed door, then leaned back on his desk. "I want to ask you something, but before

I do, I want to know you know how much I love Nick. He has my loyalty until I die. I will follow his play, whatever it is. Even when I don't agree. You know that, right?"

Donnie had been leaning over his desk, resting on his hands as he studied the map on the tablet screen. Now he stood up straight and studied his friend. "Of course."

"I'm only saying this out loud at all because you and me, Nick looks to us to advise him."

"What's on your mind, Ange?"

Conflict raged over Angie's face, and Donnie wasn't sure he'd get the words out at all. But finally, he said, "I don't know how I feel about this Trey thing."

Understanding what Angie meant, Donnie still wanted him to be clear. "What Trey thing?"

"He's not full blood, boss. He's a good guy, I like him, and I think he's good at the work. He's got growing to do, but he'll grow. If he was full blood, he'd be the obvious choice. But Nick breaks *the first rule* when he makes Trey. Forget him taking over as don someday — I'm worried about what's coming at us any time now. He's what? Twenty-seven? He's been an associate for something like four years? Sometime soon, Nick is gonna ask him to do the thing that'll give him cause to *make* him. All the way back to Sicily that shit goes. Generations back. *All* our roots go back to Sicily. That's what *La Cosa Nostra* is. Every made man everywhere, we're all bound. All family. And Nick kicks our grandfathers in the teeth when he brings a half-blood in, and *everybody* will know what he means—for that half-blood to lead this family someday. Nobody in the world is gonna stand for that. We'll be standing here in Rhode Island with our dicks in our hands while every made man in the world runs at us with fucking machetes."

Donnie didn't disagree with anything Angie had said. He was right. When Nick made Trey, he would start a civil war. Nick knew it. Donnie knew it. The whole organization—all of whom assumed the rumors to be true—knew it. This was why Nick was saving favors as if they were war bonds. They were exactly that. "You're suggesting we tell Nick that the only other man in this family who shares his blood needs to go?"

Angie sighed and stared out the window at the harbor. "I don't know. Nick wants Trey seasoned, and I back his play, but maybe we need to ask him to think harder about this. The motherland isn't just gonna roll over and say, 'Okay, mixed blood is fine now.' There's a better choice for successor. There's you."

Donnie turned and leaned back on the desk at Angie's side, looking out the window, too. "Ange, it's not a reflex decision. Nick decided this over time, and *Trey* decided him. Not because he lobbied to be made. He came in with us not expecting anything. Nick told him he couldn't advance, and Trey wanted this anyway. Nick decided he wanted to take on this fight *for Trey*. The don knows what it means. There's nothing we can tell him he hasn't already considered. When he does this, if he does it, he'll be firm. You and me, and everybody else, we'll have one choice—to stand with him, or stand against him."

"And you're okay with Trey jumping over you?"

Donnie had had a long time to think about all this and understand his feelings. They hadn't changed. "I'm with Nick. I trust him. The Pagano Brothers is his family legacy, and I'll fight at his side for his right to make it as he wishes. I'll take over if, God forbid, something happens before Trey's ready, but if that happens I'll step down when he is. But I have no burning need to be don. Where I am is enough."

Staring out at the boats beyond as late afternoon dusked to evening, Angie was thoughtfully quiet. Then he sighed. "You're right. Obviously you're right. Okay. So yeah, Trey's in tonight. That's eight. We need two more."

~oOo~

The team of ten went by water, down the coast to New Jersey. Angie re-briefed everyone on the plan during the short sail, and the men suited up in Kevlar and locked and loaded their weapons.

267

The plan was to go fast and quiet, all guns silenced, and to bring out as many men alive as possible. They would all be dead before the night was over, but Nick wanted every syllable of their information, and every drop of their blood, before they sank into the ocean.

Docked just north of Asbury Park, they met up with a small team of Vio Marconi's men. The Marconi Family were the Paganos' closest allies on the New England Council. They ran Connecticut and had their own beef with the Bondaruks. But the Bondaruks had set their sights on Nick, the head of the Council, from the go. So Marconi took a support role in this endeavor.

Marconi men handed over the keys to three unmarked cargo vans, dark grey, and took up watch over the cruiser.

The three vans split up on the road. Angie's plan was for all three to come in from different directions, closing off all access points to the video store. Their intel had it that the Ukrainians came together every night an hour after the store closed and stayed together for at least two hours.

Angie drove one van, and Donnie went with him. He pulled Trey into their ride as well. And Angie pulled Alex in. The two leaders in charge of the only unmade men on this job.

Before he put the van in gear, Angie turned and scowled at the young men. "You got a wife and a baby at home, Golden Boy." Trey reacted to the nickname he hated, but Angie ignored him and turned to Alex. "And you, kid, you live with your mamma, right?"

"Yeah," Alex answered.

"If I have to carry your bodies to the women who love you, I will be very unhappy. Do you know your job tonight?"

Both men nodded.

"Good. You keep your heads screwed tight, and your balls where they belong. You stay cool and loose and sharp. *Capite*?"

"Got it," they both answered.

Donnie turned around leveled a hard look at Trey. "You understand, Trey?"

"I got it, boss. I'm sharp."

Angie turned back to the wheel. "Good. Then let's roll."

~oOo~

The video store was about two miles in from the coast, in a corner strip mall at the edge of a cluster of apartment buildings. Across the street was an office plaza, one of those places that rented out space to hair stylists and independent accountants. At this hour, the whole intersection was quiet. All four corners were dark, and the apartments sloped down a hill behind a cantilevered gate.

Angie was right—there was room here for them to work and not make waves.

The video store—its name, so far as Donnie could see, was simply 'відео,' the green letters still illuminated on the eaves though the shop lights were down to their after-hours dimness—was two shops in from the southern end of the strip. No access in or out but the front and the back.

Angie directed Dre to use his van to block the front entrance and wait. Jake and Angie pulled around to the back, headlights dark. They cut their engines and let the vans roll in the rest of the way.

Four cars, nondescript sedans and compact SUVs, and two sport-style motorcycles were clustered near the rear door of the video store.

"We're looking for eight?" Donnie asked, considering those vehicles.

"Yeah. That's all their rides. Some of the guys don't drive."

"You're kidding."

Angie shrugged. "I guess it's different in the old country, I don't know."

Jake and Angie were stopped almost nose to nose. Jake made a 'ready when you are' gesture, and Angie turned to the back. "Do not fuck us up, children."

"We're good, Ange," Trey answered. His tone had the edge of a fight, and Angie grinned.

"Good. Then let's get this done."

Angie, Donnie, Trey, Alex, Jake, Tony, and Fezz—seven men in Kevlar, carrying silenced M4s as well as their own sidearms and ammo for it all—crept quietly to the dinged metal service door of the Bondaruk advance crew's base. Angie tried the knob quietly, but it was locked. There was a deadbolt above it, and they had no reason to believe it wouldn't be engaged as well. And it opened out, not in.

But Angie had called Fezz in on this job for a reason. Vince 'Fezzik' Bartelli wasn't the fastest or smartest guy in the organization; he was probably the slowest, in every respect. If things got dicey here, there was no question he'd be the one slowing them down. He was made, because he was loyal and would do—had done—anything Nick asked of him, but he'd never be more than a soldier. At the shipping company, he worked the warehouse and would never do anything more complicated than drive a forklift—a job it had taken him weeks to learn. His nickname had come from the warehouse guys, after the big guy in *The Princess Bride*. And it fit: Fezz was six-ten if he was a foot, and four hundred if he was a pound. They'd had to custom-order Kevlar to fit him. And, like the character he'd been named for, there was seemingly nothing that could withstand his brute strength.

271

So Angie stepped aside and nodded the big guy up. Fezz handed his M4 to Jake. He lifted one massive yacht of a foot and kicked the door. It burst in at once, the jamb splintering, the whole assembly groaning at the strain.

From then, with the Ukrainians reacting to the incursion, chaos exploded, but they'd expected as much. Their goal was to keep the fracas inside the video shop and remove all traces of their presence when they were done. The same pinch points that would hold the Ukrainians inside were bottlenecks for the Paganos; coming in one at a time, they were vulnerable to getting picked off, so they used the brief moment of surprise they had and clambered in over the broken door as fast as they could.

Angie was in first, Donnie right behind him, but bullets were already flying when he was clear of the door. The best-case scenario would have been no gunfire—the element of surprise freezing the Ukies where they sat or stood in the face of a troop of heavily armed and armored Italians. Best cases rarely happened, of course. One of their targets must have had a gun at the ready, and Donnie felt a bullet skim off Angie's Kevlared shoulder and ping off to gouge the wall at Donnie's side. Angie reacted, firing either with intent or in reflex after taking the hit, and after that, their plan changed fast.

Nick wanted live bodies to interrogate. They all wanted the men who'd envisioned horrors for their women to suffer. But by the time the brief firestorm had ended, there was a pile of Ukrainian bodies, and Donnie didn't know if any of them were breathing. Nick would not be happy.

His first concern, though, was his own men. "Are we whole?" He spun around. Angie's face was speckled with red, but it obviously wasn't his blood. There was a dark streak on the shoulder of his vest, but he hadn't seemed to notice. Jake was down, but struggling to his feet. A metal disk had implanted in his vest, on the left side of his chest. That bullet would have killed him. He'd feel the punch of it for a while.

No other Pagano man had taken a hit.

"Fuck! Fuck!" Tony yelled from the front of the store. "Fuck!"

Donnie turned to Trey and Alex. Both were whole, and Trey was holding his M4 in a way that made it clear he'd used it. "Cover Angie. Keep aimed on them. Don't assume they're dead until we check."

He ran to the front, jumping over Angie, who was starting to check for signs of life.

The trouble up front was obvious. There were two more Bondaruk men on the floor in the middle of the shop, but they'd expected some to run for the front; it was why they'd had a van stationed there. One man was clearly dead, but the other was breathing, trying to sit up, and wheezing something in Ukrainian. None of that was the trouble.

The trouble was the body lying beside and partly under the dead Ukie.

A boy. No older than eight or nine. Donnie didn't have to get any closer to know he was dead.

Tony stood and stared at the bodies, his rifle sagging from his hand. Dre and Paolo stood by the door, in shock.

"What the fuck? What the fuck happened?" Donnie demanded, going to the bodies—he knew the boy was dead, he was missing most of his throat, and his eyes were open, but he checked anyway. "What the fuck is a *kid* doing here?"

The bloody, breathing man was still yammering in Ukrainian. Now he was trying to get to the boy, and Donnie understood the grief in his voice. He was related to this dead child.

"I don't know!" Tony moaned. "They were coming for the door, and that one pulled on me, and I shot. Just a short burst. I didn't see the kid! Goddammit, boss, I didn't see the kid!"

"*Cazzo!*" Angie stood at the back of the store. "What the fuck?"

Donnie turned on him. "You said there were a couple hangarounds who might be collateral damage. Why didn't you know about this kid?"

274

"I don't know! We've had eyes on them for weeks, and there was no kid with them—ever. The only kids who came in were customers, and they went right back out. I don't know where he came from!"

The wounded Ukrainian raised his struggling voice and turned his soliloquy on them, but no one understood his language.

"He's saying it's his son, boss," Trey said. He'd come up from the back room.

Donnie wheeled around again. "You speak Ukrainian?"

"Not really. A little. Lara is teaching herself. She says it helps her, since the Bondaruks keep turning up. I'm trying to learn with her. *Miy syn, miy syn*—he's saying 'my son, my son,' I think. I don't know the rest of it."

"Can you ask him if he speaks English?"

Trey rattled off some halting syllables Donnie didn't understand. The man shook his head and wailed the same two words. Now that Donnie understood them, they weren't so different from their English counterparts.

Trey turned to Donnie. "I think you got that. He's too out of his head to make sense, anyway. But I don't think he speaks English."

"Fuck. Somebody here's got to. I hope we didn't kill them all."

"I killed a kid," Tony moaned. One of their toughest enforcers stood staring at the body of the child he'd killed and moaned.

This was not the time or place to reckon with guilt. Donnie gave Tony a hard shake. "Get your head together. We gotta get out of here. Focus! Let's do what we're here to do!"

Ten silent men focused and finished the job. Of the eleven people who were in that shop when the Paganos attacked, five were still breathing. Only three were conscious.

Of the six who were dead, one was a child.

They wrapped the dead in tarps. They bound and gagged the living. Once the dead were piled in one van and the living in another, Angie and Donnie put men on guard at the vans, and the rest went in to remove the traces of their presence. The blood was all Ukrainian, so they left it for the cleaners to come and finish the job and leave a mystery behind.

~oOo~

They brought the dead and the living onto the boat and returned to Quiet Cove, docking in a Pagano Brothers harbor warehouse, one that Nick preferred to do his wetwork in. It was already outfitted to accommodate any need he might have for the work.

As don, Nick rarely bloodied his own hands anymore. There were certain jobs he didn't delegate — when he had a personal interest in the justice, or when justice was due against one of his own men, for example — but for the most part, Donnie and Angie were his weapons of choice.

But Nick had well and truly earned his reputation as a brutal enforcer. He'd begun rendering justice in the name of the Pagano Brothers when he was fifteen years old, first on his own father. In the fifty years since, he'd become a student, and then a master, of all the methods of torture the world and its history provided.

When he arrived at the harbor that night, the men were quiet. The death of the boy weighed on them all. Six men and the boy were dead now; another man had died on the boat. Two were unconscious, including, now, the dead boy's father. Two were conscious. One of those was barely hurt. He hadn't been shot; all he had was a bump on the head. They'd found him playing dead. Neither of them would admit to speaking English.

"Where's the boy?" Nick asked once the doors had closed behind him.

"Here." Donnie directed him to the stack of pallets they'd laid the small body on.

"Show me."

Angie folded back the tarp so Nick could see the grey face, the ruined throat. Donnie watched Nick as he took in that sight. His face was calm, but his eyes flashed, and the muscles at his jaw flexed dangerously.

"I told you this had to be clean and quiet, and you bring me a dead child. You told me the only collateral damage would be hangarounds, and you bring me a dead child."

Nick's voice was low, as seemingly sedate as his expression, but danger pulsed around him like bright red heat. Donnie sensed the other men shrink back.

"I don't know where he came from, don," Angie said, quietly. "None of our surveillance showed him going in or coming out. Not once. I don't know how he got in there."

"How old is he?"

"Seven," Donnie answered, a hot rock of guilt throbbing in his gut.

Nick didn't seem to react. "Who did this?"

Tony, Trey, and Dre stood just back from Nick, Donnie, and Angie, but from the corner of his left eye, Donnie saw Tony shift, ready to take responsibility. Before he could, Angie said, "I did it."

Nick turned sharply. Donnie couldn't see the look he gave Angie, but he saw Angie's face. Saw it go pale, saw his eyes flare wide. "I'm sorry, don."

"You bring me a dead child."

278

Again, Tony moved, made to step forward. Donnie turned his head and made enough of a gesture to stop him in his tracks. It was too late to shift the blame. Angie had taken it, and it couldn't be deflected now, certainly not onto an underling.

It wasn't out of place on Angie's back. He'd planned the hit. He'd led the intel. He'd rushed the job. It was on Donnie, too, for having the idea in the first place and not insisting they triple check the plan.

It had been a good plan. Except for this child.

"Tell me you've done the work now and know if this boy has a mother."

Knowing Nick would want to know, Donnie had called Calvin and put him on the task of identifying the boy. "He does. The boy's name is Gregor Honcharenko. His mom is a waitress at the Hard Rock in AC. She's a citizen, and so was the boy. Dad is Artem Honcharenko. He's here on a green card. He's one of the hangarounds we expected."

"Is?"

"Yeah. He's alive but unconscious. Shot in the chest, but still kicking so far."

Nick's jaw worked strenuously as he stared down at the small body. "I want the boy left to be found. So his mother can bury him. Angie, that's on you."

"*Capisco*, don."

"That'll turn the Bondaruks to us, Nick," Donnie said. "They'll consider it proof that we did this. They'll say we killed a child to start a war."

"Yes. And so we have. You've brought me a dead child with a mother who'll miss him. Who'll search for him if she doesn't know. We will give her her child to bury and mourn. And now I'm at war with roaches."

"I'm sorry, don," Angie said again.

"I will cut those words out of your tongue if I hear them again. They mean nothing." Nick turned on his heel. "Trey."

"Uncle?"

"I hear you know Ukrainian."

"Only a little. Lara knows more, but—I don't ... I don't want her here." It was brave of the kid to push Nick at all right now; he was angrier than Donnie had seen him in years.

"No, neither do I. Can you say enough to get one of them to tell us who speaks English? Since they're not speaking up themselves?"

"I can try, yeah."

Trey went with Nick to the two bound, conscious men. He spoke some awkward, guttural words, but neither answered him. While Trey tried, Nick removed his jacket. He cuffed his sleeves to the elbow.

Still standing at the makeshift bier, Angie wrapped the boy's body up again.

"Angie—" Tony started.

"Shut up. You'll help me take this kid back to Jersey."

"Yeah, absolutely."

Donnie left them to that work and went toward Nick. He pushed up his sleeves. They weren't done getting dirty tonight.

When Nick was ready—sleeves cuffed, gloves on, tools out—he called Trey over. "Enough, nephew. Don't waste time on what doesn't work. Come here."

Trey came to Nick's work table, where he'd laid out an array of sharp and blunt objects.

"Take off your jacket, roll up your sleeves. You get dirty tonight."

Donnie saw the kid's Adam's apple bob with a hard swallow, but he did what he was told.

Nick chose a scalpel as his first tool. He went to the conscious Ukrainians and called Jake close with a tip of his head. Indicating the healthiest of the bound men, the one who'd played dead, Nick said, "Take his shoes and socks off."

Jake did what he was told, and Nick crouched before the man's bare feet. Donnie's toes curled in his shoes. He knew this move, and it was not pleasant.

"When information is required, the key is to make much more pain than damage," Nick said to Trey, and then slit the man's foot down the center, from the ball to the heel.

The thing about the scalpel — it was so sharp, so fine, that the first cut wasn't nearly as painful as one might think. It slid through the skin like a hot knife through butter, and on the sole of the foot, way down at the bottom of the body, the pain receptors couldn't keep up. The blood seeped almost sedately from the wound. But the scalpel went deep, through tendons and muscle, through the hard pads of the ball and heel. So when Nick set aside the cutting tool and with his fingers pried open the slit he'd made, the pain roared all the way up the subject's body. This man screamed like a soprano in the middle of her aria.

Donnie could only imagine the pain; he'd seen its effects before but had never felt it himself. Still, he doubted it was as intense as the greatest pain he'd ever endured.

Nick handed the scalpel to Trey. "Do his other foot."

"*Ni! Ni! Ni!*" the man screamed, and even Donnie knew what he meant.

"Ask him now, Trey."

Trey cleared his throat and said the same Ukrainian words. The man sobbed and screamed and stared at his quivering, ruined foot, but he wasn't ready to give up his friends.

Nick nodded at Trey, who opened the man's other foot and spread the wound wide. His hands shook, but he did what the don wanted, and he didn't hesitate.

The man broke, wailing like a siren now, and pointed to the boy's father. Artem Honcharenko. He'd denied speaking English earlier, but now that they knew the boy and his mother were American citizens, and he was a legal resident, it made sense that the father had some English. But he was unconscious.

"Anybody else?"

Trey rattled off some more shaky, incomprehensible syllables. The man gasped some back and pointed in the direction of the tarped bodies.

"Pretty sure he's saying the rest are dead."

Nick stood and went to the supine body of the boy's father. He crouched beside him and checked his pulse. When Nick's head sagged to his chest, Donnie knew that Artem wouldn't be telling them anything.

"All of this, and we have nothing. Nothing but a war I don't want."

Don Pagano stood. He went to his table, pulled off his gloves, threw them in the bin for the incinerator. He washed his hands. Dried them. Threw the towel away. Rolled down his cuffs. Fixed his cuff links. Put his jacket on.

All the while, the Pagano men around him stood silently, ashamed.

"Trey, clean up and come with me. It's not the night to make your bones. Angie, take who you need and get the boy home. Donnie, wipe this up. The rest of you, do your part. I want this erased. Everything but the boy. And I swear on my uncle's memory, if you fuck this up more, I will sink every one of you in the Atlantic."

~oOo~

It was morning when Donnie got home. Everything from his scalp to the soles of his feet ached with weariness. But the Bondaruk men had been erased, and young Gregor's body was back home, where his mother would know his fate and be able to put her son to rest. Where his body would serve as a message Nick had had no intention of sending.

Seven. The boy had been only seven years old. Donnie could barely lift the weight of the night as he walked through his house.

Mrs. Alfonsi was in the kitchen, making breakfast, and she lifted an eyebrow as she mixed pancake batter. "You were out all night. You're not getting younger, Mr. Donnie. You should take better care."

"I know. I'm sorry. I'm taking the morning off—I'll take a shower and get some sleep."

"Will you eat?"

He had no appetite at all. "Just put them in that warmer dish you have, and I'll eat them later. They smell great." He left his housekeeper to her work and went up to his room.

After a hot, scrubbing shower, Donnie sat on the side of his bed and looked down at his phone. He needed something light and good in his head before he tried to sleep, or any sleep he got would tear his mind apart. Nights like the last one tore off the lid on his old demons.

Arianna had called him late last evening, while they were preparing for Jersey. He'd let it roll to voice mail because he couldn't afford the distraction. But he'd listened to it four times in the past few hours. It wasn't anything special—just her, being sweetly awkward. *You never actually said you wanted to start a relationship. You kind of skidded out underneath that one. So just checking—you do, right? Okay, now I'm embarrassed, so I'm gonna go. I hope you call me.*

It was eight o'clock in the morning. Was that rudely early? He'd never worried about that before; when he wanted to call a woman, he called.

So he called now.

"Hello?" He'd obviously woken her; her voice was soft and unfocused.

"Hi."

"Donnie."

He smiled at the relief and pleasure in her tone. "I had a long night, and I'm just getting to bed. But I'd like to see you tonight. Are you free for dinner?"

"Here in Providence?"

"Of course." Quiet Cove was his home; it was too soon to bring her so close.

"Then yes! I have an audition late this afternoon, but then I'm free."

"I'm surprised a principal has to audition." She was quiet, and Donnie understood he'd offended her. "I didn't mean it as a criticism."

"No, I know. I'm just thinking. How would you feel about picking me up in the studio?"

"At the theatre? Sure."

"No, I mean coming in to the studio."

Now he was quiet, as he tried to understand her purpose. As much as he could, he avoided situations where attention was drawn his way, and he'd already told her as much — or at least strongly implied it. "You want me to see you audition?"

"Okay, I'm just going to be straight with you, and if you don't like this, I get it. The director and I … it's complicated, but he doesn't like me. He's being a pretty big jerk, which is why I have to audition. I don't have enough juice to deal with him on my own, which sucks, but I was thinking — "

"You were thinking you'd make a show of your Mafioso boyfriend and back him off that way."

"Sort of. Are you my Mafioso boyfriend?"

Donnie didn't answer, because he had a more important question. "What's he doing to you, Arianna?" The question reminded him of something Trewson had said, about a 'Jeremiah.' Was she having trouble that didn't have to do with him? It lightened his load a little to think he could do some good for her and not simply cause her trouble.

"He's just being a jerk. I don't want you to do anything to him, I just want him to see you, and see me with you."

"Okay." He'd pay attention to what he saw while he was there, and he'd press Arianna for more details. About Berrault and this Jeremiah, both.

"Yeah?"

"What time should I be there?"

"Like … six? Does that work?"

"As far as I know right now, it works. Unless something happens I can't push off, I'll be there. How will I get to the studio?"

"Just go to the front office, and they'll point the way. I'll tell them to expect you. And thank you!"

There was so much delight in her sweet voice that Donnie couldn't help but smile.

~ 16 ~

Ari came out from the shower and tied the sash of her kimono around her waist. She went to the kitchen, where Julian was noisily making himself a bowl of corn flakes. In case she'd doubted that his extra slamming of drawers and cupboards was meant rhetorically, he looked over his shoulder and sighed at her as she came into the room.

"Don't start already, Julian. You've made yourself perfectly clear." She hipped him aside and tore a lightly freckled banana off the bunch. "Coffee?"

He took a cup down and filled it for her. She went to the fridge and got the milk. After she added some to her coffee, she handed the carton over for his cereal. It was a dance they'd been doing in the tiny square of this kitchen for years.

Julian took his corn flakes and his petulance and sat at the bar that served as their only eating space. "Was that him on the phone?"

"It was." Ari put the milk back and snagged a carton of vanilla yogurt. She gathered up the elements of her usual breakfast and sat at his side. "Please just trust me, Julian. Let me see if this is anything with him."

"He made you cry. I don't like guys who make you cry."

"Then don't be one of them."

He turned to her, and Ari met his eyes. She saw honest worry in his, but she also saw fear of his own. He didn't want a man like Donnie in *his* life. He was afraid of what it would mean for him, too. "There was a gun pointed at you the other night. One of his men pointed a *gun* at you."

"And Donnie put himself between me and it." That was when she'd started to forgive him. When he'd shown her the diner as he saw it, and it saw him, she'd started to fall for him again.

"You can't give the guy credit for saving you from danger he brought to you. That's like thanking the guy who ran you over for calling 911."

They'd been having this same argument for two days now, and Ari was tired of it. She went back to her breakfast, and Julian hunkered over his bowl and ate his. They ate in cumbersome silence.

Julian finished his cereal and took his bowl to the sink. Ari took that moment of distance as an opportunity.

She sucked down the last of her coffee for fortitude and told him, "I asked him to come to the studio tonight."

He shut off the tap and let the bowl drop to the sink. "The studio? You want him there for your audition?"

"After it." She waited to see if Julian would catch on.

He did. "You want Bax to see you with him."

She nodded.

"You've had one date with the guy, and you're letting him fight your battles?"

Now Adrianna was pissed. "Who else will? I haven't exactly seen you step up to my side." At her friend's stricken look, she backed off. "I understand, Jule. I wouldn't ask you to fight for me. I can't even fight for myself. I'm not going to sleep with Bax, and he's going to keep humiliating me and punishing me until I can't take it anymore. But if he fires me, where do I go? To open Madame Arianna's House of Dance next to a 7-11 off the Iway? Same for you. Bax holds our lives in his hands. If we want to dance, we have to dance for him. I love what we do. Even with him looming over me, the theatre is my favorite place in the world to be. I can't lose it, so I can't fight the man who controls if I have it. But I'm dating a man that *Bax* can't fight. If Donnie wants to, he could take Bax's life in his hands and squeeze, and Bax knows it. I want him to see that I have an ally *he* can't fight. That's all I want — just for him to see."

Crossing to the bar, Julian leaned toward her. "I'm sorry, Ari. I should have your back better."

She covered his hands with hers. "You do, Jule. You're always here to hold me up."

But Donnie would stand before her. He'd take a bullet for her.

~oOo~

Baxter hated *The Nutcracker*, and most of the dancers groaned and rolled their eyes at the ballet they'd all performed more than any other. Certainly, it got to be a grind, especially since the audience was hyper-protective of the production. It had to look a certain way eternally. Every step, every costume, every ornament on the tree. Yes, *The Nutcracker* could be kind of a drag.

Except for the part of Clara. Lots of ballets showcased a single ballerina; probably *most* of the classic ballets did. But Clara scarcely left the stage for the entire ballet. Every dance, every scene, every moment was shaped by her point of view. It wasn't the most physically demanding role in ballet, it wasn't even the most demanding role in *The Nutcracker*—the Sugar Plum Fairy had more flash, and some companies put young girls in Clara's part—but it was one of the most pivotal.

It was also one that could highlight Ari's chief weakness: her trouble fading into a role. Even so, in this company, she was obviously the best choice for the role. She had the experience and the talent, and she was coming off good notices for her performance in *Phantom*. With Devonny rumored to be announcing her retirement at the end of the season, Ari should be the Rhode Island Ballet's next prima ballerina. There was no defensible reason she should be auditioning now.

So she meant not to give Baxter any defensible reason to deny her the part. And then hope Donnie showed up to put a period on the issue.

Her audition spot, not surprisingly, wasn't ideal — she was the first girl of any with a real shot at the role, so she couldn't gauge her own performance against anyone competing with her. But it didn't matter what the other girls did. Ari would dance her legs off and leave the others to stumble around in her dust.

When she'd auditioned routinely, she'd made a point of doing something unexpected. Showcasing her power, drawing attention to herself. Making everyone sit up and take notice. Back then, she'd stubbornly refused to accept the tactical error in that approach. Now she understood, and especially now, when there was more than simply her dancing in judgment, she meant to dance within the lines but do it perfectly. Grace as well as power.

Today, for Baxter, she would dance the transformation solo, when the toys come to life. She would do it in a dance studio, without other dancers or set pieces to react to, but she meant to make him forget that.

Alone in the middle of a dim dance studio, ten minutes before her audition time, Arianna danced.

~oOo~

Baxter always held production auditions in the worst studio in the theatre—it was small and poorly lit, it smelled funny, and it wasn't connected to the building's sound system for some reason having to do with the wiring or plumbing or whatever. Dancers were reduced to using an ancient portable stereo, or they brought in their own speaker for their phones and used that. He said that a worthy dancer could shine in the worst conditions.

Auditions for places in the company were grander affairs, and he used the stage itself during those events. But he liked to torture the dancers he'd already hired.

Among the many reasons Ari was reluctant to fight for herself against Baxter's abuse and advances was that he was unkind to just about everybody. Even Devonny hadn't been immune to his nasty remarks. He picked on the girls more than the boys, but overall, he was a monstrous ass. It was simply Ari's turn, and she had three times the focus he normally turned on his main target because Devonny's career was over, and that had obviously fractured their love affair. Ari, positioned to step into Devonny's pointe shoes, was enemy number one.

On top of all that, Baxter's dick was now free range. They'd been a couple when Ari had joined the company, but everybody knew that Baxter and Devonny had been director and protégé before they'd been lovers. Apparently, Ari was expected to step into those shoes as well. She could stop being his enemy if she'd become his lover. He'd as much as said so.

But nope. She had other plans. Now that preparations for the next production were getting underway and she couldn't avoid Baxter as easily as she had for the past few weeks, she was really hoping her other plans showed up tonight set things to rights.

Most of the company was crammed into the audition studio. Several of the girls were auditioning, and a few had asked some of the boys to dance with them. But really, they were all there because they were nosy.

Ari didn't care. They were set dressing and nothing more. When the time for her audition arrived and Baxter wasn't in the room yet, she stood alone in the center of the space, dressed in a filmy white gown Bastien had lent her from the costume department. Her hair was twisted into girly braids wrapped around her head, with a white satin ribbon woven through. She was thirty-one, but she could be Clara.

She stood and waited, in first position, like a doll in its box, for ten minutes before Baxter stalked in. Carrying a stack of papers and a giant travel mug, he noisily dragged a chair where he wanted it and sat down. "Let's go," he said and put the mug to his mouth.

Julian was ready at the little stereo. He dimmed the lights a bit and hit play on the CD player.

Arianna danced. She let the people in the room fade out, let the smells and sights and extraneous sounds of this crappy space dwindle to vapor. She let Baxter's impatient eyes, his uninterested posture, their tense rapport since summer, all of it waft away. She turned inward, felt every atom in her body, felt the music wind around her muscles, and she danced.

When the music faded away, she held her final pointe position for five more seconds and then came down to first position. At her side she heard a male cheer—not Julian, but Sergei. It wasn't usual for other dancers to applaud an audition, but Julian joined Sergei, and then the whole company cheered her. She blushed and tried a smile at Baxter. He didn't smile back.

But the studio door opened just then, and Donnie Goretti walked through. He wore a dark grey suit that fit him like it was genetically engineered, and a pale pink dress shirt. He wasn't wearing a tie, and the shirt was open at the neck. He looked like a man with plans after work. Ari grinned. He grinned back.

Baxter stood at once. "You can't be—" He recognized Donnie then, and changed his tone and his tack. "Mr. Goretti. Can I help you?"

Donnie ignored him and walked straight to the center of the studio. He came so close her skirt brushed the pants of his suit—there was a faint pattern in the weave—and took her hands in his. His head came close, and she had that momentary, hopeful flash that he'd kiss her, but instead he brushed his left cheek over hers, light as a whisper. Her belly quivered at the sensual graze. Almost as good as a kiss.

Almost.

"That was beautiful," he said at her ear, softly, only for her. "You are beautiful."

"Thank you."

He squeezed her hand and turned around. "Baxter," he said as if he'd only noticed his existence this second. "How are you?"

"Fine, thank you. I'm sorry—should I have expected you?"

Oh, this was brilliant. Ari had never seen the director in this condition before—if he kowtowed any more obviously to Donnie, his knees would give out.

"No, I'm not here for you. Arianna and I have plans tonight, as soon as she's finished here. I thought I'd

296

come in and watch." Turning to Ari, he said, "I tried to get here before you started, but there was traffic. I didn't want to distract you, so I watched from the door."

She didn't know if all that was a performance for Baxter, or if it was true and meant for her, but either way it was wonderful. Those mundane little details had an intimacy about them that made her fingertips tingle. She smiled and said, "I'm glad you're here."

He turned back to Baxter. "So, if she's done …?"

"Right, yes. Of course." Reclaiming some of his sense of place, Baxter turned his attention to Ari. "Casting announcements tomorrow afternoon."

Donnie looked down at her, lifting his left eyebrow. She saw a question there and understood it: he was asking if she wanted him to push harder.

She didn't. Just as she wouldn't fuck Baxter for the part, she didn't want Donnie to actually threaten him for it, either. It wasn't an edge she was after. She only wanted a fair decision. Turning to her director, she smiled. "I'll be here."

With her hand in Donnie's, she led him to the door. When she saw Julian, she remembered that Baxter hadn't been their only audience, and she glanced back to see the entire company frozen in various expressions of astonishment.

~oOo~

"Talk to me about Baxter," Donnie said, resting against the dressing-room counter.

Ari was using a locker door like a screen as she wiggled out of her costume and into her street clothes — which was dumb, since he'd seen, and been inside, her whole body, but this felt like a reboot, and she still wasn't sure they'd be having sex again quite yet. A little reserve made sense.

A shower would have been nice, but she didn't know what she'd do with him while she took one. "What do you want to know about him?"

"You know what I'm asking, Arianna."

She did, but she wasn't sure she wanted to tell him. "He's just a jerk."

"Arianna."

There was a command in his tone she didn't much like. She liked her impulse to obey the command even less, so she made herself say, "He's just a jerk," and ducked behind the locker door to get her underwear on.

Two seconds later, he was standing right in front of her. Ari froze in the act of hooking her bra. He glanced down, taking in her nearly naked body before he met her eyes. "I think you're tough enough to handle jerks on your own. Why did you need me for that performance?"

He looked really, really good in that suit. His open neckline showed the base of his throat—oh, that deep depression between his collarbones, *unh*—and a hint of the hair on his chest, and Ari's mouth managed to water and go dry at the same time. She forced her eyes up before the surge of lust fried a circuit. "It was just a performance?"

His hand settled on her hip, and his fingers squeezed lightly. "Between us, no. I meant what I said to you. But for all those people in the room, it was. That's why you wanted me here, right? To have them seem me stake a claim. Baxter Berrault in particular."

Put like that, it sounded slimy and craven. Abashed, she let her eyes fall from his. His fingers came to her chin and pushed gently, and she faced him again.

"Did he hurt you?"

"No. It's complicated, but the short version is he's been making my life hard because I won't sleep with him. You were surprised I had to audition—that's why." She felt the tension increase in his limbs, and she grabbed his arm before he could move. "He's a jerk to everybody. I'm getting an extra dose right now. I don't want you to fight this for me. I just wanted you here so he could see that I'm not alone."

"What about Trewson? He's not sticking up for you?"

Had he ever said her friend's first name? "*Julian's* just as under Baxter's thumb as I am. If he sticks up for me, he could lose his place in the company, and it's not like we can just go to a job fair and find another one."

"If he was really your friend, it wouldn't matter. If the situation was reversed, would it matter to you?"

That question might have occurred to her once or twice, but she never allowed herself to entertain it. She didn't want Julian taking heat for her. When she couldn't find words to articulate that, she simply said, "Bax has a lot of power."

"I have more."

"I know. He knows, too. So I wanted him to think it would be dangerous to keep coming at me."

"It would be."

She grinned and set her hands on his chest, under his jacket. His flinch this time was subtle; maybe he was getting used to her touch. "I like you like this."

"Like what?"

"Invested."

He frowned and took a step back, out of her reach. "I hope we both know what we're getting into. Get dressed, and we'll get something to eat."

~oOo~

She'd remembered her little black dress and her vintage Chanel flats this time, and she hadn't worked up so much of a sweat that she smelled funky or her hair looked mangy now that it was down. Walking into another of Providence's finest restaurants with her hand in Donnie's, Ari was confident. Maybe even a little proud.

The lighting in this establishment was low, and the dark décor added to the dimming effect. Most expensive restaurants she'd been in—not that it was a long list—used lower lighting for ambiance, but Ari saw things in a new way recently. Donnie liked places like this because he didn't stand out so much. Not in ways he didn't want to, at least.

In other ways, he stood out like a beacon. The staff here all knew him, and they treated them like esteemed guests, ushering them to the best table, so attentive that every need was met before it had even been fully realized. None of these servers and hosts looked away from Donnie. In his own world, his wealth and power were a mask he could wear and be seen for himself.

After they ordered and had another bottle of expensive wine at their table—*mental note to drink this one more slowly*—Donnie rested his arms on the table and said, "Who is Jeremiah?"

As always, the sound of that name struck her broadside. Tonight, now, from Donnie, the name had barbs, and Ari responded more sharply than she meant to.

"No. If all you're going to do tonight is interview me about men who've been jerks to me, I'll just go home now. This is not how I want to have a date with you. Or anybody."

"He's another 'jerk'?"

He had an uncanny knack for ruining perfect moments. "Jerk, assaulter. To*may*to to*mah*to. Almost every woman I know has at least one of them in their past, and the rest have one in their future. I'm not talking about it. Ever." She reached for her bag, because she really did mean to leave if he pushed this point. Her best defense against what that man had done to her, and all the people who'd leaned on her to let him get away with it, was to never talk or think about it or him. Period. If Donnie couldn't leave her control of her own mind, then Julian was right and she was a fool for giving him another chance.

Donnie's hand covered hers. "Just this: Is he still around?"

That question, she was happy to answer, particularly if it would close the topic before the night was entirely ruined. "No. It was years ago, and he's long gone."

He squeezed her hand. "Okay. I won't ask again."

"Thank you."

"What would you like to talk about?"

She took a sip of wine. "I want to hear about you."

He frowned and stared into his wine glass. Ari sensed something dark ballooning inside him. Then he looked up, and the shadow receded. "There are things I can't tell you."

"I know. Tell me what you can. Tell me about Quiet Cove."

He grinned. "That, I can tell you."

~ 17 ~

Before Donnie opened the passenger door of his Porsche, he did a quick scan around him. Dre was parked across the street about fifty feet down. Chubs and Ollie were on Arianna's detail tonight, but other than a regular ping to his phone, updating their location, they weren't obviously around.

He had a really excellent reason to stop this experiment in a 'relationship' in its tracks. Just last night, they'd killed a seven-year-old boy. He wasn't related to Yuri Bondaruk, but that didn't matter. Retaliation wasn't in doubt, and the bastards had already demonstrated a clear preference for going for loved ones to achieve their goals. Women in particular.

Donnie's timing, therefore, was absurdly horrible. While he'd been sitting in her dressing room, thinking about the clothes she was taking off, he should have told her right then that the danger was too great, and they couldn't see each other. He'd considered it. First, though, he'd wanted to understand the threat she faced from within. She'd wanted protection from Berrault, too.

He'd formed no strong opinions about Berrault in their few previous meetings. As one of the Ballet's top donors, Donnie was regularly invited to large administrative meetings as well as private parties and galas. He'd skipped most of the social events, but he'd attended a few meetings. There, Berrault had been a little cocky, as the artist in the room, but not so much to get Donnie's back up. He was a good choreographer, and he'd been sufficiently respectful, understanding that the people in the room held the purse strings, so Donnie hadn't thought much of him in either direction.

But he'd stood at the door tonight and watched Arianna dance, and he'd seen Berrault's performance of boredom and disrespect. Now, he'd formed a strong opinion. Knowing that he'd been leveraging Arianna for sex had made that opinion dangerous. He wasn't done dealing with Berrault, but the next time, there wouldn't be an audience.

He'd gotten tangled in his feelings about all that, and then he'd been standing there in front of her, and she'd been in her underwear, black lace over pink satin. Her beautiful, beautiful body, so small and strong, was right before him, and he couldn't leave her.

God, watching her dance. It was different in the studio than on the stage. The costumes and set dressing, the orchestra, the theatre itself was all spectacle—breathtaking, but untouchable. In that studio tonight, dressed in a simple white gown, surrounded by dancers in plain practice clothes, the experience was intimate. Arianna herself had been the only spectacle.

Sonia had accused him of having a steel cage around his heart. She hadn't been wrong. But Arianna had pried the door open. Just enough to make it hurt.

Now he had to keep her safe.

Satisfied that the area was clear, he opened the door and offered her his hand. She took it and set one elegant dancer's leg out. Her black dress was short, and she wore flat black and tan shoes shaped like ballet slippers—her legs went on forever. When her leg came out of the car, her foot was pointed. He'd noticed that even off stage, she walked like a dancer, toe to heel rather than the other way around. She glided.

He didn't step back as he drew her out of the car, and she came to her feet right against him. She didn't flinch or try to back off. She simply settled there, her body pressed to his, her face at his chest. He picked up a lock of her hair and played its sleek softness through his fingers.

"Come inside with me." She looked up at him.

At the restaurant, during the tiramisu they'd shared, he'd asked her to come with him to a hotel, but the invitation had offended her. He'd been slow to understand that it was the idea of being with him in a hotel again that had upset her, not the idea of being with him. By the time he'd grasped that obvious point, they were already on their way back to her apartment, and he'd figured the moment had passed.

"I don't want to see your roommate."

"Julian—his name is Julian, you should practice pronouncing it, since it's obviously hard for you to say—is out tonight. He has a new girlfriend. He'll be out until tomorrow."

"Is that so?"

"It is so."

"Are you asking me to spend the night?"

"I'm asking you to come in. I haven't planned the night beyond that. I'm just not ready for you to go."

He pulled her away from the car and closed the door. With another glance around, he took her hand and led her to her building.

~oOo~

The apartment was small and cluttered, but tidy. The door opened into something approximating a hallway, where a rack of hooks was mounded with jackets and bags. A low shelf on the floor beneath it held boots and •shoes.

The kitchen was a tiny, utilitarian square with a half wall overlooking the living room. A laminate bar top served as the top of the half wall, and two barstools there seemed to be the only place to have a meal.

Arianna hung her tan coat over another coat on the rack and ducked into the tiny kitchen. "Would you like a drink? I have a half-bottle of grocery-store chardonnay, and there's some Jack Daniels or vodka—Stoli, I think. Or the bottle looks kinda like Stoli, anyway. There might be a couple beers"—she opened the fridge—"Yep. There's IPA and a Stella."

Donnie grinned at her over the bar. "The Stella is fine, thank you."

"Do you want a glass?"

"I prefer the bottle." Drinking from a bottle didn't require a moment to strategize how he'd manage the mouth of an unfamiliar glass.

He turned and absorbed the insights of the living room. It had a strong starving-artist vibe. Lots of leafy plants at the windows—he'd seen those before, the few times he'd been outside, checking on her. Filmy white curtains, roll-up shades, all the way up. A futon and a couple of those big rattan chairs shaped like satellite dishes made up the seating. A raggedy old footlocker was the coffee table. The walls were covered with framed posters of classic ballets and dancers—he recognized Mikhail Baryshnikov, Rudolf Nureyev, Gelsey Kirkland, Gillian

Murphy. He'd seen Murphy dance in New York a few times.

Framed photos of friends and family were mixed in on the walls and propped on the surfaces. Donnie paid particular attention to those. There were a few of Arianna and Trewson, but they were friend photos. He saw no signs that they were more than that.

He shrugged out of his suit jacket and laid it neatly over the back of the futon.

She came in with a glass of white wine for herself and the bottle of beer for him. Before she handed him the bottle, she stood at the edge of the room, her brow furrowed but a smile on her face.

"What?"

She handed him his beer. "Just planning the night."

As he took a drink, she glided past him and went to the little unit that held a television and other electronics. She set her phone into a receiver, and music filled the room. Nothing he recognized. Something R&B, with piano and a slow, heavy beat. A woman's husky voice. Sexy.

When she turned to face him, her hips picked up a sensual sway, and Donnie smiled. "Are you seducing me, Arianna? Is that your plan?"

Her smile was slow and her eyelids low. She sipped from her glass but kept her eyes on his. "I'm just dancing. Do you dance, Donato?"

No one had called him Donato since his grandfather passed. "Nobody calls me Donato anymore."

"Nobody calls me Arianna. Except you."

"You told me you like it."

"I do. Don't you like Donato?" She'd swayed her way to him; now she set her free hand on his hip and made a lithe, writhing dip, sliding her body down his, that made his gut clench. When she wended her way up and stood straight again, her leg was between his.

He had to clear his throat before he could speak. "I don't know. I haven't heard it in a long time. Doesn't sound like me."

After a moment's study of his eyes, she let it drop. "You didn't answer my question. Do you dance?"

"No."

"That's a shame." She sidled around him, sliding her hand around his waist, letting it drop and sweep over his ass as she made her way around. "Because we're at the *Dirty Dancing* chapter. You have a world-class ass, by the way. And I know what I'm talking about. As a ballerina, I'm an expert on great asses."

Even through his clothes, her touch left electric spasms over his skin that fragmented his concentration on the words coming from her mouth. No woman had ever seduced him, not before his scarring or since. He'd always made the moves—and he would never have expected Arianna to take the lead. His impression of her was a

310

woman strong enough to live her life as she wished, but also naturally submissive. She'd readily submitted to him their first night together.

Then again, she'd asked him out that night. He never would have asked her.

"Are these movies you keep bringing up?" he asked, pulling himself out of his too-analytical thoughts.

Standing in front of him again, she laughed. The sound was musical, and her eyes gleamed. Blue-grey. Fathomless. The Atlantic on a cloudy day.

Her face was so lovely and fascinating. The features were dramatically Italian and not quite proportional — her eyes were just barely too large, as was her nose, and her mouth, its shape and color so perfect a dollmaker might have painted it on, was just a bit too small — but together, they made a uniquely beautiful woman, a balance between delicate and strong that had haunted his dreams and waking thoughts for weeks now.

"They're movies, yes. Love stories. Not your genre, I guess."

"No." He finished his beer and set the bottle on the footlocker. "Is it yours?"

"Not really."

"But you've seen them all."

"I'm an American female. I think there's a law that we have to see them all. Actually, though, I love *Dirty Dancing*."

"I wonder why."

"It's a mystery." She insinuated her leg between his again and hooked her free arm around his waist. Like that, when she began to sway to the music again, he had little choice but to follow along until they were dancing, swaying softly in the middle of her cluttered living room.

"What is your genre?" she asked, making the question sound like sex. "Please don't say Coppola."

"No. Science fiction and fantasy. And martial arts movies."

She gaped at him. "You're a closet geek?"

He chuckled. "It's not that deep a closet. I did cosplay the Phantom not so long ago, remember."

"You made a really great Phantom, too. That mask was fantastic." She finished her wine.

He took the glass from her. With his arm around her waist, he leaned down to set the glass beside his bottle. The move was almost a dip. He truly didn't dance and wouldn't have known how to plan to do it, but now that he had, he liked it, the way her body rested on his arm, the way his body loomed over her, and he didn't rush to stand straight again.

With a quiet, humming moan, she hooked her arms around his neck, pressed her hands to his head, and turned her face to his.

Her hands on his head. Her mouth on his cheek. His left cheek, on his beard, no more than an inch from his mouth. His good side, normal side. But no one touched any part of his face, let alone kissed it. In twenty years, only Bev and Carina had kissed his face, and their kisses were chaste family pecks.

Freshly minted memories of that minute in front of the mailboxes downstairs flashed in his head. He'd been far too freaked out to enjoy her touch in the moment, but since then, the recollection had been as vivid as reality, and played itself over and over in any quiet moment. Her slender, graceful hands, so soft, fluttering over his cheeks, his chin, his mouth, his horror of a nose, his stunted blob of an ear. That moment had been one of the most emotionally agonizing experiences of his life, but mixed in the pain of the memory was gentle touch and sweet care. It fucked with his brain.

"No," he said now. He couldn't take that touch. They had an agreement, and she was breaking it. Trying to take far more than he could give.

"I'm sorry," she said and let her head fall back, away from his. "I got caught up in the moment."

Grabbing her arms from his neck, he spun her around and pinned them at her sides. It was always better when he took women from behind. A thought like that about Arianna was a rusty nail in his chest, and he cursed himself for letting her in so far, so fast.

She gasped out her surprise, and her body went taut. When he grabbed the hem of her dress and yanked it up, she reared back against him. "Donnie, wait. No."

"What?" His disappointment in her honed his voice to a point.

She went very still. "You're angry."

"We had an agreement."

"I don't want it like this. Not when you're angry, and not when I can't see you."

He let her go and backed off. "This isn't gonna work."

She smoothed her dress and turned around. "I'm sorry. I didn't mean to break our agreement. This is new for me, not being able to touch and kiss the man I want the way I want. I got caught up, being so close to you, and I forgot."

"This is why I have arrangements. Nobody gets 'caught up.' There is no 'forgetting.'" He went to the back of the futon and picked up his jacket.

"Please don't go. Donnie, please."

Furious with himself, he glared at Arianna. "This is a mistake. No point in exacerbating it."

She winced and took a step backward. "I don't understand how you can do that."

"What?"

"Turn off your feelings like that. I know you were with me a minute ago. The heat between us was intense. And you can just flip a switch and be ice again?"

He wasn't ice. His chest was a boiling cauldron of emotion, but he had long experience in not showing what he felt. "Do you understand who I am?"

"Of course I do."

"You think I could have become what I am without being in control of my emotions?"

Some kind of comprehension dawned and softened the hurt and confusion from her brow. She came to him, and she set her hands on his chest, hooking her fingers in the place where his collar spread open. Donnie ignored the absurd compulsion to back away.

"I think you don't have to be a Mafioso with me."

"It's not something I put on. It's who I am."

"You need control."

He didn't answer; he'd been straightforward about that from the beginning. She clearly had a problem with it, which was why he needed to go.

"Okay. Let's make a new agreement."

"I'm done negotiating with you."

"You need control. You can have it."

"Please?"

Her eyes dropped from his and studied his throat as she answered. "If you promise to stay open and show me how you feel, you can have me the way you want."

A multiple-vehicle crash happened in his head; all he had was the word he'd just said. "Please?"

Her eyes came up. "Trust is what this comes down to. You don't trust me not to hurt you. I don't know how to change that except to trust you first. So I will." With a graceful backward step, she put distance between them. As he watched, perplexed and angry, but still aroused, she pulled down the side zipper of her dress and eased her feet from those little flat shoes.

Arianna's feet were small and slender, but they weren't pretty. He'd heard about the typical state of dancers' feet and seen some images, so he hadn't expected anything else. She had the feet of someone who tortured them daily for hours at a time. Still, he didn't find them ugly. They were the tools of her art, and her art was glorious. So her feet were, too.

While he considered the tools of her art, he heard a sweep of fabric and raised his eyes to find her in nothing but her dainty underwear. She slid out of the bra and panties and stood naked before him. Her dark hair was loose over her shoulders, tresses curling over her perfect breasts. She was a tiny Venus, and his heart throbbed.

"What do you want to do, Donnie?"

What did he want to do? He wanted to go back in time and crush that fucking Phantom mask before he could use it. He wanted never to have met Arianna Luciano. But despite all the science fiction he'd read and seen that promised it, time travel didn't exist. He had gone to that stupid fucking gala. He had met her. And now he was fucked.

What did he want? He wanted her. He wanted to be with her. He wanted to trust her. He wanted to love her.

He wanted to know her love.

It was impossible, but it was what he wanted.

"Where's your bedroom?"

Her smile was sweet and relieved. "Down that hallway." She held out her hand, but Donnie ignored it. He swept her into his arms instead and carried her down the hall.

Her room glowed. She had strands of little white lights strung all around the tops of the creamy chocolate-brown walls and swagged from the corners to a small fixture of sparkling crystals in the center of the ceiling. The effect was soft and surreal.

A few framed dance posters and a large bulletin board covered in papers and photos made up the rest of the wall décor. A queen bed without a headboard was tucked into the far corner, covered in a fluffy down comforter and several European-style pillows in lace covers. The rest of the furniture was mismatched but stylish. He had the sense that she did some antiquing in her spare time.

His own taste was much less cluttered and considerably more modern, but he liked this room. He saw her here.

He took her to her bed and laid her on it. She pushed the comforter down to the foot and settled herself in the middle.

He stood at the side of the bed and took his clothes off, laying each piece across the top of a small dresser she used as a nightstand. He took a condom from his wallet and set it on the neat pile of clothes.

Arianna lay where she was, placid and passive, and watched him. When he was naked, she whispered, "Your body is beautiful."

That was a compliment he could accept. His body was scarred, too, from the attack that had changed his life and from other violences as well, but none of those scars were repellent or particularly unusual. He worked hard — harder every year he aged — to be fit and strong.

"So is yours. Hands and knees."

She frowned. "What?"

Earlier, she'd stopped him from taking her from behind. She'd said she didn't want it. But the tempest inside him was too big now to let her see him, to have his face so close to hers, while he fucked her. He'd been caught up in the moment, too, and he'd have offered her more than he could afford, but she'd ruined that chance.

So now, he'd fuck her from behind, the way that was safest for him. She'd told him he could do what he wanted.

She'd also told him she trusted him.

"On your hands and knees."

Disappointment, and a tinge of apprehension, crossed through her eyes, but she obeyed. Donnie left the condom packet on the corner of the little dresser and knelt on her bed behind her. When he put his hands on her hips, she flinched.

She was afraid.

"I won't hurt you."

A nod and a sigh were her response.

He smoothed his hands over her hips, up the insides of her thighs, up to the bare, pink folds of her pussy. She was dry. The night at the hotel, she'd been so wet for him it had dripped down her legs, but not now.

She didn't want it this way, but he couldn't do it any other. Not now. Now, everything was wrong. He should go, but she wanted him to stay. She was giving him something she didn't want to give him, so that he would stay. But he wanted something from her he couldn't have.

He didn't want this, either. He wanted her, not this.

Fuck. He got off the bed.

"Roll over."

She looked over her shoulder. "Huh?"

"On your back. Roll over." She obeyed, frowning, and lay in the middle of her bed, her legs straight and her arms crossed over her belly. Like a corpse. "Close your eyes." She did. "Keep them closed."

Stretching out at her side, Donnie propped himself on an elbow. "Let me move you." He picked up one arm, and then the other, setting them at her sides. Her limbs were soft, without resistance, though her belly quivered with nervous breath. "I won't hurt you," he said again.

"I know."

"Shhh."

He circled the pert, perfect nipple of one small breast, feeling a weight of guilt fall off when the dark skin tightened alluringly. God, her breasts were so beautiful they made his mouth water. What he would give to taste one, to put his mouth over it and draw it in, to feel her back arch with the pleasure of his kiss.

That was a fantasy. In reality, she'd shrink back from the feel of him.

So he focused instead on what he could do for her with his fingers. He plucked each nipple to their tightest knots, pulling just hard enough, just long enough, to find her moan and sustain it, until the quivers in her belly became something better, and her muscles writhed inside a body she was trying to keep still, on his command. Under his control.

When her mouth dropped open, and her rhythmic moans became soft cries, Donnie eased away from her breast, down over the scoop of her belly, and pushed his hand between her legs. Pushing her thighs apart, he tested her arousal again and this time found what he wanted, a beautiful hot wash over his fingers. "That's it," he murmured, and surprised himself to have spoken aloud.

"Donnie ..." she gasped.

"Shhh."

She whimpered but didn't try to speak again. He played through her folds, teasing, exploring, going more slowly than before, watching her face, wanting to know every part of her, and how she reacted to every touch of his. She liked rapid flicks of a finger directly on her clit. She liked two fingers inside her, curled so they scraped her upper wall. She liked a slick, circling sweep around her anus, but tensed at any pressure there.

She hadn't moved her body except how he'd moved it, and she hadn't opened her eyes. But she trembled and spasmed and gasped and moaned. Her head thrashed, leaving her hair like Medusa's, wild and alive on the pillows.

God, he wanted her. He wanted the fantasy of her. He wanted her love. He fucking wanted it. Goddammit.

He grabbed the condom and got it on. Then he topped her, pushing her legs open, sliding his arms under hers. With his face hovering inches above hers, he said something he knew would ruin all of this, would show him reality and force him to remember what he could and could not have. With his cock nudging between her legs, swollen and aching and turned all the way on, Donnie girded himself, stared down at Arianna's uniquely gorgeous face, and said:

"Open your eyes."

He knew what he'd see. The shock of revulsion before she could master it. He was right there; he couldn't miss it.

She opened her eyes. And smiled. In the midst of her writhing arousal, with his horrific face the only thing she could see, she smiled. "Thank you," she said, and those lovely Atlantic eyes softened with unshed tears. No revulsion. No shock. Only pleasure.

Donnie couldn't think. Rocked from stem to stern, turned inside out and upside down, he could only feel. Twenty years of mastered emotion, *repressed* emotion, of relentless self-denial, pushed out and through him in a rush, and his mouth was on hers before he'd known he would do it.

They both froze at the same time, stunned in unison. Shocked and horrified at himself, Donnie broke and tried to pull away, but Arianna's hands came up. She held his face in her hands, held him in place, opened her mouth, and made the kiss real. He felt her *tongue*, oh shit, her tongue on his mouth.

All their agreements were broken again. All his rules destroyed. He was fucking terrified. This petite

322

woman, this delicate ballerina, was tearing everything he'd made of himself into pieces.

But oh God, her mouth on his. Her tongue. His mouth didn't move like hers did, he couldn't make the same sensual, spectacular contortions, but he could suck, a little, and he could find her tongue with his.

When his tongue touched hers, she moaned and brought her legs up to wrap his waist. The shift brought his cock firmly against her, and one flex of his hips had him sunk deep.

"Oh, *Donnie!*" she gasped against his mouth. "Oh yes, oh yes."

His head was a bloodbath of warring emotions, but he was inside her. She was around him. He could feel her, smell her. *He could fucking taste her.*

All he could do was chase what he needed. No control, no mastery, no concern for the consequences. He drove into her, fed on her, clamped her as close as he could get her. His guttural, desperate groans filled her mouth, a heavy beat to the sweet chorus of her whimpers and cries that filled his. He was wild, and he didn't care. The pain in his chest was like his ribs cracking open, and he didn't care. Her hands were on his face, on his scars, and he wanted them there.

He fucked her like his life depended on it. And maybe it did.

How long were they wound together like this, caught in this frenzy of fire and need? He didn't know and it didn't matter, but when her body caught its ecstasy and began to spasm and twitch, he felt crazy with the need for it. She tore her mouth from his and cried, "Oh *God!*"

With his mouth freed, Donnie breathed fully again, and the unexpected bliss of it rushed through him, supercharged his own orgasm, and sent him over with her.

He hadn't realized how impaired his breathing had been with his mouth locked with hers, and for a minute or a few, all he could do was rest his left cheek on her shoulder and breathe. The pain in his chest, the madness in his head—had it been nothing more than lack of air?

No. It was more.

But Jesus, he'd given her everything. Twenty years of everything.

Was she having doubts in the aftermath, too? Was she reliving the feel of his face now, with her physical needs sated, and feeling the disgust he'd expected?

Fuck. He'd learned these lessons already. Long ago.

He flexed back, needing distance, but Arianna's body tightened around him. "Donnie, no. Please don't go cold again."

He wasn't cold. He was a raw, fevered wound. She'd torn him open.

"Donnie, please. Please don't hurt me."

The words were barely breath. He rose up and looked down at her. Her eyes traveled over the full terrain of his face. Always she did that, looked at all of him.

Saw all of him.

"Don't you hurt me," he said.

Tears flooded her eyes, and she shook her head, a desperate promise. "Kiss me again, Donnie. Kiss me, kiss me."

He bent down and put his ruined mouth to her perfect lips.

God, it felt good.

~ 18 ~

Donnie snored.

Not obnoxiously, but definitely noticeably. She wasn't surprised that he snored, or bothered by it; his nose was impaired, so of course he'd snore. But if this became a regular thing, sleeping together — *oh please god let it become a regular thing* — Ari wondered if he'd be offended if she wore earplugs to sleep.

It wasn't only the snoring that had kept her wakeful most of the night. Just having him in her bed, right there beside her, had made her body buzz. And the cycling images of their lovemaking — *lovemaking*; it was the right word for what had happened between them. And her fear that she'd wake alone and find a frozen statue in his place again.

But he'd slept at her side, deeply, all night. She'd lain in the curl of his arm and watched him. From this position, on his left, she couldn't see his scars. Only a hint of difference at the edge of his profile. He looked as he was meant to look, and he was really handsome. A strong Roman nose, a firm chin and square jaw. A serious brow. Though he kept his dark hair fairly short, it looked due for a trim and was long enough that a bit of wave was evident. The grey at his temple glittered.

And oh, his body. Lean and perfect. Not heavily muscled, but visibly strong. Not overly groomed, but naturally masculine. His skin was a bronzy olive tone that suggested his Italian heritage was southern, like her father's — though she herself had the paler tone of her mother, whose people were from Milan. His body bore scars, too — three heavy lines over his right shoulder that seemed to be burn scars, and a few smaller, jagged creases that suggested other kinds of violence.

She was powerfully, elementally attracted to this man.

She didn't care about his scars for herself. She was surrounded by handsome men with beautiful bodies every day of her life, and she had acquired ample evidence that beauty without had nothing to do with beauty within. There was a beautiful man inside the scarred shell of Donato Goretti.

She hated his scars for the way they mattered to him, for the way they mattered to other people, for the way they closed off the man she could see in his eyes. Whoever had burned him had tortured him for far longer than the time they'd held him down. They'd tortured him for twenty years, and counting. They'd made the world see him as a monster, and he'd turned that lens on himself and seen the same, blinding him to his true worth.

A small voice in Ari's head piped up and asked if maybe she was romanticizing the damaged man—a man she knew was a killer, a man whose presence in her life required her to have armed guards, a man who'd hurt her more than once, and as recently as the night before, a man who'd told her in so many words that he was emotionally locked down. Had she bought into the clichés she'd so often mocked? Was she trying to save the unsalvageable?

That voice had been voluble in the months since her debut as Christine, since the morning after her first night with Donnie, when he'd turned something beautiful into something humiliating. She'd tried to listen, tried to move on. But when he'd showed back up, all she wanted was to reach him.

Last night, she had. He'd let her touch him, let her know him. He'd kissed her. Oh God, how wonderful it had been. Yes, it felt different, but it always felt different, kissing someone new. Beard or no beard, thick lips or thin, teeth, tongue, taste, scent—every person was a new and different kissing experience, and Donnie wasn't unusual in that regard. His mouth was a little less mobile than normal, but the result was a soft, slow, intense touch. The graft skin on the right side was a bit firmer than his natural lips, but there'd been nothing remotely unpleasant in the feel.

And oh *God*, the sheer power of the act. The blazing hot fire of it. He'd *kissed* her. He'd wanted it, and he'd trusted her. Twenty years of refusing himself, guarding himself, and he'd given it to her. She'd found the beautiful man inside the damaged armor. He'd opened himself and shown her, and he'd been on fire.

Maybe she had a romantic personality after all. Because in that moment, she'd fallen in love. If he woke and was ice again, if he regretted what they'd shared and tried to take it back, this time it wouldn't be simple humiliation and disappointment she'd feel.

This time, he'd break her heart.

Sighing, she set her hand on his chest, felt the warm skin, the soft hair, the beat of his heart.

He jolted awake and came up on his elbow. Ari held her breath and didn't move. Which man was in bed with her this morning? Fire or ice?

He cast a look around her room; she watched him wake fully and understand. He turned his head and met her eyes. Sinking into the cobalt depths of his, she tried to grab on to the man she'd known last night. *Please, please, don't close off. Please, please.*

"Arianna."

"Good morning." *Please, please, please.*

"Did I keep you up? I know I snore. I should have said something."

"You do, but I didn't mind. It doesn't matter."

He frowned, and she thought over her answer, wondering why it was wrong. Should she have lied and said he hadn't? Well, she couldn't just sit here, naked beside him, and wait for him to break her heart at his leisure.

"Donnie, are we together? Are we in a relationship?"

His frown deepened, and Ari felt cracks forming over the surface of her heart. But then he said, "You want that? You want that with me? Don't lie to me, Arianna."

He made that threat-laced demand repeatedly, and without cause. She'd never lied to him. Not even about his snoring. "I don't know how to be more clear. I want to be with you. I want you. You're what I want." He wouldn't believe her if she told him she'd fallen for him already, so she held that back. "What do you want?"

"There are very good reasons I don't do relationships," he said, his eyes dropping from hers. The cracks deepened and threatened to split apart. But then he looked at her again. "I don't know why you're different, but you are."

"What you want, Donnie?" Her voice nearly failed her.

He cupped a hand over her cheek. "You. *Stella mia.*"

He'd called her that once before, in the hotel, on the night of her debut as the star of a ballet. *Stella mia:* my star. Her heart had thrown a lasso around those two small words and hung on, but he'd never said them again. Until right now.

Ari put her hand up and cupped Donnie's scarred cheek. He flinched, but didn't pull away. He let her touch him. "Kiss me, Donnie."

"You don't mind?"

"Your kiss is everything."

His eyes left hers, skimmed down her face, and landed on her lips. Then he leaned in and kissed her. It was everything, just everything. Soft and fierce both. Needful.

Ari's heart healed and swelled. She threw her arms around him and moaned with riotous pleasure. In response, Donnie grunted and turned, rolling over her, sweeping his hand from her face, down her neck, over her shoulder and down, capturing a breast in his palm.

He tore his mouth from hers. "I have to taste."

Before Ari could protest the loss of him, his head dipped down, and he sucked her nipple into his mouth, moaning like a starved man tasting his first meal in weeks.

No — *years.*

"Oh fuck, Donnie!" She hadn't dared fantasize about this, but his kiss there was marvelous—soft again, fluttering, over and over until she thrummed and writhed. His teeth caught the tip and pulled, and Ari clutched him closer, never wanted him to stop.

"You taste sweet," he mumbled against her chest and moved to her other breast, offering it the same delights. "Like honey."

Ari held him close and thrust her hips, rocking her core on his leg, dragging her body along the forged iron beam of his cock.

He sent his hand traveling onward, and it slid between her thighs. "Ah, you're wet for me."

"Fuck me," she gasped.

He lifted his head and smiled down at her. "Kiss me, fuck me—you're demanding this morning."

Actual reasonable words were beyond her, so she simple lifted her hips higher, made herself an offering.

He laughed. Oh, she liked this Donnie, this open, unguarded man who didn't fear his feelings. She loved this man.

He reached to the dresser and pulled his pile of clothes toward the bed. With that one hand, he opened his wallet and extracted a condom—the last one, she saw.

She took the packet from him. "Let me."

"Demanding." But he let go.

Tearing the packet open with her teeth, she removed the lubed circle and brought it to the tip of his cock. First, she played her fingers over the firm velvet of his tip, caught its single needy drip on her finger and brought it to her mouth. He watched her taste him, and sighed out a hungry grunt. Rolling the condom over his girth, she felt the alluring tension in his body, in his shaking arms. He wanted her, was desperate for her.

She lay back and gave herself to him.

He sank deep. She coiled her body around his and took him all the way in. They fucked in a frenzy, wild need and pure fire. Three words filled her head in a chant matched to the tempo of his thrusts, and the little voice joined in: *I love you, I love you, I love you.*

~oOo~

"Ari, may I speak with you?"

At Baxter's question, Julian's eyebrows lifted high, and he looked over Ari's shoulder, toward the door. Ari stood shocked and wary and didn't turn around. Baxter was set to announce the cast list for *The Nutcracker* in about five minutes. What could he want to talk to her about now? It couldn't be good.

Not that she could avoid it. Nor, apparently, could she avoid being alone with him, unless she dragged Julian with her like a chaperone. Which wasn't a horrible idea, actually, but she hoped Donnie's performance the day before, making so public a claim on her, had tempered Baxter's perverse interest.

She sucked in a breath full of courage. Julian squeezed her hand and let her go, and she turned and gave her director a smile. "Sure."

She felt every eye in the company singeing her back as she followed Baxter out of the studio.

In the hallway, he kept walking, and she followed until he turned into one of the smallest rehearsal studios. Her warning system pinging like crazy, Ari let him usher her in, but when he moved to close the door, she said, "Please leave it open."

Baxter considered her, his expression serious, and let go of the door. "You're afraid of me."

"I'm wary. Just between you and me, I think it's been warranted."

"I'm hard on you."

"You're abusive." Why was she confronting him *now*? She'd been taking his bullshit for all this time, trying to save her career, and now she was going to stand up for herself?

But she wasn't standing alone, was she? That was where this courage had come from. Donnie was in the picture now, and Baxter knew it.

"Donnie Goretti—you're with him?"

"Yes." As of last night, that was true. She was with Donnie Goretti. And Donnie had her back.

"Why didn't you tell me?"

"My personal life is none of your business. Is that why you called me out of the studio? To ask about my boyfriend?"

"Do you know who he is?"

"Obviously I do." If Baxter was now going to try to play some kind of concerned friend role, she'd gag. "Do you?"

Another wince. Ari saw something interesting: Baxter hadn't had some weird epiphany about her. He didn't want to be more reasonable with her. He didn't respect her any more than he had twenty-four hours ago.

But he was afraid of Donnie. She hated that and loved it at the same time, in equal measure.

"I called you aside to let you know that I'm giving Clara to Jessi."

Not overly afraid of Donnie, then. Ari dug deep and kept herself from reacting. She stared at Baxter and hoped her eyes were cold stones.

He took a step closer. Ari wanted to stand her ground, but she didn't want to be any closer to him. As a compromise, she crossed her arms over her chest.

"I know that's the part you wanted. I know you think you deserve the lead. But Ari, you have too much body to play a little girl."

Molten rage burbled in her belly. Fucking Baxter and his absurd obsession with the fact that she had the slightest hint of a shape. She barely had the breasts for a fucking A cup. She was a fucking size 4. No one in the world thought she was fat but this jerk standing in front of her.

Holding her career in his fist.

"There's no question you're a better dancer than Jessi, but Clara isn't really the best dancer's part, is it? Clara can be danced by a child. The best dancer should be the Sugar Plum Fairy. That's the part for you."

Ari squinted at him, trying to see his scheme. Something was up. Or was he being honest? Was he trying to tell her he'd made his best judgment about the production, and he honestly didn't think she was right for the lead? Come on, no — this was Baxter. Besides which, his beloved Devonny had danced Clara for years. Ari had been the Sugar Plum Fairy for the past six years. He was full of shit. Right?

Her head began to pirouette.

"If I've been hard on you, I'm sorry, but this isn't a personal call. I'm giving Clara to Jessi because she's smaller, and she can handle the part. You're the only girl in the company who can do the *Grand Pas de Deux* justice as the centerpiece of the ballet."

The Sugar Plum Fairy's signature dance, with her Cavalier. Sergei was the Cavalier. He was an excellent partner.

"You hate *The Nutcracker*." Her thoughts were too jumbled to know what else to say.

"Indeed I do. But I always want to put on the best production we can. If you want to sic your boyfriend on me, tell me now, before I announce the parts. I know who he is, and I don't want him as an enemy. If you want Clara that badly, you can have it. I'll make Jessi the Sugar Plum Fairy, and we can all watch her legs start wobbling halfway through the *pas de deux*."

Her arms still crossed over her chest—that little bit of cleavage Baxter so despised—Ari took the time to sort through this shifting mass of feelings and information.

"Is Devonny retiring?"

The question surprised him, and he cocked his head. "Nothing's been announced."

That was a public relations non-answer. "But is she?"

"Yes. Please keep this to yourself. Dev deserves the chance to do it herself. At the wrap party in December, she'll announce. She tore her Achilles again trying to get back in shape, and it will never be strong enough to support the rigors of performance again, especially at her age."

At her age. Devonny Allera was thirty-eight.

"When she does, I want prima."

His head cocked again. *"Obviously,* Ari. Who else would it be?"

Shock and relief hit Ari so hard, she nearly went slack and collapsed to the floor in a heap. Her arms dropped from their shielding grip, and she stepped her foot out before she fell. She wanted to ask him a million questions. If he knew her value, why did he treat her so badly? Why had he come onto her, when he found her so unappealing, and if he was still with Devonny? Why did he wield his power like a mallet? Why? Why? Why?

She asked none of them. The answers didn't matter. They wouldn't undo anything. But he *did* know her value. He didn't like her, but he knew what she was worth.

Or maybe he was simply afraid of Donnie.

But that didn't matter, either. She deserved to be the company's prima ballerina, and she would have it.

"Jessi will do fine as Clara."

Baxter relaxed visibly, and Ari enjoyed watching his relief. Secondhand fear was almost as good as firsthand respect, at least when it came to the result.

~oOo~

Ari went to the kitchen and leaned on the doorjamb. "What're you making?"

Julian looked over his shoulder. "Just sautéing a couple sliced chicken breasts to put on my salad."

"Is there enough for me?"

"I can share. Is your mobster not coming?"

"He has work."

"What work do mobsters do in the dark? Kneecapping? Sending people to sleep with the fishes? Leaving the gun and taking the cannoli?"

"Don't be an ass, Jule." She stepped in and got the wine from the fridge.

"I'm just worried. As best friend, I claim the right of worry. You're in over your head with this guy, Ari. You of all people know what guys like him are like."

"Okay, either I'm in over my head or I know what he's like. You have to decide whether I'm a naïve ingenue or a Mafia princess. I can't be both at the same time."

He set the wooden fork on the skillet and turned around. "Sure you can. Being with Goretti brings you in closer than you ever were with Uncle Mel. Your uncle is a nobody, right? Your new boyfriend practically runs a family."

"Uncle Mel is not a nobody. People respect him. He's a good earner."

Julian laughed. "Okay, your highness. But did you ever need armed guards around the clock because your *uncle* is in your life?"

"The answer to that is I don't know. The Romanos wouldn't have put security on his family in any case. He's a soldier. Donnie is high enough that I get protected. So that makes me *safer*. I need you to let up on him, Julian. Respect my choice. Let me be happy."

"You really like this guy, don't you?"

Love. She loved him. But those words weren't ripe yet. "Yes." She went to the counter and picked up his work on the salad, slicing tomatoes and hard-boiled eggs, and scattering the pieces over the bed of fresh lettuce and spinach. Protein and vegetables: the mainstays of the dancer's diet.

"Tess isn't coming over?"

"She has to work tonight, too."

Ari threw a sidelong smirk at her friend. "What work does a hairdresser do in the dark?"

"She works at the homeless shelter downcity a few nights a month, giving free shampoos and haircuts to people trying to get jobs."

"Oh. Wow. That's … impressive."

"Yes." He took the skillet off the burner. "She's impressive."

"You're serious about her." When he dumped the chicken into the salad, she added some cheese and a bit of oil and vinegar, and used the tongs to toss it all together.

"I am. She's smart, and pretty, and she likes what I do but isn't obsessed with it. She's fun and funny. She's a good person. And the sex is great."

Ari had spent a little bit of time with Tess, mostly in the mornings after she spent the night with Julian. Though their conversations hadn't been deep enough for Ari to agree wholeheartedly with Julian's assessment, she'd seen enough to believe in it. And she'd heard plenty enough to know the sex was good. Julian was loud. So was Tess.

She rocked her hip into his thigh. "I like you smitten. You get blushy and deep."

He rocked back into her. "Shut up."

They set their dinner at the bar and sat side by side on the cheap black bar stools that had been their first purchase when they'd moved in together. Ari poured wine while Julian served salad onto their plates.

"You and Baxter seem to have worked things out. When he gave Clara to Jessi, I expected a different reaction from you. I thought I'd spend the night being your shoulder."

"I don't know if he was just letting me down easy, but the way he told me made it okay. He was okay today."

"How'd he tell you?"

"Basically, he said he needed his best dancer dancing SPF. He made it sound like Clara is beneath me. That made it a lot easier to take." That and telling her she'd be the next prima ballerina.

"It is beneath you."

Ari stopped in mid-chew and frowned at him. "It's the lead."

Julian shrugged. "Yeah, but it's not that hard to dance. SPF needs the stronger dancer." He shrugged again and had some wine. "I want for you what you want for yourself, but you're a spectacular SPF, and you rock the house every year. You've been the one people remember since you first danced SPF. It's your part."

"But Devonny danced Clara."

"Ari, love—you're a stronger dancer than Devonny. She's … lovely, and an excellent dancer, but what she has on you is her acting. She could be Clara at almost forty because she's so little, and because she becomes a twelve-year-old when she dances that part. You're always … you."

She was Arianna, dancing.

"I wish that wasn't a weakness."

"I don't think it is. You're a different kind of dancer—you … explode on the stage. But when you do get into a part, into the acting—love, you're *magnificent.* That first performance of *Phantom*—you stole everyone's breath. Whatever caught you that night, it made you great."

Donnie had been watching her that night. She'd been thinking of him, of meeting him later, wondering about her note, then thinking of that moment of connection, him in his box, her on the stage. She'd been thinking of Donnie.

She'd been dancing for him.

~ 19 ~

Nick's office door was pushed to, but not latched. When it was latched, even a knock would be unwelcome, but pushed to meant 'knock and lean in.' Donnie was the man closest to him, in business and friendship, but even he couldn't simply walk into the don's office when he wished. So he knocked and leaned in.

The don was at his desk, leaning back in his chair, reading his tablet. He looked up and took off his reading glasses. "Donnie."

"Can we talk?"

"Come in." Nick set the tablet aside. "Trouble?"

"No." Nothing more than Nick already knew, at any rate. In the days since their attack on the Bondaruk advance team base, there hadn't been any unexpected developments. The Honcharenko boy had been found and identified. Nick had called in one of his preciously held favors with the Domenico Family in New Jersey to direct law-enforcement interest in the boy's death, and anything related, away from family business. It was an extremely valuable favor to call in, one Nick had wanted saved for something more important. A total recalibration of *La Cosa Nostra*, for example.

The shift of legal blame meant nothing in the underworld, of course. In their world, everyone knew that Nick Pagano had erased another Bondaruk crew, and this time had killed a child as well.

Yuri Bondaruk hadn't yet responded to the loss of eight of his made men, two hangarounds, and one small child, but there was no doubt he would. Though the child hadn't been significant to him before, maybe hadn't even been known to him, he would claim the Honcharenkos as family now, to feed his case for retaliation.

Meanwhile, the Paganos were left to wait and prepare for a war with a bratva that hadn't even gotten a good foothold in the States yet. Whatever their power in Ukraine—Calvin's research indicated that they were significant players on their home turf, and had risen to power with unusual speed—they'd been unable to establish a strong base in the US.

And that was almost entirely because of Nick Pagano. They'd crossed him, and he'd obliterated their stateside operations. Twice.

Eventually, Bondaruk would stop sending recon teams and mobilize his army instead. Probably next. So the Paganos waited and prepared, and Nick seethed.

He'd calmed from his initial fury enough to keep Angie and Donnie in his inner circle, but they'd both felt a chill between them and their don these past few days. Donnie had never been so uncomfortable in the presence of his don and best friend.

He sat in his customary chair before Nick's desk. "It's personal. I need to tell you about Arianna."

"The dancer?"

"Ballerina." 'Dancer' was too vague, and vaguely sordid, for the artist she was. "Yes."

"You've got security on her still. Are you making her your *comare*?"

An uneasiness filled his chest, not far different from the tight queasiness he'd felt preparing to attack the Bondaruks, or any time he knew he'd face gunfire. What he felt for Arianna was just as deadly. Feelings he'd locked away, in a steel cage apparently, to save himself. Rules he'd made. Arrangements. All so he could survive in the world he lived in. As the monster under the stage.

He was The Face. No one had dared call him that directly in years, but it was how he was known. Who he was.

But with Arianna, he was Donnie. She saw him, and she wanted him. He believed her. If he was wrong, if she was false, he didn't know how he'd come back from that. Twenty years of repressed need had been unleashed, and if she wasn't there beside him, he wouldn't withstand the deluge.

He wasn't uneasy. He was terrified.

"Donnie?"

He cleared his throat and got back in this moment. "Not my *comare*, no." A *comare* was a mistress. A woman on the side, of a marriage or simply a life. Clear boundaries, limited connection. An arrangement.

Nick regarded him quietly. "She's more than that."

"Yes."

A smile ghosted up one side of Nick's mouth. "It's been a long time."

"Yes." There was nothing more he could say. What he felt for Arianna was too new and tender to be anything but private. Besides, under the best of circumstances, he and Nick weren't in the habit of exchanging deep secrets about romance.

"Beverly will be thrilled. She'll want you to bring her to the house for dinner. She'll probably have champagne and fireworks."

Donnie relaxed and laughed. Bev would indeed be ecstatic and effusive to know he'd opened his heart; she'd been worried about him for decades. He hoped she'd draw the line somewhere before fireworks, however. "I'll prepare Arianna for a celebration. But I'd like to hold it off for a while. She's rehearsing for her next production, and

I'm … concerned to bring her in too close until we know the Ukrainians' next move."

"She'd be safer close in. They already know she's attached to you. Seems they knew how attached before you did."

"Lucky guess on their part. Unlucky timing on mine. If I bring her here, she'd be on the road back and forth every day. That's too much exposure."

"So instead, you go back and forth to see her and expose yourself."

"Better me than her."

"She has no secrets to be dug out of her. I assume."

Donnie's jaw went slack, and his stomach filled with acid. "No. She knows nothing. And there's no depth anyone could dig in me to give you up, Nick." Realizing his hand was rubbing his scarred cheek, he dropped it to the arm of the chair and gripped.

Again, Nick regarded him quietly. Finally, he nodded once. "*Io so. Mi dispiace.*"

At the apology, Donnie swallowed down the bile that had risen in his throat. Nick rarely apologized, because he rarely made mistakes or hurt someone without intention. When he acted, even in vengeance, it was a decision, not a reaction. When he lashed out, it was a wielded whip, not a reflex. But he'd had enough thought that Donnie could betray him to form the words, and enough anger to allow them to be said.

348

Donnie was worried. "The Bondaruk hit went wrong, no question. But it wasn't a failure of the plan. The plan was good. There was no way we could know the kid would be there." The boy had come into the video store through a door that adjoined that shop with the laundromat beside it. They hadn't known the shops adjoined. Not even blueprints had shown it; the doorway was a new, and unpermitted, change to the structure. It was also hidden, nothing more than a hinged cutout in the wall. "We couldn't have known."

"Two Ukrainian-run shops side by side deserved more scrutiny."

"It's a Ukie neighborhood, Nick." But he was right. The plan *was* good, but they'd moved too fast, hadn't considered the elements of such a sweeping mission in sufficient detail. Those doctored photographs had gotten in their heads, and they'd reacted. Donnie was usually the handbrake on Angie's hot temper, but he hadn't been this time—because Arianna had been in those photos.

Nick's wife and daughters were also in those photos, but Nick held his anger inside, stoked it hot and held it close, to release on his terms.

Another long, contemplative silence, until Nick sighed. "The plan was bad. It was underdeveloped, and a child was killed because you acted without enough information. But it's my mistake. I okayed you and Angie to run with this. I should have trusted my instincts. Instead, I trusted you."

This blow was far more devastating than his earlier lash. This one was measured. Intended. Nick had just told him the trust between them, rock-solid for twenty years, was broken. The blow that had broken it wasn't betrayal, but disappointment. Worse than that—*incompetence.* It wasn't trust that had been lost, it was faith.

It wasn't fair; Donnie had proved his skill and will scores of times over the years. He'd earned his place at Nick's side. But the costs of this one mistake reached far, through the present and the future. Into Nick's legacy. "What can I do?"

"I told you this wasn't a fuck-up you come back from. Those photos are disgusting and infuriating, but they're garish. They're flash. Too outrageous and fake to be anything more than a shithead kid pissing in my yard. You took those cartoons and gave Bondaruk exactly what he wanted. He will send an army next, and then they *will* go for our women and children. *My wife. My children.* You took empty threats and filled them up. Because you feel protective of a woman for the first time in twenty years, and you acted like a goddamn scrub."

"You're right. I'm sorry, don."

"Dammit, Donnie. My faith in you was absolute." Nick sighed heavily. "We'll see what we see when Bondaruk makes his move. Do you have anything else?"

Donnie couldn't remember the last time Nick had *dismissed* him. He stood up. "No. Thank you for your time."

Nick nodded, and Donnie left his office. Rather than turn toward his own office, he headed to the exit. He needed to get somewhere alone and quiet and think.

If he'd lost Nick's faith permanently, he'd lost everything.

~oOo~

Alone and quiet wasn't getting his head clear; even racing along the coast, putting the Porsche through its paces, pulling far enough ahead of Dre to get a call of complaint from him, couldn't calm his thoughts. They clamored because there was no solution, no way to sort things to fix the problem. The only thing he could do to regain Nick's faith in him was his job. When the Bondaruks made their move, Donnie would be at Nick's side. Until then, there was only waiting.

But he had to talk to somebody, and he knew exactly who: the one person in the world who knew Nick and Donnie equally well, as the men they were at their core.

He turned turned sharply around and headed back to the Cove, leaving Dre to follow if he could.

~oOo~

Greenback Hill was what the people of Quiet Cove called the most exclusive neighborhood in town, where the houses were mansions perched on a bluff facing the ocean, and they all had expansive lawns with pools and tennis courts, and winding stairs leading to private beaches. It wasn't a large neighborhood — Quiet Cove wasn't a large town — and from just about any point in the Cove, you could look up and see those houses looming.

Nick's Uncle Ben had lived in one of the finest homes on Greenback Hill, befitting the most wealthy and powerful man in Quiet Cove. Nick was even more powerful than Ben had been, and likely wealthier as well, but he hadn't taken his place at the top of that perch. He lived just a bit lower on the bluff, in the house he'd bought as a wedding gift for Bev, when he was Ben's underboss. Valuing stability where he could have it, he'd kept his family in the same home he'd started it in.

Not that that home was a shack. It was a large, beautiful Cape Cod with a view of the ocean and an big yard with a pool. But it was homier than the Greek Revival mini-museum his uncle and aunt had called home.

After twenty years, four children, two Golden Retrievers, several smaller critters, countless sports and hobbies, and a small army of childhood friends moving through it, the house showed itself as a well-loved home. They'd done a big remodel a few years ago, once Bev decided that all the children were old enough to stop trying to destroy the house on a daily basis, but even the new construction and change of colors and fabrics hadn't shaken the essence that this was a home and life was lived well in it.

The style of the décor, and of the house itself, was too traditional for Donnie's taste, but since the first day he'd stepped into this building, he had not known a time he wasn't envious as hell of this home.

He'd been discarded by his blood family and had lived alone for the past twenty years, with no hope, until just now, that he might ever have anything more than himself. Nick and Bev had brought him into this family as deeply as they could, but he was, at best, only an honorary uncle. This home, this family, was not his, nor would it ever be.

Nick had said Donnie had behaved like a scrub because he'd acted in defense of Arianna, but he didn't understand. Nick had had love when he wanted it. He'd made a family when he'd wanted it. He got what he wanted, when he wanted it. He couldn't possibly understand what it meant to Donnie to have someone, finally, as he approached midlife, who might be with him, might love him. Might let him hope.

He hadn't acted like a scrub. He'd acted like a desperate man.

As he raised his hand to press the doorbell, he caught Dre at the corner of his eye, pulling up at the curb to wait for him.

The door opened, and Bev smiled at him, her blue eyes lighting with the pleasure of the unexpected. "Donnie! Hi!" She lifted her arms, and Donnie went in for a hug. When she kissed his cheek, he closed his eyes. Suddenly, he didn't want to talk about Nick at all. He only wanted to be with his friend and share something good with her. Speak his hope and make it real.

"You have some time to talk?"

She set him back. Snuggles, their Golden, nosed himself between them, and they both bent to offer pats. "Sure. Is there trouble?"

He shook his head. "No trouble. News."

Her eyes narrowed for a moment as she studied him. "The kids'll start wandering home from school in about an hour. Until then, I'm a free agent. Come sit in the kitchen with me. You want coffee, or something stronger?"

"Coffee's good."

He followed her into her bright, spacious kitchen and took up his customary stool at the island. Bev poured coffee for them both and pushed a plate of brownies his way.

"Careful with those. Carina put cayenne in them. They're not bad, but surprising unless you're ready."

Leave it to Carina to add hot pepper to a chocolate brownie. Donnie laughed and took a nip from the corner of a brownie. Then another, bigger bite. "That's actually pretty good."

"I was surprised, too. Sometimes, her experiments are horrifying—she did a thing with salmon and maple syrup that I still have flashbacks about—but they turn out pretty well most of the time. She's got a knack, I think." Bev picked up a brownie for herself. "So, what's the news?"

"Okay. So. I'm ... There's ..." The words wouldn't come out. The idea of announcing to anyone that he was in a relationship was too surreal to be contained in language.

Bev's eyes went round, and her grin exploded with light. She grabbed his hand. "There's a girl! Donnie, is there a girl? I mean—something real, not one of your gorgeous interchangeables?"

He grinned. "There is, yes." When Bev leapt up and hugged him, he laughed and tried to set her back. "Easy, Bev, easy. It's brand new, and I don't—I don't know how serious it is."

"If you are letting it happen, it's serious! If you're saying it out loud, it's serious! Oh my God, Donnie! That is wonderful! Tell me all about her!"

"She's a ballerina with the Rhode Island Ballet."

"A ballerina!" Bev clapped her hands like he'd given her a gift. "Donnie, that's perfect! What's her name? I want to meet her. You have to bring her to the house!"

Donnie caught Bev's fluttering hands and held them. Bev knew little about Nick's business and wanted it that way, so he had to come up with another reason that he wouldn't bring Arianna to the Cove just yet. He couldn't say that it was dangerous to bring her home.

The other reason was just as true, he realized.

He framed his words carefully as he spoke. "It's very new, and I want to keep it just her and me for a little while, okay?"

Bev calmed and let her megawatt smile dim to incandescence. "Of course. But I'm so happy for you. I've hoped for this for you every single day. I can't think of anyone who deserves this more than you do, Donnie."

She meant all those words with full-bodied love for him, but they were scaring him. Too much hope for his desiccated heart to hold. "I don't know about that."

She leaned in and set a hand on his scarred cheek. "You are the man who lay on the floor that night in horrible pain and tried to give me strength and reassurance. In the worst moment of your life, you thought

356

of someone else first. I wish you could see how deep your worthiness runs, Donnie. You deserve everything good, everything you want. And I want to know the woman who deserves what you've held so close all these years."

~oOo~

Donnie left Bev before the kids got home. He loved them dearly but wasn't in the mood for their clamor. He wanted Arianna.

She was rehearsing, dancing the Sugar Plum Fairy again this year, but he thought he could find his way to the studio again. Watching her dance would calm him.

Intimidating Berrault would calm him as well.

The front office staff smiled and welcomed him. One of them even told him which studio the principals were rehearsing in this afternoon. So Donnie went into the bowels of the theatre.

The public spaces of the theatre were elegant in a gaudy, old-fashioned way. Lots of deep red fabrics and gilt surfaces—and, of course, the giant tit looming over the lobby. The theatre itself had the same slightly decaying grace. Once the lights went down, Donnie felt as though he could have been watching a ballet, symphony, or opera— they all shared the venue, and he kept the box year-round—a hundred years or more in the past. He liked it. Though his own personal tastes in décor were different, to him this was how classical performances should be housed.

The spaces behind what the public could see, however, were dreary and utilitarian at their best, and dungeon-esque at their worst. The air was damp and smelled of mold. Old pipes moaned eerily at random times. The floor was cracked, showing concrete under antique linoleum.

None of that mattered when he arrived at the studio—one much larger than the one he'd seen her dance in before. The music for the Sugar Plum Fairy's *pas de deux* billowed into the corridor, played live on a piano. He peered through the window in the door and saw Arianna, in a dark red practice leotard and filmy pink dance skirt, pirouetting in Sergei Petrov's arms.

The Sugar Plum Fairy was not a sensual role—*The Nutcracker* was more or less a children's ballet, after all— but Donnie was jealous of these men who partnered Arianna. It had been worse watching Trewson making love to her on stage in *The Phantom*, but it wasn't easy now. There were so few clothes between them, and Petrov's hands were in places Donnie wanted only his hands to be.

"Mr. Goretti."

Donnie turned at Baxter Berrault's voice.

"Good evening. You can go in, if you'd like."

"I'll wait until they take a break."

Berrault nodded, then stood awkwardly. He likely wanted in the room himself, but Donnie stood before the door.

"Baxter."

"Yes?" The coward swallowed hard and didn't quite meet Donnie's eyes. He was used to that, people didn't like to look at him, but it wasn't distaste for his appearance that held Berrault's head down. Donnie could smell the fear on him.

"I'm wondering how much of a lesson you need to remember to always treat Arianna with respect. She's told me some things about you that make me eager to teach you that respect."

The man's complexion lost all its color. "There were … misunderstandings, I think."

"Is that what they were? Are you sure?"

"I made mistakes."

"Yes. Now the question is … will you make more?"

"No, sir."

"I hope not." He dropped his hand to Berrault's shoulder, and the man flinched hard. "I'm paying attention, Baxter."

"I understand."

"Good." He listened for a second. "The music's stopped. I'm going in. Are you?"

Berrault looked like he'd rather find a corner and cry, but he nodded and managed to straighten his spine. "Yes, I am."

Like he was the one who belonged, Donnie opened the door and ushered the ballet's director and choreographer in.

Arianna broke into bright beams of happiness when she saw him, and Donnie forgot all his worries for a moment.

"Hi! I didn't know I'd see you today!" She ran to him in that graceful glide of hers and wrapped her arms around him. He drew her close. But when she tried to kiss him, he pulled back.

He wanted to kiss her. Now that he'd reclaimed that feeling, and had it with her, he wanted never to stop kissing her. But not in front of people. Not where others might see and be disgusted on her behalf.

Frowning, she rested on her heels. "Donnie?"

He couldn't tell her that here, or maybe at all, but he smiled and cupped her face. "I missed you."

The words eased her disappointment, and she smiled again. "I missed you, too. We're in the studio for another hour or so. Can you stay and watch?"

"That's why I'm here. And to have you after." In private, he'd kiss her as much as she wanted.

Her grin regained all its brilliant power. "You are the best surprise!"

~oOo~

Trewson grinned at Donnie across the breakfast bar. "What's your poison, Donnie?"

Having already sampled the limited libations in this apartment, he'd stopped on the way. He lifted the bottle of Macallan in his hand. "I brought my own."

"Nice." Trewson reached for the bottle, and Donnie handed it over. "Rocks, water, soda, straight—how d'you take it?"

"Straight." He glanced at Arianna, standing at the stereo with her phone in her hand, selecting music. Julian's girlfriend stood beside her, conferring.

He had not intended for the evening to be a double date. However, he was very glad to meet Tess McGovern.

Arianna had said Trewson liked 'big' girls. Donnie's own tastes ran to slender, small women—ballerinas, for instance—so his perspective was maybe a little skewed. He considered Bev a big girl, especially after four children—medium height, soft curves, ample chest. But Tess was quite large—taller than Trewson, at least as tall as Donnie's six feet, and solid. She owned every inch of her look, too. Her long hair was dyed in rainbow colors and seemed to actually sparkle. Her makeup was

361

dramatic, so dark her pale eyes glowed. She wore a snug, dark blue velvety dress with black tights, and she'd had high-heeled black boots on when she'd come in. She must have stood six-four in those things. He found himself attracted — not desirous, she wasn't his type at all, but impressed. She drew notice.

Arianna looked like a china doll standing beside her, and *that* made Donnie ache with need.

Trewson came up beside him and handed him a novelty juice glass full of two-hundred-dollar single-malt scotch. "She's been happy lately," he said.

Donnie sipped his scotch and nodded.

"I just want her safe," Trewson added.

Donnie didn't respond. This man was his woman's best friend, and short of sinking him in the ocean, there wasn't much he could do about it. But as her best friend and frequent partner, Trewson got way up in her personal space, so Donnie would need, and take, some time to get right with that. He wasn't at the heart-to-heart stage, particularly not about Arianna's well-being.

The women had apparently chosen music appropriate to this awkward gathering, and Arianna set her phone in the receiver. Music he actually liked rolled into the room: The Beatles.

Arianna glided toward them, and Tess followed. Both women, beautiful in their ways, smiled at their men. Donnie pulled Arianna close as soon as he could reach her, and she tucked herself in at his shoulder. In this moment, in this room, with his troubles fifty miles away and this woman in his arms, he was happy, too.

Trewson turned back to the kitchen and picked up three wine glasses from the bar. He handed the ladies their drinks and kept one for himself. He lifted his glass and grinned at them all. With his eyes on Donnie, he said, "A toast. To bright beginnings and happy ever afters."

Donnie lifted his glass and gave Trewson a nod. "*Salute*," he said.

~oOo~

Arianna ripped at the buttons of his shirt, "Oh my God, oh my God, get this off!"

Donnie laughed and pushed her hands away. "Wine makes you horny, doesn't it?" He remembered her white-hot surrender to him in the hotel, the way she'd begged for all he gave her. She'd been a little drunk then, too. He had regrets about that night, and the morning after—he'd been too rough in the night, trying to shove his own burgeoning feelings out of harm's way, and too cold in the morning—but even so, the sex had been intensely erotic and had powered his fantasies for weeks.

He got his shirt off and shed his trousers, then grabbed her and fell to her bed, both of them still in their underwear. Arianna caught his head in her hands and dragged him down for a kiss. Donnie lost himself in that marvel. *A kiss is the seed of a romance,* Arianna had told him that morning in the hotel. Her voice had laced disappointment and hurt around the words, and he'd cast them aside.

Because of course she'd been right. A simple kiss, lips, tongue, breath, was the most intimate connection between two people.

Her hands left his face and moved between them, down their bodies, until one slid into the waistband of his underwear and took hold of his cock. He groaned at the fire of her touch and turned his mouth away. "Wait, I need a condom."

"I've got an IUD in. I'm healthy. If you are, we don't need them anymore."

He smiled down at her. The light in this room, all those tiny white bulbs strung everywhere, made her eyes sparkle like stars. "We don't?"

"We're in a relationship, right? Exclusive?"

"Absolutely."

"Then fuck me, Donnie." As he grabbed her leg and got into position, she added, "I should let you know — Julian and Tess are super loud."

He laughed. This was like when he shared his first apartment with a couple other Pagano Brothers associates, and they hung a pinup calendar on the door to say they were 'entertaining'. "Should we be louder?"

She shook her head. "I don't want to compete. I want to forget they're there."

"Oh, you will." He pushed in, skin to skin. Dear God, how good it was.

There was nobody in the world but them.

~ 20 ~

"Donnie." Ari tugged on his hand. "Please?"

"I don't like this." He stood at the corner, where a side wing met the central atrium of Providence Place, and scowled around the vast, airy space. She knew it was too bright and busy for his comfort, but it was Christmastime. Tomorrow was the premiere of *The Nutcracker*, and then she'd be working almost nonstop all the way up to a couple days before Christmas. She had only a few days that she could enjoy one of her favorite parts of the holiday: shopping!

"I thought you lived your life and didn't hide."

"I do. I don't hide. I didn't like malls twenty-one years ago, either. But it's not that. I told you, things are dangerous right now."

She turned and smiled at Dre, who stayed back about twenty feet. Keith and Ollie were in the mall, too. And Donnie was carrying as well. In her eyes, they were the most dangerous people in the place. She felt perfectly safe. "Please. Just a couple hours. I've got my list all planned out. Six stores. In, out, bang."

"Not bang, I hope."

She grinned up at him and swung their hands. "Well, not until later, anyway."

He laughed and brushed his left cheek across her forehead. He wouldn't kiss her in public. At first, she'd been hurt, but she'd come to understand that he was embarrassed *for* her, not *of* her. It hurt her heart for him, but she hadn't mentioned it. She'd simply stopped trying to kiss him unless they were alone.

"You make me stupid, *stella mia*. I break all my rules for you."

"Good. Rules are meant to be broken. Come on." This time when she pulled on his hand, he came forward, and they joined the December bustle of the mall.

She felt a little guilty, wheedling him into this evening of shopping. But it was Christmas! A mall was just about the perfect place to feel the holiday—bright, glittering decorations everywhere, carols over the sound system, people laden with tons of bags, cookies and hot cocoa, Santa, the works. She was so busy with work during December that she only got a few days to do holiday things like decorate their tree, and bake cookies, and shop, and wrap presents. This was the first Christmas in several years that she had someone extra special to enjoy her favorite holiday with, and she meant to share it all with him.

But people looked. Since Donnie had given her his lens to see the world, she hadn't lost it; she couldn't feel what he felt, but she saw what he saw. People always looked at him, often did double takes, if not stared openly. Too often, their faces twisted in cruel horror. She hated every one of those people, who knew very well they were looking at a man who'd been injured, who'd known horrible pain, and yet they behaved as if his presence in their sight was an offense.

Children stared almost always. Sometimes, they cried. Toddlers seemed the most easily frightened. Once they got to school age, curiosity tended to be their reaction, but little ones, old enough to walk but not much older, they saw a monster. And Donnie always flinched. For the most part, he was able to go on about his business and not give gawkers undue notice, he seemed easy even with sales clerks who got awkward around him, but he tensed at once when a child saw him and was frightened.

About halfway through, she pulled him to the cookie shop. Sweets were a rare treat in her life, but she loosened her leash at Christmas. The company had a long break after the holiday, until March, so she could indulge a little and not regret it too much later. A crucial part of the Christmas shopping experience was a break for cream-filled chocolate chip cookie sandwiches and hot cocoa.

Donnie looked at her like she was nuts, and he got coffee instead of cocoa, but he joined her in a bit of cookie. They sat at a table smack in the middle of the mall, with bags all around them—he'd done some shopping as well—and Ari soaked up the atmosphere. Santa was just ahead, in the very center of the mall. All those cute little babies in their red and green fancy clothes. She'd never have children; her work was too physically demanding, and she didn't have a strong drive to be a mom, anyway. But she loved other people's kids.

She watched the children dressed up like Christmas dolls for a bit, then turned back to Donnie, whose eyes were on her. Unable to read his expression, she smiled and asked, "What?"

He returned her smile. "You're beautiful."

Her cheeks warmed, and she grinned. The way he said it made the words sound like different words. Words they weren't ready to exchange yet. But suddenly, they were dancing on the tip of her tongue.

Instead, she said, "I admire you so much." Oh, ugh. That didn't sound right at all.

His smile faded, and furrows filled the left side of his brow. "Please?"

"That was an awkward way to say it. I don't know what I mean. Just … you …" She frantically searched for a word that made sense. "You astound me." AGH! NO! "God, I don't know how to say it." She could say it in three words, three true words. But she knew he wouldn't believe them. Not yet. Not after twenty years of thinking they'd never be true. "When I'm with you, I feel full of, I don't know, air. Bubbles. I'm light and happy. When I'm away from you, and I think about you, I feel the same, only softer, and I can't wait to be with you again. I'm amazed by you. You're so strong and assured, you overcome so much, but you're vulnerable too, with me, and that feels like a gift, something precious to hold close, and … I don't know, Donnie. I'm happy. I'm so happy with you. I don't ever want to lose the way I feel about you."

Horrified at her verbal vomit that hadn't gotten close to what she was feeling, Ari focused fiercely on her cookie.

Donnie's hand reached across the little table and curled over her wrist. "Arianna."

She lifted her eyes. The twinkling Christmas decorations sparkled in the deep blue of his. He didn't speak for long seconds, only stared into her eyes.

"You make me happy, too," he said at last.

Ari had the feeling that they'd both said much more than the words themselves.

~oOo~

After their cookie and googly-eyes break, they gathered up their bags and took on Round Two: her family. She always got her Aunt Anita a gold charm for her bracelet, and one of the big chain jewelers was running a sale on them, so that was her first stop.

All the clerks were with other customers, so Ari picked out the charm she wanted — a cat with crystal eyes — and browsed the cases aimlessly while she waited her turn. Donnie shadowed her as he had through most of the stores — back a few steps to give her room to do what she needed to do, close enough to be there if she needed him. Alert as always, he was another bodyguard as much as a shopping companion.

She came across a case of diamond solitaire earrings. She wore only stud earrings, and she coveted a pair of really nice diamond studs, but she'd never told anyone. They were too expensive, and she'd feel guilty. Hoping for a sale — like, a clearance-everything-must-go kind of sale, she peered close to read the tags, but no. Regular price. Her share of the rent for a few months.

"May I help you?" A clerk came over with a smile. "May I show you some diamonds?"

Ari smiled and shook her head. "Not diamonds, no. You're having a sale on gold charms? I'd like to see the little cat, please."

The clerk's perfect customer-service smile faltered a little at the shift from a four-figure sale to a two-figure sale, but she recovered quickly and ushered her to the right case. Ari selected the charm and paid for it, then waited while the clerk found a box for it and wrapped it in silver paper. When she turned, she found Donnie at the entrance, most of their bags at his feet. His hands were linked behind his back like a guard on duty.

"Okay!" She went to him with a smile. "Two more things to check off my list, and you're in the clear."

He grinned and held out one hand. On it rested a little hinged jewelry box, its lid open. Bedded on satin in the box was a pair of diamond solitaire earrings. Each one was a carat—she knew, because she'd just been looking at those earrings.

"What did you do? Did you buy me diamond earrings?"

"Well, I didn't steal them."

"You bought me diamond earrings?"

His smile wobbled a bit; her shock was the wrong reaction. He'd bought her the diamonds she'd silently coveted! He'd noticed her looking—and what she'd been looking at! And she probably didn't need to feel guilty, since he was Mr. Top-of-the-Line Porsche, Bespoke Suit, Mob Underboss.

"Oh my God! You're astounding! But shouldn't you wait until Christmas?"

"They're not your Christmas gift. I suppose they're your Christmas-shopping gift. Arianna, do you want them?"

She snatched the box off his hand. "Yes! Yes!" She dropped her bags and threw her arms around his neck. When she kissed his cheek, he flinched but didn't back off.

The customers in the store applauded and called out congratulations. They thought he'd proposed.

Ari didn't care. She felt full of air and bubbles, and she kissed his cheek again. "I love you! I love you!"

Oh God! No! She wanted nothing more than to take those words back. He wasn't ready for them. He wasn't ready.

Donnie froze completely, and all at once. He became an iceberg. The people in the store were still celebrating an imaginary proposal, and Donnie was turning into the man she most feared. The beast who hurt her with his fear.

She held on with all her might, even as his hands dropped to her hips to push her off. At his ear—his left ear, she always went to his left because he always made sure she did—she whispered, fast and desperate, "Please. Please. Believe me. I'm true, Donnie. I'm real. I love you. Please don't turn to ice now. Please. You'll break my heart."

The tension in his hands eased first; he stopped trying to push her off. From there, he thawed slowly, until she thought she could ease back down from her toes and meet his eyes. His were full and rioting. Ari put her hands on his cheeks, ignoring his flinch and the way his eyes darted to the people around them.

"I love you, Donato Goretti. *I love you.* There is no part of me that doesn't love every part of you."

Staring down at her, he took a long, slow, deep breath. He cupped a hand around her cheek. "I need to get out of here."

She understood. Too much had happened in these few moments for more shopping to follow. But she needed to know one crucial thing: "With me? You're with me?"

After terrifying seconds when he only stared, Donnie finally smiled a little. "With you."

~oOo~

In all honesty, Ari preferred dancing the Sugar Plum Fairy. The steps were more interesting, though Clara was on the stage far more. The premiere performance went well overall. Baxter was right; Jessi was the better Clara, or rather, Jessi was better as Clara than she would have been in another key role, and frankly, the talent on the girls' side was getting a bit thin. This year's company auditions would be critical for finding new talent — which meant that

Ari would be spending her winter break recruiting regionally.

Ari danced her ass off and had another brilliant performance. She always danced better when Donnie was watching.

She turned off the shower in the communal dressing room and used one of the ancient blow-dryers on her hair. Tonight, street clothes and a ponytail wouldn't be enough to return to the world. Tonight, she was meeting Nick Pagano and his family, and going with them, and Donnie, of course, for a late dinner. She was as nervous as she'd ever been. Nick Pagano was more than a powerful, terrifying don. He was Donnie's boss, and his best friend.

As a tradition, Donnie brought Nick and his family — a wife and four children — to his box for *The Nutcracker* every year. She'd also learned that Nick and his wife were Donnie's frequent guests. They'd seen her dance almost every part she'd danced in Providence. Intimidated a little by thought that Don Pagano was even mildly familiar with her, she made an effort to be beautiful this evening. A snug, shimmery red column dress with a bateau neckline. A pair of black suede pumps with a kitten heel. She hated high heels with a passion — her feet hurt enough for work, thank you very much — but the inch-and-a-half on these pumps wasn't awful. Without time to do both her hair and her face nicely, she chose her face, makeup for a night out, and caught the front of her hair in a barrette at the back of her head.

Julian came out of the shower, wrapped in a towel, and stood behind her, watching as she closed the barrette.

"Another premiere you're not celebrating with us."

She smiled at him, and then at the orange roses Donnie had sent. This time, she'd leave them here, so she could see them as she prepped for the next performances. "Sorry. Big parties aren't Donnie's thing."

"Okay." He kissed her head. "You're beautiful. Have fun."

~oOo~

The lobby was always more crowded after a performance of *The Nutcracker*. Because even the evening performances drew a younger crowd, the theatre put on a kind of winter wonderland of holiday displays. Between the glittering stations of giant sugar plums, animatronic skaters, and sparkling snowmen, and the goggle-eyed children, and adults, enjoying them, the lobby was packed well after the end of the performance. When Ari made it out, after undressing, showering, dressing, and redoing her hair and makeup, up to a hundred or so ticketholders, young and old, milled about.

And still, Donnie and his friends stood out. It had nothing to do with his scars and everything to do with the way he drew her close, body and soul. She'd loved before, but not like this. This love seemed to have changed the organic composition of her body. She loved him at a cellular level.

He saw her at once and smiled. Her belly flipflopped. Last night, after she'd spewed out the words he wasn't ready for, he'd been quiet. Not distant, not cold, but thoughtful. They'd made quiet, gentle love in her room, but he hadn't stayed the night. He'd had to be in the office first thing this morning. But she thought he believed her. He knew she'd told him the truth, and that was a better present than anything, even the diamond studs in her ears.

"You were breathtaking, Arianna." He caught her elbow in his hand and leaned in to brush her cheek with his. At her ear, he added, "And these look perfect," and nuzzled her earlobe and the diamond in it. Not a kiss, never a kiss in public, but almost as good. Enough to make her flutter.

He drew her a few steps to where his friends stood. Nick Pagano, she knew without being introduced. He was an important man in Rhode Island, known as much for his business and philanthropy as for his underworld dealings. He was an extremely handsome older man, tall and well built, with the most intimidatingly intense eyes she'd ever seen. But he smiled as Donnie introduced him, and he offered his hand.

"Very pleased to meet you, Miss Luciano. We enjoyed your performance very much."

Ari shook the hand of Don Pagano. "Thank you. And I'm glad to meet you. Please, call me Ari."

With a gallant tip of his head, he said, "Ari, allow me to introduce my wife, Beverly."

Beverly Pagano was a beautiful woman. She seemed younger than her husband but still old enough to have grown children. She was built like Ari's mother had been, and her aunt was—not really heavy, but ample in the hip and chest. When voluptuous met gravity. Though Ari didn't have it herself, after a lifetime of dedication to her body and diet, she thought of it as an Italian build.

Ari offered her hand first. "Donna Pagano. It's an honor."

Don Pagano reacted subtly to her use of the honorific. A tip of his head only, either curiosity or approval, she wasn't sure which. Had Donnie told him she had connections of her own?

"For everyone who isn't Nick, I'm Bev. I can't *tell* you how happy I am to meet you, Ari." Donna Pagano squeezed Ari's hand in both of hers. "It was a delight to watch you dance tonight. You were wonderful."

"Thank you so much." She turned and smiled at the children standing beside their mother. Only two of them seemed truly children. Two were young women who seemed about the same age. "Hi!"

"Our children," Don Pagano said. "Elisabetta, Lorenzo, Lia, and Carina."

Wow. Way to go all in on the Italian. Not that a woman named Arianna Luciano had room to marvel.

She shook hands with all four. Beautiful parents had made beautiful children. Elisabetta, tall and willowy, possibly the eldest, shook hands and smiled shyly. Lorenzo, who seemed to be middle-school age, was dark and dour. He was clearly uncomfortable in his tuxedo, and Ari could imagine him going Goth in high school. He shook her hand and mumbled, "Nice to meet you."

"And you," Ari answered.

Lia, with the fairest complexion of the group— tawny and russet while the others were bronze and sable—was plumper as well. Ari guessed her to be in high school, or maybe just out of it.

She smiled sunnily and shook Ari's hand eagerly. "You are so beautiful. You dance so beautifully! And your costume! The way it sparkled! Do you make you own? Are they made here?"

"*Gattina*." Don Pagano said, gently, and Lia settled instantly. Without a smile, her face settled into a look almost sad.

"You were wonderful," she added, much more subdued.

379

Ari had found the artistic Pagano. She smiled and leaned close. "Thank you. We have a costume department. Our designer, Bastien Quan, made my costume. If you'd like to meet him, I'm sure I could arrange that."

Lia's eyes—intense green like her father's—went wide and bright. "Oh, I'd love that!" She looked sheepishly at her father. "Papa?"

"I'll speak with Miss Luciano later, and see what we can work out."

The sun returned to Miss Lia Pagano's pretty face. Ari turned to the youngest girl, whose name she now couldn't remember. It possibly didn't matter, because the girl's arms were crossed over her chest, and she didn't look interested in meeting anyone.

"Carina, be nice!" Donnie chided. Oh—interesting. Donnie was close enough to the family that he had scolding privileges.

Ari held out her hand. "It's nice to meet you, Carina."

The girl—obviously in the full flower of new puberty, with all the hormonal attitude that came with it—finally offered a grudging hand. "Hi." She turned to her mother. "Mamma, I need the restroom."

Her father answered. "Hold on, *cara*, let me call Leo over."

"Oh my GAWD, I don't need a man to follow me to the bathroom. That's creepy, Papa!"

"Yes, you do. Be still a minute." He pulled his phone from his jacket. Before he opened it, he nodded at Donnie. "Check the exits."

"Right." Donnie gave Ari's arm a quick, affectionate squeeze. "Be right back. Stay put, please."

"This is *stupid*," Carina groused, reminding Ari that middle-schoolers were the absolute worst. "I just need to *pee*."

"Don't be a twat, Carrie," Lia sniped.

"Lia!" their mother hissed. "Watch your mouth."

Yeah, other people could have kids. Ari would observe from a distance, thank you very much.

Donna Pagano smiled and tried to recover a polite atmosphere. "How long have you been dancing, Ari?"

"Since I was three. I've been here in Providence for almost eight years now."

"Where is she?" Don Pagano was off his call, and Ari saw a beefy, bald man, squeezed into a black suit, coming their way.

Everybody looked at the place where Carina had been standing literally fifteen seconds earlier. The empty place where she'd been standing.

Ari spun around. "And where's Donnie?"

Don Pagano scanned the room in a flash and snarled, "Fuck!" He yanked his wife, his children, and Ari all toward him, somehow all at once, and shoved them at the big bald guy. "Get them to cover. Now!" He didn't raise his voice, but his alarm was clear.

Suddenly there were two giant men in black suits bustling them away, through a glittering Christmas wonderland and oblivious lingering theatregoers. Ari tried to look for Donnie, but they were pushing her too fast, off to the side, into one of the catering service rooms. Both men produced very large handguns before they closed them alone in that room.

Ari flipped on the light. Beverly Pagano and three of her children were absolutely terrified.

So was she.

And then they heard gunfire.

~ 21 ~

Things had been tense with Nick for weeks now. Donnie knew the only thing keeping him at Nick's side was the lack of anyone to replace him. The don had closed his circle so tightly around Angie and him that no one else understood how he thought or worked. Except Trey, who wasn't yet made.

There'd been no movement from Ukraine yet, so business, both day and night, had gone on as usual, with an extra layer of vigilance and preparation. The security and intelligence guys were working overtime. Everybody else was doing their usual thing.

But Nick hadn't conferred with Angie and Donnie since the death of the Honcharenko boy. He called them in and gave them orders, but he didn't ask their opinions. They'd been iced out, and Nick was alone on the tip of his iceberg.

However, Donnie was deeply immersed in Nick's family life. Bev considered him one of her best friends, and vice versa, and he was their kids' favorite uncle. All their lives, Donnie had been part of their family rhythms. Nick treasured his family's happiness, so Donnie hadn't been excluded from anything he normally shared with Bev and the kids. As the holiday season got underway, he'd spent Thanksgiving with them—missing Arianna, who'd gone home to Long Island alone for the weekend—and, as always, he'd shared his box seat with them for *The Nutcracker.*

Cold as he was in the office, in his home, where Bev and the kids could see, Nick treated Donnie as always, as his good close friend. But when they chanced to be alone, the chill took over, like the room had been dipped in liquid nitrogen.

The precarious balance of that high wire kept Donnie in a steady state of wooziness around his best friend. It needed to stop, and he had no trace of a thought how to fix things between them. Maybe he should have talked to Bev about it after all.

If Trey was a made man, he'd step down and fold into the ranks of the capos, let Nick's golden boy come to his side. But Trey wasn't made. Angie was in just as much shit as Donnie was. There was no one else to stand at the don's side.

So Donnie danced on the high wire, above raging, freezing waters.

He'd been glad to have Nick here at the ballet tonight, to see Arianna dance and know she was Donnie's woman, to introduce her and watch her charm him. Nick was a romantic, deep in his heart. He'd fallen in love quickly and fiercely with Bev, and he doted on his children — though he was also demanding of them, especially as they reached adolescence. He'd been enthusiastically supportive of Trey and Lara's relationship.

Donnie hoped that meeting Arianna, seeing her with him, would warm his feelings about Donnie's protective inclination toward her, and help him understand why he hadn't thought as clearly as he should have. He needed some room to make things right.

Arianna had made a good impression already; Donnie had seen the glint in Nick's eye that meant he'd been impressed. As he scanned the crowded, glittering theatre lobby, he smiled, thinking of his beautiful ballerina, gliding toward them in that satiny red sheath.

He checked the exits, looking for suspicious faces or movements before clearing Carina to go back into the narrow corridor that led to the public restrooms and a staff passageway beyond it. Donnie knew that passageway well now; it led by a stairwell down into the studio area for dancers and musicians. It was dim and gloomy, and Carina needed a guard on her before she went back. Which she knew; she was just being a petulant teenager irritated that she'd been forced to miss a party with friends to come to the ballet with her family.

He didn't like the way the lobby was set up for the holidays. It was pretty, lots of lights and glitter and Christmas spirit, but it made for far too many blind spots. Still, there were six Pagano Brothers men in this room, plus three more outside, not counting Nick and Donnie. To get to Bev, Arianna, or the kids, a guy would have to be literally invisible.

Not seeing anything that perked up his antennae, Donnie turned back to his group—and saw Carina, the little twerp, peel off from her family and skitter toward the restrooms. Her aspect perfectly exemplified the awkward adolescent puree of rebellion and anxiety—both 'fuck you, I do what I want,' and 'golly, I hope I don't get caught.' Muttering to himself about willful teenagers, Donnie headed straight for the same doorway. So he was looking right at the guy, dressed in an usher's uniform, who made a profoundly suspicious quick scan of the room before he ducked through the doorway right behind her, reaching into his uniform coat as he did.

An usher in a theatre. Literally invisible. Jesus Christ.

Donnie ran, pulling his Beretta as he did. In the middle of a theatre lobby, still crowded with innocent bystanders. He ducked past them, shoved through them, and got to the doorway like the fires of hell were at his heels. Carina. No fucking way was he losing her.

The hall was quiet, except for Carina and the bastard who had her. Not much taller than she was, but significantly broader, he had a hand clamped over her face, and he'd dragged her to the staff door. His other hand held a 9mm.

"Hey!" Donnie shouted, his Beretta aimed and ready.

The 'usher' froze and looked back. He put the gun to Carina's head and pushed through the staff door. That goddamn dark, narrow passageway and stairwell into the lowest recesses of the building. The dungeon where they kept the talent.

Donnie ran again, to the door and through it. He couldn't do anything else. If the guy got too far away, he'd have backup. If he got her out of this building, Donnie knew exactly what they'd do to Nick's youngest daughter. Donnie's favorite niece. He knew, because they'd done it to Lara last year. He knew, because they'd made pictures of Carina, sweet, fierce Carina, her head on a naked body nailed spread-eagle on a wood floor with a sword pushed up between her legs.

Everything was dim and quiet back here; enough time had passed since the end of the performance that the dancers had changed and gone free. Anyone still around wasn't passing from one place to the next. He heard the shuffling scuffle of someone being dragged down stairs against her will, and he peered into the weak fluorescent glow of the stairwell.

They were on the landing, two flights down. That would take them to the hall that led to the back door, which was shrouded with shrubs to keep it discreet from the public. Would any Pagano Brothers man be on that door? If this guy got out that way, no doubt there was an unmarked van waiting.

They'd done their research. They knew Nick brought his family here every year for the premiere. Because Donnie invited them. They knew, with a wife and four children, there was a nearly perfect chance one would peel off to use the facilities, or for some other reason. They hadn't targeted Carina in particular. They'd just gambled on the excellent odds of getting to one of Nick's family on this night.

The guy didn't have the gun at her head anymore; she was putting up a hell of a fight, and most of his effort was going toward keeping her in his hold.

He had instructions not to kill her, then— instructions strong enough that he was afraid to use force to knock her out.

Donnie could use that. "Hey!" he called again, before the guy could turn and drag his ferociously unwilling prey down the hallway.

He looked up and pointed the gun at Donnie. Good. Donnie put his eyes on Carina. "It's okay, sweetheart. I got you."

"Back off, man, or I'll put a bullet in her brain right now!"

The only accent this guy had was Brooklyn. If he was Bondaruk, he wasn't OG. Donnie ignored him, kept his Beretta aimed on him, and focused on Carina. The span of a floor and a half separated them, but he could see her eyes. She'd calmed, facing him, but her body remained tense with resistance. He made a show of looking downward, with only his eyes. Her brow furrowed in confusion and cleared at once as she understood, and she mimicked his gesture, looking downward with wide eyes, and then back up to him.

Donnie refocused on the man he meant to kill. "You don't want to do that. That's bigger trouble than you can afford." Subtly, rhythmically, only for Carina, while he talked, he nodded once, twice … On the third nod, she did exactly what he wanted and went completely slack. Her attacker had been struggling against her fight so much he wasn't prepared for anything else, and he lost her. She dropped to the floor, and Donnie shot that child-stealing bastard in the face.

His gun went off as he fell back, and Donnie took the blow in the gut. It knocked him back, knocked all the air he'd ever breathed out of him, and he almost dropped

389

to the floor himself, but there were more of them, there had to be more of them, so he kept his feet and ran for Carina. She was scrambling up the stairs, sobbing now, her pretty dress torn, one shoe gone.

"Uncle Donnie! Uncle Donnie!" She threw her arms around him, and pain blasted through his midsection, but he held onto her, wrapped her close, and drew her up the stairs.

"It's okay, sweetheart," he gasped. "I got you. Let's get out of here." His vision swirled into greyness. He had to get her to her father before he passed out.

"You're hurt!" she cried, seeing the blood on her own hands.

"I'm okay, I'll be okay." But he stumbled and almost couldn't make it up the steps. Her hold around him became as much about help for him as comfort for her, and they climbed together. By the time he had her up, it took all he had left to aim his gun and open the door—and there was Nick, his face contorted with wild fear.

Donnie pushed Carina to her father and fell backward, down the stairs.

~oOo~

Donnie opened his eyes to dense, swirling white fog, bright as sun. He groaned and closed his eyes against the searing light, and groaned again as he realized where he was, why he was here. The hospital. He'd been shot. Someone had taken Carina at the theatre. His tickets, his invitation, his fault.

"Donnie? Donnie?" A soft voice at his ear. A soft hand around his.

He opened his eyes again, and saw a delicate shape against the painful light. "Arianna," he tried to say, but he wasn't sure the name had left his head.

"I'm here. I love you."

Arianna. Did she love him? Did she really? Could she really?

He felt lips on his fingers, a soft cheek against the back of his hand. "I love you so much," she said, like an answer. Had he asked the question?

Agony pulsed through him from his legs to his head, a beast with its own heartbeat clawing through his body. He closed his eyes and tried to fight it off.

Another, heavier hand on his shoulder. Donnie shoved his lids up again and saw Nick at his other side. His right side. Scarred side. Monstrous. Failed. "I'm sorry," he said, and felt those words leave his lips, heard them in the air. "Carina?"

"She's well. She's safe. You saved her." The strong hand of his don squeezed his shoulder. "Donnie."

"I'm sorry," he said again, and sank back into the dark.

~oOo~

When he woke again, the light was low. No more burning white fog. His mind worked better, and he was able to put together his memories in a way that made sense. He remembered shooting the usher, getting shot by him, bringing Carina back to her father. He remembered sirens and flashing lights. That white fog. There were gaps, long spaces that felt missing, but he thought he had a fairly accurate hold on events.

Unless more trouble had happened while he'd been out.

The room was noisy with mechanical beeps and whirs. Donnie tried to rise up a bit more to see the room — oh fuck, ow. Right. Shot in the gut. His legs buzzed with a sensation of electric shock. He gave up the effort and contented himself with an inventory of the crap on him. A lot of crap on him. Over his arms, his chest. No wonder there was so much clamor in the room. They'd hooked him to every machine they had.

The door opened, and a nurse came in. "You're awake!" she said, quietly, with a smile. He supposed one of the machines had noticed he wasn't asleep. "How're you feeling?"

"Like I was shot." His voice rolled out over sand and rocks.

She laughed softly. "Well, that's a fairly common side effect of being shot."

She was whispering. While she checked his machines, he looked to see if he had a roommate, but there was only one bed in this room ... except for one of those recliner-cot contraptions, in which was curled a small body under a white blanket. A spill of dark hair over the side of the chair.

Arianna was here with him. Emotion rushed up and made his eyes burn. Clearing his throat — ow, fuck — he collected himself and turned to the nurse, who held out a thermometer. Before he took it, he asked, "Has she been here all night?"

She stuck the thermometer in his mouth. "All last night, all day yesterday, all night tonight. I don't think she's left your side, except when you were in surgery."

He'd been under so long? But she had a performance!

"Would you like me to wake her? I know she'd be happy to see you."

Watching her sleep, Donnie shook his head. She was resting, and it was enough that she was with him. She'd stayed with him.

Because she loved him.

The nurse took the thermometer back, checked the reading, and smiled. "Well, that's much better, isn't it?" He had no idea, but if she thought so, then sure. How bad had yesterday been? "You have people in the waiting room, too. If you'd like, I'll check and see if any of them are awake."

"Nick," he said. "I want to see Nick Pagano, if he's here."

Her smile faltered a little. Not much, just a twitch at a name she knew and feared. Donnie was used to that expression. "He's been here, too. I'll see if he's in the waiting room. If you'd like, I can try raise your head a little — not much, but a little. Would you like that?"

"Yes, thank you. What's your name?"

"Tammy." She smiled and pushed a button, and the head of the bed came up slowly. When pain flared through his middle with sharper teeth, after only a few inches, and that buzzing in his legs almost became a scarier numbness, she stopped and raised his knees a bit, and the pain eased. "Okay?"

"Thanks. That's good."

"Okay, I'll see if your friend is awake. I'll be off my double at seven a.m., but I'm yours until then. If you're feeling up to it, you surgeon will be in early, too, to talk about your injuries and healing."

"What time is it?"

"Almost four-thirty in the morning." She changed the whiteboard to reflect a new date. With another friendly smile, she left the room.

Donnie turned his head and watched Arianna sleep.

She loved him.

Which was fucking miraculous, not to mention lifesaving.

Because his chest was about to crack apart with loving her.

The door opened again, and Nick stood in the wedge of light. Still in his tuxedo, though his tie was undone and the collar open. More than twenty-four hours later, he was still in his tux? He hadn't left?

"Donnie. I have someone with me. Can we come in?"

Nick asking for permission was a weird phenomenon. "Yeah, of course."

Nick took a step back, and Carina came forward, into the room. She was dressed in jeans and a sweater; he was glad to think she hadn't been camped out in a damn hospital for two nights and a day. "Hi, sweetheart. Are you okay?"

She let loose a little sob and ran to the bed. Without a word, she laid her head on his shoulder and cried. It hurt, but Donnie put his arms around her, wires and tubes and all, and held on.

"I'm so glad you're okay, Carina. I'm okay, too."

She shook her head against him. "I was so stupid! I got you hurt! You almost *died!*"

"But I'm okay. I'll be fine, and you're safe. It's all that matters."

"I love you," she sobbed.

"I love you, too, sweetheart. You're my best girl."

"*Cara,*" Nick said, still standing near the door. "Come."

Carina pulled herself together. Sniffling, she planted a snotty kiss on his cheek and let him go. Nick opened the door and sent her back to the waiting room. Donnie knew by the way Nick glanced down the corridor that the hospital was full of Pagano guards. Probably every Pagano man they could spare was on the premises.

Arianna had woken during that weepy scene. She sat on the cot, the blanket pooled at her hips. She wore the red dress she'd changed into for dinner after the ballet. She hadn't left him.

She stood now and came to the bed. "Hi." Tears blurred her eyes.

"Arianna."

Leaning down, she pressed quivering lips to his mouth. "I was so scared."

"I'm okay. *Stella mia.* Don't you have dancing to do?"

She smiled, and made a sound almost like a laugh. "Well, you see, there was this incident in the theatre after the premiere. A monster tried to kidnap a little girl, and a hero saved her. But there was gunfire, and a dead monster, and the hero got hurt, and ... *The Nutcracker* was canceled for the season."

"Damn. I'm sorry."

Now she truly did laugh, though the tears spilled from her eyes. "You dope. Don't apologize for being the hero of the story. And now I'm off all month to be with you. If you want me with you."

He clutched her hand. "I do. Always."

At the door, Nick cleared his throat. "Ari, I need a minute with him."

She nodded, and kissed him again. "I love you. You astound me."

With a squeeze of his hand, she backed away. Donnie watched her pick up her shoes—the shoes she'd worn with the dress—and walk to the door. There, Nick cupped a hand around her face and kissed her forehead—a paternal gesture reserved for the women in his life for whom he felt protective affection: his wife, his daughters, Tina Pagano, Lara Pagano, and now, it seemed, Arianna Luciano.

All the people the Bondaruks had made vile pictures of.

When they were alone, Donnie said, "Did you get them?"

"We did. It was a contract hit. No Bondaruks on the ground stateside, but they contracted the Zelenkos. Four man team—you got their lead man. I've got the others on ice at the harbor, waiting for me. Angie worked them, learned what they knew. Now that you're out of the woods, I'll render justice."

The Zelenkos were a Ukrainian bratva out of Brooklyn. In Ukraine, the Zelenkos and the Bondaruks were rivals. "Bondaruk made an alliance."

Nick nodded and came to the side of the bed. "The Zelenkos have been players in the States for decades. Yuri sold out to get his hands on New England."

"And us."

"And us."

"I guess it's not a war with roaches anymore."

"They're still roaches. But they mutated."

"Nick, I'm so sorry for pulling this down on you. I don't know how to make it right."

The don set his hand on Donnie's shoulder and squeezed. Donnie had a flash of powerful memory, of blinding white fog and grey shadows, and the strong hold of his friend.

"Donnie. You saved my daughter when I did not. We're in balance, my friend."

~oOo~

When Nick left, Donnie felt faint with pain and exhaustion, with relief and love, with uncertainty for the future and hope for his life. Alone in the room, he was lonely, but not sad. Because he loved and was loved. He was forgiven. He had faith and family. He had Arianna.

He closed his eyes and floated on the spiky peaks of all that emotion. So much more than he'd let himself feel in so many years.

The room was bright with day when he opened his eyes again. Arianna sat beside him, that cot-chair thing folded into its chair shape. She still wore her red dress, but she'd coiled her hair into its familiar bun and stuck a ballpoint pen through the knot. She was curled on the chair with her phone in her hand. He could see enough of the screen to know she was texting. The diamond earrings he'd bought her on a whim sparkled in her lobes.

"I love you," he said, for the first time in his life to a woman.

She dropped her hands and turned to him. "Please?"

It had been easier to say them when she wasn't looking, but now that they were said, he embraced them. "I love you." Remembering what she'd said to him, he added, "There isn't any part of me that doesn't love every part of you."

He'd made her cry again. She jumped up from her chair and leaned over the bed. Clasping his face in her hands, she kissed him, over and over again, on the mouth, the chin, the cheeks, right and left, his scars didn't matter to her, they didn't matter.

"I love you! I love you!" she cried between each zinging touch of her lips to his skin.

Being with him was dangerous for her. The Pagano Brothers were on the precipice of a war, and he was a general. But the danger was already all around her, inescapable. She'd taken on the brand of a Pagano woman on the first night she'd known him. Putting distance between them wouldn't make her safer. Bringing her closer might.

But that wasn't why he felt what he felt right now, why he needed what he needed. The true reason was much simpler: Arianna.

Lifting his hands—it hurt but he didn't care—he caught her face, holding her as she held him, and said words that shook at the bars of their cage, crying for freedom. Terrifying words. Crucial words. This was a once-in-a-lifetime love. For him, that was certainly true. "Marry me, Arianna."

She gasped and went still, except for her eyes, which dived deep into his and searched. Then she smiled, and cried harder, and in the midst of all that soggy emotion cried, "Yes! Yes! I will!"

~ 22 ~

A .44-caliber bullet had taken a slanting path through Donnie's midsection, entering low on his abdomen, perforating his intestines and stomach, and stopping near his spine, at T10. The surgery to repair the damage had gone through the whole of the night, and he'd been comatose and feverish most of the following day. For that day, no one was sure he'd survive, or in what condition he'd be if he did. Ari hadn't felt so terrified since her mom's death.

But he'd woken early the next morning and been strong.

When he was discharged this morning, eight days after the shooting, his doctor had professed astonishment at how well he was healing. No paralysis, and the buzzing and weakness in his legs improved daily. He'd been sent home with a wheelchair, but Dre had carried it into the house. Donnie had walked in on his own power, with only Ari's arm to hold onto.

Yes, he was astounding.

Mrs. Alfonsi, his housekeeper, had set up the downstairs guest suite for him, since the stairs in his magnificent beach house were too much for him yet. Over the past couple days, as Ari had handled as much as she could to get ready for him to come home, she'd gotten to know Mrs. Alfonsi a little. She reminded Ari of her Aunt Anita—a soft, short, older Italian woman who liked to give out hugs and kisses and feed everyone who crossed her path. Did Donnie let her hug and kiss him? Or had she spent all these years that she'd worked for him building up a logjam of affection for her boss?

Because she had a lot of affection for her boss. She spoke of him like he was her son, not her employer. Knowing that his own mother had disowned him when he'd been made, Ari wanted to squeeze this little housekeeper until she popped.

Until the night he'd been shot saving Carina, and not counting the ubiquitous bodyguards, Donnie had always been alone when she saw him, and he didn't speak much about his life. As guarded as he was, as cold as he'd first been, she'd thought he'd lived a solitary life. To some degree, she supposed he had—this big, beautiful house, sleek and a little cold, was only his. Beautiful as it was, it showed little sign of a robust life being lived inside it. Mrs. Alfonsi came five mornings a week and left for a home of her own five evenings a week. Her job was to be here. Otherwise, he'd been alone.

But he was loved. Nick and Bev and their kids; other Pagano men, like Angie Corti and Trey Pagano; Mrs. Alfonsi—they *loved* him. And he loved them. The only part of his heart he'd kept on ice was the part that held romantic love.

That, he'd given to her. Only to her.

Curled at his side, she watched him sleep. Strong as he was, the ride from the hospital in Providence to Quiet Cove had made his pain flare up, and after Nick and Bev left, he'd taken a dose of Oxy.

After a while, not tired at all, Ari eased off the bed and tiptoed out of the room. The house had a cozy warmth today she hadn't noticed in her earlier visits, while Donnie was still in the hospital. The homey scent of fabric softener wafted from the laundry room. Mrs. Alfonsi came from the kitchen with a basket of folded clothes, and Ari went to meet her.

"Do you mind if I take those?"

The housekeeper frowned a little. "That's all right, dear. You don't know where things go, and it's my job, after all."

But she wanted to know. Donnie had *proposed* to her. They were getting *married* someday, and she'd learned in these past couple days how much there was of him and his life she didn't know. She hadn't yet seen his actual bedroom, and there was a basket full of neatly folded socks and underwear before her—the keys to Donnie's secrets.

Some of that must have shown on her face, because Mrs. Alfonsi smiled and handed her the basket. "Come. You can carry it up for me, and I'll show you where things go."

His house was modern and airy: pale wood floors, white walls, sleek metal and smooth wood and leather furnishings. The wall décor and other decorative accents were sparse and specific, and real art. If Ari had to guess, she thought Donnie had hired someone to decorate. Everything everywhere seemed carefully coordinated.

The huge master bedroom, on the second of three floors, fit the aesthetic. Everything was ultra-modern, in a scheme of grey and black and white, with touches of teal for accent. The windows were uncovered, showing a breathtaking view of the cove the property sat on and the Atlantic beyond it. A large art piece—an abstract acrylic painting in shades of grey—was the only thing hanging on any wall.

There was not a single photograph in his house.

The frosted-glass door to the bathroom was open, and Ari went to look—the most spectacular bathroom she'd ever scene. All pearl-grey marble, floors and walls. The tub and shower shared a big room, closed off by seamless, clear glass. A wet room. The tub must have been three feet deep and eight feet long. The rest of the space was a double-sink — vessel sinks, of course — counter of the same marble, and a small room for the toilet.

There was no mirror over the counter. In fact, the only mirror she'd seen in the house was in the guest bath downstairs.

"Miss Ari," Mrs. Alfonsi called from the closet. "Do you want to see where his things go?"

They both knew she was really up here to snoop, but his closet was most definitely snoop-worthy, so she veered over to that frosted-glass door and, not surprisingly, walked into the closet of a wealthy man: huge, full of expensive clothes, and rigidly organized. Her vibe of shabby-chic clutter was probably exhausting for him.

One wall was drawers and cubbies. The cubbies held sweaters and sweatshirts — she tried to imagine Donnie in a sweatshirt and failed. Mrs. Alfonsi was putting tidily rolled pairs of dark socks in a drawer arrayed with tidily rolled pairs of dark socks. Another drawer was open beside it, holding tidily folded boxer briefs, all in black.

Ari brushed her hand over the sleeves of his bespoke suits, in fabrics soft as a whisper. Black, charcoal, light grey. Plain, pinstripe, tone-on-tone houndstooth.

The only color in his closet were his dress shirts and ties. They embraced the rainbow and were organized by color.

"Is he so controlled in everything?"

She wasn't really asking the question for an answer, and hadn't intentionally said it out loud. But Mrs. Alfonsi closed the drawers firmly, almost a slam, and turned to her, obviously with something to say. She picked up the empty basket and said it.

"Mr. Donnie is a sad man, Miss Ari. He's been let down by people who never should have let him down. His own mamma. His own boy. I think he likes things the way he likes them because he knows they'll always be there like they should be. He let you close, so he really loves you, and that's a precious gift. I hope you don't let him down, too."

"His own boy?" Donnie had a son? Was that what she meant?

The housekeeper paled. "It's not my place to tell you things about him. Excuse me." Flustered, she pushed past Ari and left the closet, and then the bedroom.

Ari stood in Donnie's vast, perfect closet and tried to understand what she'd learned.

She noticed that one of the large bottom drawers had rolled open a couple inches, probably when Mrs. Alfonsi had closed the others with some force. Channeling Donnie's need for order, she bent to close it. A flash of

407

bright yellow caught her eyes in this mostly monochrome space, and she pulled the drawer open instead.

Ropes.

Bright yellow. Bright red. White. Black. Cobalt blue. Green. Grey. Varying thicknesses, from gossamer strands to sturdy hanks. All of a silky, flexible weave, all wrapped neatly in similar bunches. One side of the deep drawer was sectioned off, and held folded lengths of black satin, and a few black satin sleep masks.

It took her a second, but she got there.

On a quick turn, she took in this wealthy man's hyper-organized closet, and his hyper-styled, entirely impersonal bedroom.

Holy shit.

They were at the *Fifty Shades of Grey* chapter, apparently.

But yeah, no. Nope. Not her playground.

Adrenaline frothing her brain, Ari got down to some much more focused, and much less guilty, snooping. She went through every drawer and looked on every shelf and in every nook and cranny of that closet. She went through the few drawers in his bedroom. She checked the other rooms on the second floor, and went up to the third-floor loft, and didn't breathe until she was sure she'd seen everything and hadn't come upon a Red Room or a footlocker full of cat o' nine tails.

Just the ropes and blindfolds.

In the bedroom closet of a man who had to control the way he was touched or seen.

There was a sleek black bench in the second-floor hallway. Her emotions stampeding, Ari dropped onto it and stared at the blank white wall before her.

For twenty years, he'd considered himself unworthy of love. Unworthy even to be looked on, even by himself.

Mr. Donnie is a sad man.

But he let her touch him, see him. Kiss him.

He let you in, so he really loves you, and that's a precious gift.

Ari wiped her wet cheeks and got up. After a quick check to make sure she'd left everything the way he liked it, she went back down to Donnie. Her Donnie. Her love.

~oOo~

He was coming out of the bathroom, holding onto the wall. His staples were still in and covered with gauze, and he looked tired and hurt, but strong and handsome, in his black pajama bottoms and nothing else.

Ari went to him and cupped her hands around his face. Ignoring his bemused frown — but no flinch; he didn't flinch at her touch anymore — she stared hard into his eyes.

"I love you, Donnie. I love to touch you. I love to look at you. When I do, I see the beautiful, astounding man I love. I feel your strength, and I can't wait to see and feel you every day of the rest of my life."

The bemusement became seriousness, and he opened his mouth to speak. Before he could, Ari tipped his head down, rose off her heels, and kissed him.

He kissed her back, matching her intensity, until his knees wobbled, and he broke away, gasping. Remembering that he'd been shot and nearly killed, Ari swept her arm gently around his waist and helped him back to bed.

When she had him tucked in and had settled in bed beside him, he set his hand on her knee. "What brought that on?"

"Just love for you," she hedged.

He gave her a keen look. "I love you. That's all it was?"

"Isn't that enough?" Still hedging. But there were important things to talk about here.

"It is. But it feels like there's something else."

Okay, yes. There was more, and the smart, healthy thing was to talk about it. She turned on the bed so she was facing him, cross-legged. "Okay, yes. Two things. But first, an apology. I snooped. I'm sorry. I only meant to do it a little, just to see the rest of the house and get to know you through your space."

He frowned slightly, more in curious anticipation than any obviously negative reaction. "Okay ..."

"I went up with Mrs. Alfonsi and helped her put your laundry away. In your closet. In your drawers."

Understanding dawned more brightly with every word she said. "Ah."

"Yeah. I'm not judging. But ... that's ... I don't think I'd like that."

He picked up her hand and brought it to his mouth. When he pressed his lips to her palm, she rubbed her fingertips over his right cheek. He turned into her touch. "It's not for you. That was for ... before. It's not a kink, really. I don't know what to say about it. But it's not for us."

He wanted her touch. He wanted her to see him. She smiled. "Okay. You don't have to say anything else. I just ... I'm sorry I snooped."

"It's okay. This will be your house, too. There's nothing here you can't know about."

That gave her a semblance of an opening for the other, possibly even more important, question. "There's something else. I don't want to get Mrs. Alfonsi in trouble. She's wonderful, and she loves you, but she said something, and I have to ask."

Now his frown had a negative cast. "What, Arianna?"

411

"I think it sort of slipped out. She was telling me how much she cared about you, and she said something about your boy letting you down." And now he flinched, which was pretty much an answer, but she asked the question anyway. "Do you have a son?"

"Yes."

"Wow. I ... were you planning to tell me?"

He took a deep breath, wincing when it stretched his belly. "I don't know."

"Wow. But ..."

His hand still held hers; he laced their fingers and gazed down at the weave they made. "His name is Thomas. I haven't seen him since before he was four years old. He's twenty-four now."

"Why not?"

"I was never married to his mom. Melissa. We weren't ever a very good couple, and getting pregnant wasn't a plan. We didn't last long after he was born. Once she had a child, she didn't like what I did, and I had to fight a lot with her to see him."

He went quiet, staring at their linked hands, turning her hand back and forth. Ari sat, watching him, and waited.

"After I was burned, the first time he saw me after that, he screamed and screamed. He thought I was a monster. Lissie gathered him up and took him away, and I haven't seen him since."

Oh God. "Donnie ..."

He was telling a story now, and he ignored her interruption. "I didn't fight her after that. She took him away, and I let them go. He's lived in Florida most of his life. He has a stepfather he knows as his dad. And that's for the best. He's had a good, normal life." He brought sad eyes up to hers. "I supported him. I sent child support, I gave his mom extra money when she needed it, I paid for his college. I've got a trust set up for him. But I'm not his dad."

"But you *are*."

"No, Arianna. He knows who I am, and where I am. He knows he's welcome to contact me. He hasn't. I'm not his dad. Somebody else is." He tugged lightly on their hands. "Do you want kids?"

She didn't. But if Donnie asked her to give him a chance to be the father he deserved to be, she'd start up the kid factory immediately. "I ... don't know. Do you want more?"

"If you want them, I'll give them to you. I'll love our kids and be the best father I can be. But for myself, no."

"I don't want kids. I just want you. You and me, living the life we want."

Smiling again at last, Donnie pulled her toward him. Ari settled in the curl of his arm, resting lightly on his chest.

"Mrs. Alfonsi told you about Thomas, huh?"

"Please don't be mad at her."

"I'm not. It's her nature to meddle. She means well."

"She does. She loves you, Donnie. She said you've been sad."

He rested his cheek on her head and didn't answer. Ari brushed her hand over his chest, feeling the strength in his contours, the softness of his hair, the beat of his heart.

"I guess I was," he finally said.

~oOo~

A few days before Christmas, Ari drove into Providence, her omnipresent shadow shaped like a big SUV a few cars back, for the end-of-season meeting. She'd already spoken a few times to Baxter, who'd given her advance notice of three major announcements: Devonny was retiring, as expected. Arianna would take her place as the company's prima ballerina, also as expected—but YAY! And the spring ballet would be *Manon*.

That scared Arianna a little. She'd never danced any part of *Manon* before. It wasn't one of the high-profile ballets, outside the dance world. Inside dance, however, it was considered one of the greats, and profoundly

414

challenging for the ballerina who took on the title part—not only in physicality but in artistry and acting as well. She'd been hoping for something like *Swan Lake*—a super physical dual part that required some acting chops, too, but one that was familiar. Ari might have thought Baxter was setting her up to fail, staging a ballet like that for her first part as prima. But he'd been surprisingly cool and normal, talking the decision through with her, giving her the legitimate chance to say no. She was even beginning to feel like there might be more than merely fear of Donnie in his changed attitude toward her. So she'd dance *Manon*.

Which meant she needed to get back into the studio and prepare. She felt odd inside her skin lately. For the first time in almost thirty years, she gone more than two weeks without dancing seriously. Donnie had a gym in his cellar, and she was able to at least stay limber, but it didn't have a barre, or much room to let loose. He'd told her that he'd have a dance studio built down there, but she wasn't sure she wanted a studio in her own home. She wanted to dance at the theatre.

Living in Quiet Cove—which was what she was doing already—meant a much longer commute, but it was manageable, and she'd manage it. She wasn't giving up the ballet, or this theatre, or her friends, and Donnie hadn't asked her to. Once she talked to Julian, she hoped she wasn't even giving up the apartment. She'd need a place to stay in town after performances and late rehearsals.

She parked her Mini in the theatre lot and waved at Round Ollie and Keith as they got out of their shadow-truck to do their usual perimeter check. She'd gotten used to having burly men follow her everywhere she went. They were like her posse.

After changing into practice gear, she went up to the studio where the meeting would be held. Most of the company was already there, and most would, like Ari, stay after to get a workout in or finish the one they'd started.

Julian was there, working at the barre, and his reflection grinned happily at hers. He spun and came to her, wrapping her up in a warm embrace. "It's good to see you! How's your hero?"

She laughed and kissed his cheek. "He's good. Doing really well. Everything good with you?" In almost eight years, she'd hadn't had to ask Julian a question like that, because she'd been right beside him, knowing his life as it happened. But her life was moving to the next chapter.

"Yeah, it's great." He took her hand. "Can we talk a sec?"

"Sure." Ari let him pull her over to the stack of mats they laid down when corps dancers were working out new lifts. "What's up?"

His grin sloped sheepishly. "I think … if you're okay with it … since you're staying on the coast most of the time now … I think …"

416

Ari laughed. "Do you need the Heimlich to get it out?"

"I'm gonna ask Tess to move in."

"Wow! Julian!" Her friend hadn't much more success in the real romance division than she had. He'd gotten a lot—*a lot*—more play than she, but something always happened to make things crumble in a few months. Ari really liked Tess. She had her head screwed on right. And she wasn't a ballet groupie at all, or threatened by all the ballerinas he fondled for work. She had her own thing, understood her own worth.

"Your room is still your room. I don't want that to change. It's there for you as long as you want it, to use when you need it, as long as I'm still in the apartment. Tess'll bunk with me."

"Well, obviously. That's great!" Everything was changing all at once, but it was all gain—new love, new challenges, new life. The things she'd had and valued were still with her. The future was open and bright, and she would dance into it on Donnie's arm, with Julian right behind her.

"Yeah?"

"Yeah!" She threw her arms around her best friend. He laughed and hugged her back.

~ 23 ~

On Christmas morning, Donnie took a shower first thing and opened the bathroom door, drying off while he watched Arianna sleep. She always slept deeply, and when he wasn't with her, she curled up like a cinnamon roll and tucked all the way under the covers. All he saw was a puff of white comforter and a ribbon of dark hair.

Her habitual deep sleep was a blessing for more than this peaceful moment he enjoyed every morning. His snoring didn't seem to bother her much. She had ear plugs—bright pink—but as far as he knew, she'd used them only a couple times, and not at all since his pain hadn't required opiates to manage.

Getting shot in the gut hadn't been what he'd call fun, but his scale of things he knew he could endure had a very high limit. On that scale, a bullet through his middle barely entered the yellow zone. Three weeks later, the staples were out, his parts were sealed back up, and he felt pretty good. Still weak and easily tired, but stronger and more energetic every day. Some digestion problems, which the doctor warned him could be permanent, and some faint tingling in his legs, a result of the bullet making its stop in the nerves beside his spine, which would pass eventually. Considering he'd almost died and/or been paralyzed, he thought he'd come out ahead.

Particularly in light of the miracle in his bed. A woman he loved, who loved him.

And he and Nick were on solid ground again. Even Angie was back in Nick's faith. They'd worked together to render justice on the Zelenko men who'd gone for Carina, and they'd gotten good intel before they'd ended them. They faced chaos in the new year—a war against two allied bratvas—but Nick had spent his December pulling the New England families together, and calling on New York for aid as well. They were strong and ready.

It was a war that should never have been so significant. Nick's instincts had been right to ignore Yuri Bondaruk's attempts to enflame him. Angie and Donnie had been wrong to push him otherwise. The unforgivable mistake had been forgiven, but Donnie meant to continue to atone, even if it meant more of his blood.

To be ready for the Ukrainians, Nick had called in favors he'd meant to use when it was time to make Trey. He would need to collect more before he could risk a civil war. First, though, he needed to make a show of Pagano

Brothers' strength in this fight with Bondaruk and his allies.

Maybe this fight would make the next unnecessary. Maybe, when the dust settled, Nick would stand at the top of the peak, and have the power to silence tradition and do as he wished.

At Nick and Bev's for Christmas Eve dinner last night, Donnie and Angie had talked a bit about what they faced in the next year. They didn't bring it up with Nick, because it was Christmas Eve, and all his family was there, and because Nick hated to talk business in his home, ever. Inside those walls, he was a husband and a father, not a don.

That was what Donnie wanted in his home as well: to be simply Donnie here, with Arianna, and to keep her as safe as he could from the work he did in the night.

Wrapping his towel around his waist, he left the bathroom, went into his closet, and opened the drawer that held a small safe in which he kept a few incidental treasures. He keyed the code and opened it. A light blue box wrapped in white satin ribbon sat inside, with a few stacks of cash, some important personal papers, and a Panerai watch that was too precious for daily wear. He wore it only with a tuxedo. He'd been wearing it the night he was shot.

That watch had been Nick's gift on his fortieth birthday and cost more than his Porsche. More than the numbers behind the dollar sign was the value of the gift itself, from his best friend and mentor. The back was engraved: *Amico mio. N.*

What was nested in the small blue box, which Bev had slipped him last night, after conspiring with him during his convalescence to acquire it, wasn't quite as expensive as the watch from his friend, but it was at least as precious.

He picked it up and closed the safe.

Arianna was still asleep. Donnie hung his towel up in the bathroom and went back to bed, sliding in under the comforter beside her. He set the box on her pillow and settled in to watch her sleep. It was early on Christmas morning, and they had nowhere to be until they returned to Nick and Bev's for brunch and the happy chaos of family.

~oOo~

She slept another half-hour, waking when she stirred and disturbed the box from its perch on her pillow. It tumbled down and bumped her hand. Donnie smiled at the sound of her waking sigh, still muffled by the cocoon of the covers, and then her confused murmur and gasp when she woke enough to see what she was holding.

421

They were already engaged, but they hadn't discussed a ring. All their attention had been on his recovery, and her move to the Cove, and the news that she'd be Manon for her prima ballerina debut.

Manon was a love story, a tragedy about a woman who dies for her forbidden love. It was highly emotional. And, in the context of classical ballet, it was highly erotic. Donnie was thrilled for Arianna, and he'd support her unreservedly, but he was a little worried how he'd deal watching her make such emotional love to another man on stage. Sergei Petrov would be her partner. Ironically, he'd rather it had been Julian, whom Donnie knew now and was much more comfortable with.

He'd be fine, that was how he'd deal. Because Arianna was thrilled and nervous, and this was her shot. She was his, she loved him, she was marrying him, so it didn't matter one whit who danced with her. She came home to him and slept in a little cinnamon bun curl beside him, when she wasn't in his arms.

She peeked up from the comforter, her hair tousled around her head. God, so perfect. "What's this?"

"Exactly what you think it is. *Buon Natale.*"

"*Buon Natale!*" She tugged on the satin ribbon and cast it aside. Lifting the lid off the blue box, she tipped out the black velvet case it held, and opened it. The bright light in her crystal eyes, that soft gasp from her perfect lips, told him all he needed to know.

"Oh, Donnie! It's *perfect.*"

He'd let Bev guide his choice: a three-carat round solitaire on a plain platinum band. Perfectly classic, for his perfectly classic ballerina. The wedding ring was a band of small diamonds all the way around. But that was for the summer. For now, he slid the engagement ring on her elegant finger. "Marry me, Arianna Luciano. Be mine forever."

"Always!" She threw herself into his arms, and Donnie held back a grunt at the cramp through his still-tender middle. He closed his arms around her and tried to roll her to her back. Technically, he was supposed to wait another three weeks before sex or any other strenuous activity, but after three weeks of having this woman at his side every night, his patience for abstinence was at its limit.

But she pushed him off. "Wait, wait, wait. I have your present, too."

"You are my present." He tried to get hold of her again, but she was scampering off the bed and out of the room, her spectacular legs bare under his t-shirt. There was nothing under that t-shirt but exactly what he wanted.

Thwarted, Donnie and his engorged cock settled back in bed and waited for Arianna to return. In a few minutes, she did, holding a bigger, flatter box than the one he'd had for her. It was wrapped prettily in candy-cane striped paper and a silver bow that sparkled almost as much as the new ring on her finger.

Bev had great taste. The ring really was perfect. And eye-catching.

Arianna's smile when she handed him the gift shook a bit. "I hope you like it." She climbed back into bed as he tore off the paper and found a plain white box, like a shirt box. But heavy. Setting it on his lap, he removed the lid and opened the tissue.

A silver frame, sleek and solid, about eleven by fourteen. Inside the frame, under a thick black matte, was a black-and-white photograph of him and Arianna. At the theatre, in one of the rehearsal studios. She wore one of her pale practice leotards, with a soft little sweater thing she called a 'shrug' over it. Her hair was coiled in a braided version of her ballerina bun. He was in a dress shirt, two buttons undone at the throat, no jacket or tie.

Donnie absolutely loathed having his photograph taken and tried to make certain it only happened when he couldn't avoid it, and he was in charge of how it was taken. He remembered this day, during the rehearsals for *The Nutcracker*. A photographer had been present, taking photos for the annual report. Donnie had kept to the edges, out of the photographer's range, but he hadn't been too worried. He wasn't a dancer or involved in the business except as a donor. He hadn't been the subject of the photo shoot.

Or so he'd thought. But the photographer had caught Arianna and him in a quiet moment. He held her hands. She looked up into his eyes. He looked down into hers. The angle was profile, on Donnie's undamaged left side, but a little oblique, canted from the left rather than straight on. The angle showed more of his front and Arianna's back—not so much that her gaze and sweet smile didn't show, but enough that Donnie's scars almost did. Enough to know they existed.

He didn't know what to think. The photo seemed an intrusion, taken without his permission by a stranger, capturing an intimate moment that was only theirs. And his scars were visible.

But so was Arianna's love for him, and his for her. And his happiness—Jesus, he looked happy in this photograph; even he could see it.

Arianna's hand came to rest on his arm. Her ring glittered in Christmas Day sunshine. "The photographer sent me an email with this shot. When I saw it, I had to have it, for you. This shows *us*, Donnie. This is us. More than that, this is who I see when I look at you. I see love in your eyes, and in your smile. I see your scars and I love them, because they are part of your history. They aren't who you are, but they are part of the life that made who you are. You are beautiful to me. Inside and out. Every part of you. I see *you*."

Donnie cleared his throat, trying to loosen the grip of his surging emotions so he could speak. "It's perfect, Arianna. Thank you."

She studied his face, poring over every inch before diving into his eyes. "Yeah?"

"Yes. I love it."

Relief burst from her lips on a soft laugh. "Oh, I'm so glad. I was worried you wouldn't understand."

He set the box aside and pulled her into his arms. "I understand. I love you." He kissed her, turning on the bed, careful of his midsection, so he could lie over her. Enough with waiting. No more waiting for anything between them.

She was with him, moaning under his kiss, scratching her nails up his back, arching into his touch. But when he shifted to settle between her legs, his core muscles cramped painfully, and he couldn't suppress the grunt of pain.

Arianna went still at once and broke off their kiss, pushing deep into her pillows to put space between them. "No, Donnie. It's too soon. You'll hurt yourself."

"I don't care. I need you."

"I *do* care. I need you. I'm not fucking you today."

"But it's Christmas!"

She laughed at him. Hearing the petulant teenager who'd whined that complaint, Donnie laughed, too. "Well, it is."

"Next Christmas, you can fuck me unconscious. This Christmas, we can cuddle." She put her left hand on his scarred cheek. Her ring sparkled at the edge of his vision. God, the things she'd said. The way she loved him. All of him, the light and the dark.

He didn't want to cuddle. Not yet. It was Christmas, and he loved and was loved, and he wanted more. He wanted all of her. To know every part of her. Every part.

She loved him. As he was.

Donnie put a quick kiss on her sweet lips and, moving slowly, careful of his sore muscles, eased himself down her body, under the comforter. He pushed the t-shirt up.

With a soft sigh, she pulled it all the way off, then relaxed and set her hands on his head. "Okay, a little titty play won't hurt."

He laughed against her skin as he arrived where she thought he meant to stop. As he loved her beautiful small breasts, flicking his tongue against the beads of her excited nipples, Donnie smoothed his hand over her hip and belly and wondered if he should stay where he was. More than twenty years — even had his mouth worked like it was supposed to, his skills would have been lost after all this time.

But she was moaning at the touch of his mouth on her breasts. Her hands scratched at his scalp, and she writhed beneath him. He wanted all of her. To know all of her, to have her etched into all his senses. Everywhere.

Easing away from her delicious breasts, Donnie moved downward, kissing the soft flesh over her ribs, her firm, flat belly, the blade of her hip, the contour of a lithe thigh.

She sucked in a breath, and her body tensed as she lifted off her shoulders. "Donnie?" She picked up the comforter and peered down at him.

Hovering over his goal, smelling her already, as sweet as the rest of her, he lifted his eyes to hers. "Can I?"

God, if she said no …

But she nodded her head, and her eyes washed with tears. "Only if you want."

"I want. I want all of you."

With a sharp tug, Arianna sent the comforter sliding off the bed. "I want to see you."

For the first time in a lifetime, Donnie put his face between a woman's legs and tasted her. But this was no mere woman. This was his woman. Who saw him and wanted him and loved him.

Arianna thought it was only one woman who'd hurt him and turned him away from love, but she was wrong. Maybe it hadn't been any woman at all. Maybe it had been him, taking one painful moment and turning it into a life. Maybe he'd closed himself off from love for all these years. Maybe other women could have loved him if he'd been able to let them.

But only Arianna had seen what he'd needed to take the chance. She was the key. He'd been waiting for her.

She was sweet on his tongue. Her body quivered in his arms. So enraptured by the experience, Donnie forgot to wonder if his mouth felt strange to her or moved wrong for her. She moaned and whimpered and trembled and writhed. She gasped his name, and the name of God. He stayed on her, fed on her bliss, held her fast, ground his hips into the bed beneath him until he was on the verge of climax himself.

When she came, arched sharply up and keening, he drank of her, and the taste of her release, the very *fact* of it, while his face was covered with her pleasure, made him come, too.

The force of it turned all his core muscles into a knot of hot iron, and he let his head fall to her thigh and dropped his hands from her to clutch the sheets.

"Donnie?" She scrambled from under him. "Are you okay?"

"I'm good," he gasped, waiting out the cramp. "I'm okay." And he was. Unless he'd made something break open inside, he was fine. The cramp passed, and he rolled to his side and grinned at his woman. "I'm great. I just came all over the sheets like a scrub, though."

Frowning at him, Arianna leaned close. "Are you really okay?"

"I'm fine, *stella mia*. Just a cramp."

"You're supposed to be taking it easy!"

"I wasn't trying to get off. I was trying to get you off, but you're so hot I couldn't control myself. That was good?"

Her frown lost a battle with a blushy grin. "That was *brilliant*."

"It didn't f—"

Her fingers covered his mouth. "It felt like you, making me feel good. It was perfect, and now you have to do that all the time."

He took her fingers from his mouth and kissed their tips. "I will do that any time you want. Day or night. For as long as you look at me like that. *Sei la mia stella. Sei la mia vita*."

She leaned even closer and kissed his scarred cheek. "*Sono tua per sempre. Ti amo, amore mio*."

~ 24 ~

Ari got out of the back seat of the SUV and stopped where she was, still inside the wedge of the open door. As a frigid burst of January wind slapped her across the face, she pulled up her hood and stared at the house in front of her. Her childhood home.

She'd been home for Thanksgiving. Not even two months ago. But her life had taken some wild spins in those few weeks.

Donnie came up from the street and took her arm. He pulled her to the sidewalk, and Dre closed her door, which she'd been blocking. She turned at the sound. "Oh, sorry."

"Don't worry about it, Miss Ari."

Everyone who worked for Donnie called her Miss Ari. She'd told them they could drop the 'Miss,' but had been ignored. In a few months, they'd call her Mrs. Goretti, she was sure, though she meant to keep her name.

Well, at least professionally.

Dre got their bags from the back of the truck, and Donnie took them. They exchanged some words regarding security — those kinds of instructions had become background noise to her life, like the suited men who inhabited her shadow — and Dre stood with his hands crossed and his back to the car, at his post. There was another car with two more guards doing a patrol around the block. Because the Pagano Brothers were still on high alert.

But Donnie hadn't met her family yet, and they were getting married in June, so they'd driven up to spend a weekend on Long Island.

"It's a nice house. You ready?" Donnie said, hooking her bag over his shoulder so he could take her hand. He'd healed completely from the shooting and seemed strong as ever.

"I'm nervous! It's so weird."

"I'm nervous, too. I've never met my fiancée's family before."

"Speaking of meeting family ..." she nodded to the bright red Mustang in the driveway. "That's my Aunt Anita's car. You could get tackle-hugged. She gets ... enthusiastic."

He grinned. "Okay. I'll lock my knees."

They were halfway up the sidewalk when the front door flew open, and Aunt Anita dashed out, down the porch steps, and straight for Ari. "There's my baby!

There's my girl!" Ari was tackled into a bear hug. After a few back-cracking squeezes, her aunt took a short step back and grabbed her hands. "Oh! You look so good! And *look* at that *ring*! Did you eat? You look skinny! Are you eating? We missed you so much at Christmas!"

"Sorry, Auntie. I had to stay close for Donnie. This is Donnie."

Anita turned and beamed at him, but she was much more subdued in her greeting. She kept hold of Ari with one hand and held out the other. She knew who he was, what he was. Her eyes scanned his face, and dashed quickly away from his right side to focus on his left. Ari saw it, and she knew Donnie had, too. That was the way for him, meeting people. They had to reckon with his scars, which meant he had to as well. Over and over again. "Hello, Donnie. It's wonderful to meet you."

Donnie took her hand and shook it warmly. "Arianna talks about you all the time. I'm very glad to meet you, Anita."

Anita turned a wry smile to Ari. "Oh, he's charming, Ari." Back to Donnie, she said, "Oh come here, I can't stand being so damn polite. Can I give you a hug?"

Donnie took her hug with a friendly laugh and smiled over her shoulder at Ari. She grinned back. As they started toward the door again, Ari's father stepped into the doorway. She hurried up the porch steps to him.

"Hi, Daddy."

He smiled and pushed his glasses to the top of his head. "Hi, baby girl."

Before they could hug, Anita was pushing them into the house. "It's freezing out here! Come on, come on, we're heating the whole neighborhood and turning the front room into a tundra." She herded them all into the front room. There was a fire in the fireplace, and the Christmas decorations were still up.

"You didn't take the tree down yet?" Her father had a rule that the Christmas tree had to be down by Epiphany, which had been a week ago.

"I wanted you to see it," he said with a shrug.

Now she hugged him, and felt guilty tears stirring in her throat. "I'm sorry, Daddy. We won't miss any more Christmases, I promise."

He kissed her head. "It's okay, *cara mia*. I understand. I just missed you, and since you were coming so close after, I kept it up for you." With a nod to Donnie, he asked, "Will you introduce me to your young man?"

Young man. Donnie was as close to her father's age as he was to Ari's. A little bit closer, actually. "Daddy, this is Donnie Goretti, my fiancé."

Donnie offered his hand. "Dr. Luciano." Oh, her guy was good. The underboss of a major Family, and he showed her dentist father all his respect.

"Call me Art, please." Her father shook his hand. "I'm glad to know you, Donnie."

Ari turned to her aunt, who broadly mimed an impressed face and gave her two cheerful thumbs up.

~oOo~

After they put their bags in Ari's old room, she showed Donnie around. This house was full of family photographs, and he wanted the story of each one. She'd already told him about her mom, how she'd had a heart attack at the age of thirty-two, a young woman with a six-year-old daughter, healthy but for her two-pack-a-day Kool habit, and a lurking blood clot.

He considered their wedding photo: a small, smiling, pretty woman in a tulle confection of a gown, and a serious young man with a prodigious nose and thick black glasses, evidently uncomfortable in his white tuxedo jacket over black trousers and black tie. "What do you remember of her?"

Ari shrugged. "Not much. We have some videos, and all my memories feel like they came from those. Playing at the beach. Watching me at dance class and recitals. Birthdays and holidays. All the things families take videos of. That's what I remember." It was a lot — those videos meant she remembered her voice and her laugh, and the way she moved. "Aunt Anita and Uncle

Mel lived just around the corner then, and after the funeral, Anita stepped in and took over with me, and Daddy did his work, and Uncle Mel did his work, and that's how I grew up."

"He never remarried?"

"No. He still loves her."

Donnie folded his hand over hers and squeezed.

They'd made their way down the hall and the stairs, to the photos on the mantel. The front door burst open, and her Uncle Mel swept in with his usual Atlantic City flourish. "Ari baby! There's my good girl!"

"Hi, Uncle Mel!" She went to him for yet another back-cracking hug. As usual, he smelled of booze and cigars, which was more an effect of where he'd been than what he'd been doing. He ran his loan operation out of a cigar lounge.

He squeezed her cheeks and smacked a kiss on each one. Then he set her aside and strode to Donnie, who'd hung back.

"Mr. Goretti. It's a pleasure to meet you, sir."

His tone was completely different, much more serious. That was the shylock meeting the underboss. They weren't from the same families, but they were both of *La Cosa Nostra*, and rank was rank.

Donnie took his offered hand. "It's Mel, right?"

"Yes, sir. Carmelo Luciano. I guess you know I'm a Romano man."

436

"I do."

Ari stood near the door, fascinated to see this side of Donnie. She'd seen him with his guards, giving them orders, and she'd seen him with Nick and others, in casual situations like Christmas Day brunch, but she'd never seen him so obviously in *command* before. He demanded respect simply by his bearing. He wasn't aggressive at all. Power simply flowed from him, and respect flowed to him.

Mel had been made before she was born. He was respected in the Romanos and, as a good earner, was well regarded by the top brass. She knew that, had seen evidence of it. But in terms of rank, he was only a soldier. A man on the streets, whose only value was the profit he brought in. Donnie outranked him by a whole layer of atmosphere.

She *had* seen this before—when Donnie had brought Baxter to heel. Her uncle faced him with more spine, but the respect he paid was obvious. If Donnie wore a ring, Mel would have kissed it by now.

"I've been asked to talk with you about a few things, and let you know my don invites you in tomorrow."

"I'm here on personal matters, Mel. As you know."

"I understand. But this I think is important to you, and to Don Pagano."

Donnie looked past him to Ari before he answered. "I'll give you five minutes, after dinner."

"Thank you." Just like that, the tense Mafia exchange was over, and Mel was her boisterous uncle again. "Wow, it smells fantastic! My Anita is a great cook, Donnie. I hope you're hungry!"

~oOo~

Dinner—veal piccata with capellini—was delicious, because Anita could really cook. Donnie ate as carefully as Ari, but for different reasons. He was still dealing with some appetite and digestion issues from his wounds, and she would be playing the starving Manon in a few months and couldn't pack on the pounds now. But three bottles of wine had gone around the table by the time the meal was over, and the awkward, getting-to-know-the-new-boy-who-is-a-badass-mobster chitchat warmed up to more fluid conversation as their cheeks got rosy with drink.

It was her father, though, not Mel, who took the conversation to the red zone.

He leaned past Ari and filled Donnie's glass. "That black truck outside, and the one just like it doing laps around the block. That's your security, right? You got trouble so big you need three armed guys on my girl? The same trouble that got you shot?"

Her father was an educated man, and took pride in his diction. He was quiet and bookish. But when he was drunk, he talked like a guy from the block, and he scrapped like one, too.

He waved dangerously at Donnie's face. "Looks like hurt follows you around. You gonna get my girl hurt?"

Oh God. Had her father just called out Donnie's scars as *evidence of weakness*?

Donnie, for the same reasons he'd been careful with his food, had been careful with his drink. He was the soberest person at the table, Ari included. He got very still.

Ari was a bit tipsy, and Mel and Anita were as drunk as her father. All three of them, though, sobered fully up and went still as well, and they all said, in chorus, Ari, her aunt, and her uncle:

"Daddy."

"Art."

"Turo."

Her father shot an aggressive hand up. "No. I wanna know. I only got Ari left. You gonna get her took away, too?"

"Art," Donnie said, quietly. Almost gently. "I love your girl. She's the only woman I've ever loved or ever will. She's safe with me. I will put myself between her and any bad thing, for the rest of her life. I will die for her. I will kill for her. That's my vow. Those trucks that follow her around, the men inside them will die for her, too. They will kill for her before even a hair is mussed on her head. She is safe."

Loving Donnie as much for his compassionate restraint in this moment as for the vow he'd made for her, Ari put her hand on her father's and squeezed. "I'm safe, Daddy. I'm safe."

He gripped her fingers hard and pushed his glasses up onto his head with his other hand. Then he dropped his face into that hand, and Ari thought he was going to cry.

Nothing more than a loud sigh escaped him, though, and Anita vaulted to her feet. "There's ice cream! I went to 31 Flavors and got the good vanilla bean flavor, and I got that hot fudge syrup, too. And whipped cream and jimmies. Who wants a sundae?!"

~oOo~

Ari swirled one of the handled sponges that looked to her like a pink flower on a white stem over a plate, under the running tap, and handed the rinsed — practically cleaned — dish to Aunt Anita, who put it in its proper place in the dishwasher.

Her father had gone off to bed right after an awkward dessert of hot fudge sundaes. Donnie and Uncle

Mel were talking, and the women were cleaning up. Though Ari considered herself a feminist and would have laughed Julian out of the apartment if he'd ever walked away from his own dishes, she'd been raised in a home where there was women's work and men's work. Women could work outside the home if they wished, but they absolutely worked inside it as well. When she was home, she fell in line.

She had no idea about Donnie's ideas on the matter; he paid people to tend to his home. Their home.

"I hope Daddy's okay. Is he drinking again? All the time?" After her mom died, her dad had lived a few hard years, lost in grief.

"No, baby." Anita stood straight and smoothed her hand in circles on Ari's back. "He missed you at Christmas, and he's been worried since Donnie got shot, but he's been okay. Tonight was a celebration, and he just had a little too much, like all of us."

"Okay. I won't miss any more Christmases."

"You'll do what you need to do for your man now, Ari. His life leads yours. So don't make promises. If I've learned anything in all my years with Mel, it's that. In a life like ours, you don't make promises."

Aunt Anita had been a Mafia wife for almost all Ari's life. Certainly as long as she remembered. But Ari remembered her as the woman who'd stepped into the space her mother had left. The woman who took her to

441

dance class and mended her tutus, who learned everything there was to learn about the ballet so she could talk with Ari about the thing she loved, who'd learned French with her so she'd have someone to practice with. Who'd baked cookies and cupcakes for school parties and dance class bake sales, who'd sewn her costumes for Halloween and her first recitals, who'd held her when she came home from school with a bruised heart, disappointed by a boy or a friend, or just adolescence in general.

What Uncle Mel did had only touched the fringes of Ari's life, because Aunt Anita had not been a Mafia Wife in Ari's mind. She'd simply been a mother to a girl who'd needed one.

Ari looked over her shoulder and considered the general direction Donnie and Uncle Mel had gone. 'Five minutes after dinner' had turned into half an hour and more that they were sequestered in Ari's dad's office. They were talking serious business. Things like this, men going off to talk in dark corners, or leaving unannounced – those things she remembered. They were the things on the fringes of her life.

"He's a good man, Auntie."

"I know he is. Mel said he has a good rep – not just respect, but admiration. That's good. That means he's strong and smart. But men so high up, they're targets. You might have security all the rest of your life now. Can you deal with that?"

"I'm already used to it. It's been like that as long as I've known him. They're just shadows to me now. My life is exactly as I want it."

Her aunt gave her a long look. "Okay, baby."

The floor creaked, and Ari looked behind her again. Donnie was coming up to the doorway. She smiled, and saw it reflected in his own.

"You about ready to call it a night?" he asked.

"As soon as we get the kitchen clean, yep."

Anita took the flower-sponge from her. "I'll finish up. You go have some quiet time, and get some rest. I'm getting you up early so we can be at Ambricio's when they open and get their best pastries for breakfast."

"Are you sure?"

"Go! Go!" Anita kissed her cheek. "Good night, Donnie."

As he took Ari's hand, he turned his smile to her aunt. "Good night, Anita. Thank you for the delicious food."

~oOo~

Ari's childhood bedroom was caught in the neverwhere between two lives. It had the same furnishings and linens and posters and knickknacks of the teenager

443

who'd last lived in it, but none of the incidental necessities of the woman who'd left it behind. On first seeing it, Donnie had said it was like a 'dollhouse room,' and Ari thought that insightful. Decorated for a girl who was nothing more than a memory her father kept close, like a doll.

After a soft kiss and a quiet embrace, they undressed quietly, Donnie stripping to his underwear, and Ari taking his discarded t-shirt and pulling it over her bare body. She sat on her double bed, covered in a pink quilted satin spread. Donnie sat beside her and picked up her hand. "I'm going to have to do some business tomorrow afternoon."

"Okay. I figured when you talked to Uncle Mel so long, it was more important than you expected."

"It could be good, though. It could help."

Donnie didn't go into detail about the things he did, but he'd been more forthcoming about the trouble that had gotten him shot and had all the Pagano Brothers on alert all the time. A war was brewing. It sounded like the Romanos might ally with the Paganos, or provide some kind of assistance. She knew enough to know that a New York Family extending an offer of aid to a New England Family meant the war could have a huge impact.

It wasn't her place to say any of that, and she didn't want it to be. She wanted her life with Donnie to be a place where their separate worlds waited outside, like the men in SUVs.

She traced the new scars on his belly. "Thank you for being kind to my father tonight. I'm so sorry about what he said."

"It's okay. He's worried about you. So am I."

"I'm not. I know I'm safe with you."

Smiling, he brushed her hair back and cupped his hand over her cheek. "I love to see the way you see me."

"I see you the way you are."

She turned and straddled him. He groaned and hooked his hands around her hips, and his cock swelled beneath her, pressing the fabric of his underwear into her folds.

He smiled beneath her lips as she kissed him. "What are your thoughts about fucking in your dad's house? It's been six weeks today, you know."

"I know." Six weeks ago today, he'd been shot. Six weeks was how long he was supposed to wait for strenuous physical activity, including sex. But on Christmas morning, when he'd gone down on her and given her the most amazing and unexpected gift, he'd come and hurt himself badly enough he'd needed Oxy later in the day. That was three weeks ago, but Ari worried. "Are you sure you're ready?"

His hands eased from her hips, up under the t-shirt, and cupped her breasts. "Arianna, I've been ready since I woke up in the hospital and saw you sleeping beside me in that red dress. Yes, I'm ready. I feel good again. You know that. I'm strong."

She reached down between them and pulled his cock free of his boxer briefs. "Yes, you are. Strong and beautiful and mine."

As she slid down onto him, he groaned deeply, softly, desperately. He pulled his t-shirt up over her head and threw it aside, and he clutched her close and latched with ravenous hunger to her breast. Her body exploded with sparkling, earthy, needy pleasure.

Ari wrapped her arms around his beautiful head and made up for six weeks of lost time.

No. It was twenty years he'd lost.

~ Epilogue ~

Donnie tapped the screen, and the video played again. "Fuck."

Today of all days, he didn't want to be here, in Nick's office, staring at that image on Angie's tablet. Security footage from the international terminal at JFK. Bogdan Bondaruk, eldest son of Yuri Bondaruk and underboss of his organization, strolling out of Customs like he was about to embark on a long-planned holiday. As he cleared the customs stations, three heavy men in black converged behind him. They carried themselves as if they were armed, and Donnie was sure they were. People had been paid off handsomely, from Kiev to New York City, to get the Bondaruk prince into the States so boldly.

"A convoy of three was waiting for them," Angie said. "Calvin has them getting a ride to Brooklyn. He's bunking with the Zelenkos."

Nick sat back in his chair. "This is what I wanted when we turned down the meet with the Zelenkos. No more cannon fodder. I wanted Yuri, but Bogdan will do. Donnie, when it's time, you'll go in my stead. Second will face second. And we'll see what we see."

What they would see was the scope of the fight they faced. Bondaruk's decision to ally with another bratva gave him strength and weight in the US he hadn't had on his own, but it had also put his efforts on the radar of the New York Council, and now, at the urging of the Romanos, all five New York Families were in the game, aligned with the Nick and the rest of the New England Council. Ten Italian families against two Ukrainian bratvas.

The odds seemed to tip strongly in their favor, but their opponents seemed to have no code, or not one the Italians understood.

Donnie couldn't restrain his fist from punching Nick's desk. "Why did this have to fucking happen *today*?"

Nick chuckled. "It's good, Donnie. We know where he is. We know what he's doing. If he's smart, he won't make a move until he understands the land, and knows he can trust the men around him. If he's smart, he'll take more time to strengthen his position before he strikes. If he's stupid, he'll make a stupid move fast, and we'll deal with it faster. But smart or stupid, he won't make a move today. Today, you can know the day will go as it should." The don checked his watch. "Unless you're late, that is. We should get to the church."

"Don't wait on me," Angie said. "I'm gonna swing over to West Egg. Billy had trouble with tourists last night, and there was some damage."

Billy Jones had opened her Gatsby-themed nightclub two weeks before Memorial Day. Though Donnie had doubts that the name would appeal to a wide audience—he'd had to be reminded that West Egg was a reference from the book, the place where Jay Gatsby's mansion was—the club had been an instant hit with the locals, and with the summer crowd, too. Billy had a bit more popularity than she could manage, apparently.

Quiet Cove businesses paid the Pagano Brothers for protection and insurance whether they wanted to or not, but they got what they paid for. Nick would cover damages incurred.

But Nick said, "No. You come to the church. Send a guy, but I don't want you getting hung up in bullshit today. Today is for family."

Angie smiled. "Understood. I'll send Tony."

"Good. Let's go. We've got important business today." He clapped Donnie on the back.

~oOo~

"You look like James Bond." Bev fussed with the bow tie he'd just tied, though he knew damn well he'd tied it straight. He usually wore a straight tie with a tuxedo, but he'd tied enough bow ties in his day, without using a mirror, that he could do it in his sleep.

Donnie glanced down at his tux—a brand new one, custom made and classically styled, with satin notch lapels and black button covers on his plain white shirt. "Arianna has classic taste."

She laughed and picked up the boutonniere. Two identical orange rosebuds. "And you don't?"

Donnie stood still while she pinned the flower to his lapel, and let her rhetorical question go unanswered. When she was done, she smoothed her hands over his jacket, drawing them down to grasp his hands. "I'm so happy for you, Donnie. I knew she was out there waiting for you. I knew when you found her, you'd let her in."

Donnie clutched his dear friend's hands. "I think she found me. I think I was lost."

"No. You weren't lost. You just got turned around."

A knock on the door interrupted them, but Donnie didn't know if he could have replied to Bev, anyway. He felt a little drunk today, moving through a world that was brighter and more open than he'd known.

Bev dropped his hands and stepped back.

"Come," Donnie said, and the door opened.

Arianna's father stood there, in a similar classic suit. "Donnie. Can I have a minute?"

"Of course, Art. Come in."

"I'll check and make sure everything's good with Ari, and I'll see you out there." Bev lifted up, and Donnie offered his cheek for her kiss. She patted Art's arm before she left the room.

Donnie didn't want to sit and crease his suit before the ceremony, but with a wave of his hand, he offered the chair in this groom's room at Christ the King Catholic Church to Arianna's father.

"No, thanks. I just wanted to say a few words. When I married Ari's mom, her dad had a lot of things to say to me about how to treat his girl. Ari's my only, so I guess I can't call it a tradition, but I wanted to say something about her. What she means."

Donnie didn't speak; it was Arianna's father's prerogative to have words with her groom. Who they were in the world didn't matter. Right now, the man with the power was the father.

Art cleared his throat. "I don't have a problem with what you do. Mel's been connected since we were kids. I used to run errands, too, back in those days, and maybe I'd've joined up, too, if things went a different way. But I had chances Mel didn't. I did well in school. I got a scholarship to college. So I took another path. But what you do, what Mel does, I grew up with it, lived my whole

451

life with it. I've seen the good, bad, and ugly, and I'm right with it. What I'm saying is I know the life you're giving her. Ari's been my whole life since the nurse set her in my arms. On that day, I promised her I'd keep her safe and make her happy. When her mamma died, I promised her again. I told her I'd make sure she was happy again, and she'd have a good life, and I wouldn't let anything hurt her. I let her fly off on her own because home was too small for her wings, and she loves her life away. She's happy, and that makes me happy, even though she left me behind."

He stopped and let his head droop. Donnie waited, respecting the man's emotion. There was nothing he could say, no denial he could make. All he could make was a promise, and when her father was finished, Donnie would renew the promise he'd made before.

After a brisk exhale, Art faced him again. "Just because I don't see her much, don't think it means I don't love her like always. I've had her in my arms all this time, but I'm setting her in your arms now. All I ask is you keep her safe and make her happy."

"Art, on my life, I swear I will." Donnie extended his hand, and Arianna's father gripped it hard.

~oOo~

Donnie stood before Father Merkel, with Nick and Angie at his side. Across the altar stood Julian, Arianna's man of honor. Carina sauntered down the aisle, full of attitude, wearing an orange gown that made it brilliantly clear she was on her way to a wild kind of beauty to match her fierce personality. Nick would lose his mind trying to keep this girl under his wing.

As she took her place at Julian's side, Donnie sent her a smile and a wink. She stuck her tongue out at him. Still a little girl for a while longer, then.

The music changed, and Arianna came into the sanctuary on her father's arm. Her dress had been designed just for her by the ballet's costume designer, and he knew she'd been excited for him to see it. It was a thing of wonder, yes. A beautiful big swirl of tulle and satin. And he didn't care at all. Inside that dress was the woman who loved him, and she was all he could see. She glided to him, her eyes on him, sparkling with tears.

Her father put her hand in his. Set her in his arms, trusted him to keep her safe and happy.

And he would. Whatever happened, he would keep her safe.

"You are beautiful," he murmured.

She grinned. "So are you."

They'd decided on a totally traditional ceremony. Nothing extra, no writing of their own vows. They were married in a ceremony like millions of Catholic marriages through history. They exchanged rings—the circle of diamonds he'd shown her when he'd given her the solitaire, and a heavy, plain platinum band for him. They said the words, vowing to love, honor and cherish each other throughout their lives.

Except for the moment of their rings, Arianna's eyes never left his. He knew, because his never left hers. She saw him. He saw her.

When it was over, and the priest gave his blessing, Donnie cupped his hands around Arianna's beautiful face, and he kissed her. In front of everyone they knew, a church full of people who loved them, he kissed his bride.

ABOUT THE AUTHOR

Susan Fanetti is a Midwestern native transplanted to Northern California, where she lives with her husband, youngest son, and assorted cats.

She is a proud member of the Freak Circle Press.

Susan's website: www.susanfanetti.com

Susan's Facebook author page:
https://www.facebook.com/authorsusanfanetti
'Susan's FANetties' reader group:
https://www.facebook.com/groups/871235502925756/

Instagram: https://www.instagram.com/susan_fanetti/

Twitter: @sfanetti

Pagano Brothers Pinterest Board:
https://www.pinterest.com/laughingwarrior/the-pagano-brothers-series/

Made in the USA
Columbia, SC
23 October 2024